# No Longer Invisible

## Marbeth Skwarczynski

# Cover Art

By

Ranee Designs

raneedesigns.me

# Contents

# Chapter One: Counting Down

I reread the instructions in the algebra workbook and attempt, once again, to get the correct answer for number five. According to the answer key, $X=3$ but I have to show my work, and I have no idea how the people at EFC (Education for Christians) got to "3."

I push the workbook away as soon as the bell rings for lunch. The torture can wait until after I have my bowl of soup and read at least one chapter of *Love Comes Softly*, my "at school" reading book. I close my math and pull the hardcover two-in-one edition of Janette Oke's classic toward me instead.

I'm about to stand when a piece of torn and hastily folded notebook paper flips into my cubicle desk. I turn around to see Jack walking past on his way outside to the picnic tables where we eat. I slip the note under a workbook until I am sure the coast is clear. When I'm the last one in the learning center, I unfold it and read, "Sit with me tonight?" Tonight is a youth activity with a bonfire, burned hot dogs, and another attempt at s'mores.

Before Mrs. Barker, the learning center monitor, can come in and ask why I'm not outside with the others, I take a piece of clean and untorn paper and write "Sure" in my girliest script. I reread the word a dozen times, hearing that warning bell clang, but finally convince myself that if anyone finds the note, there is nothing in that single word that will condemn me.

I fold the paper into an origami heart and stick it in the school-approved reading book on my desk. I figure if anyone finds it, they'll return it to me. I've used origami heart bookmarks for years. No one would suspect there was a note inside this one.

I stand, push my chair in and pull my backpack on before grabbing my lunch bag. My eyes travel around our empty classroom or "learning center." At the room's perimeter, fold-up desks are suspended from the walls with chains that always make me think of medieval dungeons. There is space for two students at each desk. We have heavy wooden dividers between us, and each cubicle is called our "office."

Students don't interact at all except on our twice-a-day breaks and at lunchtime. Most of the others don't interact with me even at those approved times. It's when I miss my best friend, Lu, the most. My brother, Roman, has loads of friends. He plays on what passes for a football team, has a smirky smile, a rude sense of humor, and was born with the long dark lashes that I should have gotten instead of these blonde things. He's considered cool and popular. Jack, two years older than Roman and a year younger than me, is my brother's best friend. I set my origami heart at Jack's elbow as I walk by on my way to the microwave.

I put my soup in for one minute and jump a bit when I hear him whisper in my ear. "Why are you giving me a bookmark?"

"Look inside later."

"Oh." He sounds impressed.

We barely look at each other when we meet at the bonfire, but we do sit together, casually surrounded by the other teens, careful not to make a big deal about our seating arrangements.

The s'mores still taste like ashes on a shingle. Experiment 35,045 is a failure. I end up eating the ingredients separately as usual. Jack keeps me somewhat involved in the conversation of people he sees as friends and that I see as acquaintances due to proximity. Still, we laugh together and join in the group-sing and for once, I have a blast, sitting side-by-side, but never really talking one-on-one.

On Monday, I find a crudely folded rectangle in one of my workbooks. I slip it into my denim skirt's front pocket and read it in the restroom during the first break. Behind the locked door, I read, "Had an awesome time with you on Friday. Wanted to tell you on Sunday, but there were too many people around. Can you start sitting across from me at lunch? Still too many people, but at least we can talk a little."

I pull a pen out of my pocket and write, "Not at lunch. Don't want to start rumors. My parents are very strict. I'm not allowed to date until college. Volunteer for the yearbook. There are only two of us doing it now. We get out of class to take pictures, and Sheryl is always absent. I could use the company. Do you have a camera?"

I can't think of anything else to say, so I fold the paper into a heart and pass it to Jack when I go out to break.

Jack and I exchange notes for most of the year and occasionally speak to each other at youth events and church. His parents are strict, too, continually warning him against women who intend to ruin his life and reputation through seduction. He's told me about their cautionary tales of women lying to bring down great men while rolling his eyes.

Most of what we want to say to each other is done in passing or, well, with passing. We never call each other's homes, and neither of us has a cellphone. Jack never joins the yearbook.

Over time we make up nicknames for one another and the other kids at the school as well. We consider it a second layer of security in our notes. He calls me by my real name, Julia, around the others. In our messages, he calls me Ruby. He says I am priceless.

Isn't that a sweet thing for him to say?

My codename for him is slightly longer. At first, it was BE

for his blue eyes, but I didn't really like it. It was too simplistic and trying too hard all at the same time. Then I had an English workbook that outlined each of Shakespeare's plays. The first play, *The Two Gentlemen of Verona*, has a character named Proteus. For some reason, that name stuck — probably because his love interest was a girl named Julia. Like me.

And then, as our senior year went on, we found time alone. Sweet moments. Hands clasped, arms enfolding, and finally lips meeting. We made plans: finish high school, work at the same summer camp, go to the same Bible college where we can finally date openly, and get married right after graduation. It doesn't matter that we are young. My parents were young when they got married. His probably were, too. I never asked.

Now that the school year is almost over. I'm counting down the days (fourteen) until I can leave Sampson, Arizona, and begin my life somewhere — anywhere — else with Jack.

First, the day after graduation, we're going to Camp Galilee, the summer camp we've worked at for the past three years, to add a little more to our respective nest eggs. On the last day of work at the camp, when everyone else is boarding busses for home, we're going to get on a bus that takes us — I don't know where. Anywhere but here. That's as far as we've gotten with our plans. Except, we do plan to marry.

I check the clock on the wall. The bell will ring in less than five minutes, so I clean up my desk. I have three subjects that I haven't crossed through on the 5x7 card that lists my scholastic goals for each day of the week. I stuff the workbooks for those subjects into my backpack, along with a couple of pencils.

When the bell rings, a carelessly folded paper lands in front of me as Jack casually walks by and out the door — he never did learn how to make the heart. This is his second note today. I never got to read the first one since he gave it to me just after the second break, and I couldn't use the excuse of needing the bathroom. Mrs. Barker hates dismissing students immediately after a break when we "should have used the facilities," and I knew if I asked, she'd hold it against me for the rest of the day. I ended up shoving the note into the inside zipper pocket of my backpack. I slip the new message into my jean-skirt pocket. I'll read them at home.

If I could go back in time, I'd tear them up and burn both notes to ashes.

# Chapter Two: Holding On

My bedroom is my favorite place in the house. There is only one window (facing west), but when I come home after school every afternoon, my room is bright, warm, and cozy. For just a moment of every day, I feel like home is a beautiful place to be.

Then I take a step forward, and my reflection grudgingly acknowledges me. I'm surprised I even register in the glass. My pasty skin and blonde eyelashes make me look washed out in the best of circumstances. On an average day, like today, I am nearly invisible in the four-foot-long mirror over the faux Victorian dresser. When I leave here, I will finally be alive. For now, I'm a ghost standing between a bright window and a doorless doorway.

It is doorless because I "lost the privilege of privacy" six years ago when I dared to keep a private journal. I was thirteen and, while I had no desire to write about my home life, I wrote pages and pages about the most significant happenings in my little world. I'd joined the youth group at church, discovered that boys weren't as gross as I once thought, and learned that girls were much meaner than I realized. That's the year I'd learned that my classmates weren't my friends. I wrote about my heartbreak about losing relationships I probably never had in the first place.

And then I wrote about my darkest secret. I was going through what my science workbooks called "puberty." I reread the workbook twice and passed both the self-test and the final with perfect scores, but the words seemed foreign and the situations confusing. It was all about "growing into adulthood," but I had no idea what that meant. I already knew how to cook and clean and garden. That was adult behavior, right?

Any discussions at home or school concerning the functions of the human body were avoided or couched in terms so inoffensive they were useless. For years, I heard prayer requests for ladies at our church who were having surgery for "woman problems," while remaining clueless about what "woman problems" actually were.

I asked once. My mother pressed her lips tightly together and shook her head while my father snapped, "That's not something we need to talk about."

So, imagine my panic when I woke one morning to abdominal pain and bleeding. My first thought was I was going to need one of those "woman problem" operations. I knocked on Mom's bedroom door and whispered to her what had happened. "Just use the things under the sink," was all she said as she closed the door in my face. Later, she told me that I needed to watch how I acted around boys since I could get pregnant now. The whole situation left me terrorized. I wrote about my first period and my fears of having a baby at thirteen.

My father found my journal soon after that.

Found is a loose term. Dad was going through the drawers of my nightstand at the time (one of his, "It's my home, I can go where I want" search and destroy missions), and sat down for a good read. My mother approached me later and told me that Dad thought my journal was "disgusting," and how important it was not to write down anything I wouldn't want someone else to read. The fact that the journal had "private" written on the cover was immaterial. The next day, when I came home from school, my door was gone, and I never saw the journal again.

Six years later, I'm still not sure what he found so repulsive. I would think he'd be more concerned with my absolute lack of knowledge concerning the functions of my body, or at least show some sympathy for my fear of what was happening to me. But that's too much to ask from him.

Around that time, a girl from school, Lu, kind of adopted me. We're the same age, but she's a year ahead of me. My parents kept me home an extra year because I was "developmentally slower" than my peers. Even now, at nineteen, I feel like the least mature high school senior. My classmates surreptitiously talk to each other about favorite bands, games, and videos they watch online. I don't know where they find the time. Most of my home time is filled with chores. In my few free moments I read. It's the only activity I've found that lets me quietly escape. Things were better for me when Lu was still in town.

First, Lu filled in all the puberty "blanks." It was a relief to learn I wouldn't have to worry about spontaneous pregnancy. She became my best friend and made life in our close community a little more enjoyable. I poured out to her all the things I would have written in journal, and she made high school bearable by sharing my love of reading, inviting me over to watch approved movies, and simply talking to me. Lu made me laugh.

Now she's away at college, and I can't wait for her to come home for the summer. It's been a year of keeping my head down and getting my work done. I was lonely without her to talk to, so I started writing in my mind. Not novels or anything. More like sarcastic comments. I also love to play "Anywhere But Here." I've got a whole world I can imagine visiting. It's where I live when this place becomes too much.

Sometimes my fingers itch to hold a pen and fill a page with the inky strokes of deep thoughts, but except for one little thing, I've kept my writing solely for school work.

That one little thing? My notes to Jack. Those hastily scribbled words assure me that there is freedom beyond this suffocating town of Sampson. I just have to hang on.

The tightness in my shoulders relaxes when I hear my mother's car backing out of the driveway. I stand quietly in my room for a full minute after, listening for movement in the house. No one is upstairs but me. I hear the television come on, and I know that Roman has parked himself on the couch. It's safe. I pull Jack's note out of my pocket.

*My Ruby, I need to see you. I told your brother I was interested in selling my dirt bike. I'm bringing it over this afternoon. I told him five, but I'll be there at 4:30. I'll meet you outside of your garage. I miss kissing you. I love you. -Your Proteus.*

The note makes me smile. I only have to hold on for two more weeks.

# Chapter Three: Starting the Future

At 4:30, I am in the narrow space between the garage wall and the fence, kissing Jack until we are both out of breath. Then, he steps back and says, "I needed to talk to you. I was thinking that instead of going to Camp Galilee, we go someplace else."

"Where?"

"Dawes. My family went there a few years ago for a vacation. There is a university and some trade schools and a couple of factories, so we should be able to find work and eventually take some classes." His eyes burn into mine. "And we can get married. Right away."

"Yes."

He looks like he can't believe I'd agree so fast. He should have known better. I've wanted to get out of here for as long as I can remember. Our past three summers working at Camp Galilee in Crystal Falls were a glimpse into a free future.

Now that future is coming even sooner than I'd hoped.

"Hey."

Reflexively, I step away from Jack, staring at my brother, Roman, in horror.

That's right, my parents named us Roman and Julia, and no, they aren't Shakespeare fans. They get a little huffy every time a stranger brings it up. It doesn't help that our last name is Williams — as in William Shakespeare. Add to that two "Shakespearean" names, and strangers assume my parents are literary nerds — no such luck. They only read books suggested (assigned) by Dr. Jeffers, who self-publishes his "superior" thoughts six times a year.

I was named after my grandmother, my dad's mom, who hates me but loves my brother. They named Roman for the book in the Bible. He's lucky they didn't choose Deuteronomy. I would have called him Deuty for short.

Roman is looking at Jack's dirt bike, and I am hoping beyond hope that he didn't see me kissing my forbidden fiancé. He clears his throat and says to Jack, "So you said you wanted $1200 for this thing?"

Jack walks over casually. "That's right."

Roman shakes his head. "Nah. That's too much."

"What do you mean? You already agreed to it. I need the money."

"I know. I can give you $800."

I interrupt. "Roman, what are you doing?" I know Dad gave him the full amount to buy the dirt bike. It was Roman's reward for being the family's crown prince.

"Trying to keep you from making the biggest mistake of your life. Do you honestly think Dad and Mom are going to let you run off and get married?"

I want to point out that the "run off" part would mean that Dad and Mom wouldn't have much say in my wedding, but Jack beats me to it.

"They don't have to know anything about it. You don't have to say anything."

"And I won't — if you sell this to me for $800." He gives his usual oily grin that somehow turns the knees of the girls in the learning center to jelly but makes me cringe. He looks like our father when dad is trying to be charming. Fortunately, that doesn't happen much.

"It's not up to me. My dad is the one who set the price," Jack explains.

"He set the price, but he's giving you half, right?"

"Yeah, to put in the bank for college."

"Doesn't sound like you're planning to use it for college. Why don't you call him? See if he's willing to deal?"

Jack looks like he's about to pound Roman into the

ground, but he rolls his eyes and shrugs. "Fine."

Roman's greasy grin grows wider as he motions Jack toward the back door. "I'll be right in," he says.

I lead Jack into the house and pour us glasses of iced tea while he sits at the kitchen table and calls his father from our house phone. Most of the kids at our school don't have cell phones, myself and Jack included. There's a big, bad internet out there, and our parents and teachers want to protect us from any information they can't control.

Jack says, "Hi, Dad," but breaks off when the dirt bike roars past the window. We watch Roman race down the driveway and into the manzanita forest across the road from our place.

Jack lets out a huff of frustration and gets back to his dad while I shift from foot to foot, wondering what I should do. I'm not supposed to be alone in the house with a boy. But, of course, I already broke the spirit of that rule when I arranged to meet Jack outside for stolen kisses and secret engagement. A glance at the clock reminds me that Mom will be home soon, but not before Jack finishes his call and goes outside again. As soon as he gets off the phone, I'll tell him he can take his iced tea on the porch while he waits for Roman to return. In the meantime, I'll get started on the list of chores Mom keeps on the refrigerator door for me.

"Wash and peal the five-pond bag of potatoes for potatoe salad tonite."

Mentally, I corrected her spelling, then dump the bag of potatoes into one side of the sink and cover them with water and a few drops of vinegar before grabbing the vegetable brush to scrub each before peeling.

I'm halfway through the pile when I feel Jack's warm arms encircle my waist. I close my eyes and lean back into him, breathlessly awaiting his sweet words.

"Wow. That is a lot of potatoes."

It catches me off guard, and I laugh. Turning around, I plant a quick kiss on his lips. "My dad likes potato salad."

"Ugh. Can't stand it."

"I'm not a fan either, but what 'Daddy wants, Daddy gets.'" I know he'll get the reference. It's from a song the Junior Church girls sing every Father's Day.

"That is the creepiest song."

"Tell me about it. Now, get your tea and sit on the porch until Roman comes back. I've got to get these done and in the pot before mom gets home."

"One more kiss first."

I gladly oblige, enjoying the sweetness and strength of my wonderful Proteus. When we move to Dawes, I won't mind living in a crummy apartment or a broken-down trailer as long as I am with this man who loves me — and far from my parents.

It is a sound like a pistol shot that wrenches us apart. My mother stands at the kitchen island, the contents of her purse scatter from where she's slammed it down on the granite. Fury pours off of her in waves.

# Chapter Four: Assuming the Position

It is warm for mid-May, but my arms crawl with goose-flesh. My bedroom window is open, so I hear the cars arriving and then the heavy tread of cheap dress shoes on gravel.

A knock and then the doorbell. No one in this town does one or the other. It's always both.

Names are acknowledged in gruff disappointed voices instead of pleasant hellos. The front door closes with a va-cuumed *whoosh*, and "all is silence," to quote Hamlet — a guy I'm relating to, and even envying, right now. At least he had some power and autonomy.

Unfortunately, my situation is closer to Ophelia's.

I don't want either's ending. I want to live my life.

*Anywhere but here. Anywhere but here. Anywhere but here.*

The game's name repeats through my mind, but for once, I can't project myself into one of my fantasy locals. Some-times it's a cabin in the mountains, at others, a shack at the beach. Sometimes, it's even a castle in Denmark. Usually, it's a large, modern apartment in a big city, but right now? Bupkis. Bupkis was one of my friend Lu's words for awhile. She always mades a popping sound with her lips after announcing that something amounts to bupkis (pop!).

I used that word once at dinner to describe the final score of our volleyball game at school. As in, "I thought we were finally going to score, then Alenna ducked away from a spike, and it left us with bupkis." I left off Lu's pop.

Mother's lips drew into such a thin line that they practi-cally disappeared. "I don't think we need to use that word in our house. It doesn't sound very nice."

It was her go-to declaration for anything she didn't understand and therefore considered worldly.

"I don't think you need to read that book. It doesn't look very nice." So I returned *Cinder* to Lu without reading it.

"I don't think we need to watch this movie. It doesn't look very nice." *Well, no, it's about the Holocaust, so it isn't a "nice" movie by definition.* But I don't say anything as I eject *The Boy in the Striped Pajamas* from the DVD player and put it back in its case.

I wonder why she didn't object to today's meeting. "I don't think we need to gather all the decons from church to delve into our daughter's love life. It doesn't seem very nice." I hear the top stair squeak as I think this, and Mom is at my door.

"They're ready."

Her eyes rake over me to make sure I at least look respectable — an ankle-length denim skirt made from my brother's out-grown jeans, a half-dozen layered t-shirts, tights, and flats. My coarse light-blonde hair is pulled back tightly from my face and French-braided down the back, tied with a bit of glittery elastic. No makeup. No nail polish. No jewelry. In other words: perfectly presentable.

Mom jerks her bleached blonde bob toward the stairs, and I follow her down.

Seven deacons, my father included in the number, are crowded together on the couch and love seat. Dr. Jeffers is in my father's recliner. Dad sits next to him in a kitchen chair, a deposed monarch. Dr. Jeffers gestures to the ottoman in their midst, and I gingerly sink into its tufted top, studying my folded hands so I won't have to look at their faces.

Dr. Jeffers suggests we begin with prayer. He asks God for wisdom in dealing with me and the terrible situation I've gotten myself in. As soon as his courtiers echo his "Amen," he jumps right in.

"We've talked to Jack and his father already."

*Really? That was quick. It's only been an hour and a half since …*

"So we have a pretty good idea of what happened. Jack's parents were surprised to learn that the two of you were in a relationship. He told us this has been going on for the past eight months."

My father's glare turns my blood into crystals of ice.

"Mr. Carter searched Jack's room and backpack while we were there and found these." Dr. Jeffers reaches into his jacket pocket and produces a half-dozen sheets of notebook paper that were once origami hearts. "Do you recognize these?"

I mean to nod, but my head is too clumsy for quick motion. Instead, it hangs forward, too heavy to rise again. I wince as I hear the rustle of paper as the pages shuffle. Jack and I were stupid to assume that no one would figure out how we were communicating. Or that we *were* communicating.

As I sit, staring at my hands, the feeling comes over me, that strange phenomenon of being in a play — a very badly written, poorly performed play — acted by people who take their roles much too seriously. What is my big crime?

I kissed a boy.

I kissed my boyfriend.

My fiancé. (I carefully keep even the shadow of a smile off my lips.)

For that sin, I sit in a circle of judges who look like they are preparing to deliver a death sentence.

"'My dearest Proteus.'" Dr. Jeffers stops, and I imagine his smirk at my nickname for Jack, but he clears his throat and continues reading, "'I can't believe you smiled the whole time Mrs. Barker was yelling at you for sitting on the girls' side of the table during lunch. I know you were only goofing around, but she didn't get the joke. She doesn't get any jokes. She's a crab, but I don't want to see you get into trouble, and I don't want the girls to get in trouble either. During P.E., Barker told us we shouldn't flirt so much and then gave Magpie the stink-eye while all the other girls smirked at me, giving me side-eye, saying that I'm too ugly to worry about getting a guy in trouble. Polly picked that up right away and yammered about it the whole time she led calisthenics. She ran me into the mud when we were doing laps, and I'm pretty sure Magpie took my pink water bottle.'" Dr. Jeffers stops and waits until I look at him. "Who are these people you mention? This Polly and Magpie?"

I try to swallow, but my mouth is experiencing drought conditions. "They're just nicknames," I finally rasp.

"Nicknames for who?"

I silently corrected his question to end with "whom" and try to get him off that track. "I — I don't — they don't have anything to do with this." It comes out in a dry breath. My voice cracks from the utter lack of moisture.

"And yet you wrote about them smirking at you and giving you 'side-eye,' whatever that is."

I feel like "side-eye" is self-explanatory, and I don't offer to enlighten him. I go back to observing my hands and realize that they aren't moving at all — like they don't belong to me anymore.

The hand on my shoulder snaps me back to the present. My fingers, my hands — all my limbs — tremble.

"Come." The grip goes from firm to crushing. "Don't make me repeat myself."

I lurch off the ottoman, each step faltering as I follow Dad into the kitchen.

"Hands on the table."

Muscle memory takes over. Fingers splayed, palms supposed to act like suction cups on the old pine tabletop but too slick with sweat to grip. I hear the sickening scrape of the oversized decorative spoon lifted off its hook on the wall. When my friends talked about getting spanked with a wooden spoon, I thought they meant the large old-fashioned wall hangings like dad used on me. But no. They were talking about the little ones, like what I use to make cookie dough.

The first swat knocks me off balance — my pelvis slams into the edge of the table. Pain shoots through me, and I accidentally yelp — the word "no" involuntarily escaping my lips.

He pulls me back from the table by my braid and hisses, "You set your feet!"

I do as I'm told. I firmly plant my feet a shoulder's width apart and, after wiping my hands on the front of my skirt, replace them on the table and lean forward into the palms of my hands.

Smack.

"When Dr. Jeffers asks you a question, you answer it!" His voice never rises above a mutter, but his tone is like he's shouting.

Smack.

"When you go back in, you give him those names!"

Smack.

Smack.

A pause while he adjusts his grip.

Smack.

I hear the water in the sink slosh and a sopping wet dishtowel lands in front of me.

"Wipe your face and get back out there."

I pass the towel over my face, and, as gross as it is, I suck in some of the water. It tastes disgusting, a combination of potato dirt and vinegar tinge, but at least it gives my dry mouth some moisture.

Dad flippantly hangs the spoon back on its hook with the flare of a basketball player who shoots a basket as he walks off the court at the end of a winning game.

The crushing hand directs me back to the living room.

# Chapter Five: Facing the Accusers

"Who are Polly and Magpie?" Dr. Jeffers continues his questioning in a calm voice as if I hadn't just had the tar beat out of me in the next room. His uncaring expression makes me angrier than the beating. For the first time — ever — I speak up.

"Aren't you going to say anything about what just happened?"

I see Dad shift, ready to stand, but he settles when Dr. Jeffers waves him back and says to me, "What just happened?"

"My father just beat me." I can't help the indignant tone. I'm an adult woman whose father just spanked her.

An adult woman. I've never thought of myself that way before. I like it. But then again, this probably isn't the best time for an emotional breakthrough.

Dr. Jeffers looks at me from crown to foot with an arched brow. "You don't look like you've been beaten. I don't see any bruises or marks. I heard you screaming at your father. And it sounded like you were throwing a fit. Now answer the question. Who are Polly and Magpie?"

I'd read the phrase "he felt like the wind was let out of his sails" and knew what the idiom meant, but for the first time, I know how it feels. My brief moment of "adult" realization evaporates as different apprehensions begin to crowd my mind. The first is that none of these men are going to help me. That thought alone should cause me to panic, but it pales compared to problem number two: the adrenaline from the beating is wearing off. Usually, I'm sent directly to my room, where I can cry and wallow without witnesses. Instead, I find myself surrounded by human jackals and am expected to answer stupid questions in the proper "spirit of submission." I clench my fists as the pain spreads over the back of my thighs and my pelvis.

"Polly is Candice." The words come out in a gasp.

"Why call her Polly?"

I pause a hair too long as I breathe through a new wave of stinging welts rising on my buttocks and see my father lean forward again. I hurry on, "It's — it's because she repeats everything like a parrot. Everything the teachers say." I try in vain to breathe slowly, willing the needles to subside.

"So you don't like her because she supports the teaching staff."

I look up, blinking at the spin he gives my answer. "I like Candice — most of the time. It's not a big deal. It's more of a — an idiosyncrasy. We'll all agree with what is said, but she'll quote Mrs. Barker word-for-word and act like she's just thought of it herself — like she forgets she has a mind of her own."

"Who told you it was okay to have a mind of your own? You should have the mind of Christ."

I don't know what to say to that, and I try to suss out Dr. Jeffers's reasoning. Didn't God give us our minds? Did having the mind of Christ mean we were supposed to be brainless drones?

"Who is Magpie?"

That is a question I don't want to answer — mainly because Magpie's father is sitting to my right. I shift on the ottoman and gasp at the sharp stings on my thighs. Dad broke the skin again.

"Who is Magpie?" Frustration creeps into Dr. Jeffers's voice.

"Magpie is Alenna." I know Deacon Chase's eyes are boring into me, but I keep my own on Dr. Jeffers, knowing he'll ask the follow-up question.

"Why do you call her that?"

*No one's going to help me the way they always seem to help you, Alenna—so I'm just going to say it, and if fire rains down on your head, all I can say is — it's about time!*

The pain is bringing out my carefully suppressed anger.

"She's a thief." None of the men say anything, but I get the impression that no one is shocked. I should leave my statement to stand on its own, but the explanation spills out anyway. "When our class was in second grade, Mrs. DeVoe brought in a bird expert. He talked about magpies — about how they steal little bits of shiny metals and materials. One of the kids said, 'Oh! Like Alenna!' We've been calling her Magpie ever since."

"You're accusing her of stealing? Stealing what?"

"Anything and everything she can get her hands on."

"Have you ever told anyone that she takes things?"

"Of course."

Dr. Jeffers sits up a little straighter. "Now, Julia, I'm not only your pastor, but I'm also your principal. Alenna has been in our school since kindergarten. She has never, as far as I know, been in trouble for stealing."

I know that is a lie.

I also know it is true.

Students complain about her all the time, but the teachers won't do anything. Instead, they roll their eyes in frustration and quietly instruct us not to leave anything out where Alenna can take it. The common reasoning behind the special treatment comes from Alenna herself. Deacon Chase is one of the biggest givers at the church. It is why he is allowed to be a deacon even though he'd divorced twice and is now on his third marriage — a no-no for our church's leadership until Deacon Chase paid to have the roof replaced. Then the Scripture was re-interpreted to read that a deacon should be the husband of one wife at a time.

"You need to apologize to Deacon Chase for lying about his daughter."

"I'm sorry," I lie. *Sorry about not being sorry for calling your klepto daughter Magpie.*

Deacon Chase nods his acceptance of my false apology

then pulls a crookedly folded piece of paper out of his shirt pocket. "My daughter found this." Then, without breaking eye contact with me, he hands it to Dr. Jeffers.

Dr. Jeffers takes it between his index and middle fingers as if it were a flat cigarette. "You want to tell me what this says?" he asks me.

I shrug, beads of sweat popping all over me. "I don't know." It's not like I can see through the paper — what a stupid question.

"It was found at the school today," Deacon Chase supplies, and I instinctively know it was the note Jack passed to me at the end of the second break. I'd put it in my backpack. I know I had. How did Magpie get ahold of it?

"So instead of doing your schoolwork, you and Jack have been passing notes in class."

"No, sir. Jack and I never exchange notes during class. He handed me that one when we were coming in from the last break. I put it in my backpack to read later — at home." I had been so excited about seeing him at 4:30 that I had forgotten all about it.

"So it fell out of your backpack." Dr. Jeffers flips it open.

"No, sir. It couldn't have. I put it in the inside zipper pocket." I watch his eyes to see if they will look over at Deacon Chase and acknowledge that Alenna had gone into my bag and taken it, just like she steals every other thing she touches. I can't figure out when she did it. I know better than to leave my stuff unattended at school. The only time my backpack is out of my possession is when I'm at P.E.

Magpie must have gone back into the building while the rest of us attempted to play volleyball on the windy field.

Dr. Jeffers's eyes drop only as far as the note. He shakes his head and begins to read out loud. "'My Dearest Ruby,'" He begins, glancing up long enough to ask me, "Another nickname?" I nod once, and he continues. "'It tears me up having you so near and yet not being about to talk to you, touch you, hold you …'" his voice fades for a second as his and seven other pairs of eyes express their disapproval. "I know you're not allowed to date until college, but even then, we won't be able to do much more than sit together to talk. I wish we could skip college and just get married.'"

While I try to keep my face serene, my heart stutters, and I silently pray that Jack hasn't written our entire plan into the note.

"Four more years is four years too many. Love Proteus." Dr. Jeffers folds the note. "Why Proteus?"

"It's — it's from Shakespeare."

"You read a lot of Shakespeare?"

"Just what is in the English workbooks." *And any other plays or sonnets I can get my hands on via yardsales or the few forgotten paperbacks hidden in the school bookcase.* "He wrote about two characters named Julia and Proteus."

"It's not Julia. It's Juliet."

"The play wasn't *Romeo and Juliet*. It was something else. *Two Gentlemen from Verona*."

Another head shake of frustration, this time with his lips pressed tightly together. I imagine him saying, "That doesn't sound nice," in my mom's voice.

"These marriage plans — are they why you had him over to your house when your parents weren't home?"

Finally, a chance to explain. "No. I didn't invite Jack over. He came to the house because Roman said he was interested in buying Jack's dirt bike."

"Roman isn't buying any dirt bike," my father interjects.

I know better than to contradict my father's outright lie to Dr. Jeffers. One word, one head shake, and I'd be back at the table, having the welts on my legs opened up even further. Instead, I continue to speak directly to Dr. Jeffers. I'm afraid of the man in a very different way than I am afraid of my father.

"He told Jack he'd give him $800 for it. Jack told him he'd have to ask his dad since the price was supposed to be $1200." I already threw Alenna under the bus. I might as well send Roman to join her. "Originally, Roman said he'd pay the $1200, but he saw us together and told Jack to agree to $800, or he'd tell."

"So Roman knew." Dr. Jeffers pursed his lips.

"Yes." *That's what you get for being such a jerk, Roman.*

"He caught you kissing in the house — before your mom came home?"

"No, we were ..." *Oh, rats.* "We were outside when Roman said he'd only pay $800. Jack came into the house to use the phone to see if his dad would say it was okay."

"And what were you doing while he was on the phone?"

"Washing potatoes."

"But when your mother came into the kitchen, he wasn't on the phone, and you weren't washing potatoes."

"No."

"And your father says that your brother isn't buying a dirt bike." Dr. Jeffers suddenly rises from the recliner and stretches out a hand to me. I put out my own automatically, and he jerks me into a standing position. I wince and bite my lip. The pain in my thighs and buttocks is nothing compared to the pain in my pelvis. Dr. Jeffers ignores my ragged gasp of pain. "I think that's all we need to hear. Please excuse yourself while we talk to your parents."

No one says a word as I hobble up the stairs. I know the decons are likely waiting for the sound of my bedroom door closing. If that's the case, they'll be waiting a long time. So at the top of the stairs, I go into the bathroom instead. I make sure the door shuts with an audible click.

# Chapter Six: Enduring the Aftermath

The whole way to school, my eyes leak tears. Sitting is worse torture than the second beating I endured after Dr. Jeffers and the deacons left last night. My bandages pull as I gingerly climb out of the back seat, and I wince. I feel the dampness and know that some of the welts have begun to seep again.

No one attempts to catch my eye as I hobble into the learning center. No one even glances in my direction. Someone, probably Mrs. Barker, set up all of my things at the end of the grading table. The table is a heavy brown eight-footer that has its feet sunk into wooden blocks so that the top is waist-high. When it's time to grade our workbooks, we walk up to the table, pull the appropriate key, grade the checkups and self-tests, put the key away, and go back to our offices to frantically "correct" our work before we forget what the answer key said.

Since my stuff is at the table, I know someone called ahead and let the school know to make arrangements. No one heard the beating. No one saw any evidence of a beating. No one acknowledged that a beating took place. But somehow, everyone at the school knew I wouldn't be able to sit down at my office.

I stand all day, shifting from one foot to the other, trying to focus on my work while everyone around me treats me like a ghost.

Except for Mrs. Barker.

I remember when she was in high school, and she would help out in Jr. Church. She always went out of her way to talk to us church kids. Back then, we called her Miss Sofie, and we all loved her. She was one of our own. She grew up in our church and attended our school. When she graduated, she'd left home to go to college and taught at a Christian school in California. Then, she came back to marry Thomas Barker. None of us could figure out why in the world she'd want to marry him. He's kind of scuzzy. All the girls know never to be alone with him. Even the boys think he's creepy.

Everyone at church went to their wedding, not that we had a choice since it was held at the end of a Sunday service followed by our annual Fourth of July potluck. She talked to us girls who would be promoted into the Secondary Learning Center in the fall, telling us she would be our new teacher. We talked and played board games with her most of that day while her new husband played horseshoes with the "men of the church." The older women sat in clumps socializing with each other with disapproving shakes of their heads the way they always did.

Now we call her Mrs. Barker, and she's one of the meanest people I've ever met. It's obvious that she hates it here and takes it out on us. This year, though, she's kicked it into high gear. I think one of the reasons for the change is her promotion. She monitors the secondary work center as usual but is now Dr. Jeffers's personal assistant too. His old assistant, Mrs. Taft, was fired last summer when she let one of her daughters play rock and roll music at her wedding. So none of the Tafts come to our church anymore. Mr. Taft was nice, and I knew their youngest daughter, Amy, who graduated from the Secondary Learning Center the year I started. I kind of remember their oldest daughter, Caroline, but we didn't have much contact. She was shy and quiet and always looked uncomfortable in her own skin. Just before she moved away to go to college, at the same time Mrs. Barker did, she lost a bunch of weight and suddenly all the adults went out of their way to be nice to her. Then she came back from her first semester fatter than ever. Her mother was furious. The women at the church went out of their way to sympathize with her over her daughter's "lack of self-discipline," sometimes right in front of Caroline.

I remember feeling sorry for Caroline while everyone else felt sorry for Mrs. Taft. After that winter vacation, Caroline didn't come back.

Now Mrs. Taft and the rest of her family are gone too.

I don't miss Mrs. Taft. Her one expression was disapproval tinged with disgust. Now Mrs. Barker has the same look. Maybe it's a requirement for the personal assistant job.

After a service one Sunday night, I'd overheard Mrs. Barker tell the elementary monitor that she had hoped she wouldn't have to "babysit" the secondary students this year. Unfortunately, the deacons weren't able to hire a replacement in time, so she's doing double duty.

And it makes her crabby.

I swear the woman has demerit slips always within easy reach. She's why I was so careful about our notes. Passing notes was automatic detention. I haven't had many detentions this year, but most days, I come close.

Three demerits equals a twenty-minute detention at our school, usually writing out the verses we're supposed to memorize for the month. More demerits than three mean more time and harsher punishment — cleaning bathrooms, vacuuming, emptying trash, scrubbing walls, pulling weeds, etc. Followed by a guaranteed beating at home.

Too many mornings, I've walked in the door with at least one demerit for incomplete homework. Algebra is killing me. I have no idea what I'm doing or even what the workbooks are asking for, so by the time I have to go to bed, I've given up on math, shoved my workbook back into my backpack, and pick up a book to read before I go to sleep. I spend the rest of my school days monitoring my behavior even more closely than Mrs. Barker because I've already got a strike against me.

Today, I come into the learning center trembling. I'd tried to get as much homework done before Jack showed up at my house, but I still had math and science to do when I took a break to see him.

And then, everything fell apart, and homework wasn't even a blip on my thought radar.

I'm walking in with homework in two subjects undone, which means two demerits. If I get one more demerit, that means detention and yet another beating. I pray that Jack doesn't try to slip me a note when I'm so exposed up here at the grading table. I look in the direction of his office and realize that Jack is absent.

I add a new block of worry to my emotionally unstable tower.

Having to stand all day and dealing with the ever-present pain (no drugs allowed at school — not even Tylenol) makes it hard to concentrate. As a result, I'm much farther behind than I usually am when it's time for P.E. at the end of the school day. Finally, I catch Mrs. Barker's attention and, in my most submissive voice, say, "Would it be okay if I stayed inside today to finish up my work. I don't think I can do P.E."

"Do you have a note excusing you?"

"No."

"Then you need to change out and take the field." Mrs. Barker prides herself on treating everyone "fairly," which in her mind is torturing everyone the same amount. "It wouldn't be fair for you to stay inside when everyone else has to run laps." Then she frowns like she's not happy about what she's going to say next. "I'll let you walk your laps today."

I'm angry, but I don't let it show. In the bathroom, I slip out of my skirt and into my culottes and P.E. shirt. Calisthenics open every new welt, and by the time I finish my single lap, my soaked bandages are leaking. Mom puts down a towel in the backseat before I get in at car lineup. She doesn't want me to get blood on her upholstery.

She doesn't say anything to me on the ride home. Instead, Roman fills her in on what's happening in his privileged world. After she parks in the driveway, she walks past me to unlock the front door. By the time I get in the house, she's disappeared. I'm relieved. I'm not in the mood to talk about this ghastly day. I get a glass of water from the kitchen, then take the stairs one at a time. I toss my backpack inside my doorway before detouring to the bathroom for some pain reliever. I swallow four. Too many, I know, but I don't care. I drop my skirt and try to tape new bandages over the worst of the seeping welts using the mirror on the back of the door.

I hobble back to my room and stand in my doorway, my favorite part of my least favorite place on the planet. For a moment, I take in the warmth of the sunshine as it shines through my westward window, then I hobble forward where the mirror catches my reflection. It doesn't look like me — not like how I picture myself in my mind with rosy cheeks and sparkling eyes and shining blonde hair beautifully styled. Instead, I look like who they force me to be — an ugly, pathetic loser with long, braided hair, riddled with split ends, whose usual pasty skin has the addition of red-rimmed eyes. I haven't been crying. I'm just exhausted. I turn from my reflection and stand in the middle of my room, staring out of my window. This spot may be my favorite place in the house, but I'd rather be anywhere but here.

Anywhere.

Swinging my backpack onto the desk, I pull out my math, English, and history workbooks. I organize the booklets. Math will take the longest — and I hate it with a fiery passion, so I use it for my foundation, piling language and history on top of it. History won't take long, maybe five minutes.

I push the chair away from the desk, preparing to stand in its place to finish my work. But the hour of P.E. paired with hours of standing during the school day have taken their toll. My legs are jelly, and I know I can't stand a minute longer. So I decide to work stretched out on my bed.

After two minutes of reading and answering questions, my history is complete. I pull the English workbook closer and jump when I hear, "Why are you on the bed?" Mom is standing in the doorway, glaring at me. She's a stickler for conformity, and everyone knows homework should be done at a desk.

"I'm — just doing my homework. Would it be okay if I do it on the bed? My legs were starting to shake."

"It's fine — this once. Be downstairs in an hour to help with dinner."

"Yes, Ma'am."

The English packet is literature, thank goodness. Hand me a great story and get out of my way.

Unfortunately, this isn't a story. It's the historical background of George Eliot. I continuously lose my place as I search for words to fill in the blanks of my checkup while keeping an eye on the time. At the end of the assignment, I discover that I'm supposed to read Silas Marner. I hope it isn't very long since I need to get this packet done before graduation. Tomorrow I'll borrow it from the bookcase that comprises the school library.

Before I shove the workbook back in my bag, I turn to page thirteen and erase the lightly penciled circle around the page number. I turn back one page and carefully encompass the number twelve. Only twelve more days of school. The only thing left to do is about three packets of math. Mrs. Barker has already told me that I won't be graduating if I don't complete them by next Wednesday with at least an 80% on my tests. Knowing how long it takes me to complete a math book, I will be pushing that deadline. But I have to make it. I've got to get out of here.

It's only 4:45, but I decide there's no point in getting started on the last of my homework with only fifteen minutes left before dinner preparation. So instead, I gingerly slide off the bed, holding onto the edge of the mattress while waiting for the stiffness in my legs to loosen up. Then I'm off to the bathroom, followed by a tortuous journey down the steps. By the time I make it downstairs, it's five on the dot.

"Mom?" No answer. I peek out the window. There's no car in the drive. Out of reflex, I look for a note on the fridge. All it says is: "Meetloaf, baked potatoes, corn on the cob, salid, brownys." I pull the ground beef out of the fridge and dump it in a mixing bowl with a sigh. I bite my lip when I double-check the digital readout on the microwave. It takes an hour for meatloaf, and I'm already behind. As quickly as possible, I chop an onion and toss it in with the meat, two eggs, bread crumbs, and tomato sauce. Five minutes later, it's mixed, kneaded, shaped, and in the oven.

Next, I scrub potatoes, stab them, microwave them for eight minutes, and then throw them onto the top rack just above the meatloaf that doesn't even look warm yet. Wash down counter. Shuck corn, start a pot of water. Tear lettuce, cut veggies, put the completed salad back in the fridge next to the freshly made ranch dressing.

I open the brownie mix box and dump the powder, oil, egg, and water into a bowl. As I stir the ingredients, my hands begin to shake. I know that the meatloaf isn't even close to being done. The oppressive dread threatens to telescope my vertebra as I stare at the clock between the oversized fork and spoon hanging on the wall. If my room is my favorite part of the house, the kitchen nook is my least favorite.

If that clock shows that dinner is late — and I was the one responsible for getting it on the table — Dad will pull the giant spoon off the wall, tell me to set my feet, and begin swatting. Afterward, he'll expect me to sit in my chair, eat my dinner, and answer questions about my day — all without "attitude."

"Oh, God, let him be late today," I pray while wiping away the tears that are flooding my face. I can't stand another beating.

God answers my prayers. The family cars don't pull into the driveway until 6:30, a good half-hour late. By the time mom and dad come in, I've got everything on the table.

No one acknowledges me. Dad doesn't even wait for me to ease myself into my chair before beginning his formulaic prayer. I'm glad because it hurts like fire when the seeping welts stretch, and I can't keep the grimace off of my face

"Looks good, Mother."

"Thank you."

I sit quietly, pretending not to be annoyed as they purposely exclude me. Of course, dad knows that "Mother" had nothing to do with this meal.

"We had another meeting with Dr. Jeffers today."

It takes me a second to realize that Dad is addressing me. I nod to show I'm listening.

"He's decided that you're done."

I don't know what that means, but I know better than to ask. Dad's not finished, but he's going to make me wait for more information until after he's finished topping his baked potato with butter and sour cream. He pulls the two halves of the potato apart, slops the toppings onto each side, then picks one half up and bites off the end like it's finger food. I know I have to pay attention, but I don't want to look at Dad while he chews. He's not great about keeping his mouth closed.

"He gave us your diploma. You won't be walking at graduation." He sprays a little of the spuds as he mutters through his mouthful.

Oh.

Done.

I try not to smile when I realize it's over — thirteen days early. I accidentally flick a look at my brother.

"Don't look at Roman!" The tenuous calm of the room dissipates like it has experienced a lightning strike. My stomach clenches as he revs up. "It's not his fault you had to act like such a whore!" He tosses what was left of his potato back on his plate and wipes his fingers with a paper napkin. "I can't even eat with you sitting there. The rebellion rolling off you is smothering. Go to your room!"

I push back my chair, refusing to wince as I stand.

"Here. Take this with you." He pulls a crumpled paper from his front pocket and throws it at me. I catch it and hold it in my clenched fist as I back out of the doorway. As soon as I am away from his eyes, I smile and hobble up the stairs.

The math workbook lay closed on my bed, a pencil resting on top. Without pause, I pick it up and toss it in the trash, pencil and all. The English and history packet join it. I uncrumple the ball of paper that Dad threw to me. It's my diploma.

Now I just need to get out of here.

# Chapter Seven Relishing Freedom

I don't expect a holiday after getting kicked out of school, but I also don't expect Mom to nudge me awake the following day, complaining that I had overslept my alarm.

I didn't oversleep the alarm. I hadn't set it. I saw no reason to get up at six if I wasn't going to school.

Silly me.

Mom's agitated voice instructs me to hurry up and get in the shower. We have to leave in thirty minutes. I can grab a granola bar on the way out since I missed breakfast.

I don't jump out of bed. It's more of a cautious crawl. The raised welts are nearly gone, but they have left scabs and contusions in their place. My pelvis feels much better. The bruise is already yellow, so I know it will be gone soon. I slept all night on my stomach with my legs straight. Now, stiff all over, I "mummy walk" to the bathroom.

I assume it's a "mummy walk," Since *The Mummy* didn't "sound like a nice movie," so I've never seen it.

After my abbreviated shower, I throw on a few t-shirts and a heavy denim skirt. I don't even want to think about bending over or sitting down to put on shoes. I don't know where I'm going, but I hope it's flip-flop-friendly.

In the back seat on the passenger side, I pretend a feeling of indifference and try to angle my face directly behind the headrest in front of me as we pull into the school parking lot. My brother exits the front seat with a gruff "bye" to Mom and a slam of the door. I pretend I'm somewhere else while my former fellow students stare at me and whisper to each other. I guess my time as a ghost is over. I avoid their eyes, and my mind echoes the familiar refrain:

*Anywhere but here. Anywhere but here. Anywhere but here.*

A flicker catches my eye, and all pretense is gone. Jack walks by without a glance. A couple of guys from our class slap him on the back. Magpie welcomes him with a girlie giggle. He disappears into the doorway, and our car lurches forward.

I have no thoughts. No coherent ones anyway. They won't stop swirling long enough for me to pin any of them down.

When we pull into Walmart, I'm stunned. It's a half-hour away from the school, and I don't remember a single mile of the drive.

Mom thrusts a page from a yellow legal pad at me. "I have a hair appointment. I need you to pick up everything on this list." With that, she's out of the car and walking into the store. I'm thankful to find a cart nearby. At least I can lean while I walk.

The place is buzzing. Weird for so early in the morning. Senior citizens crowd the grocery section, so I scan the list to see if Mom needs anything from the rest of the store, which is slightly less packed.

I skip the vitamin aisle — it's three deep — and head for makeup. I'm not allowed to wear it, but Mom keeps her vanity table stocked. I get the makeup remover, mascara, and blush from the list and add a bottle of face wash and emergency spot treatment for me. The stress of this week has played havoc with my already bad complexion. My jaw and chin itch from all the little bumps under the skin, just waiting to erupt.

I jostle through the hair-care aisle and swing my cart toward body washes and deodorants. There's a sudden crescendo of voices, and I peek around the corner. As if called by some silent whistle, all the old people in the store have joined the snake-like lines at the two express lanes. They sound like they're either visiting with friends or grumbling about the wait — or both, I guess. I check the vitamin aisle for the third time, and this time it's empty. Ghost-town empty. A lone bath pouf goes rolling by like a tumbleweed.

Not really, but you get what I mean.

Iron, multivitamins, calcium, and I'm gone. Off to produce.

I get the grocery shopping done in record time and touch base with mom at the salon. She's going to be at least another thirty minutes, so I take a stroll to electronics. Very few kids at school have cell phones yet, myself and Roman included. We can't afford it. Or it's not good for me to have one. I'm not sure which, if either, argument is the valid one. Mom talks about tight budgets. But every time Dr. Jeffers preaches on the evils of the internet and tells parents to be vigilant since kids now have access to the internet right on their cell phones, Dad agrees with a bellowing "AMEN!" and smirk in my direction.

Nevertheless, I'm supposed to get one for graduation to have it for college — I guess that's the magic age when cell phones no longer threaten my well-being. As I caress every cell phone at the counter, it hits me that no graduation will automatically translate to no cellphone. After a flash of disappointment, I tell myself I'd rather buy my own phone anyway — after I leave home, of course.

Working my way to the front, I stop by a display of t-shirts. It's almost time for me to restock my collection. I look for any colors I don't already have. I have to wear them in layers so my bra straps don't show through. Mom checks. I find a navy v-neck that can replace the one that got ruined at the last bonfire — a victim of yet another attempt at s'mores — and mentally add it to my list of things I need for camp this year — or for what my parents will think of as camp this year.

Instead, I'll shop for camp, get on the bus for camp, get off at the next station, and then get on a different bus with Jack and begin my life as a married woman. Somehow I don't feel wrong scamming my parents into buying me a few t-shirts before I say *sayonara*.

A white sundress with an abstract peach-colored flower blooming over it catches my eye, and I check the tag. Only fourteen dollars. I mentally add it to my "new-life" shopping list. It would make a lovely wedding dress.

I'm looking for a shrug or cardigan to wear with my future dress — can't have bare shoulders, you know — when I see mom exiting the salon. Her hair is glowing. Radioactive, even. She's a natural blonde, but it's the same color as mine — a shade that Dad refers to as "dirty-dishwater." He willingly pays for her to get it "brightened." She says it's a golden blonde with platinum highlights. It's a brassy yellow with streaks of white, and it costs a small fortune every month. I'm pretty sure it's the real reason I don't have a phone.

Mom empties the cart onto the conveyor, clucking her tongue at some of my choices as if paying five cents more for a can of corn is going to break us when she just laid out over $200 at the salon. I keep my face neutral and reload the cart with bags of groceries while she pays with a card and a flick of the wrist.

She drops me at home with the purchases and takes off again to "run errands."

"After you put all the groceries away, you can have lunch. No T.V. You can get started on the laundry too. I'll be back in a few."

I don't ask, "a few what?" From the verbal list she gave me, I know it's hours.

Hours.

Alone.

Freedom!

I hustle to get the laundry in. I know "get started on the laundry" is code for "have it washed, dried, folded, hung-up, and put away before I get back." The groceries are easy. Lunch. Yes, please! I'm starving, but if you think I'm going to eat it at the kitchen table, you're crazy. Every time I look up and see that stupid wooden spoon, I shudder. I make a peanut butter and honey sandwich and head to the living room, snagging *The Wonder Book* from the family bookcase on the way.

My parents have never read *The Wonder Book*. I'm glad

because they'd probably chuck it. They don't like things they don't understand, and they don't read much of anything unless Dr. Jeffers assigns it to them. Our bookcase is crammed with glossy-covered self-published paperbacks by other honorary doctors and Christian college administrators. *The Wonder Book* isn't glossy or a paperback. It's old — like it was my great-grandfather's old. And it's a hardback covered with faded red fabric. Mom keeps it on the bottom shelf because she thinks it's ugly.

It's anything but. I discovered it a year ago when I read about Nathaniel Hawthorne in one of my school workbooks. I was assigned *The Scarlet Letter* and loved it. Mrs. Barker was surprised at my reaction. She confessed that she hated giving it to students because they constantly whined and complained. I had to return my copy of *The Scarlet Letter* to the school when I finished the language workbook, but I asked my parents if I could buy a copy for myself since I wanted to re-read it. They looked at me like I had two heads.

"Why do you need to read a book more than once?" It sounded like a question, but it wasn't. Instead, Dad was letting me know it was a stupid idea.

"We can't afford a lot of unnecessary purchases right now." Mom backed him up with her go-to argument.

That evening, while watching *Wheel of Fortune* with the family, I noticed the shabby red book on the bottom shelf. In gold print on the spine was the word "Hawthorne." When Mom and Dad went to the kitchen for ice cream, I grabbed the book and took it straight to my room. My brother didn't notice. He was busy playing a game he'd downloaded onto Dad's phone. Dad has an unlimited plan, by the way. So much for the evils of the internet.

That night I opened my new find. It was a kid's book, but I didn't mind because it drew me in immediately. I thought Eustace a ridiculous name, but so is Roman. I'm glad my name is somewhat normal.

*Oh, my goodness! Just imagine someone named "Normal"!*

Getting back to *The Wonder Book*, it's about this family that gets together for holidays, and the oldest cousin, a guy named Eustace, entertains the younger kids by telling stories from Greek mythology. It's a great book. I've read it four times so far. One part of the book really gets to me. One of Eustace's older male relatives insists that Eustace tell the adults one of the stories he's been relating to the little kids. Eustace tells an engaging, sweeping saga about "The Three Golden Apples" in the Hesperides' garden. Mr. Pringle condescendingly smiles when it's all over and declares that while it is very entertaining, the stories Eustace tells are far from educational, so they're like "bedaubing a marble statue with paint." I had to look up the word "bedaubing."

I admit it. Every time I get to the part about Mr. Pringle, I picture him with my father's face and hear his voice.

I know I should love my father, but I don't.

I wish I did, but I can't.

I've tried.

I want to get out of here and never see any of these people ever again.

I hate myself for saying that.

What is wrong with me? Why can't I love them?

I can obey them — usually. I try to be obedient. I swear, I do.

I can even honor them. I've sung the creepy song on Father's Day. I add extra touches to the meals I make. I complete every chore they give me to the best of my ability. I do all of this to — to — honor them?

Maybe.

Maybe the reason I do all those things is to prove to them that I'm worth loving.

Is that so wrong?

My reading is interrupted periodically by dings from the washer and dryer, prompting me to get up, add fabric softener, or fold the warm laundry. By 3:30, I've put everything away, and I've gotten a head start on the chocolate cake I'm making for dessert tonight. Mom's car pulls into the driveway just long enough for Roman to pour himself out and slouch into the house, and then she's off again.

He ambles past me to the laundry room and comes out in only his boxer briefs. I keep my eyes on the cake batter. It drives me insane when he strips down and walks through the house. He's been doing it since he was old enough to walk. It wasn't so bad when he was a toddler, but it's just icky now that he's sixteen. Just once, I'd like to hear dad give him the same "modesty" speech he gives me.

"Mom said for you to wash my uniform and P.E. clothes." His voice echoes back to me as he clumps up the stairs.

Of course she did. Goodness knows precious little Roman can't wash his clothes.

I check every pocket before his clothes go in the wash, holding my breath the whole time. The boy needs to get a little closer to the deodorant in the morning. Once the soapy water starts foaming up over the clothes, I close the lid and pick up his P.E. bag. I hear a crinkle. I don't usually go through my brother's stuff, but I can't seem to help myself today. In one of the pockets of his bag, I find a crookedly folded piece of notebook paper. I open it just enough to see "Ruby" scrawled near the top and quickly shove it into my skirt pocket.

My hands shake as I pour cake batter into pans, put on oven mitts, grab a couple of potholders as well, and set the rounds in the preheated oven. I hear the T.V. on in the living room, so I know where Roman is. Still — I have to be more than careful. I set the timer for the oven, wipe down the counter and then head upstairs to the only room with a locking door.

Sitting on the toilet, the cold seat feeling good on my bruised thighs, I pull the note from hiding.

*Ruby,*

*I can't believe how twisted everything got. I heard you weren't walking at graduation and couldn't believe it. I offered to leave early too, but they said it "wouldn't look right" for the valedictorian to mess with what they already have planned.*

*I want you to know I'm sorry about everything. It's like that book we read at camp last year — I can't remember what its title is. So frustrating, but it's all the same.*

*It's gotten so that I'm not even looking forward to camp. This is not the way I wanted to end my senior year — alone on a bus.*

*I hope you're doing well then. I wish I could go back in time and switch. Maybe I'll see you — even if I can't sit with you on the bus.*

*-Proteus*

*P.S. People at school miss you. Is there anything from your office that you want? Tell Roman to tell me. I'll see him Saturday at 2. Or he can give me a call. It's a little tense between him and I. I'm rebuilding our relationship the best I can. Not sure if this is something we can over come. Can't wait until it's over.*

*-P*

I wipe a stream of tears from my eyes with a wad of toilet paper. So much for running away, I think. I stand and splash some water on my face, then stare at myself in the mirror. Good grief, I'm ugly. I wonder what Jack sees in me. I have the expression of a girl newly jilted. I'm in shock that it's over, but have to acknowledge that he was too good for me anyway.

I think about his note. It is apologetic but cold and doesn't sound like Jack at all. His notes tended to be crooked and sloppily written, but his grammar and spelling were always on point. And what was the deal with the book? We'd only read one book together — a kid's story we'd read with some campers last year. I can't remember the title either. It wasn't well written, so I'd let my mind drift whenever it wasn't my turn to read. I recall something about a group of kids pretending to be spies, and — I watch my red-rimmed, blonde-fringed eyes widen in the mirror and sit down as quickly as I can. I scan the letter again and feel a smile stretch over my face.

The characters in the kid's novel underlined sentences in books. The last word in each sentence was their code. Rereading Jack's note, it says, "Got it planned. Everything same. Camp bus. Then switch bus." The P.S. is "Want me to call? I can come over."

Now my tears are happy ones as I tear his note into teeny-tiny pieces and flush the confetti down the toilet.

# Chapter Eight Changing Plans

The cake still has twenty minutes left to bake, so I pull my duffle bag off the top shelf of my closet and do a little pre-packing. I am excited about "camp." I'll still have to wait a week and a half for school to let out before mom grudgingly takes me to Walmart to get me summer clothes, but there are a few things I can pack now. All my sweaters, for instance. Camp nights can get cold, especially at the beginning and the end of the season, so mom won't think it strange that I've packed them ahead of time. I purse my lips, looking over my wardrobe. It is primarily long denim skirts (made from the jeans Roman has outgrown) and tees. I wear the same thing to school, church, and camp. I think about the dress I saw in Walmart and can't wait to buy it once I get to Dawes. A real dress! Floaty and light and feminine. And a pair of jeans. I've always wanted a pair of jeans. I hope that when we marry, Jack will be okay with me wearing them.

That prompts me to lift the lid of the decorative teapot on my dresser. Inside is my stash of babysitting cash. My camp money from previous years is in a joint account at my parents' bank and earmarked for college. It would be nice to withdraw it, but I'm not sure if I can do that without my parents knowing about it. I'll go to a bank branch near the camp and remove it just before Jack and I take off into the sunset. Another plan is made.

I lay out my pile of small bills and grimace at the $73. It isn't going to get me very far, but I put it in the front pocket of my duffle.

The smell of chocolate cake fills the house, and I hustle

downstairs to check on it. Mom still isn't back, but, as usual, tonight's menu is on the fridge. Another potato dish. Shocking. When I leave, I won't eat potatoes for at least a year. Mom pulls in just as I finish all the prep work. I roll my eyes at myself when I realize I forgot Roman's clothes in the washer. I don't bother to start the rinse cycle over again. Instead, I open the door and throw them in the dryer without a dryer sheet. I can't bring myself to care about his static cling.

"You didn't finish the laundry?" Mom's greeting was barbed with a dramatic sigh.

"I finished everything but Roman's P.E. clothes. They're in the dryer now."

"And dinner isn't done."

I look around the kitchen in confusion. Creamy mashed potatoes are in a pot on the back of the stove, the broccoli is in the steamer waiting to start cooking for precisely seven minutes before it needs to be on the table, the chicken thighs, coated in breadcrumbs, are baking in the oven, and the chocolate cake is frosted and on its stand. It's still fifteen minutes to 6:00.

"Go upstairs, and I'll take over here." She clucks in frustration as I leave the room. "Don't bother coming down for dinner."

"Yes, Ma'am." I don't mind missing dinner. I'm hungry, sure, but not so hungry that I want to sit at the table of stress and torture.

My relief is short-lived. Dad demands everyone be at dinner. Mom isn't happy about being overruled, but she doesn't argue. "Set the table," she barks.

I am accompanied in my habitual placing of flatware and plates by the sound of my brother's frantically fishing through every pocket of his P.E. bag still in the laundry room. Yet, I keep my face serene, knowing he'll never find the note from Jack.

I silently pray he won't realize that accusing me of receiving a note from Jack is enough to get me in trouble.

At 6:00, we are seated, Dad's complete concentration on his plate, mom's lips still in their disapproving tight line, and Roman pouting. I eat as invisibly — and as quickly — as possible. We are almost fifteen minutes in before the drama starts. All I can think is: at least I ate all of my chicken.

"Roman," Dad starts without preamble, "You'll be taking Julia's place at Camp Galilee. Julia's staying home this summer."

I stay silent though my thoughts are swirling. Roman isn't so careful. He sputters a protest before Dad's glare brings him up short. "We don't think it's wise for Julia to spend the summer with Jack at camp, but it wouldn't be fair to Brother Topher to leave him shorthanded. So we told him we were sending you instead. Julia can tell you what your job is."

I feel my upper lip curl ever so slightly before I get it under control. There is no way Roman would want to do my job at the camp.

"Well?" A bellow from dad. I swear the man has only two sets on his volume control — menacingly quiet and roaring like a bull. I blink when I realize he's addressing me, demanding I tell Roman his camp duties now.

I reel them off. "I helped in the kitchen with all of the prep work, cutting up fruits and vegetables, opening cans, hauling meat out of the coolers. Last year I also took over the salad bar. During food service, I was the hostess in the dining room. I monitored food availability, letting the kitchen know when things were about to run out. I also kept an eye on the trashcans. They have to be emptied before they get too full. After meals, I wiped down the tables and chairs in the dining room and swept the floor. After dinner, it needs mopping as well. Sometimes, the staff is tagged to help take care of campers. We'll lead them in a devotional, read a book with them, or take them on a hike while their regular councilors are in meetings. But that doesn't happen very often." I nudge a tiny cloud of mashed potatoes off my corn and slip a forkful of niblets into my mouth. We don't eat corn directly off the cob — "It doesn't look very nice."

I concentrate on my plate, so I don't have to watch the rest of my family's faces after my announcement. I don't need to. I can sense their confusion. Roman isn't skilled enough to do even the simplest task in the camp kitchen. I wish I could watch someone hand him a number ten can and direct him to the giant manual opener attached to the end of the prep table. He wouldn't have a clue how to use it. Maybe I should write a note to Chef Dan at Camp Galilee. An introductory letter like in Jane Austen novels.

*Dear Chef Dan,*

*Since I am currently a disgrace to my family, I send you my brother in my place. He is, unfortunately, an arrogant oaf who has never been trained in a single life skill. He has never swept or mopped a floor, taken out the trash, or washed a dish. However, I can guarantee that he will mope, sigh, pout, and grumble at every opportunity. I wish I could assure you that his best friend, Jack, will be there to guide and help him in his first foray into the workforce, but, alas, Jack and I will be running away to Dawes, where we will marry and live as adults instead of as adolescent children always swayed by the whims of our parents. May you have a pleasant summer.*

*-Julia*

Poor Chef Dan.

"May I be excused?" I whisper to my mother, and she nods. I rinse the potatoes off my plate and put it into the dishwasher as quietly as I can, listening to my dad give Roman advice on convincing Brother Topher to provide him with more "manly" duties. I don't offer the information that the kitchen crew has many guys — including Chef Dan. It's a pretty equal mix. Last year, on the girls' side, were my best friend, Lu, a prepper who cut mounds of fresh fruit and vegetables every day and kept the refrigerators, freezers, and pantries in order, Brother Topher's wife, Ms. Denise, and his daughter, Sylvie, who acted as the camp's bakers, and me — second prepper, dining room hostess, and general gopher to all the kitchen staff.

The men assisting Chef Dan were Douglas, the kitchen

staff manager, two line-cooks, Tyler and Marcus, and two dish-washers, Nick and Andy, who also did all the cleanup after hours — in the kitchen anyway. Lu and I did the cleanup in the dining hall, with some occasional assistance from Nick and Andy.

The work was hard, no doubt about it, but it wasn't difficult to learn — for most people.

It would be nearly impossible for Roman. He hated manual labor. He didn't mind working out or playing sports, but hand him a broom, and his lips curl in disgust as he comes up with all the reasons why he shouldn't have to sweep the floor. The only person who can make Roman do anything chore-like is Dad, and he isn't much for manual labor either. The camp supervisors aren't going to put up with Roman's excuses. He is in for a rough summer.

I finally let a smile slip as I move up the stairs, but it disappears before I hit the top step. Mine and Jack's plan was contingent on us slipping away from the group on the way to camp and hopping another bus to Dawes.

I sit in the back of the church during the Wednesday night prayer meeting. My parents are two rows from the front, and Roman is seated next to Jack among the youth group on the auditorium's right side. When I had attempted to sit in my usual spot, Mrs. Brand, the youth leader's wife, touched my shoulder and asked me to find a seat elsewhere. So I plunk my butt on the back row and stifle a yelp of pain. I had forgotten to sit carefully.

I stand and open the hymnbook to the announced page at the music leader's direction, but I sing with my eyes closed. I've sung these songs since I was a toddler, and I love them. So I let the words and notes soothe me while I drink in the beauty of the carefully crafted lyrical poetry.

When the song finishes, I open my eyes to find Lu standing next to me. I give her a quick hug before easing back onto the pew. We don't say anything, hyper-conscious that we're being stared at by creepy Mr. Barker, who is slowly pacing the back of the sanctuary.

If someone comes in late, Mr. Barker helps them find an empty seat (and there are plenty of them), but he also keeps track of who leaves to go to the bathroom and directs them to a back seat when they return so they won't be distracting. If a child starts crying, he'll suggest the nursery. If people talk, he'll shush them.

We don't have many returning visitors.

Lu and I wait patiently for prayer requests to be announced and expounded upon before everyone separates into little groups. We are ignored, which is fine with us. Before we pray, I notice my parents facing each other in their usual seats, bowing their heads serenely, a perfect picture of a spiritually mature couple, still in love after two decades of marriage. Suddenly I wonder how many other illustrations of spiritual leadership around here are fake. Finally, I bow my head, and Lu begins to pray.

"Dearest Heavenly Father, be with my wonderful friend, Julia, who has recently received the distressing news that she won't be graduating with her class. Help her remember that you have her best interests at heart and that it's only another week before we go to camp together where I will be both her boss since I got the promotion for kitchen staff supervisor and her roommate. So be with us as we meet at her place tomorrow morning. Give her guidance and blessing, oh, Lord, and help her as she goes through this trial, Amen." She squeezes my hand, and I begin.

"Heavenly Father, thank you for bringing Lu home safe from college. I've missed her so much. Thank you for blessing her with the promotion at the camp. Help her not to be too disappointed that I won't be joining her this year." There is a little gasp from Lu, but I go on. "Help her as she trains Roman to take my place and help him to do his best work for her. Be with Brother Topher as he sorts everything out. Be with all of us this summer. Amen."

A piano starts quietly playing as people break from their groups and go back to their seats. The youth group files past me on their way to the youth room, where they will play a game and listen to a sermon about what clothes they should wear and what music they should avoid. Most stare at me curiously, but a few refuse to glance my way. Jack gives me a smile that disappears so quickly that I wonder if I imagine it. Roman looks past me at Lu and raises his eyebrows at her as he licks his lips suggestively. I hear her disgusted groan. He hears it too, and he grins as he mouths the words "Hey Lu-ser." His nickname for my best friend.

There is something seriously wrong with that boy.

Lu and I sit through the sermon and the final hymn. Then, as the congregation dismisses, she gives me a hug and whispers, "See you tomorrow," before sliding out of the pew and through the back door.

With mom's permission, I sit in the car while everyone visits. I go over as much of Lu's prayer as I can remember. She was promoted and arranged for us to share a cabin at camp. That would have made for a fun summer. Almost as good as getting married.

Then I give a laughing snort as I realize Lu is going to be Roman's boss. Lu got her promotion because she's a natural-born leader. If you're on her team, you perform. She drives her workers to perfection.

By the time summer is over, Roman will be whipped into shape.

# Chapter Nine Reconnecting

Lu knocks and rings the doorbell just minutes after Mom and Roman pull out of the driveway. "I waited until the coast was clear," she jokes.

"When did you get back?" I ask with a hug, then lead her into the kitchen, where I was beginning breakfast clean-up.

"Yesterday afternoon, around four. I ate dinner with the fam, heard about the implosion of my best friend's life, was grilled about my own, and went to church — you know, the usual." The look she gives me doesn't match the off-hand, casual tone of her voice. She is concerned about the mess I've made of my life.

"Coffee?"

"Coffee? Really?"

"Yep. Fresh pot and everything."

"You're not going to tell me what happened?"

I shrug as I pull a mug out of the cupboard and fill it. "You already know what happened."

I don't expect the little hitching sob at the end of my sentence, and I'm certainly not anticipating the full-on ugly cry as Lu pulls me close in a fierce embrace. When I show signs of slowing, she steers me to a barstool, looking confused when I don't hop onto it. I'm still a couple of days of healing away from that. One thigh is especially sore, and the skin feels tight all the time.

Lu tears off a few sheets of paper towels, thrusting them into my hands so I can stem the flow of snot and tears that pour over my face.

"You sure you don't want to talk about it?" Lu's look goes

from hopeful to defeated as I shake my head no.

"I want to know what you've heard," I squeak out.

I feel Lu's eyes study my face as I attempt to hide behind my wet towels. "Okay," she finally agrees. "Grab your coffee, and we'll sit outside." Lu grabs the paper towels off the dispenser on her way out of the kitchen with her usual flair.

The cushioned gliders on the front porch are much more comfortable than our conversation.

"So — the note thing — that I understand. Jack, not so much. Trust me, if you wait for college, you'll be a part of a larger dating pool, and it will be easier to identify and separate the good guys from the dweebs we have around here."

"Jack isn't a dweeb," I say quietly, not used to defending my fiancé. Everyone loves Jack. He's the captain of both the football and basketball teams, valedictorian, and the best-looking guy at school. I shift uncomfortably as the thought I so often push down comes roiling to the surface — what does he see in me? It's got to be love, right? Why else would he choose a pasty thing like me for his future bride? Yeah. Why?

"You okay?" Lu takes a sip of her coffee, her eyes peering over the mug to my face.

I nod and take a sip of my own. "Well?" I finally prompt, "What else have you heard?"

Lu's information is surprisingly accurate. She even knows about the beating. I ask if her dad told her since he's on the deacon board and had been an eye-witness to my humiliation, but no, she'd heard it from Jack. That makes me sit up a little straighter.

"You've talked to Jack?" I wonder who told him. Roman maybe?

"Last night after service." She pulls a folded note out of her pocket and hands it to me. I snatch and unfold it all in one motion.

*Dear Ruby,*

*I love you. I can't wait for us to be married so we can start our lives. I need to see you. Let me know the best time for me to come over. This time, we'll make sure no one is around. You can get a message to me through Lu.*

*I'm still trying to work out our plans. I'm not sure what to do. Now that you're not going to camp, I think we should leave earlier. When can you go? I'd go tonight if I could, but I should stay for graduation. The class is counting on me. We NEED to meet and discuss our final plans.*

*-Proteus*

I run through each sentence to ensure that he isn't using the secret code, but it's a straightforward message. Finally, I fold the note and begin the ritual shredding. Lu looks alarmed. "Bad news?"

"No." Then I stop short. "Yes? I mean, we're still trying to figure things out, but he still loves me, so that makes everything okay, right?"

"You asking me or telling me?"

My brain fogs and I can't think of how to answer her. Fortunately, she continues without my input.

"Because if it's a question, the answer is no. I've spent the last nine months surrounded by girls who are all on the Great Husband Hunt, crying their eyes out when the guy they decided was 'the one' asked out someone else. On the other hand, I know of three girls — three — who signed up for piano lessons the first week of college because they met a guy who said he'd prayed for a piano-playing wife. But they didn't say that they were learning piano because they wanted to impress him —it was because they loved him and knew he was the one God had chosen for them."

"Wait, I'm confused," I break in. "Was — were they all after the same guy?"

"Well, those three, yeah, but I saw dozens of girls twisting themselves up for guys they said they loved. It turned them into crazy people."

"You think I'm crazy?"

Lu sighs and drains her mug. "No. I think you're acting like a teenager."

I bristle at that. Lu is the same age as me, technically a teenager herself.

"But not crazy," she continues. "It is everything else that is insane. I mean, who gets expelled from school for passing notes? Or even for kissing her boyfriend? And why isn't Jack kicked out too? I mean, I know why, but it's nuts!"

I know why too. It's because Jack is a boy. That's all.

Lu keeps ranting. "This whole 'boys are best' garbage has to stop. I shared a dorm suite with five other girls who were all straight-A students. They were all involved in extra-curricular activities. All played instruments. All sewed —."

"You do all those things."

"Yeah. I do. I learned to do all of those things because I enjoyed them, but when I got to Palmdale, I realized I was in the middle of this big group of girls who spent years training to be wives — like that was their life goal. I felt like I was in some crazy Jane Austen novel with an invisible mom crying, 'Mr. Collins!' after every pimply-faced boy that walked by."

It feels strange to laugh, but I can't help myself. The six-hour *Pride & Prejudice* mini-series was our favorite, and we tended to bawl out that line at each other for a week or so after watching that episode. "So, what did you do?"

"I went to one mixer — one — where my fears were confirmed. And then I pulled an 'Elizabeth.'"

Translation: she read.

"Even with all of the homework and papers and hours of required 'ministry work,' I read twenty-seven books over the last nine months. I spent all of my free time in the library, reading a little bit of everything. As a result, I've never felt more clear-headed." She gives me a frank look. "You should try it."

"You don't think I'm clear-headed."

"Question or statement?"

"Does it matter?"

"No and no."

She lets me absorb that for a minute.

"Maybe take this summer to ask yourself what you want

out of life. Is it a marriage at nineteen? If it is, fine, do it. If you want something else instead of, or as well as marriage, now is the time to figure that out. Don't float along with the stream just because it's the easiest choice." She stands abruptly. "I've gotta get going. I've got a mountain of laundry waiting at home — all the bedding from school as well as my clothes. I put laundry off during finals week, and now it's out of control." She looks down at me and smiles. "You're going to be okay. Just take some time to think. And if you need to borrow any books, let me know."

I stagger to my feet and lead her back inside to grab her purse, but instead of taking it and leaving, she drops a small bomb even as she hands me the coffee mugs, and I load them into the dishwasher.

"Just so you know, I have a boyfriend now." She blurts it out as if there is no easy way to broach the subject, so she might as well get it over with. I stare at her, my mind trying to wrap itself around the information. She'd just spent the last half-hour going on and on about the dweebs in college and how my own choice of boyfriend was suspect.

She nervously hands me a plate from the counter, and I slip it into the dishwasher's rack. "It's Sione," she adds.

I close the appliance door and wash my hands before turning back to her. This news deserves my full attention. "You and See?" Sione, the head lifeguard at Camp Galilee, is a six-foot-four, heavily muscled Samoan guy whose family moved to the mainland when he was ten. He's not much for small talk. He runs a tight team, ruling the pool from his exalted perch and keeping an eagle eye on swimming campers. But after a long day of keeping campers safe, he keeps to himself. Even at meals, he spends his time reading rather than taking part in the dinner conversation. The guy always has a book in his pocket, ready to read whenever he gets some downtime.

Things become suddenly clear. "Is that why you spent all of your freshman year in the library?" I ask. Lu blushes.

Lu's always been a reader, but it was usually YA, dystopian stuff. The only classic lit she read was the books assigned to her in school.

"It was at first," she confesses. "Last year, near the end of the season, I decided to gut up and talk to the guy. I figured he likes to read, I like to read, not the same things, of course, but maybe we could find some common ground. Turns out he'd read most of the books I had and then suggested others with similar storylines that he thought I'd like. Those I'd read that he hadn't heard of, he typed into a memo on his phone. Every time he finished one of my recommendations, he'd text me at school, and I'd do the same for him. We reconnected at Supervisor Orientation Week at Camp Galilee during spring break and decided we had enough in common to explore a deeper relationship. He called my parents last night after we got home from church and asked if they would mind if we dated. My dad was on board immediately. On the other hand, Mom had a few choice questions — good questions — things I hadn't thought about asking, but she eventually gave her blessing. Now, if anyone asks why I'm such a freak, why I choose to read rather than go to some lame event where rapid-fire interview questions pass for conversation, you tell them that I already have a boyfriend."

"I had no idea." I'm grinning now, so ridiculously happy for her.

"Well, you were kinda googly-eyed over your dude. I don't think you would have noticed if your hair was on fire."

My smile fades. Had I been so obsessed over Jack that I'd ignored my friends? I already knew the answer: yes.

"I'm sorry. I haven't been a good friend."

"Nah. Don't worry about it." Her eyes, however, say she agrees with me, and it makes my heart hurt. I think of all the times I meant to write to her at college but forgot. I was too wrapped up in my own little world.

"Well, next year will be different," I assure her. "We'll share a dorm room, and I'll have your back any time someone wants to call you out for being a wallflower." I give her what I hope is a light-hearted smile.

She doesn't return the grin. Instead, she looks at me with sadness, anger, confusion, and pity flitting over her face in rapid succession. "I thought you were running away to get married."

I try to laugh it off and blame it on not having enough coffee, but I can't help the alarm I feel. The truth is I had forgotten. I'd forgotten Jack and our plans and, at the same time, recognized how badly I had betrayed Lu. She and I had spent years planning our college days, from the décor in our shared dorm to the classes we would take to the socials we would attend. And she completely slipped my mind the moment Jack proposed. No, before that. When Jack flipped that first note into my office, all of my attention had turned to him. Then, just as quickly, I'd forgotten Jack when I'd tried to assure Lu.

What is wrong with me?

Well, that I know. I'm the "slow" one in the family — the embarrassing dummy.

Lu casually reopens the door to the dishwasher and adds detergent before closing it and turning it on. I'd forgotten that too. Then, finally, she faces me. "Look, I need to go, but," she draws in a deep breath and slowly exhales, "I know you're upset about camp, I get it, but it may be for the best. You need some time to think about what you want to do." She raises a hand as if to stop me from interrupting even though I'm still shocked into silence and stillness. "You get so attached to people. You grab on and go wherever they take you. You need to find your own feet. Walk alone for a bit. Decide what is best for you. It may be Jack. It may be college. It may be waitressing or working at Walmart, I don't know — but neither do you. You're like Nick Carraway in *The Great Gatsby*. You go along with the crowd, not judging them, but not making good judgments for yourself either."

I nod. Even though I'd never read *The Great Gatsby*, I understand what she is saying. She slings her purse over her shoulder and lets herself out.

I realize I'd forgotten to give her a note to deliver to Jack.

∞ ∞ ∞

"Have you seen Lu since she's been home?"

Mom asks the question so innocuously that, of course, I think it is a trap. We don't have everyday conversations around the dinner table unless we have guests. So I keep my face pleasantly blank and nod while I force down a bite of my daily potatoes.

"Yes. I saw her last night at church," (her lips began to thin) "and then she dropped by this morning, and we had coffee on the porch. She didn't stay long. She had laundry to do, and I needed to get back cleaning up after breakfast."

"That's nice."

*Really? What is going on here?*

"I talked to Misty at church last night."

Misty is Lu's mom, by the way. She was obviously named in the seventies.

"She's very concerned about Lu. Unfortunately, it turns out she didn't go to any of the special events they have for freshmen at the college."

*False.*

"She just hung out in the dorm the whole time."

*Library.*

"Misty's not sure what to do about her. She's afraid that Lu's hiding in dorms is a symptom of depression. So many kids come down with that these days."

*Oh, good grief! It's not like it's a head-cold that gets passed from person to person.*

"No young man is going to want to marry a girl with depression. Misty is afraid that Lu is going to move back in with them after she graduates."

I use the cheese sauce from the au gratin potatoes to trap my peas and ready them for spearing. I keep track of the conversation as it continues and mentally correct and comment as it goes on and on. I've heard some twaddle (now there's a word that doesn't sound very nice but so adequately describes most of the conversations I hear) in my time, but this fake concern over a non-problem grates on my nerves. Another pea gets it straight through the heart.

"If she's that bad off," Dad gives Mom a knowing look, "maybe we should let Dr. Jeffers know. He could talk to her. Let her know it's time to grow up and take on the role of a woman." He looks almost joyful at the idea of getting Dr. Jeffers, and possibly the deacons, to pry into Lu's business. I can practically see the wheels turning in his head. He's going to find a way to twist everything he's just heard into a plan to destroy Lu's reputation.

"Actually, she has a boyfriend," I break in. I can't let their speculations and plans to ruin Lu's life go on any longer. Besides, Lu said I could tell.

Mom looks at me sharply, "Do her parents know?"

It isn't concern in her voice, and it isn't relief that Lu is "normal." It is an accusation. It's the assumption that Lu is keeping secrets.

"They know. He called her parents last night after they got home from church."

My parents eat the rest of their meal in disappointed silence, and for that, I am thankful. No one should have reason to doubt Lu or accuse her of not being on the right path. She knows where she stands better than any of us.

# Chapter Ten Taking the Win

I wake Saturday morning to the slamming of a bedroom door and the heavy tread of Dad stomping down the stairs. Every move the man makes is designed to intimidate. I wait for the front door to bang shut and his car roar to life. He's off to prayer breakfast with the guys.

The clock reads 7:00. It feels good to sleep in. I could use a few more hours — days — of snoozing, but I get up and shuffle to the bathroom for my morning routine.

There's no note on the fridge, so I make what I want. In twenty minutes, I've got biscuits in the oven and various toppings on the counter. I like butter and honey. If Roman or Mom wants to make theirs into an egg sandwich, I can whip that up in no time.

It promises to be a warm day, so I fill a jar with cold water and ten tea bags and haul it outside to slow brew. Summers and sun-tea go together, although I guess it's technically still spring. The mailman pulls up to the end of our driveway, and we awkwardly wave to each other. I wait until he motors down the street before retrieving the mail.

It's the usual collection of bland-looking bills peeping through cellophane windows and brightly colored circulars for the local grocery stores. And then a thick purple envelope that is addressed to me in glittery purple gel pen. I smile when I see Nana's handwriting on the front. Nana is my mom's mom, and I adore her. She's the polar opposite of Mom — than all of my family, actually. She's relaxed, fun, and adventurous. Before I open the card, I check the biscuits. They still have a few minutes to go, so I tear open the envelope and read the graduation card.

*My Dearest Julia,*

*It's hard to believe the little girl I held in my arms just yesterday is old enough to graduate! I am so proud of you. You're a sweet young lady, and I know you will succeed in all you do. I'll see you at graduation!*

*Love,*

*Nana*

Inside the card is a check for $200. I slip it into my pocket just as the timer dings. I pull on oven mitts and grab a couple of potholders (I always use both) before opening the oven door to remove the golden brown biscuits. Mechanically, I plop them one-by-one into a napkin-lined basket and cover them. The whole time, I'm thinking about what Nana said. She's coming for graduation, but I won't be graduating. She's going to be so disappointed in me. I wipe down the counters and leave the kitchen, taking the pile of mail with me.

There's a system for everything in this house — even the mail. On the table in our entryway, there's an old brass letter holder. Bills and business letters go in the back of the fancy metal rack, and personal mail goes in front. The fliers go in a neat pile on the black-enameled tray next to the holder. I take my card upstairs.

I'm not sure what to do. Should I call Nana and tell her not to come? Wait for her to arrive and then spring the bad news? That doesn't seem right. I add the check to my money stash in the duffle bag. My gut clenches at the thought of giving that $200 back. I know Nana can't afford it, but I need it to get out of here. I can't possibly keep it — can I? As much as I hate to admit it to myself, I'm going to have to ask Mom for advice. I'll tell her about the card, but not the check.

The conversation with mom does not go well. There is no clear answer as to what I should tell Nana, just lots of reminders of all the ways I've disgraced the family.

Once she breaks down my walls of self-control and has me ugly-crying into my pillow, she leaves. She quashes my glimmer of hope that my guilt trip is nearing its end when she tosses a dozen unopened greeting cards onto the bed.

"You need to write to everyone who sent you a graduation card and let them know why you aren't walking. Also, make sure you return any money they may have enclosed. You have until 1:00. I've got to go to the post office today anyway so I can drop the letters off for you."

The rest of my morning is opening cards, reading about how family and friends are "Proud of me," or "Happy for me," and wish me "Good Luck!" or "God's blessings," and informing them that I had broken the school's rules and therefore would not be walking at graduation. Thanks for the kind words, but I cannot accept the generous gift you sent.

I wish writing were as mechanical as cooking or cleaning. But, instead, every stroke of the pen is another jab at my heart.

I put all the envelopes on the red enameled "to be mailed" tray (I told you there was a system for everything), and return to my room until Mom leaves for the post office. The house is empty. Dad's car is gone. I have no idea where Roman is. I take a deep breath go downstairs to bring in the sun-tea. It's delicious over a glass full of ice and a teaspoon of honey. I set the jar in the fridge and notice the chore list already written out and waiting on its magnetized pad. It's a doozy.

I tear a blank sheet from the pad and attempt to reorganize the list so that I can get everything done. It's impossible. Still, I have to try. My actual butt is on the line. As soon as that thought crosses my mind, I glance up at the wooden spoon. It is waiting for me to fail.

There is not enough time to do everything correctly. The weeds in the garden get a cursory uprooting and raking. The hardier ones are chopped quickly with a hoe, their truncated stems covered with a sprinkling of soil. I throw the garden trash into the compost bin, spray it with a bit of water and stir it. I set the sprinkler in the garden and head for the garage.

I don't clean the garage in the traditional sense. Instead, I quickly move the boxes in a very general spirit of organizing. At least all plastic tubs are stacked one on top of the other against the outside walls. I set the few cardboard boxes on top where they are less likely to be damaged from flooding or mice. A quick sweep and I deem the garage passable.

The bathrooms are already clean since I scrubbed them yesterday, but I give them a quick wipe-down. Then I've got to get dinner started. I've been rushing all day, but the lasagna I need to make is time-consuming. I get the bags of shredded mozzarella cheese out of the freezer first thing, so it has time to defrost. We buy it whenever it's on sale and freeze it until we need it. Next, I start a pot of water boiling to blanch the pasta — Mom refuses to buy the oven-ready noodles. In the pantry, discover the box of lasagna sitting lonely on the shelf. I know there had been two cans of spaghetti sauce next to it. I put them there myself. Now they are gone.

Something kicks in. I had known from the first glance at the chore list that Mom was setting me up. I had been frantic all afternoon, but now I'm just plain angry. I start another pot of water boiling, then race out to the garden. I grab every ripe tomato I can find — not easy since it is so early in the season. They won't be enough for the amount of sauce I need. I check the pantry for the little cans of plain tomato sauce. I find four. Then I notice the ketchup — a big, family-size squeeze bottle. "You come with me," I mutter as I gather all of my tomato-based ingredients on the counter.

I put a lid on the first pot of boiling water. I'm not ready to deal with pasta just now. I dunk the tomatoes one by one into the second pot until their skin is blistered and prepared to slide off. I cut each one, seed it, and set it on the cutting board where I begin to mince. Fresh tomatoes, tomato sauce, and ketchup all join together in the second-largest pot, along with a ton of garlic, oregano, and onion powder. I set it on simmer and pray the whole time I'm cooking the pasta. Once the noodles are in the colander, I dip a spoon in the sauce and give it a quick taste. Still sweet because of the ketchup, but not horrible. I add a little salt and pepper and a dash of garlic powder, giving it another stir. It will have to do.

The lasagna goes in twenty minutes late, but I'd made sure the noodles were thoroughly cooked, turned the oven up another fifty degrees — and prayed.

When everyone sits down at the table, the lasagna is an animated centerpiece, still bubbling around the sides. French bread is sliced and in a basket to the side, and the iconic green parmesan cheese container sits above Dad's fork. He looks pleased, despite the meal's complete lack of potatoes.

My first bite is tentative, but I immediately relax. It's pretty good.

Mom accepts the compliment from Dad for the delicious lasagna and takes a bite herself, her forehead creasing in confusion. I can tell by the way she refuses to look at me that she isn't happy.

I win this round.

# Chapter Eleven: Dreading the Day

The rest of Saturday night is uncomfortable. Mom refuses to talk to me and leaves the room as soon as dinner is over, leaving me alone to do the cleanup. I had done most of it while the lasagna was baking, so it is just the dishes from the table.

When I finish, I make some cinnamon muffins with a crunchy topping for the next day. I've just put them in the oven when Dad bellows my name. I'm expecting it, as it happens most nights. I immediately approach his Lazy-Boy throne.

"Yes, sir?"

"Bring everyone some ice cream."

"Yes, sir."

I return to the kitchen and open the ice cream container I already had out on the counter. As I said, I was expecting it. By the time I've delivered the bowls of ice cream to my father and his favored subjects, the smell of cinnamon fills the house.

"What are you baking?" Mom asks, her forehead in its usual crease.

"Cinnamon-topped muffins for tomorrow."

"When they're done, bring a couple out," Dad commands. Any argument Mom might start is immediately quashed. She cannot go against his majesty. I fight the urge to curtsey and instead blandly say, "Yes, sir," before escaping back into the kitchen.

After delivering the muffins, I don't want to join my family in the living room, so I ask permission to get ready for bed. I guess I've impressed Dad because he nods without asking for a bunch of other stuff first. I crawl between the sheets and read until I hear the first steps of a family member on the stairs. It is nice.

∞∞∞

I wake with dread pushing me down into my mattress.

I don't know why.

Yes, I do.

It's Sunday.

I've disgraced my family and myself, and everyone at church knows about it like it's their business.

Sundays are always busy. Everyone in the family has a billion things to do, and we all have to leave the house at the same time. The schedule is tight. Usually, I jump out of bed and into the shower first so that my gears don't jam against anyone else's, but not today. I lay in bed a good five minutes after the alarm goes off. I mentally check my entire body for indications of illness, but no stuffy nose, no sore throat (I clear it a few times to make sure). No fever. Nausea? Yes — but not from the flu. Nothing but a still-sore thigh, but I know that will pass. I decide that the only thing wrong with me is nerves and finally throw back the covers with a prayer for strength and motivation.

Dressed in my bathrobe, I go downstairs and peel two potatoes and two carrots per person (so many potatoes), put them in the bottom of the extra-large crockpot, cover them with water, and place a seasoned hunk of raw beef on top. Then, I turn the slow-cooker on high and trudge back upstairs, thankful that dinner prep is already done.

Roman beats me to the shower, so I have to wait. I grab my Bible and try to have devotions at my desk, getting more anxious with every minute that passes. I need to get ready for church.

*Bang!* Dad's out of his room and stomping down the stairs. "Where's the coffee?" he yells.

The adrenaline kicks in, and I run downstairs, silently

berating myself for forgetting such a basic thing. Most mornings, I drink a cup myself. I lie to myself that my lack of caffeine is why I couldn't concentrate on my devotions. "Sorry, Dad, I forgot." Water in the tank, fresh coffee grounds poured into a clean filter, basket pushed in, and "on."

"You forgot? Who forgets coffee?" He sounds miffed but not out-of-control angry, so I'm relieved. I warm a muffin for him and pour him a coffee as soon as there's a cup's worth in the pot. He grunts and takes a sip, his eyes never leaving the newspaper he has spread before him.

∞∞∞

Church goes about as well as expected. I make my appearance in the youth room and am immediately redirected to the College and Career class with the comment that if I plan to live as an adult, I should sit with the adults. I surreptitiously wave to Jack as I leave, feeling a little bitter that he gets to stay.

On a more positive note, I get to sit near Lu. The two of us have a chance to chat before class starts. She notes my wet hair pulled back in its usual braid. "The dean of women at Palmdale hates it when girls show up to chapel or classes with wet hair. She thinks it's too sexy — that if a man sees wet hair on a woman, he automatically imagines her in the shower," she finishes with a snort.

"Well, I got out of bed five minutes late and missed my window for the bathroom. Roman made it in ahead of me, and by the time the shower was free again, I only had fifteen minutes before it was time to go. You're lucky I'm wearing shoes."

Lu shrugs, and I feel like she's summarily dismissed my problems. I push the feeling down and sit quietly, waiting for class to start.

After Sunday school, I walk with her to the choir room and draw my black binder out of the pile. I try to ignore Mr.

Coleman's steady gaze, but he eventually walks over to me and says, "I think it would be wise for you to take a break from the choir until everything settles down." He takes the binder from me, and I'm on my way out the door.

I hide out in the bathroom for a while. Sitting in a locked stall while people run frantically in and out trying to take care of business and then get in their places on time is liberating. Finally, the room is empty, but I sit for another five minutes, enjoying the silence before forcing myself to leave the stall, wash my hands, and get back out into the real world.

Through the windows of the swinging doors leading into the sanctuary, I see the congregation standing for the first hymn and the choir filing into the loft. I pause at the nursery door and note that someone crossed my name off the schedule posted there. So I guess I don't have nursery duty tonight.

I make it to a seat on the back row just as the first hymn finishes.

During the sermon, I take notes in the margins of my Bible. I always turn to the passage Dr. Jeffers calls out and then systematically write a three-point devotional for myself (complete with cross-references, thank you very much). That may sound weird, but I started doing it a couple of years ago when we learned to write a sermon or devotional for speech class. If you're wondering about the difference between the two, a sermon is presented by guys only, even if it is preached to both men and women. A devotional is written by a woman and delivered only to women, usually at some over-decorated function where everyone drinks fruity teas. Other than the audience and the speakers, sermons and devotionals are pretty much the same.

I enjoyed the project. I wrote about Mary and Martha. Most preachers focus only on the first story written about them and ignore their other appearances in Scripture. I discovered that their three stories go together.

I also decided that Martha got a raw deal. Preachers constantly criticize her despite her hard work, and they praise

Mary for her quiet discipline. But, in the following story, Martha openly declares her trust in Christ, while Mary's total lack of faith makes Jesus weep.

Sometimes Dr. Jeffers gets off to a good start only to use the text as his jumping-off point to discuss hunting, sports, politics, and those he'd counseled "in the past," like it is okay to betray someone's confidence if it happened long ago or in a different church. I do not doubt that someday I'll be an example in one of his sermons. Today's he's preaching out of First Samuel.

I quickly sketch out the life of Abigail — a woman married to an abusive fool (Nabal) who, after the idiot dies, runs straight into the arms of another man that she had met only once. I had always heard of (and thought of) Abigail as a heroine, but now I question her life decisions. Why get remarried at all? Or at least she could get to know the guy first. This woman was an excellent manager, had impressive people skills — why not take over the farm for herself? That is my starting question. Of course, the truth is I already know the answer, but I think it through anyway.

There's no mention of kids belonging to Abigail and her husband, so I assume that there aren't any. If Nabal the Fool had a brother, the land would go to him, and he would also have a crack at Abigail. If the two of them married, their first son would carry Nabal's name (Fool, Jr.) and inherit the property. Some men chose not to marry the widow of their brothers and arranged for them to marry someone else. In that case, the woman had the chance to spit in the brother's face (I ran across that little gem this winter when I was still at the beginning of the Old Testament on my annual read-through-the-Bible devotions). Of course, I don't know any of Abigail's motivations absolutely — the Bible doesn't come right out and say any of it — but when I look at her extreme response to her husband's death, I can't help but speculate.

The weird thing is I've never thought of it as an extreme response until today. Now I wish I could go back in time and ask Abigail why she said yes to David's proposal. The one time she met him, she saw him at his worst — when he was on his way to kill Nabal and his entire household in a fit of rage. Abigail heard about it and met David on the road. Abigail freely acknowledged that her husband was an idiot and went so far as to offer to take Nabal's punishment for him to protect all of the people on the estate. David told Abigail that he'd planned to kill everyone, but he'd go in peace since she brought him food and apologies.

After the danger passed, Nabal had a feast during which he got sloppy drunk and ate like a king (and I'm assuming the preparation of all the food was done by Abigail), after which Abigail told him she took supplies to David. Then, Nabal had a stroke or heart attack or something and died ten days later. David heard about Nabal's death and immediately sent a marriage proposal to Abigail. She accepted it (!), moved out of her home into David's camp, became ONE of his wives (!!), and had a son with him.

See, it's that decision to accept David's proposal that bugs me. Yes he was a godly man — at least most of the time — but when she met him, he was on his way to take out an entire household of people because of one man's foolishness. He was angry. He was potentially violent. She did some fast talking to keep him from shedding innocent blood. And she said yes. Yes, to spending her life with him!

Was it because she knew that he was God's anointed and the future king of Israel? (After all, she prophesied precisely that when she confronted him.) Or was it that her life was so chaotic that living with David seemed peaceful and sane. How awful was her experience with Nabal? How potentially bad did she see her life becoming after his death? Was she escaping? Was David the only way she could see herself getting out of a horrible situation?

I make one last notation, then close my Bible and stand to sing the invitation hymn. This time I ignore the song's lyrics. I'm stunned by what had snuck out of my pen and onto the page:

"Was David Abigail's Proteus?"

# Chapter Twelve Waiting for It

I get to the car before everyone else, so I have a perfect view of my family as they exit the church, happily shaking Dr. Jeffers's hand, then smiling and talking with friends. Just last week, I had been part of that. Over there, under the eaves, I had slipped Jack a note and even shared some pleasant words with Candace, AKA Polly, who'd had a few original thoughts about looking forward to summer. It was nice not to hear her usual canned responses. Then Magpie had turned the corner and walked toward us, brazenly chugging a bottle of iced coffee she'd stolen from the Senior Saints Sunday school room.

Strangely, none of the youth group are hanging around this week. I scan the property and see Jack and Roman near Jack's family car, deep in conversation. I have no idea where the girls are.

When my family finally gets in, they're displaying a variety of moods. Roman looks angry and nervous, Mom is holding steady at her usual level of annoyance, and Dad is gregariously loud and happy — one could almost say manic. So that I don't attract the attention of any of these nutcases, I'm making myself sit as still as possible, hoping they don't see me, feeling like I'm stuck in a strange version of Goldilocks and the Three Bears.

∞∞∞

Mom's cell rings as we walk in the door. "Oh. Hello, Mother."

I sidle past her toward the stairs. I usually change into a less formal denim skirt and layer of t-shirts. But not today, I think, as Mom grabs my shoulder when I walk past her, and I find myself turned toward the kitchen as she takes the stairs herself.

Roman is the first one back down. He looks around the kitchen, taking in the now-set table and the smoking hot platter of roast beef and veggies.

"Where's Dad and Mom?" I ask.

He shrugs, his face shadowed with worry. "Mom's still on the phone."

"Maybe I should cover the food." My reply is calm, but my heart is fluttering with apprehension. What is Mom talking about with Nana? Had she received my letter already? It only went out yesterday afternoon.

I erect a foil tent over the roast before I join Roman at the island. I'm finally able to sit on the elevated chair, my welt pulling only a little. It's still tender, though, so I put most of my weight on my other thigh. I stare at the veins running through the stone countertop. Neither Roman nor I say anything. We don't even look at each other as the tension in the room builds. Something is up.

Finally, there is the slam of a door. I wait for the expected footsteps on the stairs. I shoot a look at Roman, whose face is colorless. I can read the question in his anxious eyes. *What is going on?* I shiver. We'd been through variants of this before, but I'm usually the target of their wrath. I wonder what Roman has been up to. He looks terrified. I know I do too, but for me, it's my normal state.

Suspense builds as the minutes tick down. I toy with the idea of putting the roast in the oven, just to have something concrete to do, but I sit. I am quiet. I am invisible. I am nothing that will attract their attention, but the air around the void I attempt to create is a frisson of anger about to explode. Despite the danger, the desire for the suspense to end is strong. I wish for whatever is coming to happen already.

Roman is barely breathing. He isn't the usual target of our parent's anger or "discipline," but he's as terrified as I am today. I squeeze my fingers between my knees to stop their trembling.

"Julia!" Mom's voice screeches down the stairs.

I gasp, and Roman exhales, his shoulders lowering in relief. Before I can get off the barstool, Dad is in the kitchen, grabbing the spoon off the wall and gesturing for me to get upstairs. My legs are gelatin, swaying and shimmying up every step to my room. Mom stands in front of my open duffle, holding a wad of cash and a folded piece of paper. "What is this?" She gestures to the bag at her feet with both hands.

I try to speak, but not a sound squeaks out. Suddenly, I'm face-first on the bed, my rear-end sticking up over the footboard. My almost-healed pelvis is grinding into the wood. I try to turn my face to the side to breathe, but the heel of Dad's hand keeps me immobilized and wheezing.

"Answer your mother!"

The one good thing about nausea that comes from nerves is that it fills my mouth with water. I swallow and gasp out, "It's the bag I packed for camp — before I found out I wasn't going."

"What about the money?" Anger edges Mom's voice.

"Babysitting." I croak with my remaining air. I try to breathe in, but my mouth and nose are still smashed against my bedspread.

"And a check I specifically told you to return?"

I'd forgotten to include it in Nana's envelope, and the realization adds yet another layer of panic to my breathlessness. The memory of the sunny yellow rectangle with Nana's "I'm so proud of you" in the memo line wavers and darkens. Everything goes black.

I wake face-up, my blurry vision clearing until my bedroom's popcorn ceiling comes into sharp focus. I'm on the bed, but my head isn't on my pillow. My legs are hanging over the footboard. I struggle upright as sibilant whispers filter through the air.

Dad is suddenly in front of me, pulling me into a standing position. "She's awake," he mutters over his shoulder and turns me around, so I'm facing the bed again.

Mom thrusts the check into my face. "Why did you keep this?"

"I forgot." I'm too woozy to soften my voice.

Mom steps closer. "You watch your tone! I told you — I specifically told you to send back all the money in those graduation cards!"

"I'm sorry," I lower my eyes to the open bag. It was as good a place as any to look so I wouldn't have to see Mom's face.

"Sorry isn't good enough. You deliberately disobeyed me. Bend over."

I stand unmoving, thinking that I should have just walked out the door instead of sitting at the kitchen island, waiting for the inevitable to happen. Instead, the crack of the wooden spoon against my backside knocks me face down on the bed again. The covers slip under my hands, so there is no way I can brace myself. I have no control and am unable to stop the mewling cries of pain and the wracking sobs.

I open my eyes, close them, and then open them again. My foggy brain tries to comprehend why, even with my eyes open, I remain in darkness. The clock reads 8:00, so I guess I slept through the afternoon. The house is silent and dark. I realize that my family left me alone and went to church.

The pressure on my bladder is intense, but I'm fused to the bed. The slightest movement makes me whimper. I can't stay here, I tell myself. While I ease myself off the mattress, I examine that thought.

I can't stay here.

It isn't just about not wetting the bed. I can't stay in this house.

I finally get my feet on the floor and lumber to the bath-room. The cold of the toilet is exquisite on my bruised thighs, and I sit longer than I need to as I attempt to come up with a plan. I don't have time to spend a summer in quiet reflection, deciding what I want to do with my life. This was my third beating in a week.

"And you just sat there, waiting for it," I mutter to my-self. "You could have walked out the door." The house is empty. I'd leave now if I could do more than shuffle my feet. As soon as I can, I'll get out of here. But where do I go? Do I pack the rest of my stuff and hoof it to Lu's? I try to think of something else, but I've got nothing. I finally grab the edge of the bathroom sink to steady me as I stand up and flush. There is blood on the seat. I clean it off and wash my hands before taking a good look at my bottom and thighs in the full-length mirror on the door.

There are blotches of black where the blood has pooled under the skin and jagged tears where the skin split open. Most of the wounds have started closing, but they're still gooey. I get the antibiotic ointment out of the medicine cabinet, but every-thing hurts too much to touch. I dab a little here and there, but I can't cover the myriad of new and newly reopened welts — we don't have any bandages that big — and the sores end up sticking to the inside of my skirt. I pull the fabric away from my backside as I make the mile-long trek back to my room. I'm not going anywhere for at least a few days.

When I finally make it to my doorway, I flip on the light switch. The drawers of my dresser are open and empty. My closet holds only a skirt, a sweatshirt, and a pair of sandals. My camp bag is gone. My bookcase is empty, and every knick-knack has disappeared. The only thing left in my room is the furniture.

I already knew my money was gone, but my clothes? My books? All because I'd forgotten to send back the check? Is that why they'd done this?

I make the return trip to the bathroom to blow my nose

(they took my box of tissues too). I catch my reflection in the mirror over the sink. I hate that girl. Almost as much as my parents seem to. The blubbering, red-eyed, snot-nosed mess that her parents don't even want. "You'd think they'd be glad to see you go," I accuse the mirror image.

I understood them wanting to save face when the notes came to light, but why lose face by calling Dr. Jeffers and the deacon board in the first place? Why forbid my going to camp? Why prevent me from running away by taking my ready cash. I could have been out of their hair days ago. Why were they keeping me?

Why had they kept me in the first place?

Even when I was little, I wondered about that. I'd go to Nana's for a week, and before five days were up, they'd arrive to take me home. I'd beg Nana to let me stay, but Mom would remind her that if she interfered with their decisions, she wouldn't see her grandchildren at all. Nana quickly learned to do all of the fun stuff at the beginning of our visits.

I realize that there is no rhyme or reason for these people. "Because they're nuts!" I mutter as I mince my way into their room. It is a forbidden zone, but it is a forbidden zone with a phone, and I suddenly know what to do.

I punch in the number.

"Hello?"

"Hello, Nana? Can you please come to get me?" I almost get the whole sentence out before my throat closes, and the tears start again.

"Julia? Are you okay?"

A slash of light flickers in the doorway. Headlights are reflecting off the front windows. "They're home," I whisper. Then louder, "Don't call back. I'll call you tomorrow." I hang up the phone and make it to the bathroom just as I hear the front door's hinges squeak. I flush the toilet and run the water in the sink to strengthen my alibi.

# Chapter Thirteen Drifting Along

The alarm doesn't wake me — they took the clock while I was asleep. I guess my parents missed it in the first sweep of the room. It is nature's call that gets me moving. I don't make it this time, so on top of the painful shuffle, I have to clean the floor, take a stinging shower, and wash my urine-drenched clothes.

They left me home alone again, and I don't care a bit. I don't mean to look at the chore list, but it's reflexive. It's just instructions for dinner. It seems I have the day off.

I bypass the usual coffee — already in the pot made by someone other than myself — and opt for hot chocolate instead. Do I care that it's already the end of May and 80° outside? No, I do not. Hot chocolate is soothing, and I need some soothing right now.

There's a knock/doorbell combo, and before I even turn from the counter where I'm pouring hot water into my cup, Lu bounces in. "Hey! I called, but there was no answer. You weren't at church last night. I figured you were sick."

I'm not looking at Lu. I'm staring at the space behind her where the wall phone used to be. They'd removed it, leaving behind nothing but a plastic plate screwed into the wall around a jack. They probably took the one in their room, too — no chance of calling Nana again. The hair on my head stands up as I wonder if they found out I'd called her.

"Julia?"

"What?"

"Are you sick?"

"No. Want some hot chocolate?"

Lu's face scrunches in mild confusion. Being in church whenever the doors are open has always been expected except in cases of illness. "Uh, no. I'll take some coffee, though." She pours a mug-full. "You don't look so good. Are you sure you're not sick? Is that why you weren't there for the service?"

Last night, after I made the decision not to stay, I also decided to stop covering. Now I did something I'd never done before. I turned my back to my friend and started pulling up my skirt.

"Julia!" I can hear the shock in her voice, but I don't stop. "What are you — oh, Lord!" The surprised panic drains from her voice and ends in a whisper. "Who did that to you?"

I mean to spin around to glare, but it's more a tottering, stiff turn. "Who do you think?" I snap as I carefully let my skirt slip back down.

She collapses on a kitchen chair. "But — why?"

"Why?" I can't believe the question. "Does it matter? I guess it was because I kissed a boy, or maybe it was because I wrote some notes, or because I didn't answer Dr. Jeffers fast enough." I can't stop the frustration rising in my voice. "Or maybe it's because I forgot to return a check to my Nana. Or maybe it's just that they hate me! Maybe they never wanted me but can't let anyone else have me. Maybe I'm a disappointment or evil or frustrating to be around. After all, I'm just floating in the stream, right? Just latching on to whatever floats by? Well, guess what, Lu?" I hear myself screaming, but I can't stop, and the rest comes bubbling out, "When you're drowning, you grab onto whatever you can to survive! If I'm lucky enough to find a guy who wants to marry me and get me out of this place, I'm going to latch on with both hands!"

Lu's face is shockingly pale, and her eyes are glistening. "You should," she whispers, then swallows and repeats the words, "You should. You should ignore everything I said before and go. Just go. Let me — what can I do to help?"

"I don't know." I knuckle the tears off my face. "Uh — my Nana. I called her last night and told her I'd call her back today, but they took out the phones."

Lu spins to stare at the space on the wall. "Who does that?" she whispered.

"Can I use your cell?"

"Of course!" She pulls her phone from her back pocket, unlocks the screen, and hands it over.

I stare at the screen, my mind goes momentarily blank, and I close my eyes, praying for clarity. I open my eyes again and thumb in the number. It goes straight to voicemail. "Hi, Nana, it's Julia again. Sorry I missed you. I'll try again later. Don't call the house, okay? Love you. Bye." I hit end and hand the phone back to Lu. "I got her voicemail."

"Can you call her house phone?"

"That was her house phone."

"Then call her cell." She attempts to hand the phone back to me.

"I don't know that number."

Lu sticks the phone back into her pocket with a frustrated sigh. "Okay. We'll try again later when we get to my house." At my quizzical look, she says, "You can't stay here."

"I know." The words hang between us for a moment until Lu clears her throat.

"Okay. I'll pack a bag for you." She is off before I can stop her. Out of habit, I rinse our mugs and put them in the dishwasher.

The doorbell rings. No knock. I shuffle to the front door and sob with relief when I see Nana's face through the window. I open the door and fall into her arms.

"Those monsters!" Lu's yell from upstairs makes Nana jump and pull me closer.

"Who is that?" Nana asks.

"Lu. My friend."

Lu's stomp down the stairs rivals my dad's. "They took all your stuff?" She stops short when she sees Nana.

Nana nods in her direction. "What happened, girls?"

"They beat her." Lu's voice is outraged. "Julia, I'm so

sorry." I turn to her and see from her expression that she is begging me to understand. Her eyes bore into mine as if trying to deliver her sincerity straight to my brain. "I didn't know that they really beat you. When you talked about it, I thought you were talking about spankings — you know, swats. I didn't know that they ..." her voice drifts into a choking sob.

Nana holds me at arm's length so she can look into my eyes. "Are you okay?"

"Her legs," Lu starts, but I interrupt.

"I'm okay. A little sore — very sore — but I'll be okay in a couple of days."

"Show her," Lu urges.

I feel my face warm as I turn my back and lift my skirt again. Nana gasps, and I smooth the material back down.

"We need to go to the hospital," Nana's voice is calm but determined. She turns to Lu. "Can you get ..."

"There's nothing to get," I interrupt.

"They took everything but the furniture out of her room. They even took the phones!" Lu's indignation is back.

I pluck at the front of my sweatshirt. "I have this outfit and one in the washer."

"Leave it here. Let's go." I guess Nana can be no-nonsense when she needs to be.

Lu helps me into the front seat of Nana's compact car and squeezes into the back. She tells Nana, "When you pull out of the drive, go right. Take a left at the first light." Nana nods and heads down the drive.

I don't say anything. I guess you can say I am drifting — letting my life-savers carry me along the turbulent river.

# Chapter Fourteen: Telling the Truth

The nurse at the ER is sweet and concerned. "Let's get you into a gown and up onto the table." She stops short when my skirt hits the floor. I hear her shocked intake of breath, then a couple of snaps as she puts on a pair of gloves. Her touch is light as she examines the backs of my thighs. "How did this happen?"

"I — got hit."

"Who hit you?"

"My father."

"It looks like — it's more than one — instance. You've got the beginnings of infection here." She gently touches me, and I know from its location, her finger is on one of the welts from last Monday that had broken open on Tuesday at P.E. and again during Sunday's beating — the one that never stopped hurting. She makes a note on the chart. "Do you think you can get up on the exam table?" She holds my hand, and I lift my foot to the step. I groan when I feel one of the sores open. "What?" the nurse asks, and I put my foot back down, gesturing to the back of my thigh. She looks and says, "Oh, my. Just stand there, and I'll get the doctor."

When Dr. Mendax walks into the exam room a few minutes later, I know I'm in trouble.

"Hey, little lady, missed you in church last night."

I'm not sure how to respond to that. No one else does either since the room stays silent while he makes some notations on my chart.

"Hop up on the exam table. Let's find out what's going on."

I edge to the table, more to get away from him than trying to obey him. Nana shakes her head. "She can't get on the table, doctor."

"Sure, she can. Here." He grabs my elbow and propels me forward roughly. My gown swings open, and I pull my arm free to cover myself. He pushes me closer to the step. Either I raise my foot, or I knock it with my shin. An automatic response takes over, and I lift my foot again, this time feeling multiple welts separate. Dr. Mendax ignores my yelps of pain and continues to pull me along until I am stretched out on the table, my panty-clad bottom exposed to the room.

I can't stop crying, but I try to keep it quiet. Nana is next to me, her expression confused as she looks from me to the doctor. "I know it hurts, honey. I'm so sorry. The doctor is here to help you."

I shake my head at her, but she's watching Dr. Mendax poke and prod roughly at my tender thighs.

"What happened here?" He asks in a light tone. "Try to slide down the stairs again? You don't need stitches this time." A hint of hardness creeps into his voice. "I keep telling you to knock that foolishness off."

Nana's objections barely register over the clanging of instruments on a tray. I'm too embarrassed, too frightened to correct her assumptions. How could Nana know that Dr. Mendax already knows about the beatings? That he's given lessons at the church on the best ways for parents to spank (beat) their children and what stories to concoct if the children betrayed their parents and ended up in the emergency room — or if the punishment went too far, and the child needed medical treatment. A slip and fall down a set of stairs. A spill off a bike while doing a wheelie. Falling off a flatbed truck during a hayride. Each of those excuses had been used for me over the years.

"It's obvious she's been beaten," Nana insists.

He moves up to the head of the table and grabs my chin with his blue-gloved hand. He lifts my head so he can see my whole face. His coffee breath floods my nostrils, his mouth smiles genially, but his eyes are black with anger. "Doesn't look like she's been beaten to me."

"Maybe we should let the police decide that."

"The police will concur with my findings, I can assure you."

"I'd still like them called."

"It's not necessary."

"Actually," the nurse breaks in, "They're already on their way. I called them as soon as she said she was hit." There is silence for a few seconds, then the nurse insists, "We are required to report." It sounds like the nurse is standing up to Dr. Mendax.

Dr. Mendax sounds annoyed but not angry as he answers her. "Fine. We'll waste some officer's time." He gives me a light slap on my outer thigh. "Or you could just come clean and tell Nurse Longo that I've treated you for years and know that you are equal parts klutz and liar." He turns his conversation to the nurse. "We attend the same church, and I happen to know that she comes up with some new drama every year to get attention." Back to me. "Did you tell Nurse Longo that the school kicked you out with only two weeks to go? Shall I go on? I will if you want me to, or I can prescribe some antibiotics and something for the pain and send you on your way."

My eyes beg my Nana not to believe him. Nana nods at me and lays her hand on my shoulder. To Dr. Mendax, she says, "We'll wait for the police, but we'll go ahead and take those prescriptions."

"I'll call them in," Dr. Mendax says with a tight smile. "The nurse will get you bandaged up." With that, he strides out the door.

I hope I never see him again.

The nurse blows out a breath and says to Nana, "Let me show you how to bandage her. She's going to need some help changing her dressing for the next few days. I close my eyes as Nurse Longo smooths a numbing cream over the backs of my thighs and bandages them in yards of gauze.

She is almost done when I hear the door open. "Again?" the cheerful voice grates on my ears and digs into my brain. I can't take any more of this. I start to cry again.

"Hello, officer," I hear Nana introduce herself to Mr. Hereford — Candace/Polly's father.

"It's nice to meet you, Ma'am. I'm sure the Williams are glad to have you here." His voice lowers, but I still hear him plainly since he's only a couple of feet away. "This one has been breaking their hearts."

Nana doesn't say anything. I don't know if she's stunned, angry, or finally believes what everyone is saying about me and second-guessing her decision to take me with her. We should never have come to the hospital. We should have gotten in her car and gone anywhere but here.

*Anywhere but here.* The thought calms me. I can leave. I can walk out of the ER and drive away and never come back to this town.

A tugging on my bandages brings me back to the humiliation of the exam room.

"Looks like they're on there nice and tight. I don't want to disturb your work." Officer Hereford says to the nurse.

"It's no problem," she says. "I can unwrap them."

"Nah. Not necessary. I have a pretty good idea of what happened here."

I feel his breath on my hair, and it makes me shiver. I can't move, but I shrink from him inside my skin. "You don't want to make a bigger deal of this than it is." It isn't a question. "Your parents are in the waiting room."

My fingers reflexively crumple the paper on the table under me.

"I can send them in, or I can arrange for you to go out to your vehicle without seeing them."

I understand what he isn't saying.

"I want to leave," I whisper, non-verbally agreeing not to press charges. I don't care at this point. I want to leave town and never return.

"Good idea." I can hear the smirk in his voice. "Get dressed, and I'll escort you out."

Nana and Lu help me as Officer Hereford breezes out the door. "Honey," Nana begins tentatively, "You really should press charges."

I can't think anymore. I finally understand the true meaning of the word "overwhelmed." I'm drowning, and I need air. "We shouldn't have come here," I gasp out. I shiver into my sweatshirt and jean-skirt and shuffle out the exam room door, not bothering to wait for Officer Hereford to come back and escort us. I don't want to see him — or any of these people — ever again.

Nurse Longo jogs after us to hand Nana my prescriptions and a care package of bandages and gauze for the road. We all thank her. Nana even hugs her, and Nurse Longo wishes me luck as she points us on our way through the maze of hallways back to the ER waiting room. I'm almost to the door when I see them. My parents are sitting on a two-seater bench in the corner. I pick up my shambling pace, but I see the fury in their eyes as they watch me pass.

I'm stiff-legged and limping, but my whole body leans forward, desperately trying to propel itself outside.

"Slow down, Julia," Lu says, grabbing my elbow as I stumble.

"My parents are in the waiting room," I wheeze.

"I know."

"Let's keep going," Nana urges. "My car is right over there."

Lu and Nana get me into the front seat and assume my gasp is one of pain rather than the result of my parents' sudden appearance just behind them. Mom, with her usual tight-lipped disapproval, and Dad with his face red and gathering spittle in the corners of his mouth.

As soon as the seatbelt clicks, Dad bumps Nana out of the way and boxes her out with his body, squeezing himself between the car's frame and its open door, his face swooping in and stopping uncomfortably close to my own. "We talked to Dr. Jeffers about this latest stunt of yours. We're going to stand aside and let you go. It's the only avenue left open to us. We've done everything we could to raise you right, but you've stubbornly clung to your own will. We can't do anything about these seeds of rebellion you harbor in your heart."

Mixed metaphor, I think to myself, wondering at his strange cadence and word choice. It sounds like he's quoting from a script. Now that I'm listening to one of his faux concerned rants from the safety of a getaway car, I feel less anxious than I usually do. I know he can't hurt me anymore.

"Yes, you go your way," he continues, unaware that I am barely listening, "but don't bother coming back."

Not a problem, I silently agree.

"But keep in mind, you take nothing with you. Your mom and I had planned to pay for your college — no more. If you can find a college that will take you as a high-school dropout, you're paying for it yourself.

"I'm not a dropout," I counter, then bite my lip, wishing I hadn't engaged.

He gives me his smarmy smile, "The school has no record of you graduating."

"My diploma ..." I trail off as I remember my ransacked room. "I guess this means you stole the money I earned at camp as well." I accuse him, careful to keep my voice matter-of-fact.

"Not stole. Withdrew. The bank account was in my name too. I have every right to it."

The car starts moving backward, and my dad and I share surprised looks that morph into outrage and serenity, respectively. Dad's face is furious, but he has no choice other than to back up as Nana pulls neatly out of the parking space and exits the lot. I shut my door with a smile.

# Chapter Fifteen: Finding Freedom

Lu sits with me in the car as Nana fills the prescriptions at the drugstore. Nana hands me a water bottle and encourages me to take my first dose of antibiotics and painkillers right away. The painkillers kick in quickly, and I'm pleasantly numb as we pull up at Lu's house. Lu opens the car door to hug me goodbye, but Nana gets out to embrace Lu and thank her for all of her help. We're a half-hour out of town when I realize I'm still holding the paper Lu pressed into my hand when we dropped her off. It's her address at the camp. She made me swear to write to her. This scrap of paper is the first tangible thing I focus on in my new life.

Nana's music is different from my parent's. It's lilting and light with lyrics that hover in the air and echo through my brain. According to the digital readout, it's a band called Arctic Life. I find myself floating on the notes and poetic images as we finish the twists and turns out of the foothills surrounding my hometown and hit the straightaway road through the high desert.

The desert is empty, framed on either side by wooded mountains, with a big, black road cutting it into two hemispheres. It feels like a runway, and I'm ready to fly.

I am flying.

Nana suggests I recline my seat and take a nap. I don't wake up until we stop, and Nana quietly leaves the car without a word. It's 5:00 in the afternoon, but the spring sun is still high in the sky. Nana parked the car in front of a hotel — a nice one. I've never stayed in one like this before. My parents based our motel choices on the bare minimum they had to pay. More times than not, it was two double beds, one for my parents, one for Roman, and me on the floor in a sleeping bag. It was always stressful with Mom's constant reminder that it wasn't something we could afford. I wonder why Nana chose such an extravagant place.

When she returns, I see the exhaustion on her face — no wonder we've stopped. The guilt doesn't creep in — it slams into me as I realize what I've done. As she opens her door, I'm wiping the tears off my cheeks.

"We're all checked in — what's the matter, honey? Are you in pain?"

I shake my head and blurt out, "I'm sorry!"

Nana slips behind the wheel and hands me a tissue all in one motion, "Sorry for what?"

I gesture at the hotel. "For everything. For calling you and making you come to Sampson, and now you're tired, and we had to get a hotel, and you can't afford it."

"Who says I can't afford it? That's nonsense. Plus, I'm in a points program, and I get a bunch of perks. Let's get inside and relax. Don't worry about what I can afford. I've been saving up for this for the past couple of years."

She's out of the car again before I can say anything, so I obediently open my door and follow her. "Don't forget your medicine," she reminds me, and I reach carefully back into the car to get the stack of stapled paper bags from the pharmacy. I follow Nana into the glass-fronted hotel. Embedded in the marble floor is a sunburst of different kinds of stone. Not a sunburst, I correct myself, a wind rose — a compass used on maps. It's pretty, I think, as I pass over it.

Nana stops at the desk, picks up a little plastic bag from the clerk, then nabs some menu brochures from the table opposite the elevator, scanning their contents as we rise to the second floor. But when she passes a hand over her eyes, I know she wants to rest.

I do too. Despite my nap in the car, I'm still feeling woozy. My stiffened legs are screaming for another dose of pain killer.

The room is gorgeous. The bathroom has the same marble floor as the lobby. Nana hands me her toiletry case and the plastic bag containing a travel toothbrush, toothpaste, and some beige squishy things that I think might be earplugs. I set them and the bags from the pharmacy on the sparkly granite countertop. Nana's alarm goes off in the other room, and she says, "It's time for your meds." I open the paper bag and take one pill from each plastic container.

Nana is unpacking her bag in the main room, setting her clothes in the dresser's drawers. I look longingly at the beds. They are huge and covered in snowy white linens and piled high with pillows. Sconces hover over dark wood nightstands.

I hold back from throwing myself face first on the billowy comforter, mostly because I know it will hurt like fire, but Nana has no such compunction. She sinks onto the bed with a sigh, then looks at me ruefully. "I shouldn't have done that. Now I don't want to get up." With a groan, she stands and opens the dresser drawer again. "Here's a t-shirt for you," she sing-songs as she tosses it to me. "I'm going to get changed for bed. I'm wiped out, and it looks like you are too. Let's order in. Take a look at those menus and decide what you want to eat." She hands me the brochures on her way into the bathroom.

I try to choose between Italian or Mexican, but my eyes keep drifting to the pizza ad next to the phone. The gooey cheese looks so good.

"Would you rather have pizza?" Nana has materialized next to me, wearing a pair of grey yoga pants and a long-sleeved pink t-shirt. She looks adorable. I nod. "Sounds good." She picks up the phone and punches in the number. "What kind?"

"Cheese."

Into the phone, she says, "Okay," then to me, "I'm on hold. What kind of crust?"

I shrug. "Whatever you like."

A half-hour later, I'm in an oversized tee and fresh bandages, sitting under a fluffy comforter, eating a deliciously greasy pizza, and feeling amazingly happy.

Nana tosses a gnawed crust back into the box. "So good, but I've got to get some sleep. I drove straight through after I got your call, and I'm exhausted. I got some earplugs at the front desk, so feel free to watch TV or read if you want."

"I don't have any books anymore." That was the worst part about losing my stuff.

Nana hands me her phone, tethered to an outlet by a charger cord. She shows me her Kindle app and invites me to peruse her library while she heads off to the bathroom again, saying, "I'm glad I packed some antacid." I'm still scrolling through her massive collection when I hear deep breathing coming from her bed. I didn't even notice her come back in.

There are tons of books on the app — more than we had in our entire house and at my school combined. I had tried to get a phone for years because Lu had one, and I wanted to text her and Jack — but now I want a phone, so I too can hold an entire library in my hand.

Finally, after scrolling through the list multiple times, one title jumps out at me. I swipe to the first page, and the story instantly sucks me in. By midnight, I've turned the last page, and I sigh with pleasure at the beautifully written novel.

I continue to think about what I've read as I work my way off the bed and shuffle to the bathroom. While I'm in the cool marble room, I take my next dose of medicine. My legs are stiff, but I'm already feeling better than I usually do after a beating. I brush my teeth, telling myself that I need to relax and get some sleep, but the story from Nana's book keeps playing in my mind.

After laying back down, I pick up the phone again to read the author's note and discover that she based her character's struggles on her own and how God showed His love to her the whole time she wrote. She ends her note with, "This is a story of freedom from the bondage of shame."

I lay the phone face down on the nightstand and turn off

the light, smiling as I feel the pain meds take effect. I snuggle deep under the covers, and as I drift off, I think, *I'm free.*

# Chapter Sixteen: Healing Day

I wake to the sound of crying and Nana rubbing my arm, saying, "Wake up, honey." I open my eyes and discover I'd been weeping in my sleep. "It's time for your meds again," Nana says. I take the little pills out of her hand and place it on my tongue. She hands me a water bottle and helps me sit up a little so that I can drink, then gently lays me back down. "I'll leave the water on the nightstand. Drink as much as you can. I don't want you to get dehydrated." I nod at her in the still-dark room and then drift off again.

The sun is peeping in the crack between the curtain panels when I wake again. "Stupid bladder," I mutter as I struggle to get my stiffened legs over the edge of the bed.

"Here. Let me help," Nana says and materializes at my side. As soon as I am on my feet, I'm shambling to the bathroom, closing the door behind me. I'm about ready to burst, but I can't bring myself to sit on the seat. I have the irrational fear that I will open every wound on my thighs if I sit right now. I compromise by standing over the toilet bowl and squatting just a little.

I wash my hands and face and brush my teeth, half-wishing for a shower but without the energy to take one. I shuffle back to bed instead.

Nana is sitting in her bed, reading something on her phone. She looks up and smiles when I come in and gets up to help me back to bed. "It's time for your medicine again."

"I just took it," I remind her.

"When? In the bathroom just now?"

"No. When you woke me up, remember?"

"That was six hours ago."

"Oh." I look at the bedside clock. It's a little after twelve. "When is checkout?" I'm confused. Whenever I stayed in a hotel with my parents, checkout was a time to be feared. "You don't have time for a long shower — we have to check out!" "Get your stuff packed — it's almost checkout!" "Hurry! Get your stuff in the car. Your dad is checking out now!"

Nana gives me an amused smile. "Our checkout isn't until Friday. I thought we'd spend some time in Dawes before heading home."

Dawes? Are we in Dawes?

Nana encourages me to try sitting up for a while, piling pillows behind my back and head until I'm almost upright. She's so gentle that the bandages don't pull at all. "I'll get you a new water bottle."

"That's okay. I can drink this one." I unscrew the cap and down the room temperature water. As soon as it's empty, Nana has placed a cold, frosty bottle on my nightstand.

"Drink this one too. You haven't had enough over the last day."

I nod obediently, but even as I argue with her in my mind that I'm not thirsty, my hand reaches for the new bottle. The water is cold and sweet. It's the best thing I've ever tasted. I drink it to the last drop and turn to put it on my nightstand, but a replacement bottle is already there. Nana takes the empty from my hand. I wonder where she's pulling all of these cold water bottles from when she opens the mini-fridge and pulls one out for herself. The refrigerator is full of water, and I notice there's half a case on the luggage rack next to it.

"I put in an order at Walmart this morning and snuck out to pick it up while you were sleeping. We've got plenty of water, as you see, as well as granola bars, popcorn, some frozen meals, and a few fruits and vegetables. Are you hungry?"

I'm starving. I start pulling back the covers, but Nana stops me. "No, no. You stay there. What would you like?"

I want everything — all of it. I try to narrow down what

I want first. "Um — granola bar?"

Immediately, Nana hands me the variety pack of chewy bars with the encouragement to eat whichever ones I want. I give a little shimmy when I see the S'Mores flavor and pass it by for peanut butter. Nana goes into the bathroom with a grocery bag, and I hear the water running for several minutes. When she returns, she's carrying the ice bucket full of freshly washed apples, oranges, and pears. She sets it within easy reach on the nightstand. I select an orange and start peeling.

Nana says, "I'm going to make my ravioli." She goes to the minifridge and holds up her frozen entrée. "I got one for you too. Do you want yours now?"

"Yes, please." Then I see the pizza box on the dresser. "Is there any pizza left?"

Nana flips open the lid. "Two slices. Want them heated up?" I shake my head, and Nana hands me the box. The cold pizza is a perfect accompaniment to the smell of the microwave ravioli, which I devour minutes after the timer dings. Nana sits on her bed eating hers and chatting with me while I feel like I'm eating everything in sight. I find myself getting anxious. Like I should apologize for enjoying the food. For enjoying anything. Nana breaks into my thoughts with, "Want to watch a movie?" I nod, and she flips through the movie options, practically squealing when she sees an adaptation of William Shakespeare's *A Midsummer Night's Dream*. "Have you ever seen this?" I shake my head. Lu would invite me to her house to watch at least one movie a week, but my movie days ended when she left for college. At our place, it was all game shows and true crime. Nana gets excited over the movie, promising that I'll love it. I smile, and nod and she pushes play.

She's right. I love it. It's hilarious and sad and a little naughty in places. Mom's lips would be a straight white line through the whole thing, and I don't care. Nana and I laugh at Bottom the Weaver's ego and Puck's mix-up in the forest around Thebes. I get a little frustrated with Helena, who is so thirsty for Demetrius' love she acts the fool. I wonder if that's what Lu saw when she looked at me.

That makes me wonder if Jack knows I've left Sampson and if he's okay. I should have given Lu a note to deliver to him. I was so loopy from stress and pain meds that I forgot to let him know I was leaving. I try to stop my thoughts there. I don't want to admit to myself that I hadn't thought about him since I left. I pull my focus back to the movie.

After Puck finishes his last address to his viewing audience and the music swells with the credits, it's time for me to head to the bathroom again. This time, I'm moving easier. Still, there's a slight pulling depending on how I move, but I'm much more comfortable than I was this morning. This time I can actually sit down.

My walk back to the bed is somewhat normal. No more shuffle! I notice that Nana moved the bucket of fruit off the nightstand, replacing it with rolls of gauze, pads, and ointment. I guess it's time to change my bandages.

"Feel up to a shower?" Nana asks, catching me off guard.

"Um — I guess so." Although what I'm going to change into afterward has me stumped. My denim skirt and tees aren't exactly clean, but I guess I can wear them one more day. It's my underwear and bra that need changing more.

Nana hands me a shopping bag. "Don't worry about your bandages getting wet since we're going to change them after anyway. I picked up a few things for you to wear. I went for comfort over style, but hopefully, everything fits. Oh, you won't need these just yet." She pulls out something in a cozy shade of gray before handing me the bag of clothes and sending me off to wash.

Hot water is a miraculous blessing from God. I let it flow over me, getting used to the sting of my cuts until they don't bother me anymore. I didn't realize how disgusting I felt until I started washing. I washed my hair twice, using Nana's full-sized shampoo since the sample provided by the hotel wouldn't be enough to clean the massive mop on top of my head. Mom bragged to people that she never cut my hair. I never understood her pride in that. My hair is awful. Yes, it's long, but that doesn't automatically make it pretty. The dirty-dishwater blond hanging in bumpy, awkward skeins down my back isn't attractive. I wasn't allowed to have bangs, so my hair was always pulled back from my face by barrettes, a headband, a ponytail, or a braid. Mom fussed about how much shampoo I went through, but it takes a palm-full to wash all of this mess.

I rinse the last of the shampoo out and follow it up with conditioner. I leave it in while I scrub every inch of me not covered in gauze. Rinse, rinse, rinse, and rats. No facewash. I shrug and ring out the washcloth, soap it up again, and clean my face. It's the best I can do for now.

I wrap my hair in a towel, the ends sticking out to drip down my back, and I use a second towel to rub myself dry. In the bag Nana gave me is a fresh pack of underwear in pastel colors. I slip a pair on. They're a little big on me, but they're clean and new, so I'm not going to complain. She also bought me some sports bras. I put on the pink one. It fits just right and perfectly matches the tunic tee that is long enough to cover my bottom. I realize now that it was a skirt Nana took out of the bag. I wouldn't need that yet because of the bandage change, but I still feel self-conscious walking out in a t-shirt and panties, which is weird since that's pretty much all I've been wearing since we arrived in the room. Still, I pull my damp towel off the rack and wrap it around my waist.

Nana has pulled back the covers of my bed and straightened the bottom sheet. "Let's change those bandages, and then you can rest again."

Obediently, I drop the towel and lay down on my belly as she cuts away the gauze and lets my healing wounds "air out for a few minutes." She assures me that my legs are looking much better and asks how I'm feeling.

"Exposed," I joke, and she laughs. "The shower felt great, but it wore me out. The pain is nearly gone, though."

"That's great. Maybe tomorrow we can go out for a little bit."

"Yeah. Maybe." I don't want to force Nana to hang out with me in a hotel room, no matter how nice it is, but I'm not sure about sightseeing.

"We'll see how you feel tomorrow. There's no hurry." At that, Nana starts the process of smoothing antibiotic ointment over my hurts, strategically placing non-stick pads over the worst sections and rewrapping my thighs. When she's done, she helps me stand and works a pair of gray sweatpants up my legs.

My first ever pair of pants.

"Want to get back in the bed?" She asks, ready to assist me.

I'm still looking down at my legs covered in soft material. I walk a few steps. It feels nice. My thighs don't stick and rub together like they do when I wear a skirt with no tights. And I don't have a fabric crotch hanging two inches below my own the way it does when I do wear tights — just low enough to encourage a nasty inner-thigh rash.

"Or, maybe you'd like to take a walk; get out of the room for a while."

At that, I nod. I locate my flip-flops while Nana straightens things up a bit, and we're out the door to take a stroll down the hotel's long hallway. At the end are a couple of vending machines and an ice dispenser. Next, we take the elevator to the lobby. The clerks greet us cheerily. Nana indicates that I can head outside while she makes a detour to the front desk. She's back at my side a minute later. "Shall we follow the sidewalk and see where it leads?" It dead-ends at the pool, blue and sparkling in the afternoon sunshine. We turn and go back the way we came until we go around the three sides of the hotel and end up at the other entrance to the pool.

My legs feel good, but I'm tired. Nana must see it in my face because she suggests we go back to the room. While we walk, we talk about the movie we watched, which leads us to Shakespeare. Nana is a fan. I told Dr. Jeffers that I'd only read the Shakespeare made available in the language workbooks, but I'd read a couple of his plays that I bought at yard sales as well as others I found crammed into the bookcase at school. Nana asked if I understood them. I did because they were annotated versions that explained the text as I read.

"What was your favorite?" Nana asked.

"I loved Hamlet."

"Great play. One of Shakespeare's best."

"What is your favorite?"

"Macbeth. I guess we both have a thing for tragedies."

When we return to the room, we discover that both beds are made up with fresh linens, and clean towels are sitting on the shelf in the bathroom. Nana pulls the covers on the bed back for me. I kick off my flip-flops and get in. Nana puts the fruit bucket and a new bottle of water on the stand.

"What would you like for dinner tonight?" she asks.

I feel like I've been eating all day, but I'm hungry again. "I chose last night. You choose tonight." Talking to Nana is like talking to Lu. She's my friend, but a friend I look up to. A friend I trust to lead me on the right path. A friend I love.

I love my Nana.

I never loved my parents. I tried, but I couldn't. I said I did, but I didn't. My parents let me know that they didn't love me and never would. I just mirrored their behavior.

Now I'm mirroring Nana.

She loves me. She genuinely cares about me. She doesn't watch over me or provide for me because she's afraid of what others will say about her if she doesn't. She doesn't demand I act or dress or speak a certain way. She only wants the best for me. I love her for it.

I hope that someday I'll be able to show her how much I love her back.

# Chapter Seventeen: Hiding Me

In the morning, Nana and I are both up and raring to go by eight. While she showers and dresses, I brush out my hair and weave it into a tight french braid. When finished, I clean out the brush I borrowed from Nana and collect all the hair that I'd shed on the bed and floor to throw it away. I wrap my braid around my head while I take a quick shower and brush my teeth before dressing. Nana changes my bandages again and hands me another pair of sweats, these in deep black. Today's tunic tee is light turquoise. My flip-flops remain the same. Nana is wearing jeans, a bright red blouse, and a pair of open-toed slides. She's adorable.

We sit down to enjoy the complimentary breakfast at the hotel. And it's not just a Little Debbie Honey-bun and a cup of bitter coffee, either. Instead, this is a buffet of fresh fruit, yogurt, oatmeal, bagels, muffins, and even waffles!

Nana and I are the only ones dressed casually in the hotel's breakfast area. Everyone else is in business suits. As we sit down, a team of six people walks in, dressed in khakis and polo shirts. I no longer feel so underdressed.

"I was thinking," Nana breaks into my people watching. "That today we could find the local mall. We can walk around for a bit — there should be plenty of places to sit when you need to rest — and even do some shopping." That sounds great to me, and a half-hour later, we're standing in the center of a glass, chrome, and marble palace accented with potted plants.

"Ooh, they have a Vivid!" Nana breathes excitedly. "We'll stop by there before we leave."

"We can go there first," I suggest. I don't know what

Vivid is, but I also don't know what any other stores contain. I do all of my clothes shopping at Walmart. Mom always insisted that the nearest mall was too far away (I think I went twice in my whole life) and far too expensive (but then she said the same thing when I bought a can of corn that wasn't on sale).

It turns out that Vivid is a store for "full-figured" women. I never thought of Nana as big. She's kind of short and always looks put together, but "plus-sized"? Not really. More blocky than anything.

The woman who waits on us, however, is definitely plus-sized. We're talking busty, hippy, and tall — really tall. Let me unpack my vocabulary words: she's voluptuous and gorgeous and Amazonian. I am instantly intimidated — and captivated. I find myself wanting to look like her. My hair is longer, but her's is glass-smooth with heavy bangs that stop just short of her big, heavily mascaraed eyes. I'm still a bland blob of near invisibility, and I cast a look of disapproval at my spotty reflection in one of the many mirrors in the store.

While Nana tries on a dress, I wander around picking up clothes and putting them down. I find a few dozen things I'd love to wear, but nothing in my size — everything is size twelve and above. I think I'm size ten? Maybe eight? I don't know. I usually go by small, medium, and large. I wear medium everything. Humdrum medium, I chant silently.

I check out the shoes. Finally, something that fits! I'm looking at the reflection of my feet encased in a pair of the cutest booties, ignoring the inner "Mom-voice," which insists that "only hookers wear boots," which is why I spend every winter with chapped legs and purple toes. I take a few steps. They feel good. I glance toward the changing rooms to see if Nana's made a reappearance and notice the giant posters adorning the tops of the walls just under the ceiling. I wonder how I haven't noticed them before.

The model is flirty in dresses that show miles of legs, sharp in tailored jackets, sporty in swimwear, and seductive in lingerie. Her short hair is a breezy tangle of platinum blond waves, making my long braid feel heavy and lifeless. I wonder how that hairstyle would look on me. The clerk heads my way. If can't pull off the short shag, I might be able to replicate the clerk's long tresses with heavy bangs.

"Is there anything I can find for you?"

I can't help mirroring her smile, but I shrug. "Everything is really cute, but there's nothing in my size." I glance down at the booties still on my feet. "Except these."

"And those are on sale. Good eye."

Just then, Nana comes out in a sky blue dress with a blousy bodice and calf-length skirt, cinched in at the waist with a wide belt. She looks fantastic.

I sift through the collection of graphic tees on a nearby display table as she and the clerk select a few more items.

"It's why I love this store," I hear Nana say. "My whole life, I've had to cram myself into clothes not made for my body type. When my husband and I were first married, I would steal his clothes to wear around the house because they fit me perfectly. He encouraged me to buy some men's clothes and make them feminine, but it just felt weird to me. I kept looking for something decent to wear and then, 'bam!' I walk into a Vivid, and there are racks of clothes for an 'I' body type."

I puzzle over Nana's little confession and move to a rack of dresses. I notice that all of them have a tag with a letter. I turn one of the tags over and discover that the clothes aren't just organized by size but also by shape. Nana said her letter was "I," so I rifle through the rack until I found the matching tag. It turned out that "I" women's bodies are straight up and down — same size bust and hip with little to no waist. That doesn't sound like Nana. I look at her standing at the counter, wearing straight-leg jeans and a cute red peplum top. It dawns on me that her clothing gives her the appearance of curves, of softness.

In a way, it's encouraging. I don't have any curves either. As Lu said, "the breast-fairy lost my address." However, Mom insisted I wear a bra and hide it under layers of dark t-shirts.

I grew up hearing that girls shouldn't wear boys' clothes, but my skirts didn't start as women's wear. They were Roman's old jeans repurposed for my wardrobe. Their one benefit was that their waists and hips fit my body perfectly.

For a while, Mom insisted I tuck in my t-shirts to give at least the illusion of a waist, but the bulk of all the extra material made it look like I was smuggling inner tubes under my clothes. They went back to being untucked, and any shape I may have had was well hidden. Even the sweaters and sweat-shirts Mom bought me were always bulky and unstructured.

I catch my reflection again: a shapeless mass topped with frizzy blonde blandness. No matter how tightly I braid my hair, the split ends poke their way out. I am so ugly.

This is not how I see myself in my head. I think of myself as prettier, with darker eyes and defined cheekbones. I look up at the confident woman on the poster and wish I was her.

No. I wish I were really me. The me I see in my mind.

I wander over to the counter near the back wall. Shiny gold cases hold makeup in a variety of colors. The powders and blushes pressed into the shape of roses catch my eye. I love pink. It's my favorite color.

"Ready?" Nana holds two black bags with "Vivid" scrawled on the sides in gold script. She's flushed with excite-ment. I've never felt that way about clothes shopping.

"Sure. Just let me put these back." I hold out a foot to show her the boot I'm still wearing.

"You can wear them out," Nana says, eyes twinkling.

The clerk approaches with another bag. "I put your san-dals and the box for the booties in here. I'm glad you found something you liked."

"Thanks." It comes out as a whisper, and I hope they understand I mean more than I say.

I see the clerk ask Nana a silent question, and Nana nods. The clerk turns to me with her million-watt smile. "Would you like a free makeover?"

# Chapter Eighteen: Shopping Spree

I can't stop looking at my reflection in the windows of the stores as we walk through the mall. This is me. The real me. The me I always knew I was inside. The way I pictured myself.

Nana is reading the names of the stores while I'm fascinated by my new look. She steers me into a boutique that caters to "juniors." I guess that's me. Shopping isn't half-bad! It was frustrating at first to find jeans that fit. Yes, you read that right! Jeans! Nana encouraged me to try on a pair made for men, and they fit perfectly. We paired them with feminine blouses, and the whole look came together. By early afternoon I have an essential wardrobe of clothes that are both cute and non-layered. I've found another aspect of freedom!

Nana insists she's starving but suddenly veers into a used bookstore on the way to the food court. I thank God that my Nana's a bookworm — and that she's awesome.

Nana heads for classics. I aim for YA. I pick up a copy of *Cinder* that I couldn't read last year and wonder if Nana would have any objections. I doubt she will, but I mosey over to ask anyway.

"Ooh, looks good. I want to read that when you're done." She walks me back to the YA shelves. "Have you read this?" she hands me a copy of *The Hunger Games.* I say no, and she adds it and the two sequels to the stack. "What about this one? Or these?"

With every shake of my head, Nana adds a new book to my stack. The clerk comes from behind the counter and offers to keep them on his desk until we are ready to check out.

We hit the Christian books section next, and I get other

novels by Ginny Ytrupp, author of the book I read the first night, and a couple from the *Love Comes Softly* series and three books by a new-to-me author, Anne Mateer.

Soon we're back at classics, and I've got my copy of *Scarlet Letter* — no *Wonder Book,* though; Nana muses that we might have to look for it online. *Animal Farm, Frankenstein, Uncle Tom's Cabin, The Call of the Wild, White Fang*, and a collection of *Edgar Allen Poe* stories make it to the counter before Nana takes a breath and murmurs that we might be finished.

"At least I know you've read all the children's classics." I nod, but she can tell from my blank look that I have no idea what she's referring to.

"You know — all the books I sent you when you were growing up. Roald Dahl? Fred Gipson? C.S. Lewis? Any of those ring a bell?"

"Sorry, no."

We are back out of line and in the children's section. Nana hands me *James and the Giant Peach* and *Charlie and the Chocolate Factory.* "Read *Charlie* first." A few others by Dahl make it to the stack. *Old Yeller* and *Harriet, the Spy,* are next. Then I hear Nana gasp, and we sweep across the room to the fantasy section where she selects a five-book collection called *The Belgariad.*

"Ah-maze-zing!" she announces, "You'll love these!" I can't help smile at her enthusiasm — and all my new books.

Nana is eyeing the mystery novels when I see our clerk from Vivid sashay into the store. The woman should seriously take up modeling. She sees the guy behind the counter and flashes him a gorgeous grin. He smiles back, but he's helping out the customer at the desk, so she comes over to talk to us.

"Hi, ladies! It looks like you found some good stuff."

Nana looks up in surprise, "Just rebuilding my granddaughter's library."

"Nice." The model clerk looks at the first book of the *Belgariad* at the top of the stack. "*Pawn of Prophecy.* Looks interesting."

Nana gives her a brief synopsis, trying not to drop any spoilers before I get a chance to read the book for myself. Nana finds another copy and hands it to her.

"Thanks. I'm intrigued. Oh. It looks like Michael is free now. It was great to see you again. Drop by anytime you're in town." With a wave, she pivots, calling to the clerk, "Michael! Got a minute?"

Michael grins. "For you, Ally, I've got all the time in the world." Then he pulls a book from the shelf behind the counter and adds it to the book Nana suggested. I wonder if they are a couple, but when she waves at us again on her way out, I decide they aren't. Michael looks too regretful as he watches her leave to be that woman's boyfriend.

By the time we finally check out, he's back to his smiling self and chatting with Nana. He suggests a book journal, and Nana has him throw it in the box — yes, box! We have too many books for even several plastic bags. Just before Nana swipes her card, I grab her elbow. I hadn't asked for any of the books she bought me except for the first one, but now, I suddenly remember a book I desperately need.

"Nana, wait." I swallow hard before asking Michael, "Do you have any Bibles?" He gives me a huge grin and pulls a brand new Gideon Bible out from behind his counter. "Free of charge. The Gideons give me a case a couple of times a year for moments just like this. Need a pen for notes?" He slips a pen with his store's information into the box when I nod. "Bookmarks?" Grinning, he adds a set of four, all different colors, with the store's logo and information, to the box. I nod again, this time struggling to keep my smile in place. I haven't made an origami heart bookmark since my notes were discovered.

I don't think I'll ever make another one.

Nana thanks him and swipes her card, the transaction over in a moment without grumbling, arguing, or guilting me into an apology.

Michael says, "Why don't you let me hold onto this for you while you pull your car around to the back door. I can load it into your trunk for you."

"Thanks, that would be wonderful. It might be a while, though. We're going to the food court. Can I get one of your cards? I'll call you when we're ready."

While Nana and I are eating lunch at the food court, the excitement of the day catches up with us. "We shouldn't have sat down," Nana muses. I nod because I'm too tired to speak. And because that little flash of sadness connected with my old bookmarks came out of nowhere. On top of my emotional and physical exhaustion, my thighs are throbbing. I wish I had brought my painkillers. "How about after we eat, we go back to the hotel and relax? Honestly, I could use a nap."

"Me too."

"Were you able to get any sleep last night?"

"Some." Then I admit sheepishly, "I went to bed at midnight."

Nana gives me a sympathetic look. "Hurting?"

"Reading."

That brightens her face. "Really? What book?"

"*Words*."

"I love that one. Where are you at in the story?"

"I — uh — I finished it."

"All in one shot? Wow. I have another one of her books on my app."

"*Invisible*?"

"Yes."

"I read it the night before last."

"That's my girl!"

Without warning, my eyes prick with hot tears. They catch me by surprise, and I hurriedly blink them back. Nana places her hand gently on mine.

"What's wrong, honey?"

"You used to say that to me when I was little. I've missed it. I've missed you."

"I've missed you too, honey. I'm so sorry about everything. I knew your parents were odd, but I had no idea they were hurting you. If I'd had known, I would have gotten you and Roman out of there sooner." I can see she's still worried about Roman. It's weird. I haven't thought about him at all.

"Roman will be okay," I assure her. "They like him." I take a bite of my sandwich, wishing the silent part of that statement was one I could ignore. Yes, they like Roman — but they also hate me. I swallow and take a sip of Coke. "But now I'm with you." Nana gives me a strange look, and I realize I hadn't spoken my entire thought process aloud, so it came out as a non-sequitur. I don't clarify; just keep eating.

We discuss *Words* and *Invisible* over the rest of our lunch, then head for the car. Nana pulls up behind the mall to the back door of "Twice-Turned Books" and calls Michael on the phone. He pops the box of books into the trunk no problem — obviously something he frequently does — and wishes us a great rest of our day.

At the hotel, I select a half-dozen books I might want to read while waiting for the pain meds to kick in, but I've barely been introduced to Charlie Bucket when I drift off.

# Chapter Nineteen: Reviewing History

I wake from my nap and hobble as fast as I can to the bathroom and check my face in the mirror. Good. My makeup is still in place. I smile at my reflection. There I am. The real me, finally allowed to come out.

Nana insists I wear one of my new outfits to dinner at a restaurant called "Olive Garden." I've seen their commercials on TV but have never been to one. I'm pretty excited. I choose to wear my dress — an actual dress! It's black with a scattered purple flower print. It's so light and free-feeling that I attempt a spin in the bathroom. It doesn't go well since I'm still at the hobbling stage. Oh, and get this! No tights! Just bare shins and my brand-new booties.

I try doing something with my hair, but I don't have any barrettes, and my one hair elastic breaks as I pull it off the bottom of my braid, so the mop has to be loose. Waves from the earlier braiding help disguise my split ends. I push the side strands behind my ears and borrow Nana's hairspray to keep it in place. As soon as I can, I'm getting my hair chopped off. I'm sick of it.

The restaurant is lovely. Nana encourages me to get an actual meal, not just the cheapest thing on the menu. I get soup and breadsticks and lasagna. Nana gets the salad and mushroom ravioli. I focus on the food and try not to think about how I'm bleeding this poor lady dry.

Nana clears her throat, and I look up, surprised to see her looking so serious. "I need to ask you something." I nod at her, and she continues. "At the bookstore, you were—you hadn't read most of the books we bought, but you're no dummy," she breaks off when I let an eye-roll slip. I feel an immediate frisson of fear. The last time I rolled my eyes where an adult could see me, my father smacked me across the face and then blamed me for provoking him.

"What?" Nana wants to know.

"I'm sorry." It comes out in a whisper. She doesn't say anything, so I continue, even though I know it's better just to apologize and then shut up. "I shouldn't have shown disrespect. It's just that I already know I'm not as bright as other kids ..."

"Where in the world did you get that idea?"

I look over at her in surprise. She should know my early history even better than I do. She'd had greater contact with my family when I was little. "It's why I started school a year late," I prompt. "Because I was developmentally behind."

"You were no such thing," Nana practically growls. "You were always light years ahead of other kids your age. You were walking at nine months and reading at three years. By the time you were four, you were reading *Little House in the Big Woods* by yourself, mainly because your mother was busy with Roman. The only reason you didn't start kindergarten until you were six was that your mom didn't want to drive back and forth from the school for 'just one kid.' She made you wait until Roman was old enough to go to the three-year-old's preschool on campus. Paw Paw and I thought she was selfish and ridiculous, but we couldn't convince her to let you go. Your dad didn't have a problem with you staying home as he didn't have to pay tuition for another year and, as he told your Paw Paw, 'Girls don't need much education anyway.'"

"Oh." I wasn't slow. Wasn't developmentally behind. I purposely keep the information on the very surface of my brain. If I let it sink in, I won't be able to control my emotions.

"You speak as if you're well-read ...," Nana is saying, but I jump in. It's easier to focus on the conversation than on the bombshell she just dropped.

"I do a lot of reading, but it's the same books over and

over again. There wasn't much variety in the school bookcase and even less at home. I got a few books from contests and a couple of yard sales, but I had to run everything by Mom, and she's not much of a reader. I won the rest of the *Little House* series by Laura Ingalls Wilder when I memorized one hundred verses for a Sunday School class, and Mom was okay with those because she has the whole TV series on DVD. And I've read everything by Jane Austin and Louisa May Alcott and a few things by Nathanael Hawthorn and a couple of Shakespeare's plays — pretty much anything mentioned in my language workbooks. Except for *Moby Dick*. I wasn't allowed to read that. Mom didn't think it sounded very nice."

Nana's spontaneous guffaw catches me off guard. It takes the other diners by surprise too, but no one seems annoyed. They smile at this beautiful older woman tickled by something hilarious. Her laughter is contagious, and soon I'm chuckling too. While at a table, eating dinner. I'm enjoying a meal and not feeling the slightest bit of fear that I'll say the wrong thing and either be sent away from the table or beaten. It's a measure of safety I've never felt before. Have I mentioned that I love my Nana?

Finally, Nana dabs at her eyes and draws in a cleansing breath. "Oh — goodness — I haven't laughed like that in years." She sighs in happy relief. "Back to books. You said you never got the children's books I sent you?"

I shake my head. "I didn't know — I never got any books."

"I sent you and your brother books every Christmas along with a check for whatever big gift your parents might want to get for you." Her eyes narrow shrewdly. "I know they got the packages. They always cashed my checks. What?"

I try to pull my expression back to its normal neutral reset but can't. I remind myself that I'm not going to cover for my parents anymore. "Mom and Dad always told us you and Paw Paw didn't send us gifts because you couldn't afford them. And then, after Paw Paw died, you were scraping to get by so not to expect anything from you."

"Those liars!" Nana sputters. I'm shocked to hear it stated so blatantly, but I can't argue against it. "When your Paw Paw died, he left me with a very — um — generous insurance policy. I put it in a special account and let it collect interest. I'm self-employed as an antique and collectibles buyer. It keeps me busy and lets me pay off the few bills I have. I've already paid off my house, and I have very few expenditures. My guilty pleasures are occasional dinners out with friends and buying movies and books. I can easily cover those expenses with what I earn and still put money in the bank every week. Why in the world would your parents lie to you about me like that?"

"Pride." The word slips out without thought.

"That I believe." Nana agrees. "I think that answers every question I've ever had about your parents."

"What was Mom like when she was my age?" It's an awkward segue, but when Nana talks about my parents, it rattles me — like Mom is a stranger and not her daughter.

"When she was your age, your mom was normal. She loved school — great at math but was a terrible speller. She enjoyed antiques and art even then."

I didn't know my mom liked art and antiques.

"I bought her tons of books about collectibles and even arranged for her to work at the antique mall where I had a shop. She told me she wanted to work as an apprentice and learn how to appraise stuff, planning to work at the store instead of going to college. Your Paw Paw and I weren't happy about it at first, but we realized it was her passion and gift, so we gave her the go-ahead. Her youth leaders weren't pleased with either her or us. They even came over to the house and tried to convince us that it was somehow sinful for her to miss out on going to a Christian college. Paw Paw had always wanted your mom to finish her education and worked hard to provide her with a college fund, but he'd come to realize that college wasn't for her. He pointed out to her youth leaders that she wasn't doing anything immoral or sinful. She was still attending church regularly, and she was faithful to her daily devotions, and no one had any right to tell her they knew God's will for her life better than she did herself.

"After that, the youth leaders pretty much cut her off. The only time they spoke to her was to point out something she did wrong. Most of the time, the "wrong" things they accused her of were simply the leaders' opinions — she wasn't wearing the right clothes, her music wasn't acceptable, her hair was too short, just ridiculous stuff, but their coldness hurt her. She bent over backward to ingratiate herself to them, and that's when they started encouraging her to pull away from us. They implied that we held her back and led her farther away from God rather than closer to Him.

"Your mom worked her senior year as an apprentice and was up for full-time employment with the store after graduation when she, under pressure from the youth leaders, went to a college and career outing with the young people from church. It was a big rally on a college campus, and that's where she met your dad. I don't know how he got a hold on her so fast, but after that weekend, she quit her job at the antique store, applied for the same college he was already attending and planned out her whole future to match with his. It was an obsession, pure and simple. Your dad called to get permission for the two of them to date, and Paw Paw had none of it. He said no. Period.

"Your mom stopped talking to us. Her youth leaders came into our home and told us we were standing in the way of God's will. They told us we should encourage her in her new relationship because, hey, at least she'd be going to college. But, we still weren't sold and had to ask her youth pastor to leave."

"Your dad came for her high-school graduation. He just showed up on our doorstep, expecting us to welcome him, give him a place to stay, and feed him. We arranged for him to stay at the youth pastor's house. We figured if he was so anxious to have our daughter marry this boy, he could get to know him. We'd already made up our minds. Meeting your father solidified our opinions. There was something about your dad, right from the beginning, that we didn't like. He said all the right things, but he was calculating. He was manipulative. We prayed your mom would see it, but she was so blind, and every effort to point out his flaws made her cling closer to him."

"He visited for three days and left for his summer job on the college campus. Your mom's whole focus was on getting her stuff ready for school, but she got sick — really sick — migraines, nausea, vomiting." Nana stopped. She didn't resume eating but didn't look like she was going to continue the story either.

"What was wrong with her?" I finally ask.

"She was pregnant." Nana's eyes still hold the hurt she must have felt when she first heard the news. "She'd been around your dad for maybe ten days at the most, and she was pregnant." Nana shakes her head in confusion. "Just the logistics of the thing is mind-boggling. We made it a point not to leave them alone when he was visiting. The only thing we could figure was that it happened during the rally the month before. Or maybe at the youth pastor's home."

"It wasn't me. I couldn't have been me. I wasn't that baby."

"I'm sorry, honey, but it was." Nana reaches out to pat my hand. "Paw Paw called your dad and arranged for him to fly back so we could discuss everything face to face. Your dad was unapologetic and demanding. Your parents married in a private ceremony at the church, the youth leader did the ceremony, and your mom wore my wedding dress. There was no reception. They got into their borrowed car and took off for their one-night honeymoon in a local motel. We waved goodbye and then had a meeting with the pastor. He claimed he had no idea what the youth pastor was teaching, which we thought was odd. So we filled him in. We brought up all the standards and rules the youth leader had made up based on his opinion but passed off as biblical doctrine. The head pastor didn't seem surprised because he agreed with most of what the youth pastor was teaching and how he was leading his group. So we

MARBETH SKWARCZYNSKI

withdrew our membership and never went back.

"When your mom and dad came to our house the next day, Paw Paw took your mom to the bank. He was planning to take his name off her college fund and put it solely in her name. Your dad invited himself along and insisted your mom add his name to the account.

"Your parents flew to your dad's college the next day, but the news of their pregnancy and rushed wedding had gotten out. The school expelled your dad and revoked your mom's acceptance. So they went to Sampson, your dad's hometown. They used her college fund to put a down payment on the house there. Your dad got a job at the paper plant, working at his home church in his off-hours, and your mom became the church secretary until you were born. After that, she stayed at home until you and your brother started school full-time. Then she went back into selling antiques."

I shook my head at that. "Mom doesn't have a job."

Nana's confused look must mirror my own. "She's an appraiser. She works at Dewey's Antiques."

Dewey is the neighboring town to Sampson. It's where we go to Walmart.

"How did I not know my mom had a job?"

Nana shrugs one shoulder. "Your pastor has some strange ideas about women working outside the home. Unless it's at the church, of course, I guess that's acceptable. Your parents probably keep her job quiet."

"Very quiet," I agree, finally understanding her long hours away from home running "errands."

"So they ended up married and in Sampson by default. No wonder they hate me."

"No, honey, you shouldn't think that way. Your parents made their own choices. It has nothing to do with you."

"But it does. My parents hate me because they think I ruined their lives. Just like they ..."

"Hate me?" Nana lifts her glass of iced tea. "Here's to us both being hated by two of the most prideful, obnoxious people on the face of God's green earth. May we always be great company for each other."

I clink my glass against hers and smile, but deep inside, I mourn for our disillusionment.

# Chapter Twenty: Exploring

After the restaurant, we go straight back to the hotel, where I immediately announce that I need a shower. Under the noise of the heavy stream of water, I sob for all of the years I'd believed I was not only ugly but stupid. I was so far behind my peers and thought it was because there was something wrong with me. Tonight I'd discovered it was because my parents had designed me that way. I cry until the sadness is replaced with righteous anger, then with determination. It's not an "I'll show them!" resolve, but an "I'll prove my worth to me!" Once I get that thought firmly in the front of my brain, I wash my face with my newly purchased facewash, then step out and towel off.

Nana doesn't say much when she changes my bandages, but we chat for a few moments before we both select books to read and retire to our beds. She and I are in a good place emotionally, and the silence in the room doesn't feel weird. I don't read for long. I'm exhausted.

We sleep in on Thursday morning and miss the complimentary breakfast. Nana isn't as disappointed as I am. "We needed the sleep," she says. "Let's get ready and have brunch — or lunch — whatever you want."

I'd washed my hair the night before so it would dry overnight. I'd used a blow dryer a couple of times in my life and had trouble keeping my hair out of the fan. I give the hairdryer on the wall a curious glance, but I decide not to try it. The smell of burning hair that always accompanied my earlier attempts at blow-drying is nauseating.

My hair is still a little damp this morning, so I brush

through it as it finishes drying. It's almost smooth, but I still can't pull it back, so it just hangs around my face.

I lay out my first pair of jeans ever (yea!) and a beautiful peach-colored blouse with lacey cap sleeves. It's so beautiful. I want to cry. There are no camisoles or t-shirts to go under it, just a new perfectly fitting bra in a matching shade.

Before I dress, I get out my new makeup and attempt to recreate the look from Vivid the day before. It's not too bad. Nana points out I have a foundation line and helps me fix it, but I get the blush almost right. The eyeliner is tricky. Nana suggests I watch a few tutorials on YouTube and tells me I'll get better with practice.

When I walk out of the hotel room this morning, I feel like a new person. I feel like me for the first time.

At the suggestion from the clerk in the hotel lobby, Nana and I head for Historic Dawes and walk the six blocks of the district. Instead of brunch/lunch, we end up eating street food from the vendors who seem overly excited to see us. I have funnel cake for the first time. Nana and I share it because it's enormous. We sit on a bench together, people watching while we eat what is basically a waffle whose batter is poured through a funnel into a deep fryer instead of onto a press. It's delicious but so filling that we both insist that we won't eat for the rest of the day. Nana gets a hand-wipe out of her purse and hands me one too. We clean up and head for the first antique store on the street.

Nana heads straight for the glass. I wander away because I want to see everything. I've never been to an antique store before. There are old toys in excellent condition and tea-cups blooming with roses, and even oil paintings on the wall. One shelf contains delicate matte blue, pink, and purple ceramic objects with scenes in white depicted on their surface. I run my finger carefully over the raised white figure on a pink heart-shaped box. It's three women standing together in long robes. They look like they might be friends or sisters. I pull my hand away carefully. I don't want to be responsible for knocking anything off the shelves. Then I carefully reach back and lift the lid. There is a tree on the inside. I replace it and look more carefully at the leaf detailing around the edge of the box. I'm about to turn it over to see how much it costs when Nana joins me.

"You've found the Wedgwood."

"Oh." I guess all of this pottery is Wedgwood, then. I've never heard the name.

"Is there one in particular that you like?"

Without thinking, I point to the pink heart. When Nana reaches for it, the guilt starts to build. What if she buys it for me? She's already purchased so much. The clothes I needed, so I can talk myself out of feeling guilty for those, even though she could have bought my wardrobe from Walmart, and I would have been just as happy. Well, almost as happy. Walmart's clothes aren't nearly as cute as the blouse I'm wearing right now.

Nana inspects the box, then carefully examines several other pieces on the shelf. I see her head nodding slightly. "Julia, would you ask the lady behind the counter to come here?"

I squeeze past her and see the woman who greeted us is already on her way. She must have heard Nana. I stay back while Nana asks her questions that I don't understand. I wander off and find some old books. I'm reading the spines, but none of the titles or authors sound familiar. Then I see it. Locked in a glass case is a copy of *The Wonder Book*. It's in better condition than the one I had at home. The cover is still red and gold, but the fabric is shiny. I itch to open the case and hold it in my hands. Then I see the placard next to it. It's an English first-edition decorative cloth volume. Price: five hundred dollars. I back away slowly and return to Nana, who is at the counter checking out.

She and the woman, who I now realize owns the store, smile and chat like old friends. The two of them even exchange business cards. We walk out of the door empty-handed. The owner has offered to hold Nana's purchases until the end of the day.

At a kiosk selling star-topped wands and flower crowns, I swallow my anxiety and ask Nana if she would please buy me some ponytail holders. Nana doesn't bat an eyelash. "Which one do you want?" I choose the cheapest pack of elastics available, and we're on our way again. The next time we sit to rest. I finger-comb my hair and put it back in its usual braid. So much better.

After another hour of walking the district, the funnel cake is a long-lost memory, so we stop at a truck for the best tacos I've ever had.

After throwing away our empty plates, we decide to head for the car, stopping just long enough to pick up Nana's stuff from the antique store.

Back at the hotel, Nana says, "I think I'll swim for a bit. You can bring a book and hang out if you want."

We'd discussed swimming before. But, for me, it was a no-go since I (A) don't have a swimsuit, and (B) my thighs are still recovering. So instead, I stretch out on a lounge under the pergola near the pool and finish *Charlie and the Great Glass Elevator* while Nana does laps. I completed *Charlie and the Chocolate Factory* yesterday and loved it. So I went into the sequel with anticipation, only to be disappointed. Nana assures me *James and the Giant Peach* is top-notch, though.

It may seem weird that I'm reading kids' books as a nineteen-year-old, but I feel like I'm catching up, you know? Like I'm finally getting to experience childhood.

I finish the last page of *Elevator* and pick up *Peach* just as Nana steps out of the pool. "I'm hungry, but not for anything heavy. How do you feel about salads tonight?"

"Sounds good." I'm ready for some veggies.

"I'm going upstairs for a quick shower and change, and then I'll order. You can stay down here if you want to keep reading."

"Okay," I agree and get back to poor James. I could "get" Charlie's story — wracked with poverty, unable to participate fully in the world around him, and yet surrounded by a family who loved him — but with James? He has me reliving some stuff. If anyone needed to cling onto a piece of driftwood as it floated by, it was James. I had Nana to carry me away, and, to my relief, James has a magical peach with a stone filled with an odd assortment of critters that immediately adopt him as one of their own. I read until the peach rolls over the cliffs of Dover and into the sea. I'm shocked to find I am already at chapter 19. I set my bookmark and get up to see if the salads have arrived, snagging a complimentary apple on my way through the lobby, wishing it was a peach.

The salads are delicious, and we eat them while watching a movie adaptation of *Charlie and the Chocolate Factory*, but I'm starting to get restless, and I think Nana is too. I'm looking forward to leaving Dawes tomorrow morning and creating a life in Posting with Nana.

# Chapter Twenty-One: Going Home

Nana and I wake early, both raring to get on the road, but we don't want to pass up the complimentary breakfast. I get my peach this morning — in yogurt form, though. Afterward, we return to our room with the rolling cart and collect all the stuff we've accumulated.

"It looks like the next thing we need to buy you is a suitcase," Nana says, looking at my pile of shopping bags.

I brush my teeth and add my plastic baggie of toiletries to Nana's case. "Are you done with the stuff in the bathroom?" I call.

"Yes."

I close the clasps and add the toiletry case to the cart.

Nana is slipping her makeup bag into the outer pocket of her suitcase.

"You look nice," I say, studying her face. I'd seen Nana without makeup for the first time during this trip. To me, she was always pretty, but the cosmetics accenting her eyes and cheekbones make her look beautiful.

"Thanks, hon. It's amazing what a little makeup will do."

"You're pretty even without it."

"You're sweet. Let's go check out."

After leaving Dawes, we drive through the mountains for a good hour, never coming across another city as big as that mountain town. Jack had made a wise choice. I could live in Dawes. Maybe get a job at that used bookstore. Jack could get a job at — I don't know. I hadn't paid much attention to where he could work. The truth is, I haven't thought much about him at all since I left home. I'm a horrible fiancée.

"Mind if we listen to a book?" Nana breaks into my thoughts, and I agree immediately, excited when I hear the first line of *Pride and Prejudice* coming from her car's speakers. "You said you liked Austen, right?"

"Love her!"

Approximately three hours and twenty-one chapters later, we are pulling into Nana's mid-century modern house on a quiet street in Posting. I'd always loved her dark purple front door with its brass knocker. Now I am coming here, not just for a suddenly cut-short visit, but to live. I can't keep the grin off my face.

Nana leaves her stuff in the glassed-in entry and leads me to my room. I expect the kid's room I stayed in when I visited her as a little girl, all pink and ruffly, but Nana has redecorated. It's a self-contained studio apartment in cool shades of white and grey. I set my bags on the space-age recliner near the giant window, looking out into the side garden, and turn slowly to take it all in. "Nana, this is gorgeous!"

"Did you see the bathroom?"

Gone are the yellow duckies and the pink tub from years past. In its place is an oval soaker tub surrounded by sparkly white quartz. "Nana! When did you find time to do all of this?" I ran my hand over the quartz counter surrounding the vessel sink.

"Uh — let's see — about three years ago? Yeah. That's about right."

"Oh." Three years ago, I'd started working at the camp. "Wow," I whispered. "Has it really been three years since I've been here?"

"Four, but you're here now!"

"Nana, I'm so sorry." Not only am I a terrible fiancée, but I'm also a horrible granddaughter and, according to my parents, a disappointment as a daughter. What is wrong with me?

"All those home-improvement shows on cable inspired me. So I hired a woman from our church, a decorator, to help me strike a balance between mid-century modern and — well

— modern-modern. She did an awesome job. I love it. Come on; I'll show you the rest of the place."

The house looks and feels bigger than it is. Nana's suite is just slightly larger than mine. The third bedroom is decorated in a masculine black and blue, "In case Roman wants to visit."

Then she shows me the best thing ever. She has a whole library in her house. Three walls are floor-to-ceiling built-in bookcases. The fourth wall, across from the door, so it's the first thing you notice when you walk in, is all windows lined with glass shelves holding a small (or maybe an enormous) fortune in glassware. "Marie, she's the designer I told you about, encouraged me to show off my collection. Most of it is Fenton." I've never heard of Fenton, but from context, I assume it's a glass manufacturer. The late afternoon light causes the colored glass to glow. "You should see it in the morning," Nana says. "The sunrise makes this room look like the inside of a kaleidoscope."

The rest of the house is a great room where the kitchen looks out over the living and dining room space. "I hated being stuck in the kitchen while everyone else was talking and laughing in the living room or around the dining table. So I asked Marie to take out the walls so I could be a part of every-thing. Now I can watch *Jeopardy* from the kitchen while I cook my dinner."

The kitchen is as white and sparkly as the bathroom but with dark purple accents. It is Nana all over.

That night we steam some rice (I haven't had potatoes for almost a week now) and stir-fry some veggies in her wok while Nana shouts out *Jeopardy* answers. I do better at *Wheel of Fortune* when it comes on next. After eating sautéed veg, rice, and egg rolls, we are stuffed and settled in on her comfy couch for a *Poldark* marathon on one of the many streaming services she has. It's the most relaxing evening I've ever had.

"Well, that's it for me," Nana finally announces at eleven. "I've got work tomorrow, so I'd better hit the sack. Stay up if you want to, but turn everything off before you go to bed. Love you." With a hug and a kiss on my cheek, she leaves the room.

I start the next episode, but instead of sitting, I pick up the living room, folding the blankets we'd snuggled under and putting them back in the storage chest that doubles as an ottoman. In the kitchen, I toss the paper plates Nana insisted we use for easier cleanup, scrub and put away the wok, and wash the glasses and silverware before wiping down the counters. I stop the show halfway through. Unfortunately, I haven't been paying attention to it, so I'll have to re-watch it.

In my "apartment," my window glows with light coming in from my private garden. It is tiny — only six feet wide at the most — terminating in a seven-foot-tall cinderblock wall that separates Nana's property from the neighbors. Yet, it is a patch of paradise. Wrought iron plant holders holding colorful succulents cover the wall. A trellis at one end contains night-blooming jasmine, while on the other end, morning glories are napping, waiting for the sunrise. Around the edge of the patio are solar globes of crackled glass, welcoming moths to their subtle light.

I take the bag of clothes off the chair. At my dresser, I deposit three bras and the rest of the package of panties. I stop short when I see the pink heart-shaped box on the dresser's top. Nana is too good to me.

I hang up two pairs of jeans and five blouses. I sniff the dress. It smells like Olive Garden, so it goes into the dirty clothes hamper. I strip off the clothes I've worn all day, and they join the Olive Garden dress. My new boots and flip-flops go on a shelf. Before I leave the closet, I'm in the oversized tee Nana lent me that first night. She told me I could keep it. It has a giant mug printed on the front with the words "TEA SHIRT." Nana is punny.

I brush my teeth, looking with longing at the soaker tub. It's so inviting. Spit, rinse, resolve — that tub is calling my name. I carefully peel away the gauze and take a look at my thighs. No more open wounds. That's a plus. There's just the scab from that one truly nasty welt. I sigh. I'll have to wait for

it to finish healing before I attempt a soak. I smear some ointment over the backs of my legs and wrap the gauze around. It's
not as neat as when the nurse or Nana's wrappings, but it will
keep the cream off the bedsheets.

I should have gotten a glass of water from the kitchen
before coming back to my room. I need to take the antibiotic. I
use my hand to slurp up water from the sink instead — no need
for the pain pill. I'm feeling much better.

I'm exhausted.

I'm not even going to read tonight.

Well, maybe one chapter. Or two. Three at the most.

∞∞∞

Nana tells me to take the day off as she leaves for work, but
I've already had so much "relaxation" that I'm getting antsy.
I'm pain-free, well-rested, and unrestricted.

I haven't a clue what I should do, so I crawl back in bed
and read for a couple of hours. Lu is right. It clears the mind
and helps a person to focus.

I take my sweet time getting dressed, putting on
makeup, and braiding my hair before slipping on my flip-flops
for a walk around the block. It's an older neighborhood with
mature pines and palm trees lining the streets and wide side-
walks, some of which are buckled by roots rising too close to
the surface. During my walk, I pray. I ask for guidance. I think
about Jack and realize that he'll be graduating in four days. I'll
see if Nana can get me a card to send to him.

I love being with Nana. Love the house. Love my room.
But I hate that I'm still dependent. Yes, I'm free from a — an —
abusive — is that the right word? — situation, but I still need
someone else to take care of me. I have no job, so I have no
money. Not even for a graduation card for my fiancé.

I finally understand what Lu was talking about. That
need for independence. She has it. She wants me to have it too,

but it isn't something you can wish for someone else. It has to come from within a person. I walk faster on my way back to the house and slip in the back door that I left unlocked.

Searching for a pen and paper in my room, I come across an entire little kitchenette I didn't even know was lurking behind some giant cupboard doors. Once the doors are open and slid back into the wall, they reveal a countertop, a mini-fridge stocked with water bottles, a microwave, and a cabinet full of snacks. I grab a granola bar then close the doors, thinking I might revisit this little stash tonight.

I check the library. I've missed sunrise, but Nana is right. Colored light dots the entire room. I sit and observe, then remember why I'm there. In the top drawer I find what I'm looking for — a purple legal pad and a pen, which is also purple. Dark purple with glitter. Nana cracks me up.

I make a list for myself, a real one that won't just be words swirling around and around in my head. This one will be in black and white — well, dark purple glitter and lavender.

Things I Need to Do:

1) Get a job

And I'm stuck.

I mean, I know I need a job and to make money, but for what? And where? I'm supposed to get married to Jack, but he's — I double-check Nana's desk calendar and nod that I was right before — he's four days from graduation. And then what? Is he coming here to get me? I realize he doesn't even know I'm here unless Lu told him. Somehow I don't think she has. I'll have to write and ask her.

2) Write to Lu

3) Write to Jack

Writing to Jack might not be such a good idea. His parents are likely thrilled that I'm no longer in Sampson. They won't want him to get a letter from me. They probably won't even be thrilled with the graduation card I plan to send. Maybe I could call him? I'll ask Nana before I put any weird charges on her phone. Maybe I could get Lu to pass on a message. It might be the best move. But she's probably already at Camp Galilee. I wish I had a phone.

4) Buy a phone

I sit at the desk for another fifteen minutes combing through my brain for more ideas. Then, finally, I grab the legal pad and meander about the house. I eat an apple before starting a pitifully small load of laundry.

5) Buy more clothes

I straighten the comforter on my bed and wipe down the sink, shower, and toilet in my bathroom, arranging my miniature toiletries on the vanity.

6) Buy shampoo, conditioner, toothpaste, toothbrush, dental floss, mouthwash, face wash, deodorant, leave-in conditioner, hairspray, brush, ~~ponytail holders, barrettes~~

7) Get a haircut

In the living room, I peruse Nana's impressive DVD collection. Yes, the woman streams, but she's also a collector — and a literature nerd. There's a whole section of movies based on Jane Austen's work — including multiple versions of the same stories. She not only has the six-hour miniseries of *Pride and Prejudice*, but she also has the newest remake and even a Bollywood version that I immediately put in the DVD player. It's not bad. A little cheesy for my taste.

When I try to return *Bride and Prejudice* to the shelf, I drop the case, and when I bend down (carefully) to pick it up, I notice the Shakespeare section. *Two Gentlemen of Verona* start the shelf, followed by some titles I've never heard of, two copies of *Taming of the Shrew* next to *Ten Things I Hate About You* and multiple *Romeo and Juliettes*, and then *West Side Story*. Nothing is in alphabetical order, and there are classic plays mixed with modern rom-coms. Most of the DVDs look recent. *Macbeth*, *Hamlet*, and *Much Ado About Nothing* (two versions) have actors even I recognize.

8) Watch Nana's DVD collection

Standing back, I realize she's grouped the whole thing according to the authors of the books on which the movies are based. I take the first DVD off the shelf, *Little Women*, based on Louisa May Alcott's novel — one of my favorites. While it's loading, I pour myself a glass of iced tea. I decide I like having a day off. I'm about to make my way back to the living room to hit "play" when Nana's car pulls into the driveway. It's only three. I wasn't expecting her for a few hours yet, but I'm excited to see her — and it feels weird. I catch myself looking around the kitchen to ensure I've got my chores done, then grin when I remember I didn't have any. I get another glass and pour her some iced tea, too, greeting her with a smile.

"Hi, Nana!"

"Hi! Oh — tea! Thanks!" She takes a long drink. "What did you do today?"

"Um — read a little, took a walk, made a to-do list, watched a movie."

"Really? Which one?"

"*Bride and Prejudice*."

"Ah, Bollywood meets Austen. Good one."

"I was going to watch *Little Women* next. Want to watch it with me?"

"Sure. Let me change into comfy clothes. I'll need to work on this while we watch." She gestures to a stack of file folders. "It won't take long, though." She leaves the folders on the counter but takes the tea with her to her room.

While Nana taps on her laptop, I watch the friendship of Jo and Laurie bloom and implode as the two of them find love not too far from one another. I love it and tell Nana so. She's done with her job and had watched the last half-hour with me uninterrupted by her "homework."

"I love this version," she agrees. "But one of these days, I'll break down and get the black and white with Katherine Hepburn." She gives me a wry look, then makes a few taps on her phone. "It will be here in two days."

I chuckle. "Just like that?"

"It's my one vice. One of my two vices. Books and film. I can't get enough of them. Did you like Laurie in this one?"

I nod. Laurie is the cute and charming next-door neighbor in *Little Women*.

"He's fantastic in the Christopher Nolen *Batman* trilogy."

"I — I've never seen that."

"You said you were planning to watch through my collection, right?"

I nod. I had told Nana my goal when she'd sat down.

"Then you'll get to it. It's under K for Bob Kane, the original creator of *Batman*."

"Oh. So they're alphabetical by author." I already knew this.

"And then ordered by the release of the source material. So *Little Women*, then *Little Men*, and so on."

"Ah."

"Think that's weird?"

"Not really."

"Then you're the only one. My friends think it's nuts. It gives them something to tease me about." She grins to let me know she doesn't care at all that they think her strange. "Everybody has something odd about them. So you might as well enjoy it. What would you like for dinner?"

I am not usually asked that question, and my brain goes blank. I shrug, and Nana sighs. "I don't know either. Let's go hunt."

We settle on spaghetti. Not the cleverest of meals, but it tastes good. I show Nana my to-do list while we eat.

"I can get you a phone, no problem."

"Oh, no, you don't need to do that." I feel embarrassed, but it's not like I had been hinting around for her to get me one.

She shrugs. "I was planning to anyway. It was supposed to be your graduation present. Your parents asked me to send the money, and they'd buy it up there, so I mailed the check with your card. Next thing I know, I'm getting yelled at for sending it to you instead of to them."

"I'm sorry."

"You had nothing to do with it. Don't apologize."

"But now you're out $200."

"No, I'm not. I stopped payment on the check. We'll go get your phone tomorrow." She looks at me. "Nah. Let's go tonight. We're both presentable. All you need is your shoes, and off we go." We clear the table and do the dishes first, but then we get into the car for a spontaneous trip to the phone store.

Before I go to bed, I read the instruction manual from cover to cover. Then, I select the wallpaper and send my first text:

*Nana, I love you. Thank you so much for the phone, the clothes, the books and everything you have done for me. I owe you my life.*

# Chapter Twenty-Two: Starting Over

The next morning in the shower, I pour myself the usual handful of shampoo and slop it onto the top of my head, completely forgetting that most of my hair is gone.

After we left the phone store, Nana pulled my purple to-do list out of her pocket and headed for Professional Styles, the salon she frequents. At my confused look, she waved my list at me. "Go do number six!"

I didn't want to go in alone, a weeny move, I know, but sometimes freedom is a little scary. "Um — want to go with me?"

"Sure, honey," she says. "I was going to anyway. I want to introduce you to Georgi, my stylist."

While Georgi and my Nana chat, I flip through a lookbook and find a shag cut that looks a lot like the posters I saw in Vivid. I show it to Georgi, and she raises an eyebrow at me. "You do realize that once it's cut off, it can't be put back on?"

I bite my tongue to keep from saying, "Really? I had no idea!"

She offers to trim, layer, and style it, but when I insist on a short style that calls for zero to no maintenance, she sighs.

"You said you wanted a no-maintenance look. I can give you that cut, but you'll need to invest in a curling iron and some good styling products since you have straight hair. It's not a wash and go look."

Maybe someday I'd be into doing my hair, but right now, I just want it off. I keep flipping pages — and there it is. The shortest little pixie cut in the book. I tap on it decisively. Georgi's eyebrow goes up again, so I turn in my chair and show it to Nana. Her brows shoot up too, and she turns a little pale. I watch her eyes moved swiftly from the book to my face and back again. To my relief, she finally nods. "That would look great on you. Not many people could pull it off, but you have a good jawline."

"I have one more question before I give you that cut," Georgi breaks in. "Who are you mad at?"

I'm stumped. "What?"

"Usually, when I have someone in my chair asking for a drastic cut like that, they're angry with someone. They've gone through a bad breakup or are angry with their spouse — probably not your case — or are frustrated with their job or school."

"Mostly, I'm frustrated with my hair," I assure her. "I've never had it cut, and it looks awful." She doesn't argue with me. "I've just turned nineteen *(six months ago)*, and I want to choose my own hairstyle finally."

"Fair enough." Georgi gathers the length of my hair in one hand. "Last chance. Are you sure?"

"I'm sure."

With a sharply indrawn breath, the stylist begins to saw through the mass with her scissors. When I see her standing with the detached hair in her hand, I grin. It is gone!

It takes almost no time to rinse the globs of shampoo — I guess there isn't enough hair for it to hide in — and apply a small amount of conditioner over the short back and the longer bangs in front. Next, I use a bath pouf to smooth delicious smelling body wash over me. No more "boy soap" picked out by Roman. I chose the sweet pea scent because it was the girliest — and it's pink! Nana bought me the body spray to go with it — and everything else buyable on the list. I tell myself not to write down shopping lists, so Nana doesn't have to feel obligated to purchase stuff for me, but Nana doesn't seem to mind. She acts like it's perfectly normal. I decide I'm going to enjoy her generosity, thank her often, and not expect anything but appreciate everything. Oh — and keep her house as neat as a pin, so she doesn't even have to think about it.

Next on today's to-do list: makeup tutorials from You-Tube. Nana's idea. She showed me how to download the app. I search for "natural" makeup techniques after a few glam presentations get out of control. I finally find one I think I can go with, but even without her makeup, the brunette looks much better than I do on my best days. I search for "Natural Makeup for Blondes," then I backspace and type in redheads.

That's right! After Georgi cut off my nearly three feet of damaged beyond repair hair, she encouraged me to try a different hair color too. She suggested a deep strawberry blonde. It's pretty close to my natural color, but with just a hint of red. It turned my dirty dishwater color into a bright, happy tint. While the dye was doing its thing, Nana told me to go ahead and get my eyebrows waxed and shaped. Georgi even dyed them. They're a little darker than the hair color, more brown than red. I'd never really thought about my eyebrows before — probably because they're practically invisible blonde — but now that they frame my eyes, I can see the difference it makes in my look.

I'm still scrolling through videos when bingo! There's a girl who — still pretty — has reddish-blonde eyelashes and brows and skin as pasty as mine (but without the zits). I follow her directions as best I can with the makeup Nana bought me, and the result isn't half bad. It's pretty good, actually. I feel — more like myself. By the way, I LOVE mascara! And my shiny pink lip gloss.

I decide to wear my new yoga pants and an extra-long t-shirt, slipping on my new tennis shoes for a bit of a walk. I only go two blocks around Nana's house — still a little afraid of getting lost and not knowing how to get back to her place — and again using the time for prayer.

I kick off my shoes at the back door when I return and get a glass of water. Yesterday's list is on the counter, and I look it over. Nana insisted I fill out the electronic job application while we were at Walmart. So I guess now I have to wait to see if they call or not.

I get the purple pad and pen and begin my letter to Lu. I could call her, but I know she will be busy this week getting the camp ready. I could text, but I have too much to say. I let my pen go as it faithfully records everything I'd been up to since I left Sampson, ending with asking her to send on any information she has about Jack. Five pages later, I'm hunting through the desk for an envelope and stamp and then through my pile of books, looking for her address. I find it in my copy of *Hunger Games*. I'd been using it as a bookmark. All of the other bookmarks the guy from Twice Turned Books gave to me were being used.

Before I take it to the mailbox, I get out the card I'd bought for Jack last night. Using a fresh sheet of lavender, I write what I want to say and then reconstruct it in innocuous sentences so no one would suspect our code. If we had been doing this all along, we probably wouldn't have gotten into so much trouble — or we would have. I can't tell anymore.

*Dear Jack,*

*Congratulations! You completed four years of math, science, English, history, and sports (even if they're not full-contact)! You did it despite me. So glad you made it all the way through. I heard you were doing well the last time I saw Lu. She's doing well to. Sorry about the notes; thought they'd be more appreciated than interrupting the class with talk. I was wrong to assume I knew what I was talking about. I'll be thinking about you and the rest of the class in your final our. Good luck in the future.*

*Your friend, Julia*

I read the draft through twice and decided that it will have to do even though it is a little stilted. Besides, it's the code that was more important: "Contact me through Lu to talk about our future." I'd had to misspell a couple of words, but I know he'll get it.

The letters get into the mailbox just as the letter carrier is tooling up the street. I mosey back to the porch, stopping at the flowerbed to pull a half-dozen weeds that are just beginning to send up their second leaves. I search for more, but Nana keeps her gardens pretty tidy. Once the mail truck takes off, I go back to the box to get today's stuff. A bulky envelope from Amazon, some junk mail, some bills. Inside, I look for a place to put them and decide to leave them on the desk in the library. While there, I make another list for myself. A chore list. Nana won't do it — doesn't even expect it — but I need to do something for my wonderful grandmother, who took me in and cares for me in a way I've never been cared for before.

By the time she comes home, I've swept the floors, cleaned the kitchen, and have dinner in the oven. I've made baked chicken and shredded zucchini topped with garlic and cheddar cheese. On the stovetop, there's a light and fluffy rice pilaf. Not a potato in sight.

"Julia?" Nana calls as soon as the door opens. "Oh, my goodness! What smells so good?"

I jump off the couch where I'm watching *Sense and Sensibility* and meet her in the kitchen. I pour her a glass of tea and give her the rundown for dinner.

"Sounds so good. I'll change, and then we can eat." She takes a sip and sets her glass down on the counter. "Oh, and I've got some news. Remember when I told you about our church's youth pastor, Mr. Andrews? His daughter is getting married in two weeks, and they've been struggling to get everything done. I saw him today, and he asked if I knew of anyone who could help them out. They're willing to pay $10 an hour. I told them you might be interested. You can talk to him on Sunday. I'll introduce you." I cut off Nana's words with a giant hug. Number one on my list was about to be crossed off.

On Saturday, Nana and I take a drive to a larger city about twenty miles away. Redland's historic district is much more modern than any other I've been to and is the home of a weekly farmer's market. We walk past blocks of booths, stopping here and there to look at handmade wares and to buy a jar of local honey before I follow Nana up a side street to a sunny-fronted restaurant called Martha Green's The Eating Room. Nana walks right in. The place is busy, but doesn't feel over-crowded. My flip-flops squeak on the terra cotta tile floor as we follow a bubbly server to a wooden-topped table.

I try to scan the menu, looking for something inexpensive to order, but the punny names of some of the dishes make me smile and I end up reading all the descriptions too. Nana doesn't rush me, even though it's obvious that she's already decided. Instead, she reads along with me, laughing at some of the sillier names of dishes and pointing out things she thinks I might like. I finally settle on the pulled pork sandwich with a side of fresh fruit. It's saucy and delicious and there is no way I can finish it all. Nana encourages me to take the rest home and boxes up her leftovers as well.

Before we leave, we stop at the bakery in the front of the restaurant. Nana encourages me to pick out a dozen cookies from the case.

Nana looks pretty wiped out after lunch, so I suggest a movie marathon. Her eyes light up, and she turns the car toward home.

A box is waiting for us on the porch, so I offer to take it inside. Nana thanks me and says, "Go ahead and put it on the coffee table. I'll get a pair of scissors."

She slides a blade of the scissors through the tape on top and pops open the flaps. "Here you go," she says and tosses a blur of black to me. The old leather purse I'd had since the fifth grade is suddenly in my hand, the long strap swinging. "How?" There's nothing else to that question. It is just "how."

"I called your mom the day we went to the mall in Dawes. I realized you weren't carrying a purse with you, which means you had no wallet, no driver's license, and, very likely, no social security card. Things you need if you're going out into the real world."

"And she just sent it to you?" It didn't sound like something either of my parents would do.

"No. I threatened your parents with legal action. I figured all of your stuff combined wouldn't be worth much in dollar value, so I told them if they didn't send your things, I would take them to small claims court, where they would be forced to pay cash out of pocket, and their behavior would be entered into the record. She texted back the next day that they'd get the box to me by the end of the week. They just made it."

I peer inside and find the contents of my room. It had all fit in a "small" packing box from Home Depot. My teapot's spout is broken, not surprising since it was tossed into the box without newspaper or bubble wrap, but it doesn't bother me. I'd bought it for fifty cents at a yard sale. I do peek inside, though, to see if they'd returned the money. Then I remember that I had taken it out and put it in my camp bag. The bag isn't here — just my few books (including *The Wonder Book* that I guess they didn't remember was theirs), some school supplies, and my spare pair of ninety-nine-cent flip-flops. At the very bottom is a note.

*Heres all the stuff from the room. We didnt include any cloths since there already donated to Goodwill.*

No salutation, no "love Mom and Dad," not even the mention of my name. Or Nana's. Only a poorly written note. I get angry at my eyes for burning and making tears I don't want to cry. I know they didn't want me — had never wanted me — but it hurts. Nana pulls me close, and we cling together for a minute.

I put everything back in the box and haul it up to my hip. "I'm going to put this stuff away. Mind if we do the movie marathon a little later?"

"Not at all. I might lay down for a few."

In my room, I set my *Little House* set of books on the shelf next to my "childhood re-creation" collection and *The Wonder Book* near my new copy of *The Scarlet Letter*. I'm not in the mood to look through the rest of them, so I stack them in an empty spot on the shelf. I don't toss the teapot. Instead, I put it on my dresser, the broken spout next to it. I'll glue it back on later.

Opening that box sapped my energy, but I don't want to sleep. So instead, I fill the soaker tub with hot water. I'd checked my thighs this morning — no scabs, just shiny worm-like scars that will hopefully fade over time. Before getting in, I grab my copy of *Hunger Games* to read while I bathe.

Why is every YA novel fraught with danger, violence, and confusion? Because those things are totally relatable. Some people think they're metaphors for puberty. I believe they are metaphors for life in general.

# Chapter Twenty-Three: Working

Scott Andrews is a pretty cool youth leader. Not fake in any way, not looking to take over the "big job" of leading a church. In Sampson, we had a new youth director every two to three years. It was like we were the training ground for guys who wanted a couple of years of experience before they went out on their own to head up their own churches. I met his wife first, and she invited me to sit in Mr. Andrew's class this morning, even though I'm actually in the college and career class. He is already a real pastor, and he sees his youth group as an integral part of the church, not just a place where teens are stored until they are shipped off to an approved college.

Mrs. Andrews, Cheryl, invites Nana and me over for lunch. Burgers in the backyard for Sunday dinner sound great to me! That's when I meet Lauren and Dave, the bride and groom. Lauren is like no one I've ever seen before. She has black — not dark brown, black — hair smoothly pulled back in a French twist, framing her flawless face. Lauren heavily lines her dark brown eyes but wears a beige eyeshadow that contrasts with her ruby lips. She's vintage glam and gorgeous. If I could pull off that look, I'd give it a try.

"It's not a fancy wedding," Lauren assures me over her veggie burger. "The decorating won't take very long, but the church building is used for so many activities that it's in desperate need of a deep clean. We can't even start setting things up until after the Wednesday night service. We're trying to get all the stuff ready to go so that when we finally have access to the rooms, all we have to do is decorate."

Mrs. Andrews swipes her phone open and starts reading

out the list of things to do. Aside from the deep cleaning, most of the chores are easy but time-consuming.

"When do you want to start the cleaning?" I ask.

"We have to do it at night since the church is hosting summer day-camp Mondays through Fridays. I was thinking about starting tonight with the kitchen. It's pretty gross. It gets used all the time and wiped down afterward, but it never really gets a good scrubbing."

"Not tonight," Mrs. Andrews says firmly. "Enjoy the last bit of Sunday off. Monday will be soon enough."

"I can help you with the cleaning," I assure them both. I think over the other things on the list. "And the thing with putting the transfers of your initials on the bubble bottles and making the bird-seed bags? I can do that at home while Nana's at work."

"You're hired," Lauren says without even a glimpse at her parents for confirmation, but from the way everyone is smiling at me, I guess they are okay were her decision.

Her fiancé, Dave, breathes a deep sigh. He looks exhausted and doesn't say much. All I've learned so far is that he is tall, handsome, muscular, very much loved by the entire Andrews family, and has a giant tattoo on his neck that says DESTROYER.

I know there has to be a story behind that.

Before we leave to go home for the requisite Sunday afternoon naps, Dave and Mr. Andrews load plastic-wrapped trays of bubbles, a manila envelope of transfers, a partial bolt of white tulle, several spools of narrow satin ribbon, and a ten-pound bag of birdseed into Nana's car.

"Need any help unloading all this?" Dave asks.

"No thanks, I can manage," I tell him.

"Okay, then."

"Before you go, let me give you my cell phone number," Mrs. Andrews says. "Text me when you start working on a project for the wedding and again when you're done so we have a record of how long you've worked so we can pay you."

Lauren gives me her's too. "Thanks so much! You're a lifesaver," she says as she gives me a heartfelt hug.

"No. Thank you," I say. "I needed this job. Call me anytime you need me to do anything. I'm always available."

She laughs and tells me she'll remember I'd said that.

I get in the car, grinning while Nana says her goodbyes to Mrs. Andrews.

I've done it — completed my list (everything but watching Nana's entire DVD collection). Mission accomplished.

On to the next thing.

Monday morning dawns bright and sunny as usual. I jump out of bed, take a quick shower, put on full makeup (I love makeup!), yoga pants (yea, pants!), and t-shirt (just one!), and text Mrs. Andrews to let her know I'm at work. I go to You-Tube to find a tutorial on making the birdseed favors, but I find myself making faces at the video. They have a dozen people all working to put these things together. I think about how I'm supposed to hold and tie the little net baggies simultaneously. I decide I'll think about it while I'm working on the bubbles. Those are easy. I'm putting a sticker on a bottle, going over it with a wooden stick, and pulling off the plastic backing — ta-da transfer complete. I watch a movie while I work. And then I watch another one. It turns out it takes a long time to decorate two hundred bottles of bubbles. I move the four flats of party favors to the entryway to load them more easily into the car tonight.

By the time I'm done, my shoulders and back are aching. I text Mrs. Andrews that I'm taking a break and go for a walk, thanking God for the beautiful day, my Nana, and my new job. As I near home, I think I've come up with a solution to my birdseed bag problem. I walk faster, anxious to see if my idea will work.

I unwrap a foot of tulle off the bolt and use a dessert plate as a template to draw a perfect circle with a pencil. I cut it out, line a juice glass with the fabric, add a quarter cup of bird-seed, and then run to the library for a tiny binder clip. I saw a whole bunch of them in the drawer and wondered what in the world they would be suitable for; they were so small. It turns out they are perfect for this project. I gather up the edges and give the baggie a little twist and hold it with the clip until I cut some ribbon and tie it around the neck of the bag. Done. I do a silent fist pump.

I move everything into the living room and put in another DVD before I text Mrs. Andrews to let her know I'm back on the clock. By the time Nana comes home, I am seventy-five bags in. I know because I counted them — repeatedly, making little piles of ten to measure my progress.

"Wow. You got a lot done today!"

I nod, concentrating on tying the tiny bow before releasing the clip. "I'm not going to be able to finish the rest until tomorrow, though."

"I'm sure that won't be a problem. Do you know what time you're meeting Lauren tonight?"

"At 8:30."

"You'd better eat first, then."

"Yeah." Then I turn, my stomach sinking with the realization. "I'm so sorry! I didn't make anything!" How could I be so careless? So thoughtless?

Nana's response is wary. "Are you okay? You look like I'm about to fly off the handle." She trails off, and I drop my eyes to my hands, not surprised to see them shaking. I know my Nana would never hurt me, but my body responds to the situation as if I were still at home, and it is one of my parents in front of me. "Oh, honey, I don't expect you to cook every night. It's a lovely surprise when you do, but I didn't bring you here to be my servant." I feel her arms envelop me. "How about I make dinner for the two of us tonight? You look like you could use a break. Read or something. Relax a little." She gestures to the mess I'd made of her living room. "You can leave all this here until you've finished the project. I won't move anything."

I nod against her shoulder, but instead of curling up on the couch and letting my mind drift, I help out in the kitchen. I find myself smiling when Nana shouts answers to the *Jeopardy* questions. We chat about our days as we make dinner. Spending time with her is the best cure for anxiety. Twenty minutes later, we're snarfing down tacos, and I'm guessing *Wheel of Fortune* puzzles like I came up with them. Nana and I alternately trash talk and cheer each other on.

When the show is over, I get cleaned up, and Nana tosses me her car keys. "Don't forget to lock the front door when you get home."

"Okay." It feels weird to have this much trust.

But I like it.

Do you know the saying "time flies when you're having fun"? Trust me; it zooms when you have a job with a definite goal and someone friendly with whom to work. I like Lauren. She's a bit of a clean freak, but I don't mind. She has concrete ideas of what needs to be done in the church kitchen. About an hour in, I ask her if our scrubbing out the top cabinets is vital for the wedding.

"Not at all. But it needs to be done. Everyone in full-time ministry here has so many big things they're responsible for that the little things get lost. So when they told me I could have the wedding here free of charge as long as I arranged for the clean-up afterward, I decided to use the opportunity to do some of those 'little things' as a way of showing my appreciation for all they've done for me."

In no time, we have every cabinet cleaned. We look at the pile of cupboard contents spread out over the kitchen work-table. "Throw away anything out of date and everything that looks sketchy." Lauren holds up a battered and dirty box of toothpicks and trashes them. "Oh. And Cheryl wanted me to make an inventory list of everything. I have the feeling she's planning to restock this place. It needs it." It really does. Most of the items on the table look like they haven't been touched in a decade. Most of it goes in the trash, and the rest is stacked neatly back inside the freshly scrubbed cupboards.

The oven is surprisingly clean. "They only use it for heating casseroles during potlucks," Lauren notes. The fridge, on the other hand, is disgusting. "I am not opening a single one of those Tupperware containers. I'm tossing them all." (Lauren had posted a note on the fridge door, threatening to do just that so that anyone who wanted to save their stuff could get it out before she came to clean). Lauren even has us move the refrigerator out from the wall so she can scrub behind it.

We talk the whole time we work.

"Have you lived in Posting long?" I ask her.

"About two years. I came looking for my Dad. I lived with my mom and didn't have any contact with Dad until I became a legal adult."

"That must have been hard." For her. Mr. Andrews was a nice guy. I could have gone without my dad for eighteen years.

"Yeah. Sometimes it was. But I didn't know what I was missing until I met him. It turns out he was waiting for me — but preparing for me too, you know? He and Cheryl even had a room for me in their house."

"Huh — my Nana did that too."

"Yeah, I know. Dave worked for the contractor who did it. It was actually his first real job as part of a crew."

"Oh — well — it's nice. Beautiful. I love it."

She stops scrubbing the wall behind the fridge and sits back on her heels to look at me. "It's an amazing thing to be loved by a family. I'd never really had that before I met my Dad. I mean, I love my Mom, but I was always an afterthought. I was who she wanted to be with when no one else was available. But Dad and Cheryl — it's a completely different vibe in their house. There is no — I don't know — compartmentalizing? Partitioning? Their love is just — inclusive. They love each other, they love their children, they love me, and they love Dave like it's a part of their nature."

"I wonder why," I muse, half to myself as Lauren disappears behind the fridge again. I understand what she is saying. My Nana is the same way. She'd enfolded me in her love without a second thought. So why isn't everyone like that?

Lauren pops her head back out. "I think it's because they're Christians. I mean, it was because of how they showed me God's love that I decided I wanted to follow Christ too." She ducks back behind the fridge

"My parents are Christians, but they don't act like that."

Her head pops out again. "What?"

"Nothing. Where are you going for your honeymoon?" I figure if I change the subject, she wouldn't realize I'd slipped up and talked too freely about my parents. I won't protect them anymore, but I don't feel the need to offer any information about them, mostly because I don't want to think about them.

"We've been offered a place up in the mountains for a week. It's kinda cool. It belongs to the woman who's making our cake, Caroline. Her husband and brother-in-law own an event hall, and we went to check it out when we were planning our wedding. It was way too expensive for us. My grandparents — Scott's — I mean, Dad's — mom and dad — offered to pay for it for us, but that idea didn't sit right. While we debated it, Caroline called us all apologetic that the last spot for the summer had been booked. Their next opening was in September, but that didn't work for us since we'd planned to move at the end of June so we could get jobs and get settled before our classes start in the fall. We didn't mind. Dad was sure the church would be cool with us using the facilities. We said we still wanted to order our cake from them — Caroline makes the most amazing cakes — and that's when Caroline and Ty asked about our honeymoon plans. We didn't have any yet. We were just going to pack up and go to Dawes.

"Dawes?"

"Yes. That's where we're going to school — at the university there. But it's an expensive place to live, so we wanted to get a head start on getting jobs and hunting around for a cheap apartment. That's when Ty and Caroline offered us their cabin. Ty had set it up for Caroline when they got married last year, and they liked the idea of helping us out. So it's their wedding present to us.

"That's sweet."

"Yeah. They remind me of Scott and Cheryl that way." She blushes a little. "It's the kind of marriage Dave and I want."

It's after midnight before I return home. I snuggle into my comfortable bed, wondering if I will ever have that kind of love with Jack. I want us to have the type of love where we consistently care about how the other feels, about what we can do to make the other person happy, and extend that love to other people in our lives.

That's when it hits me that I've already failed. I tap the phone to bring up the display. Sure enough, it is already Tuesday morning. I missed graduation night. I thought I'd be an emotional wreck thinking of my classmates, walking down the aisle in their caps and gowns and especially Jack giving his valedictory speech, reaching that milestone without me. It hurts worse that I hadn't remembered it at all.

# Chapter Twenty-Four: Reconnecting with Lu

The past two and a half weeks have been nothing short of backbreaking. Cleaning the church kitchen was only the beginning. First, Lauren and I scrubbed the entire church — every single room — until it was white-glove-inspection-clean. Then, on the Wednesday before the wedding, as soon as everyone left the church building after the mid-week service, Lauren, Dave, and I began shampooing the hallways, classrooms, and the fellowship hall carpets. They'd rented three Rug-Doctors to accomplish the task, and it still took us until early Thursday morning. I question the sanity of people who insist on putting carpet in a fellowship hall — the home of receptions, AWANA games, and potlucks — where a hard floor would make for much easier cleanup. Strangely, the floor of the sanctuary is polished concrete. I ended up doing the whole room myself since I was the only one who'd had experience running a buffer, thanks to three years of helping run the Camp Galilee dining hall.

I sleep in on Thursday, then work for a couple of hours putting return addresses and stamps on thank you note envelopes so that all Lauren and Dave have to do is write the actual messages inside and mail them off. After that, I'm on my own, wandering around Nana's house like I had the first few days I lived there. I don't even have work to look forward to tonight. Lauren is taking the evening off to rest before the next big wedding push of decorating the church.

I flop onto my bed and text Lu.

*Hey, Girlie. I've got the day off. What are you up to?*

To my surprise, she buzzes back right away.

*L: On break. Ready to clunk some heads together. The crew is GREEN this year. I REALLY miss you. I'd trade three of my kitchen staff for you.*

*How is Roman working out?*

*L: He's my prep person. He's up for trade. I'd even throw in a shiny nickel.*

*Sorry.*

*L: How in the world does he function? I'm surprised he can tie his shoes.*

*He used Velcro until sixth grade.*

*L: I had to teach him how to cut a melon. Seriously. A melon. You know, stick a knife in it, cut it from end to end, scoop out the seeds, slice into crescents, and cut off the rind. It took a ½ dozen cantaloupe for him to figure it out. He kept cutting them the short way.*

*He's never learned much in the way of cooking.*

*L: Melon cutting isn't cooking!*

*He might be better at emptying trash.*

*L: Not by much. After the third bag, 'just exploded!' Chef Dan had to explain to him that he couldn't drag a full bag on the ground on the way to the dumpster. You would think that after he'd had to clean up the mess over and over again, he would have figured it out for himself.*

*Sorry, he's such a pain. How is Jack doing?*

*L: Um, okay, I guess. Hasn't he been texting you?*

*No. Does he have my number?*

*L: Yeah. I gave it to him.*

*Does he even have a cell phone?*

*L: He got one for graduation. He and Roman are ALWAYS on their phones!*

*ROMAN has a phone?*

*L: Yep. Sorry. I was pretty ticked when I saw him with one. I know you weren't allowed to have one until after you graduated.*

*Can you give me Jack's number?*

*L: Sure.*

She sends me his information, and I add it to my contacts immediately. Then my phone buzzes again.

*L: Maybe it's a good thing if he doesn't contact you right now. It will give you a chance to take a breather from toxic relationships.*

*Ha, ha. Except ours was one of the few NON-toxic relationships I've had. How is he really?*

This time there is no response. I get a buzz, but it is from my bank. Nana set me up with a checking account so the Andrews could put my pay directly into the bank. It is up to $500. That makes me smile. All the hard work is putting cash in my pocket, and I haven't completed my job yet. Starting tomorrow morning, I'll help decorate. On Saturday, I'll assist the wedding planner, who turns out to be Nana's decorator, Marie, and do whatever little jobs she has for me until the wedding is over. Then I'm on the cleaning crew.

Since I still haven't heard anything from Lu, I figure her break is over. So I type out a quick text to Jack. It's a no-pressure note — just my contact information and an "I miss you!" I make sure my notifications sound is up and slip the phone into the back pocket of my jeans. It's time for a walk around the neighborhood, followed by a late lunch and an afternoon sunk up to my ears in bubbles reading from a stack of books.

The phone buzzes as I'm walking out the door.

*L: Jack's fine, I guess. A little weird. He's not talking to me, but he does come into the kitchen all the time to talk to Roman. I don't remember him being so underfoot before.*

*Huh. Last year it was hard to get him to the mess hall on time for meals because he was so focused on his work at the stables. Is there a new manager there? Is he not as strict as Frank?*

*L: Nope. Frank still runs the stables, and he's frustrated at Jack too. Had to pull him out of the kitchen yesterday to do a job.*

*So weird. Maybe you'll get lucky, and Frank will take Roman off your hands to work with Jack.*

*L: I don't think Frank wants Roman either. No offense, but your brother hasn't proven his usefulness to the staff as of yet.*

*Here's hoping he gets it together.*

*L: Amen, Sister. Gotta go. TTYL.*

I Google TTYL and discover it means "Talk to you later." Of course, I also realize there are a bunch of acronyms I'll need to learn if I'm going to completely embrace texting as a form of communication.

My day goes as planned, and it is glorious. My long soak leaves me with a book-induced clear head. That night, I enjoy a scrumptious veggie lasagna Nana and I make together. We finish our evening with a Scrabble game during which she trounces me so badly that I began to question my literacy.

By 10:00, I'm in my room, and my phone is ringing. "Hi, Lu!"

"You would not BELIEVE the day I've had!" Lu explodes without preamble

"'Sup?"

"'Sup? You turning gansta out there in Cali?"

"Yo."

"How about you get your gangster behind up to Camp Galilee?"

"Wish I could." And suddenly, I know I want to go.

"Your brother is a donkey."

"Tell me something I don't know."

"He's trainable."

"Did you hit your head?"

"No, but I almost clunked Roman's and Jack's heads together tonight. Maybe if I do it hard enough, I'll get them back to factory resets." Lu's tone makes me laugh.

"Okay, I'll bite. What happened?"

"Jack came into the kitchen again, taking up space, trash-talking with Roman. I asked him NICELY to leave because we had to get prep done for lunch. He said something under his breath to Roman, who laughed hysterically. Chef Dan was standing at the flat-top, back to us, just shaking his head, waiting for me to deal with it. So I did. I ordered Jack out. He rolled his eyes at me and left, BUT ROMAN WENT WITH HIM!"

I sit up at that. "Wait. Did Roman quit?"

"Nope. Just walked out. The two of them went into the dining room, continuing their conversation like it was no big deal. I pushed between them and got in  Roman 's face, ORDERING him back into the kitchen. He just SMIRKED at me and went back in. I was so ticked, but we had lunch in like fifteen minutes. After service, I talked to him and told him NICELY that I'd appreciate it if he talked with his friends on his own time and not during prep or service. He was immediately apologetic, told me he was sorry, acted human for once. I told him I appreciated his willingness to work on things and that we could start with a clean slate tomorrow. He suddenly snapped to attention and SALUTED ME, saying, "Sure, chief!" I mean — what am I supposed to do with that?

"I don't remember him ever being that bad. He was always the sneaky kind of disrespectful."

"I know what caused it."

My heart drops. I assume Lu's about to say, "It's all Jack's fault!" Jack has always influenced Roman, but I had always thought it was for the better. What had happened after I left?

"He's got a crush on Sylvie."

My thoughts and Lu's words matched up wrong. For a long second, I thought she was telling me that Jack has a crush on Sylvie, Brother Topher's fourteen-year-old daughter who worked with her mom in the camp's "bakery" (the back section of the open kitchen). I have to remind myself that we'd been talking about Roman.

"What makes you think that?"

"Because that's when his personality changed. He went from apologetic to macho man in the blink of an eye when she entered the room. So I think he's trying to impress her."

"Then, I guess that's how you 'fix' Roman."

"What do you mean?"

"The next time you need to tell him off, let him know

that Sylvie doesn't like rebellious guys. That if he keeps up his rotten behavior, you'll have to report it directly to Brother Topher, Sylvie's dad."

"That's cold — and brilliant. But, you know I'd never go directly to Brother Topher. I was hired as the supervisor of the dining room and kitchen staff. I report to Chef Dan, and I won't even go to him with this. It's my mess to clean up."

"I get that, but Roman wouldn't. So basically, you're reminding him who gave you the authority you have."

"You're sneaky."

I'm a little shocked by that.

"But in a good way," she continues. "I'll talk to him first thing tomorrow. I need to get him focused and working with the group before camp opens next week. I mean, if I'm having this much trouble when we're just serving staff, imagine what it will be like when we have four-hundred little kids running around."

I don't have to imagine. I'd been there and done that and loved every second of it. "You'll do fine. Let me know what's going on with Jack when you get a chance. It seems so weird for him to act that way."

"Not really." Lu's voice is casual. "He doesn't like having women in charge any more than your brother does."

I'd never noticed Jack being disrespectful to women. I would have seen that, right?

"Remember how he tormented Mrs. Barker?" Lu continues. "He'd always prank her and then stand there with his head cocked to one side like a puppy whenever she'd try to discipline him. She'd say 'stop talking,' and he'd stop just long enough to say, 'I wasn't talking.'"

"But he was just joking around," I protest. Of course, I had noticed those things, and I have to admit that yes, they made me uncomfortable, but I still didn't think of Jack as anti-woman.

"Yeah, he was joking, but after a while, it's not funny anymore. Once you're a boss, you'll understand it better. It's ridiculously difficult to do a job when your employees, or in Barker's case, the students, are constantly making fun of you. That's why I'm so frustrated when Jack comes into the kitchen to hang out. I'm trying to teach Roman how to do his job, and Jack is undercutting me, teaching Roman that he doesn't have to respect me or my position as his boss. And they're both doing it for Sylvie's benefit as if driving me crazy will make her want them more. As I said, I'm about ready to clunk their heads together."

"I'd be okay with that."

"I think Chef Dan would be too." Lu laughed. "Okay. My rant is pretty much over. Thanks for letting me get that off my chest. How was your day?"

I give her only the most basic rundown of my fantastic day, not wanting her to feel any worse than she already does, and end the call with a reminder that I'll be pretty busy over the next few days due to the wedding.

"Getting any good ideas?" she prompts.

"About what?"

She sighs dramatically. "About your own wedding, ya big goof. Although why you'd …" Her voice drifts off. I understand what she left unsaid. She doesn't get why I want to marry Jack. I pretend she didn't almost say it, and we end the call on a good note. As I lay in bed, waiting to drift off, pictures of Jack flit through my mind. I'll make it a point to think of him every day, pray for him, and attempt planning how we can get back together so we can marry, but it is an exercise, a discipline. It isn't like I'm so drawn to him that I can't keep him out of my mind. He doesn't make me obsess like Bella obsessed over Edward. He doesn't make me angry the way Mr. Darcy infuriated Elizabeth. He doesn't make me question myself like Peeta made Katniss confused over who she was and what she stood for. Jack is just an average guy who stepped up when my best friend went off to college and left me all alone. He wrote me notes when he saw I was having a bad day. As for Mrs. Barker — well, nobody liked her, not even the other teachers, even Dr. Jeffers was annoyed at her motto of "Academics before athletics."

No, Jack is fine. A perfectly nice boyfriend who cared about me when no one else did. If I was going to compare us to any literary couple, I could kinda see just one aspect of Bella and Edward's relationship in Twilight. Bella was a plain Jane, just like me, and Edward saw something in her that no one else did. He fell in love with her heart. That's what Jack had done. He'd picked me to be his girl when he'd had a half-dozen better-looking girls to choose from.

While I'm contemplating our dynamic, my phone buzzes again. Jack has finally answered my text.

*Hey, Ruby, thanks for sending me your number. I probably won't do much texting since I'm knee-deep in work at the stables. I hope you're enjoying your visit with your grandmother. I'll text back when I get some free time. Right now, though, I've got to get to my bunk. I'm asleep on my feet! Thinking of you. Love, Your Proteus*

I drift off to sleep, wondering what he'd think of my new look. Then I remember that he hates short hair on girls. I mentally shrug before I turn over and immediately conk out.

# Chapter Twenty-Five:
## Too Much Work

I think Jack and I were on the right track when we decided to run away to get married. Weddings are too much work. And this comes from someone who doesn't mind putting in the effort and is being generously compensated.

Trust me. Weddings are too much work.

I arrive at the church at nine in the morning to help Lauren's wedding coordinator, Marie Swanson. She suggested I wear jeans and tennis shoes as she and I would be running to do the last-minute setup. I hadn't realized she meant actual running. For the life of me, I couldn't figure out what we were going to do at the church that early. Lauren's crew (myself included) had already set the tables for the reception the night before and got the auditorium mostly decorated. As far as I can tell, everything is almost ready to go.

I am wrong.

The fresh flowers arrive. I put the bouquets and boutonnieres in the newly scrubbed refrigerator and then run (yes, run) to the auditorium to help Ms. Marie put little bouquets (she calls them nosegays) in holders already set up at the end of each pew. I add water to the holder, plop in the little spray of flowers, wipe up any drips, and move on to the next row. Then there are flowers for the stage. And for the stand holding the guest book. And for the front doors. And for the swinging doors that lead into the hallway connecting the auditorium to the fellowship hall. And for each table in the fellowship hall.

I've never seen so many flowers in one place.

Ms. Marie says, "This large centerpiece goes on the bride and groom's table, and those four little ones go on the cake table but wait until it arrives. The cake should be here any minute."

As if she spoke it into existence, a catering van pulls into the parking lot. The man from the driver's side is tall, with a chiseled jaw and a brilliant smile. He opens the passenger door for the plump, pretty lady that must be his wife. He laughs at something she says, and they share a quick kiss. She steps back while he moves the passenger seat forward and reaches behind it to the oversized cab's back seat. I smile when he hands her a baby carrier.

"Good morning, Caroline," Ms. Marie greets her as the baker hauls the carrier up the ramp toward us.

"Good morning, Marie!" the dark-haired woman almost sings the greeting. Then she gives the wedding coordinator a quick hug and pulls aside a blanket to reveal a tiny dark baby with shockingly blonde hair.

"She's adorable," Marie gushes.

She is. But it's a little strange seeing a baby that looks like she has a dark tan.

"She's our surfer girl," Caroline chuckles as if she can read my thoughts. She turns to her husband and two other men, who are carefully unloading a masterpiece of a cake from the back of the truck. We silently stand while they pass by us and then follow them in. As soon as the cake is safely on the table, Caroline lets out a sigh of relief. Her husband flashes her a smile and then laughs.

"You always do that," he teases. "I've never dropped a single one of your cakes."

"I can't help it." She shrugs and smiles back at him. The two are ga-ga for each other, and frankly, it's a little embarrassing, so I turn my attention to the cake.

Four tiers high, it is white on white swirls of buttercream topped with a perfect recreation of the ivory and blush flower arrangements in frosting. I straighten a wrinkle on the tablecloth and set up the four small flower arrangements, plates, napkins, and dessert forks, careful not to jostle anything.

While the couple chats with Marie and takes a quick tour of the fellowship hall to admire the decorations, I can't help but feel like I've seen the baker before. At one point, she laughs at something her husband says and looks up at him with a sweet smile. That's when I recognize her. It's Caroline Taft. Her mother had been the church secretary/pastor's assistant at my church in Sampson for years until Mrs. Barker took over the job.

Caroline looks and acts very differently now. I only knew her by sight when we attended the same church. I always thought she was pretty and admired her dark skin and glossy brown hair. But, she was quieter then and always looked uncomfortable in her skin. I remember her constantly tugging on her skirts, smoothing them down, sometimes holding the seams on the sides, like it was a nervous tic or a security thing. She and her sister Amy often wore the same outfits, but while Amy, four years younger, looked cute and fresh, Caroline would either look frumpy or like she was about to bust out all over.

The last year she was home, though, she was all everyone talked about. She'd lost a ton of weight, and everyone at church went out of their way to tell her how good she looked. It was as if she were visible for the first time. Her mom even got her a whole new wardrobe.

Then she went off to college. When she returned home for Christmas break, the curves were back, and everyone went back to ghosting her, except to mutter phrases like "self-control" and "no discipline" whenever she was around. I remember that she still had to wear the clothes her mom bought her before she left, even though it was evident that they didn't fit anymore. I felt terrible for her but didn't say anything. I was only about nine or ten at the time.

It's hard to believe she's the same person, but I know without a doubt that it's Caroline Taft. She's happier now than I've ever remembered seeing her and, while she's still curvy, her clothes fit her perfectly and add to her beauty. I almost introduced myself to her, wondering if she'd even remember the pasty-faced thing from her home church when I freeze. The thought of news, any news, about me getting back to Sampson and specifically to my parents makes me hold back. My life is better when they aren't a part of it. I don't need any ties to my old hometown, no matter how tenuous.

After Ms. Marie hands them a check and walks them out, she comes back looking more relaxed than she has all morning. She flicks her wrist and checks her watch.

"It's nearly 1:00," she tells me. "Go home, get a shower, change, and be back here by 3:00 so we can finish up before people start arriving."

I run to the car, dash into the house, rush through my shower, take my sweet time with my makeup (still working out the kinks), and put on an ombre dress Nana bought me for the occasion. The colors range from a shocking pink at the knee to a beautiful blush pink at the neck and shoulders. If Jack could see me now, it would knock his socks off.

The ceremony is beautiful. It almost makes me want a big wedding, but then as soon as the last soloist gets up, Ms. Marie taps me on the shoulder, and I move to the fellowship hall to take my place behind the crystal bowl of fruit salad at the end of the buffet table. A dozen women from the church who volunteered to help out join me. They share information about how Lauren and Dave have known each other for two years, earned associate degrees at the community college, and will attend the university in Dawes together, Dave studying architecture and Lauren writing. None of that is news to me. Lauren had already told me most of it. But I did learn that Mrs. Andrews was a coupon queen, and she'd kept the cost of the wedding low with her wily shopping habits. A couple of women make disparaging remarks about the expense of so many fresh flowers (always a few curmudgeons in every church, I guess). But they are shut down quickly and informed that Lauren's grandparents purchased the flowers. They hadn't seen her since she was a baby and reconnected with her when she came to Posting looking for her dad. Lauren had told me that she and Scott had been unable to see each other until she turned eighteen and that she thought her dad's parents were the sweetest in the world. I think the flowers are even more beautiful now.

Ms. Marie comes in the double doors of the fellowship hall, pushing down the stoppers with her foot so they'll stay open. She gives a last look around the place, notes the readiness of all the buffet stations, then nods her head silently and goes back out. Almost immediately, guests began to trickle in to find their assigned seats.

I smile at each person who comes by my station and give them a scoop of fresh fruit salad. One guy comes with two plates, and as I carefully place the mixture so it won't topple onto the rest of his food, I look up at his face and almost drop the spoon. "Brother Topher!"

He straightens a bit and stares at me. I can tell he doesn't recognize me, but he gives me a nod and smiles anyway. I figure he thinks I'm one of the campers from Galilee. So many of them see him on stage, welcoming them or leading them in worship, and they feel like they know him. Then, later, when they see him walking around the camp, they'll flock to him, talking to him like they're old friends, even though he doesn't know them at all.

"It's me. Julia."

The blank eyes and generic smile disappear in an instant. "Julia? I can't believe it! What — what are you doing here?"

"I'm living with my Nana now." Then I gesture at the room with my now-empty spoon. "And I'm working this wedding," I finish with a grin.

He sighs. "I wish you were working for me. We get our

first campers on Monday, and ..." he drifts off, noticing the line forming behind him. "Hey, when you get a break, come see Denise and me. We're at table six."

After I serve everyone in the line and guests come back for seconds, Ms. Marie suggests taking a twenty-minute break. I make my way to table six and say hi to Mrs. Stade, although we all call her Ms. Denise.

She seems shocked to see me, and I can tell that Brother Topher hasn't warned her I was there so he could see her reaction. "You look amazing!"

I take a step back. I wasn't expecting that. Ms. Denise fumbles, putting her napkin on the table, pushing back her chair so she can stand up. She envelops me in a tight embrace then holds me at arm's length. "Look at you! I love your hair! And your makeup! It's gorgeous!"

I have to laugh. Ms. Denise is a woman who is enthusiastic about hair and makeup. I mean, really. She could have her own YouTube channel. The woman lives full time at a campground and never leaves her cabin without being completely done up — hair, makeup, false eyelashes, perfume, and perfectly tailored clothes (most of which she makes herself). She is the most glamourous camp baker you could imagine.

"What are you doing in Posting?"

After explaining that I live with my Nana, I see my grandmother waving at me from across the room. "Come on. I'll introduce you."

Brother Topher joins us, and I get to introduce my Nana to my former bosses — and two of the nicest people on the planet. They all hit it off immediately, and Nana invites them over for Sunday dinner. My alarm buzzes. My break is half over. I give the Stades and Nana quick hugs and excuse myself. I need to use the restroom and get back to work.

The bride and groom leave at 8:00. The guests are gone by 8:30.

I stay behind to help clean. I don't get home until midnight and I flop into bed, fully dressed.

Weddings are too much work.

# Chapter Twenty-Six: Weak Spots

There is no trace of the wedding on Sunday. I sit in the morning worship service and congratulate myself on a job well done while trying not to nod off. The message is good, but I'm exhausted. I don't even have the energy to write my own sermon, but then I don't need to. Pastor Kris is pretty focused.

Lunch at Nana's perks me up. Brother Topher goes ga-ga over Nana's DVDs, and Ms. Denise admires her library, so Nana likes them even more than she had the day before. The roast beef is delicious, but that could be because I didn't have to make it.

Nana isn't offended when I politely decline a potato and take an extra carrot instead.

After dinner, we sit in the living room and talk about camp.

"I wish you were working for me this year," Brother Topher repeats his thought from the day before. "I'm not looking forward to tomorrow."

"What's tomorrow?" Nana asks.

"First camp of the season. When we left on Friday, things still weren't ready. Usually, everything is organized, stowed, and ready to go, and our staff is wandering around looking for something to do. Every year, we take the staff out the Saturday before the season starts."

I nod my head. I loved those celebratory days out. Last year it was a lazy day at the lake. Lu and I had laid in the sun until we felt ourselves start to bake, then spent the rest of the day in the shade of a cabana. I'd read *Love Comes Softly* for the dozenth time. Jack spent his day on the water racing jet-skis with his friends. I'd noticed him, he was always on my radar, but it was before we'd gotten serious.

"I told Chef Dan that if all of the other department heads agreed that everything was ready to go by Saturday afternoon, they could take everyone out to dinner in town. Of course, even Dan didn't think that would happen. I've never had a crew like this."

"What's so different about them?" Nana seems confused. I would have been, too, if it hadn't been for my phone call with Lu.

"They don't know how to work," Brother Topher says with a tone of disbelief. "It's not like they don't want to do the jobs — well, some don't — but that they can't. They don't even have the most basic life skills, and when their supervisors try to train them, they become hostile. Unfortunately, their attitudes have spread to some of my more seasoned workers. So, now, I not only have untrained people who need constant supervision, but I also have experienced workers who now somehow think their jobs are beneath them. My supervisors are good — but they're running ragged because they end up picking off the slack on top of battling their employees." He turns to me. "I'm sure Lu is missing you right about now."

Nana smiles at me. "Lu, your best friend? The one who helped us when we left?"

"That's her," I say. "She's supervising the kitchen and dining room workers this year. I was supposed to work with her this summer. Instead, Dad and Mom sent Roman in my place." I notice both Brother Topher and Ms. Denise take long drinks of their iced tea so they won't have to say anything. "He's been giving Lu a hard time."

Brother Topher looks surprised. "You know about that?"

"Lu and I have been keeping in touch." I gesture with my phone, which rarely leaves my person.

"Ohh, can I get your number?" Ms. Denise pulls her cell out of her purse, and I give her my contact information. She calls me immediately and hangs up. "There. Now you have mine too."

"And you be sure to call her if you change your mind," Brother Topher interjects. Then, when I give him a confused look, he elaborates. "If you want a job at Camp Galilee this summer — or any time really — you just give us a call. I'll find a place for you."

"Thank you." I'm more than surprised. I'm grateful and touched. I'd always like the Stades, but I hadn't realized that they liked me too.

"Who else from your church is working at the camp?" Nana asks me.

"Um — Jack."

"You're boyfriend, Jack?"

I'd told Nana about Jack when I asked her to buy me his graduation card. That was the only conversation we had about him. She hasn't asked for more information, and I haven't thought to provide any.

Ms. Denise cannot stop the look of shock that passes over her face at the mention of Jack's name, and I find myself embarrassed. I nod but don't say anything.

"I didn't realize that you and Jack were dating." Brother Topher says in a sober voice.

"We — we know each other from school and — wrote notes to each other and sat by each other at youth group activities and stuff like that. But, we've never actually been on a date." I feel embarrassed that I don't have a stronger argument for my and Jack's relationship. Why couldn't I just come out and say that we've known each other for most of our lives, but over the past year, we fell in love? That he asked me to marry him, and I said yes without hesitation? That I can't wait to spend the rest of my life with him?

Because I can wait, that is the problem. I have no desire to leave Nana's, and from Jack's few texts, it's apparent that he isn't ready to quit camp. So postponing our elopement for the fall wouldn't be difficult for either of us — not that we've mentioned our elopement since I left Sampson. I tell myself that we are two mature people who understood the meaning of timing. Except, we haven't talked about changing the timing.

"Is that why your parents didn't want you to work at the camp?" Brother Topher asks.

I work hard to keep my face neutral and nod, not wanting to elaborate.

Ms. Denise clears her throat and softly speaks as if she's afraid of spooking me. "Are the two of you still going out?"

"Yes," I say firmly. "We're both busy with work, so we haven't had much time to talk to each other, but we're keeping in touch through texts." I don't tell her he'd only texted me twice since he got my number two weeks ago — or that he is my fiancé.

Ms. Denise nods, but the apprehensive look doesn't leave her face. "Well, hopefully, the two of you can get to know each other better this summer through correspondence. Do you have the camp's address? If you write to him, we'll be sure he gets your letters."

I see Brother Topher's eyebrows go up at that suggestion. I ignore his reaction and smile, keeping my eyes blank. "I have it. Thank you."

As much as I like the Stades, I'm ready for them to leave. I hate how they were quick to discourage me when the subject of Jack came up. Jack is a great guy. Every adult at my home church in Sampson says so. He doesn't deserve the words of caution, the worried looks, and the meaningful half-conversations where the message is clear, "He's not a good boy."

I know he's a "good boy." He was there for me the entire last year I was home. No, we hadn't officially dated because neither of our parents allowed it, but that doesn't mean we didn't get to know each other. When Jack wrote to me, he was sweet and wonderful. He was exactly who I needed. I loved him — I mean, I love him. I am going to marry him. No one is going to talk me out of it. Any doubts are gone now in my desire to protect my Proteus.

Ms. Denise wisely leads the conversation onto a different

path, and an hour later, we end the visit on a good note. The Stades leave mid-afternoon to get on the road back to Camp Galilee.

"Tomorrow is going to be a busy day." Brother Topher groans. "First camp of the summer. This is where we find all the staff's weak spots. I have a feeling that this week is going to be a doozy." He shakes my hand before he exits the door. "I meant what I said. Any time you want to work at Camp Galilee, you just let us know."

"Thank you." My brief snit is gone, and I appreciate his offer.

After they leave, I help Nana with the cleanup and then go to my room for the obligatory Sunday afternoon nap. I text Jack.

*Hey, Proteus, I've thought about you a lot lately. I hope you're having a good summer so far. I'm so sorry that I'm not there with you. How's Camp Galilee?*

I hope that's enough for us to get a conversation started. First, we need to talk about our upcoming wedding. I'm assuming it's pushed to fall since Jack took the job at Camp Galilee. I've got a checking account with nearly a thousand dollars in it already and the ability to work all summer to add to it.

Next, I'll see if he'd consider moving to Posting instead of Dawes. It would be nice to live near my Nana. I have so many questions to ask and news to share. I fall asleep, waiting for the phone to buzz.

There is still no reply when I wake up to get ready for the evening service.

# Chapter Twenty-Seven: Working at Love

I've decided not to wait for Jack to text me back. It's time for me to be the fiancée I should be. I'm willing to stand up for him — for us — to Lu, my closest friend, and Mr. and Mrs. Stade, people I respect, but I haven't stood up to my apathy.

It's the part of me that I wish I could fix. I try, I really do. When Lu and I were in school together, we talked all the time. If I made cookies, I always brought her some. I encouraged her when she was down. I was a good friend. Until she left for college, then it was like I forgot her. I didn't really, but I didn't actively reach out to her either. I think I sent her six letters the entire year she was gone.

I love my Nana, but I didn't write to her as often as I should. I can't believe it had been four years since I'd seen her. I was so focused on myself that I didn't even notice the passing of time.

I'm always saying to myself, "What is wrong with me?" but it's pretty obvious. I'm a selfish, self-centered person who is always waiting for someone else to make the first move.

I hate myself for being this way.

Lu sought me out at school. Nana was at my doorstep less than a day after I called her for help. Jack dropped notes on my desk and gave me hope that last year at home.

I don't want to be the way I am. So I'll push myself to be better.

I check my phone display — still no answering text.

Jack is probably busy getting everything ready for this week's campers.

Jack works in what they call "the stables," but it's more of a garage. The camp got rid of its horses years ago and replaced them with ATVs, dirt bikes, skateboards, and BMX racing bikes. Right next to the stables, there are three racing tracks and a skate park. Jack's job is to help maintain both the equipment and the "action zones." He'd even helped design the dirt-bike track since riding motorized bikes is one of his all-time favorite things to do at home, and he knows first-hand what riders are looking for. Last year, his boss forced him to leave work and get to the dining hall to eat during mealtimes. Jack made it obvious that he had a strong work ethic.

That's one of the reasons the Stades got me so miffed. They know Jack is a hard worker, so why would they act like our dating is horrible?

Okay, not horrible. They didn't say that. Brother Topher and Ms. Denise weren't horrified, just — disappointed.

I'm still puzzled at what Lu said about how Jack is always hanging out in the kitchen this year. He'd stressed that he had tons to do at the stables. Besides, I'd worked the past three years with Jack, and he'd never hung out in the kitchen before. I'm sure it's because Roman is there. He's trying to encourage his friend from home.

I open my phone and type, *Good morning, my Proteus! I know today is the first day of camp and that you will be super busy, but I wanted to tell you I love and miss you. I'll be praying for you and texting you throughout the day. So text me back when you can. No pressure. TTYL.*

Still in my jammies (a pair of shorts and a tank-top that make me feel amazingly free!), I walk to the library to get some writing paper and an envelope. I write to Jack all of the details of my life since I left Sampson. I don't tell him about the new hair and my forays into makeup. I want to surprise him.

I set the letter on the table by the door before making myself peanut butter toast and hot chocolate — the breakfast of the newly unemployed.

*Proteus, I just wrote you a looooong letter about my life after Sampson. You should get it in a day or two. I hope you're having a good morning. Love you, Ruby.*

I have devotions. My Gideon Bible is still in its "new book" stage, so I have to hold onto both sides of the book at every moment, keeping it from shutting on its own. I miss my old Bible with its soft vinyl cover that lay flat on my desk when I wrote in its margins. I especially miss all of the notes I had amassed over the years. I wonder why Mom and Dad didn't include it in the package I had gotten from home.

*Proteus, for devotions this morning, I read Psalms 40. I especially love verse 5 — Many, O Lord my God, are thy wonderful works which thou hast done, and thy thoughts which are to usward; they cannot be reckoned up in order to thee; if I would declare and speak of them, they are more than can be numbered.*

*I'm blessed with my wonderful Nana, my best friend Lu, and you, my wonderful Proteus. Love you, Ruby.*

Instead of lying around all day, I sweep all of Nana's hardwood floors with a dust-mop, intent on cleaning the entire house before she gets home in the afternoon. I make it with an hour to spare, and it's a good thing because, after all of that housework, I need a shower.

I strip off my sweaty clothes and pick up my phone on my way into the bathroom.

*Dearest Proteus, I spent the day cleaning and thinking about you. I want to apologize for leaving Sampson without a word to you (I wasn't thinking straight) and then not contacting you for days after I got to Posting. I hope you can forgive me and that today's texts help prove that I am serious about our relationship. I've been selfishly looking after myself when I should have been focused on us. It's something I promise to work on.*

I send the text determined to believe everything I've just said. I'm sure it will come in time. I want to be in love, and I want that love to be fantastic love, like what Lauren and Dave have. I don't have that yet, but hopefully, it will come if I work at it.

I try to shut out the nagging voice that tells me I shouldn't have to work this hard to convince myself that I'm in love with Jack.

I set the phone down on the sink's vanity and reach for the shower faucet when the text notification chimes. I smile when I see the name "Proteus" and open the text.

*Julia, give it a rest. I'm trying to get some work done, and every fifteen minutes, I get another notification. Sorry you're lonely, but I really can't deal with that right now. I'll text you when I have time.*

Huh.

It is strangely painless. I put the phone back down and turn on the shower. I'm stunned but not crushed. Shouldn't I be crushed? I'm actually more confused than anything. Jack has never talked like that to me before. He always asked me how I was, encouraging me, saying little things to make me laugh. The part about me being lonely — that I don't get. I didn't say anything to him in my texts about being lonely. I'm not lonely. I'm happier than I've ever been. Had that not been clear?

I keep the shower short and text Lu as soon as I get out.

*Hey, Lu. When you get some time, could you text me?*

There's an immediate buzz.

*L: 'Sup, girlie!*

I'm thankful she's not irritated with me like Jack is.

*I just heard from Jack. He's annoyed at me for texting him so much today. I was trying to encourage him, but I guess I overdid it. I didn't mean to bug him — I figured he'd text back when he had the time, but he wasn't happy about getting four notifications from me.*

I send my paragraph of self-flagellation.

*L: Four? He's complaining about four? Four in a DAY? Good grief, when Sione and I text, it's more like four an hour — on a slow day.*

I'm thinking about what to say to that when the phone

chimes again.

*L: He hasn't been all that busy today anyway. The first group of campers was late. All they've had time to do is claim their cabins, eat lunch, and go to the welcome service in the chapel, where they hear the camp rules. The stable isn't even open until tomorrow.*

*Maybe he had to get things ready for tomorrow.*

*L: I wish. He spent the morning in the doorway between the dining room and the kitchen. I told him he could no longer hang out in the kitchen with Roman. It is his smart-aleck way of getting around me. It's so stupid. Chef Dan is not amused.*

*Was he there all morning?*

*L: Pretty much.*

*What exactly is he doing? He can't just be standing there.*

*L: He can. He does. He is. I had to push by him to take my break just now. As for what he's doing? He's talking to Roman, pretending to be all macho as they compete for Sylvie's attention.*

*THEY are competing? Does Jack like Sylvie?*

This time the answering ding isn't immediate.

*L: I don't know if he likes her or if he's flirting just to make Roman mad. You know how those two are.*

I know. They are best friends but fight and scrap like two stray dogs. Jack may be winding Roman up just to mess with him.

The quiet, mature part of my brain asks me why I want to be with a guy who acts that way. The romantic part of my brain tells Ms. Quiet & Mature to shut up.

*I guess so. Sounds like them. I'll let you go. Call me tonight?*

*L: I'll try. If you don't hear from me, assume it's because my crew couldn't handle the first night of actual camp, and I ended up having to do everything myself, and I'm too exhausted to dial the phone.*

*Got it. When you get the energy, contact me. Love Ya!*

*L: Love you too! I'll call tonight around ten. I'll make it a point. I'll probably need to rant anyway. BTW, this was way more than four texts.*

I don't expect another chime. This time it is Nana.

*I'm craving chips and salsa. Get your eatin' pants on. I'm taking you out to dinner!*

I love my Nana.

And just like that, I can put Jack away in the little box in my brain reserved just for him. I'll worry about our relationship later.

I slip on my jeans and a sparkly peasant blouse and am at the front door when Nana pulls into the driveway. I see the envelope addressed to Jack on the table. I fold it in half and stick it into my purse. I don't want to mail it just yet.

# Chapter Twenty-Eight: Work Ethic

Is there anything better than Mexican food? I mean, really? Chips and salsa, giant burritos, fluffy rice — who can ask for more?

Nana has me cracking up with stories from the antique mall where she works. I share some funny things that happened when I worked at Camp Galilee. It's so much fun to laugh and enjoy an evening out.

Nana surprises me by ordering deep-fried ice cream for dessert. It is amazing! Whoever came up with the brilliant idea should be given the Nobel Prize for sweets. I'm going in for another spoonful when, out of the blue, she says, "Do you want to go work at Camp Galilee this summer?"

I sit stunned, my spoon hovering over the crunchy brown crust leaking vanilla bean deliciousness.

"Oh — I — I can, I guess. Do — do you need me to go?" I feel embarrassed that I had just assumed I lived with Nana now.

"No. I don't need you to go. My home is your home. You stay as long as you like. I'm not in any hurry to get rid of you. I love having you as a housemate. No. I thought this is a guaranteed job when jobs — especially summer jobs — are hard to find. I know you like the place, and the Stades are sweet people. Plus, it's nice to keep the old resume up to date."

It sure sounds like she wants me to go. I take another bite while I think.

"I don't need you to go." She says again, emphasizing the word "need." "But I think you should. You have some stuff to figure out."

I wonder if she means Jack. "You sound like Lu."

"Lu's a bright girl."

"Yeah. She's pretty awesome."

"You don't have to decide tonight. Maybe take a few days to think about it and let me know what you decide. I might even be able to drive you up myself."

"And we can finally finish *Pride and Prejudice*."

"There's that. Always a good excuse for a road trip."

At 10:00 on the dot, Lu calls, and the ranting begins. Aside from the occasional "Uh-huh," I don't contribute much. I listen to her every word while simultaneously thinking about Nana's suggestion that I go to camp. When Lu's frustration finally fizzles, I broach the subject.

"Hey, Lu? Want me to come up and help?"

"Do. Not. Mess. With. Me! Of course, I want you to come up and help! Get on the bus and get your butt up here!"

I laugh. "I'm serious. I saw Brother Topher at the wedding, and he told me that it was mine if I wanted a job. I just had to call."

"Want me to hang up right now so you can call him? Please? I'm begging you — take the job! Save me from these morons!"

"You make it sound so appealing."

"You want me to lie to you? Fine. Come on up to Camp Galilee. All of the workers are kind and competent and go out of their way to make my life a blissful breeze of contentment. If you show up, I promise you double rainbows, puppies, and a million-dollar contract."

"How can I pass that up?"

"Just in case you can pass that up, let me try this: Please come up and help me. I need you."

"I'll call Brother Topher tomorrow."

"Whoo-hoo!"

"Do me a favor, though?"

"Anything."

"Don't tell anyone else I might be coming up."

"Might? We're back to might?"

"I don't want to presume."

"Fine. By 'anyone else,' I assume you mean Jack?"

"And Roman. I don't need him calling Dad and Mom so that they show up when I arrive and try to drag me back home."

"Yikes. You're right. My lips are sealed."

"Thanks, Lu. I'm gonna go to bed."

"Me too. Thanks again for letting me rant."

"No problem."

∞∞∞

Nana is filling her travel mug full of coffee before leaving for work when I tell her that I've decided to call Brother Topher about working at Camp Galilee. She doesn't seem surprised. "Let me know when he wants you to come up so I can make arrangements. Saturday would be ideal, but I might be able to work something out if you need to go sooner."

"I'll call you as soon as I find out."

"Thanks, honey." Nana hugs me on her way out the door. "I am going to miss you, though."

As soon as she leaves for work, I pull up the contact for Ms. Denise and make the call.

"Hello, Julia!" Her voice is chirpy as if she adores answering the phone at eight in the morning. "I'm so glad you called! We've been praying you would."

"You have?"

"Since we left your house on Sunday. Did you decide to work for us again?"

"Um — yes, if it's okay."

"It's more than okay. When can you come up?"

"Saturday. My Nana said she could drive me."

"Wonderful! Text me your email, and I'll send you a contract for the summer. We look forward to having you up here.

You've always been such a great team member."

"Really?" I can't keep the skepticism out of my voice.

"Really." Her voice is serious now. "From your first year, we knew we'd been blessed. You have an amazing work ethic and are one of the sweetest spirits of any team member we've had. We were disappointed when we heard you wouldn't be back this year — but now you're on your way, so disappointment over! We've always appreciated the way you are willing to not only do whatever is asked of you but go above and beyond. Your parents did a great job raising you."

My skin grows cold, and goose pimples break out all over my arms. I breathe deep, even as my stomach churns.

"Julia? Are you there?"

"Yes," I whisper.

"Is everything okay?"

"Uh-huh."

"All right." Now it's her turn to sound skeptical. "Send back the contract as soon as possible, and we'll arrange a bunk for you. I assume you don't mind sharing a room with Lu?"

"No, I don't mind. Thank you."

"You sure you're okay."

"Yes." Then, "Could you do me a favor?"

"If I can."

"Don't tell anyone else that I'm coming."

"Well, I'll need to tell Topher and Chef Dan. You do still want to work in the kitchen, right?"

"Right. I just meant the other workers."

"Sure. I'll let your arrival be a surprise."

"Thanks."

"I'll send the contract right away. Call me if you have any questions. See you on Saturday!"

"See you Saturday," I echoed.

I hang up the phone, mulling over her words, "Your parents did a great job raising you."

∞∞∞

*Buzz.*

I don't bother to uncurl my body from where it lay on the bed as I open the notification.

*I'm going to the store after work. What would you like for dinner tonight?*

I double-check the time. I've been moping all day. *Pizza.*

I get a thumbs-up emoji in response.

The next thing I know, Nana is waking me. "Julia? You okay, honey?"

I nod but then start crying. Nana cuddles me the way she did when I was a little girl, and my parents called to tell her they were coming to take me back early. I hated that phone call, and after three or four days of bliss at Nana's, I would get nauseated every time I heard the phone ring, afraid it was them.

"Want to talk about it?"

Right now, I can't talk. I'm too busy trying to keep from falling apart. It feels like my parents are in the room, berating me, telling me I'm a fool, an embarrassment, worthless — and that they were only doing what they did for my own good.

"Someday, you're going to thank me for being so strict." I hear the echo of Mom's voice in the room, bypassing my ears and assaulting my brain. It isn't just one instance, but one of dozens that somehow all run together.

"Mrs. [Fill-in-the-Blank] spoke at [one of many women's conferences Mom attended], and she said the biggest problem in our churches today was girls who didn't want to be lady-like. They always talk about things they shouldn't, hang out with the boys, and even dress like men! When asked what they want to do when they grow up, the answers are always careers instead of staying at home to create a family that will serve the Lord. She was invited to a home where the mom was having trouble getting her pre-teen daughters to obey. Mrs. [Fill-in-the-Blank] and her husband went over after church one Sunday night for cake and coffee. The girls didn't even help get dessert on the table or with the clean-up afterward! They stayed in their rooms until they were called to the table, and when they did show up, they were wearing pajama bottoms — pants! Right away, Mrs. [Fill-in-the-Blank] knew where the parents had gone wrong. They were confusing their daughters, making them think they were boys with all the responsibilities of manhood looming in their future, instead of girls who were supposed to be soft, gentle creatures who ran the home. Mrs. [Fill-in-the-Blank] suggested that they dress their daughters only in girls' clothes — no pants — and train them to be little housekeepers. She said that the next time she visited the house, the girls were in the kitchen and dining room helping their mom while still wearing their pretty Sunday dresses. They hugged Mrs. [Fill-in-the-Blank] before she left and thanked her."

There was an awkward pause right after Mom stopped talking, and I knew Mom was waiting for me to thank her for not letting me get the cute pajamas I was looking at in Walmart. I didn't say anything, just nodded and moved on to the nightgowns. I hated them because they stuck to the sheets when I turned over, twisting around my body in ever-tightening loops, making me feel claustrophobic. My lack of appreciation put Mom in a bad mood for the rest of the shopping trip while I mused about how those girls got "pretty Sunday dresses," and I got my brother's hand-me-down jeans that were converted into long skirts.

I make a mental list of all the things my parents insisted I be thankful for in their quest to be "strict." There was: a complete lack of privacy ("So secret sin does not so easily beset you"), limited contact with kids my age ("Your biggest influences should be your parents, not your friends), the back-breaking housework ("We're raising you to be a Proverbs 31 woman — 'her candle goeth not out at night'"), and even my plain-Jane look ("Boys don't want to marry pretty girls anyway

—they're too high maintenance"). I remember shooting a look at my mom when Dad let that one slip. She'd just gotten her hair "brightened" when he said it, and while Mom didn't seem happy with his statement, she didn't object. I wondered if he thought she was "high maintenance." I certainly wasn't.

I'm still not; at least, I didn't think I am. I spend even less time on my hair than I did before. The makeup doesn't take all that long. I'm not drop-dead gorgeous, but I'm not the doughy lump I had been before either.

"Julia?" Nana's voice breaks through my fog. I'd forgotten she was in the room. I sigh a little.

"Yes?"

"What's going on?"

I pull myself into a sitting position, my back against the headboard of the bed. Nana sits next to me, waiting for me to talk.

"I got the job at camp."

"That's great, honey, but if you don't want to take it, you don't have to. I don't want you to feel like I'm asking you to leave."

"That's not it. At the end of the call, Ms. Denise said that Dad and Mom raised me well."

"Oh."

"It made me wonder if they had."

No comment from Nana, so I continue.

"The camp wants me because of my work ethic. I didn't tell Mrs. Stade that the reason I have that work ethic is that my parents beat it into me." I cringe a little on the word "beat." It was always the word I used in my head, but usually, in the few times I told people about the beatings, I used words like "spank" or "swat" even though they were inaccurate.

"Do you believe that?"

"Where else would I have gotten it?"

"You were always a strange kid," Nana says in a tone that is much more comforting than the words she speaks. "Even when you were a baby, you wanted to be in the kitchen helping. At two, your favorite thing to do was empty all of my bottom drawers and cupboards. You'd get the big pot out from under the stove and root around for a wooden spoon and then chatter the whole time you were 'cooking' in the middle of the floor. Your PawPaw and I would sit at the kitchen table and watch you play. Then, when she came to pick you up, your mom would object — unhappy that we allowed you to put the clean dishes on the floor. Paw Paw assured her that it was the easiest thing in the world to pick everything up and put it in the dishwasher. She told us she didn't let you in her kitchen because you were always getting things out. Paw Paw and I talked about it later. We couldn't understand why she wouldn't just let you play. So we got you a little plastic kitchen for your third birthday."

I gasp. "I remember that! I loved that kitchen!"

"It was maybe a week later, your mom sent us a book in the mail, *To Train Up a Child*. No note or letter, just the book. I read it and was horrified. I had your Paw Paw read it. He was ready to hunt the author down. He called your mom and asked if she was 'seriously following that nut's advice?' She hung up on him. After that, our visits were always cut short. We never knew when they were going to end. It was a power play, but we didn't want to say anything for fear we wouldn't see you at all."

"What did the book say?"

"It — hmm — it was how to train a child to behave. It was almost like a dog-training manual in some places. There's no real love or compassion expressed. It was cause and effect and the idea that parents are always right, while the children are always wrong."

"Do you still have it?"

"It's in the library."

"Can I read it?"

"Of course." I could tell she's trying to sound confident, but her voice shakes a little. "But, please, keep in mind that while, the author uses Scripture to back up his ideas, he's twisting them to fit what he's teaching." The bed bounces and bobs as she gets up. I hear her flats clack on the wood floor as she crosses the hall to the library. She comes back and puts the book into my hand with a worried frown. The cover is a simple black and white illustration of a horse-drawn buggy. "He got his inspiration for the book from watching the Amish in a nearby community," Nana says. She waits for a few beats. "Are you hungry?"

"Not really."

"I'm going to start dinner because I'm starving. Come out when you're ready. Food will be waiting."

I hold the thin white paperback in my hand. I've seen this book before. It is on my parent's bookshelf in their living room. I dusted that shelf several times a week as part of my chore list. It was near the top, meaning it was a book they referred to often.

I open Nana's copy. The binding creaks, letting me know it hasn't been read much. I turn to the first page and begin.

# Chapter Twenty-Nine: Training Sessions

The introduction is only one page, so I read it, even though I usually skip anything printed in a book before chapter one. Right from the beginning, the author clarifies that his book is not about discipline but training. That proper training will reduce instances of discipline. In the first chapter, he points out that a child doesn't need to reason to be trained because even mice and rats can be taught without reason. He gives examples of parents giving him glowing recommendations and telling him how happy their home is now that they've used his methods. The parents are relaxed, the children are loving, the home exemplifies love and peace.

I'm beginning to wonder what made Paw Paw so mad, so I keep reading. It doesn't take long for indignation to kick in. The man's methods are brutal — and oddly familiar.

Want to teach a child to obey his father's voice without a second thought? Place a toy or sippy cup on the floor in front of him and when he reaches for it, tell him, "No, don't touch it," and when he reaches for it, hit him lightly on the legs with a switch. It's not discipline. It's training.

Want to teach a baby not to upset a bowl on his highchair tray? Sit it in front of him, and when he reaches for it, say, "No, don't touch it," and thump his hand. It's not discipline. It's training.

Want to teach a child to come when you call? Set aside an evening for training, bring out your child's favorite toy, wait until he becomes engrossed in playing with it, then call the child. If he doesn't come to his father's chair, the father should go to the child, explain that the child should come when called, and walk him to the father's chair, then back to the toy. Do this three times. After that, if the child doesn't immediately come when called, the child should be spanked. Do this repeatedly throughout the evening until the child learns to go immediately as soon as his father calls.

A little sweat pops out on my upper lip when I read that last example. I had no idea those were "training sessions." Up until I left home, Dad would call me from something I was doing. I'd get to his easy chair (throne in my mind) and stand in front of him, waiting for him to tell me what he wanted. It was usually something silly. "My water's warm. Get me some ice." I'd take his glass into the kitchen, wondering why he'd called me away from loading the dishwasher to freshen his drink when Roman was on the couch next to him playing a video game.

I'd return the glass and wait to be dismissed, then get back to my evening chores. When done, I'd sit on the couch on the opposite end from Roman. As soon as I snuggled in and opened a book, I'd hear, "Julia!" Keeping my face blank, I'd close my book immediately and go to stand in front of him. "Go get everyone a bowl of ice cream."

Off I'd go into the kitchen again. I'd give everyone bowls and wait for my dismissal. "You can go to your room now." I'd nod and stop by my seat on the couch to retrieve my book. It was easier to read it in the quiet of my room anyway, but then he'd say, "No. Leave the book."

"Yes, sir." I'd perfected the robot voice by now and didn't even grit my teeth or make a face until I was walking up the stairs even though I was furious. I knew it wasn't over. I'd quickly get into my nightgown and throw my robe over it.

"Julia!"

I'd scamper down the stairs as quickly as I could. "Take the bowls out and wash them." As soon as they were dried and back in the cupboard, I returned to Dad's chair. "You may take your book and go to bed. Goodnight."

"Goodnight," I'd respond politely, inside wishing he — no — couldn't think that of my father.

I would crawl into bed, trying to get lost in the stories of Laura Ingalls Wilder while keeping my ears open for my father's demanding, petulant voice. When I heard the squeak of his easy chair echo off the landing upstairs, I knew to turn off my light. I'd gotten drug out of bed before for reading after I was "sent to bed." I had disobeyed because I hadn't gone right to sleep. But then another time, I had fallen asleep and had gotten drug out of bed for not coming when called. I found it easier to stay awake until his squeaky chair let me know he was on his way upstairs.

Now, I'm reading the book he had used as his blueprint. He did the "training" long after I was a toddler. It didn't seem like training to me at all. Instead, it was an exertion of his power over me. He let me know who the boss was and, more importantly, that I was the least essential person in the family. He let me know exactly where I stood in his eyes.

As far as I knew, Roman had never gone through the training.

I flip through the pages of the book, not wanting to dig much deeper, but my eye catches the heading "Hot Stove." It's another training session where the author heated up the woodstove in the winter and invited his toddlers to touch it. Then, he'd yell "HOT!" at them when they burned themselves (he assures his reader that the stove was not yet hot enough to raise blisters, just turn the skin red). He'd do this several times until, from then on, "If I wanted to see them do a backflip, all I had to do was say, 'HOT!' and they would turn loose a glass of iced tea."

Suddenly, I remember this training session too. It's been years since I'd even thought about it, but Nana reminded me about the toy kitchen she and Paw Paw bought, and now this book brought it all back.

We didn't have a wood stove, so Dad and Mom used the oven. Mom had set up my play kitchen from Nana on one side of the island, so I'd be under her watch but not in her way while she cooked. I cooked right along with her, trying to imitate everything Mom did. I remember even trying to press my lips into that straight line she always had. One evening, Dad came out and saw me taking some pretend muffins out of my pretend oven with my bare hands. He yelled "HOT!" at me, and I just stared at him in surprise. I offered him a muffin, but instead of taking it, he grabbed my hand, pulled me to the actual oven, and pointed at it. "HOT!" I nodded. I knew it was hot. I tried to take my hand out of his because he looked scary. He swatted my bottom for trying to get away. He pointed to the oven again. "HOT!" and then he pressed my hand to the oven door. I screamed. He just kept yelling "HOT! HOT!" over my cries.

When he finally pulled my hand away, my palm was ringed with blisters. He and Mom got very quiet, very fast, but I kept wailing. I still remember the pain. Dad insisted that I grab a piece of ice and hold it, but Mom, never directly contradicting him, ran my hand under cold water instead. There was some whispered discussion of the hospital, but they treated me at home with burn cream and bandages. I didn't stop crying until they gave me children's Tylenol, and mom rocked me to calm me down. Then, as I was drifting off, Dad stood over me where I lay in Mom's lap and said, "And that's why you never touch a hot oven."

It was years before I would go near the stove. Then, when Mom wanted me to learn how to cook, she called Dad in to swat me over and over again until she finally got me near the range. I still use both hand mitts and potholders to take things out of the oven.

It's my most complete early memory. I have little flashes of memories from earlier, but I remember nearly everything about that day. I had forgotten about my play kitchen, though. When Nana talked about it, I'd wondered what had happened to it. Now I remember. After that "training session," I refused to go near it. Mom sold it at our next yard sale.

As for the burn marks on my palm? It took them years to fade, but now all evidence of that training session has been erased.

I flip the book end-over-end across the room, then sigh and go to pick it up. I'm not sure where it goes in the library, so I carry it out to Nana.

"You okay?" are her first words to me.

I nod and hand her the book.

"Did you finish this already?"

"I read as much as I wanted to."

She gets up to put it away while I spoon some spinach salad onto my plate. "There's pizza in the oven," Nana calls from the living room. I stare at the oven door. I don't want to touch it. I add another spoonful of salad to my pile and head out to the living room couch. "You didn't want any pizza?"

I shake my head.

"Don't you like that kind of pizza?" I can hear the confusion in her voice. I'd had no problem eating it before and had even requested it for tonight.

"Julia! What's wrong, honey?"

I'm surprised at the panic in her voice, and when I turn to look at her, the alarm is on her face too. "Are you okay, sweetie?" She takes the plate from my suddenly nerveless hands and pulls me close. I hear strange coughing wheezing sounds and realize it is me. My whole body convulses and shakes as I sob in Nana's arms. I don't know when I fall asleep, but I wake with my head in Nana's lap and covered in an afghan.

I sit up. "I'm sorry," are the first words out of my mouth.

"You have no reason to apologize." The digital clock on her entertainment system reads 1:37.

"Oh. It's so late. I'm so sorry. I didn't mean to keep you up."

Her arms encircle me again. "I'm always here for you. It

doesn't matter the time of day or distance. When you need me, I'll be there." Then she adds, "From now on." She pushes me back a little so she can look at my face. "I'm sorry I wasn't there for you before when you needed me. I had suspicions, but I was too afraid of what I would lose to ask the important questions. I was a coward …" her voice ends in a papery rasp, and I watch in horror as her sweet face collapses in sorrow. Now it's my turn to hold her.

"You came when I needed you the most," I remind her, my voice rough with tears. "I can never thank you enough for what you've done for me."

She gives me a panicked look. "What about Roman? We need to get him out too. He isn't safe."

"We can ask him if he wants to leave. He might not want to go."

"But — if they're beating him …"

"Roman doesn't get beaten. He's gotten a few swats and gets yelled at, but that's about it. I don't even think he's gone through a training session."

"Training session?"

"Like the ones in the book."

"You remember those?" Nana's voice is thin and wavering. "That training is for tiny children — children who are hardly able to walk. By the time your parents gave us the book, we had thought you were too old for those, and we took comfort in the idea that you were so young you wouldn't remember them."

I tell her about Dad's usual call and response scenarios, and, without meaning to, I tell her about the oven. I had never told anyone about that before. Not even Lu. Nana alternated between hugging me and looking like she was planning my Dad's beat-down, but when she spoke, it was about her daughter.

"I can't believe she stayed married to that idiot. What kind of a woman watches her children undergo torture in the name of 'discipline.' She knows — we taught her — that discipline isn't about punishment, it's training — but not the kind of training that moron author was pushing. Jesus had disciples, disciplined people, and didn't beat them up or spank them or hold their hands in the fire. He taught them. He encouraged them. Discipline is about walking with someone to show them the right way to live. She knew that. We raised her that way, and she still chose an abusive jerk for a husband. She still watched her kids get hurt. She still refused to reach out for help. What is wrong with her?" A little gleam of hope sparked in her eyes as Nana asked, "Does she need help too? Is it that she doesn't feel she can leave? Is she being abused?"

I know what Nana is thinking. If Mom is being held against her will and covering for Dad's abuse, Nana can rescue her. Then Mom would be an unwilling pawn and not a monster Nana and Paw Paw had accidentally created. I know Nana wants it to be true, but I have to shake my head.

Mom wasn't so much about hitting or screaming, but she was scary in her way. She required much more than what I, as a child, could do, muttering and complaining that my best wasn't good at all, making me do the same task over and over again. When I cried from exhaustion, she'd set me up with a beating for Dad. She let me know I was ugly, that I was "built like a boy." When I showed interest in the romances played out on the *Little House on the Prairie* DVDs or in any Jane Austen movie, she'd imply that I had a dirty mind and say I was "only interested in sex." The first time she said that to me, I was ten and wasn't even sure what she was talking about, but I kept quiet, not asking her to explain. I knew from her tone that it was terrible.

I don't say anything about Mom to Nana, but she reads my face. She sees the truth there and turns away to weep for the daughter who is lost to her.

# Chapter Thirty: On the Road to Galilee

After prayer meeting/small group study on Wednesday night, Nana and I drive to Walmart with my list of "suggested items for camp" in hand. It had been sent the day after I'd filled out and returned my contract by email. But Tuesday was all about crying and dealing with horrible childhood memories, so tonight is the first time we could get to the store.

Our emotions are still raw, but Nana and I try to keep things light with banter and oh-so-many hugs. I'll be working in the kitchen and my clothes for that job in years past were jean skirts and t-shirts (shocker, right? As if I didn't wear the same clothes for nearly everything). The idea of going back to that lifelong wardrobe is repugnant, and I say as much to Nana. She shrugs like it is no big deal and drives the cart straight to men's jeans. "You only have two pairs at home. Get five more, so you only have to do laundry once a week." I pick the cheapest pairs in my size.

Now for blouses. Not t-shirts. Blouses. Nana takes me to business wear. "These are the ones I get for work." She held up a button-down dress shirt with three-quarter sleeves and nipped in at the waist. I shrug. They aren't for me. Or kitchen work.

Finally, we find a rack of blouses that are like those I've admired on others. They're made out of t-shirt material but cut differently in a variety of styles. Some have lace inserts on the shoulders, others have crisscross straps across the back yoke, and bright, colorful prints and patterns spangled all over with glitter or clear sequins. Nana keeps encouraging me to "get one more" until I have a dozen in the cart. Instead of basic grey or navy sweatshirts, Nana leads me to a rack of hoodies in pastel colors. I choose lavender. Nana chooses turquoise, "For when you have to wash the purple one." My yoga pants and oversized tees at home will do for pajamas, and I'll take my two new dresses for church, and for if the staff pulls it together and we get to go out for an end-of-the-year celebration.

I'm passing the endcap of sundresses when Nana asks me to wait. She pulls a white cotton dress with abstract pink flowers scattered over it. "This would look great on you." Nana selected the same one I did when I was still living in Sampson — the one I'd thought about it for an impromptu wedding dress. "It's on sale for ten dollars, down from fourteen. Want it?" I nod, but I don't want to wear the one I once picked out for a quickie wedding. Instead, I reach for the light blue with a pink, purple, and black print that looks almost like butterflies. It's more me. The new me. The real me. Nana nods and returns the white dress to the peg, and I deposit my new sundress in the cart.

"Let's get you a new purse. That one is looking pretty worn out."

My first new purse! I bought my trusty old black one at a yard sale for a quarter. Tonight, I touch every bag in the department until I land on a steal-of-a-deal. A dark blue four-piece set for $20. The tote is plenty big enough for a book (an absolute necessity) and there is also a smaller purse and a "wristlet" (I didn't even know that was a thing) and a brand new wallet to boot.

Our last planned stop is the shoe department, where I get another pair of tennis shoes (required for working in the kitchen), and a new pair of flip-flops (mine are on the verge of breaking and the ones my parents sent from home aren't much better), and, at Nana's insistence, a comfortable pair of dressy sandals.

"What about a swimsuit?"

I blink at her. I've never swum at camp. I haven't swum anywhere for years. There is a beautiful pool at Camp Galilee, but I'd always sat on one of the lounges, reading a book when visiting it with Lu. Even then, I wasn't in a swimsuit. Instead, I'd be in my usual "sportswear" of t-shirts and my P.E. culottes from school. I follow Nana silently as she roots through swimwear. Finally, she shows me a simple one-piece in Navy blue. "How about this one?"

"Sure."

"Want to try it on?"

"I guess I'd better." Blouses were easy, humdrum medium, and for jeans, I just looked at the label of the pairs I bought in Dawes, but a swimsuit? This is new territory for me. Nana hands me one that says 8-10 and one that goes from 10-12. I decide to try on the 8-10 first.

I take the swimsuit into the dressing room and strip down. I don't bother to look in the mirror until I've pulled the straps up over my shoulders. I am immediately confronted with the reminder that the "breast fairy" (as Lu called the phenomenon of bust-development) hated me and avoided me during those confusing puberty years. The top of the suit sags a bit, and the built-in cups are just empty promises destined to remain unfulfilled. I'm ready to take the suit off when I notice the reflection of my back-side in the mirror.

Between my bottom and my knees are countless squiggles of pink lines. I slip the one-piece off, then drop the underwear I'd kept on underneath. The squiggles continue up over the fleshiest part of my butt to my lower back. I'd caught glimpses of my scars in the full-length mirror at home, but I didn't usually look unless I'd just gotten a beating and was trying to apply antibiotic ointment and bandages.

I pull my underwear back up and get dressed. There's no point in trying on the other sizes. I can't wear a swimsuit in public. I hand the tag with the number of items I'd taken into the dressing room back to the clerk, and she hangs the suits on the go-back rack. Nana is waiting with a smile and another selection.

"I was thinking — since you and I have pretty much the

same build — the one-piece probably won't fit exactly right. Years ago, I switched to tankinis. You might prefer them too. Want to try this one out?" Nana holds up a tank-style top paired with long shorts. It might work.

Back in the dressing room, I slip on the knee-length shorts, tagged as "bike-shorts," and they cover my scars beautifully. The tank top has some gathers just under where my bust is supposed to be, adding the illusion of a waist. The upper part is tight enough and much higher than the one-piece, so there is no gaping. This will be my first ever swimsuit since before puberty. I like it, and I smile as I dress in my regular clothes. I refuse to look at the back of my legs again.

"I like this one," I tell Nana, not ashamed of the excitement in my voice.

She tosses the tankini into the cart, encourages me to get a couple of beach towels as well, and we're off to the checkout. I have a mild panic attack at the total, but Nana pays for it all with a smile and a flick of the wrist, swiping her card and pushing buttons like she's having an excellent time.

The next morning, I wash all of my new clothes (except the swim suit), and while they are in the dryer, I pack up my unused toiletries and makeup (I'll keep my open stuff here for when I return in the fall) as well as my new flashlight, sunscreen, and insect repellant. Each item of clothing is then folded and placed in my new rolling suitcase. Everything that passes through my hands is an "I love you" from Nana.

I don't pack the clothes I got in Dawes (I have to have something to wear before we leave for Camp Galilee on Saturday) except for the dresses. Nana lends me a garment bag for those.

∞∞∞

Thursday and Friday go by much too fast. After Nana takes me to the salon for a touch up on my hair, I go to bed early on Friday night, but I can't sleep, so I spend a few hours reading.

We are on the road, with coffee and homemade breakfast burritos in our hands, by 7:00 Saturday morning. While we eat, we listen to the melodic cadences of Jane Austen's writings. Lizzy visits her friend Charlotte and discovers that Mr. Darcy is visiting his Aunt, Lady Catherine, just down the lane.

We make a few comments on the story, especially about the worst proposal in literary history, but we listen in companionable silence for the most part. Finally, after two hours, Nana pulls over, and it is my turn to drive. There is something so very peaceful about going on a gently curving road into the foothills surrounding a mountain. The trees grow taller, the underbrush is greener, and the blue sky hovers overall. Nana turns off the air conditioner, and we open the windows, letting the wind pull at our short hair and bring us the scents of the pine forest. We see a few deer in a meadow, and I sigh at the beautiful red-rock outcroppings decorating the high desert. Later, we stop for burgers in a small town that seems about to tumble off its mountainside. Nana insists she needs to stretch her legs, and we wander around for an hour looking into shops set up for tourists passing through.

One last stretch at the lookout where we'd parked our car, and we are back on the road. Nana grins as she swoops around the curves going out of town. I hold on to my seatbelt and giggle at her. She is hands-down the happiest adult I've ever met — even when I take our mutual melt-down on Tuesday into consideration.

The last words of *Pride and Prejudice* echo through the car when we are still a half-hour away from camp. We both remain silent for a few minutes until Nana draws in a breath and says, "Count it." At my questioning look, she elaborates. "Write it in your reading journal. Audiobooks count as books you've read. Now, read off the titles in my library so I can pick something to listen to on the way home." Nana decides on *Vanity Fair*. For the rest of the ride, we listen to her Spotify playlist with Nana announcing the bands and songs and offering trivia tidbits about each one. Some of the songs are the floaty ballads I remember from our escape from Sampson, but others are more upbeat, and some even have an edge. I'm in shock when she openly dances while sitting in the driver's seat, encouraging me to do the same. I shake my head no automatically. It's hard to let go of years of "be still" teaching.

In my church and home, I was taught that music that wasn't specifically for the worship of God was evil and sinful. If a song made you want to dance, it was a sign of demonic influence. Now that I'm out of that oppressive atmosphere of "home," I reevaluate that teaching using my observations. My parents never had music playing. Dad even muted commercials that were too "rocky." According to the church, they were right. But they were also two of the most miserable, angry, frustrated people I've ever met.

Looking over at Nana while she dips and sways, rapping along with the lead singer of some band featuring what sounds like a giant drum, all I can see is someone who is irrepressibly happy. Spending time with Nana, I know she's godly. She loves Jesus. She reads her Bible and understands it, refers to it in her conversation all the time. She has no connection with my childhood church and is all the better for it. She's found joy in many aspects of her life — in books, films, friendship, family, and music. No one can tell me her happiness doesn't glorify God. I start nodding my head to the beat of the drum, grinning while Nana smoothly recites the fast-paced poetry of the music blaring from the speakers. I guess music is her third "vice" after books and movies.

As instructed, I send a text to Ms. Denise when we pull

onto the five-mile-long gravel road leading to the camp. I get an immediate response telling us to park in the spaces behind the office. Ms. Denise is watching for us and opens the back door as we pull in.

"Welcome back to Camp Galilee!" She gives me a hug then gives Nana one too. She gestures for us to sit. "I've got your contract already in the file. So you can start right away. I've put you in Lu's room — she's so excited. We haven't told anyone that you'd be arriving to work this year, and Lu wanted me to run something by you." She takes a deep breath before she continues. "I told Lu about your makeover — that we didn't recognize you at first — and she had this idea that maybe you could get a better feel as to what has been going on around here if people didn't realize it was you."

My confusion must be evident on my face because she chuckles.

"She wanted to know — and I think it's a pretty good idea — if you'd be willing to go by a different name to start."

"Oh." I get it now. I'd be the undercover operative. I would see what was going on behind Lu's back because I would be just another worker. "Of course. That would be fine."

"I thought we could use your middle name. It's Rose, right?"

I nod. "Right. Easy to remember and respond to; I get it."

"Exactly." Ms. Denise takes a beat, then says, "We haven't told Roman that you're coming back."

"That's good," I assure her. "I understand he's been a big problem for Lu."

"Um — yes." Ms. Denise gives Nana an embarrassed look, uncomfortable about criticizing her grandson so openly, but Nana puts her to ease with a smile. I know Nana is relieved that no one (especially not Roman) will contact my parents about my presence just yet. That was probably the only thing she'd been worried about with me coming back to camp.

"Do you need a guest cabin for tonight?" Ms. Denise asks her.

Nana shakes her head. "I'm driving straight back. I'm subbing for a friend's Sunday school class tomorrow. Do you want me to drive Julia's — sorry — Rose's things to her cabin?"

"We can manage. Plus, we don't want anyone to recognize you," Ms. Denise says with a grin.

The only one who would recognize Nana, other than Lu, was Roman. That thought makes my stomach lurch.

I hold Nana tight before letting her go, thanking her again, reminding her I'll see her at the end of August. Her smile is shaky as she pulls out of the parking space, and my eyes water as she leaves. I brush a tear off my cheek with my thumb and shoulder my garment bag. Following Ms. Denise to my cabin, my suitcase bobs and weaves behind me on the gravel path.

# Chapter Thirty-One: Roman

Ms. Denise walks me around the dining hall to the back, where a simple wooden staircase leads up to the attic rooms of the building. At the top is a wide veranda sheltering three doors. My new home is behind the center door. The places to the right and left are storerooms. I'd been in those rooms plenty of times, organizing and cleaning, as a part of my job. But I'd never been in the dorm before.

I'm surprised at its small proportions, no bigger than a single-wide trailer with one open living space and a bathroom. Ms. Denise flips a switch, but the overhead lights do little to break up the gloom.

There is a single bed on each side of the room. I roll my suitcase to the one that is just a bare mattress, thankful when I see the light on the nightstand. I'll be able to read in bed.

"The bathroom is back there. So go ahead and unpack and make yourself at home. I'll let Lu know you've arrived as soon as the staff meeting is over."

"Thank you." I put every ounce of gratitude I can into those words.

"We're so glad to have you here." She pulls me in for one more hug before closing the door behind her.

I have my bed made in no time. When Lu walks in the door, I'm coming out of the bathroom, where I was stowing my toiletries. She stops dead in her tracks and blinks rapidly.

"Julia? Is that really you?"

I laugh. "Yeah, it's me. Fresh haircut and a little mascara. Okay, a lot of mascara — and a bunch of other makeup."

"You look amazing."

I like my new look too, but it's getting embarrassing how she's looking at me like an art exhibit. Then she grins, and she's suddenly my old friend again. "You're wearing jeans! And that top — it's perfect! No one is going to recognize you. This is going to be awesome!"

Lu takes her twenty-minute break sitting with me in our new dorm, catching up. "Want a soda?" She nods to the mini-fridge under one of the two windows at the front of the room. She hands me a diet strawberry soda and takes one for herself. "One of the perks of the promotion," she says with a grin. I know she means the mini-fridge, not the soda. That she would have had to purchase herself. I share the granola bars I brought from Nana's, and we munch while we talk. Twenty minutes later, she and I enter the kitchen where dinner's meal-prep is in full swing. She's already caught me up on everyone working there, so I spend the first couple of seconds registering who is present.

I know the dishwashers. I've worked with them in years past, but they're in a room off the kitchen, so we only work to-gether when cleaning the dining hall. Ms. Denise winks at me from the baking corner, and Sylvie smiles at me warmly. She doesn't recognize me. Chef Dan has his back to the kitchen, his focus glued to the flattop. The only other person in the kitchen is Roman. He pushes off the prep table where he's leaning and comes our way. He barely flicks a look at me on his way past as he heads for the walk-in, and I know he didn't see me. "Hey, everybody," Lu addresses the room. "This is Rose, our new crew member."

There is a diffusion of "Hey, Rose" from the group.

"You'll be assisting Chef Dan," Lu says, walking me to-ward the prep table next to the flattop. Chef Dan wipes his hand on his apron and turns. He looks startled but shakes my hand, openly staring at my face.

"Nice to meet you, Rose. Have any experience in the kitchen?"

"Some."

"Then you're already ahead of the game." He gives me a smile that sends a wave of warmth through me. I know they had let him in on the sting. I smile back.

"What can I do to help?"

"I'm making stir-fried rice tonight, so I'm going to need the onions, mushrooms, and cabbage cut up."

"No problem." I get an apron from Lu, select a knife from the magnetic holder on the wall, and make my way to the prep table where the freshly washed veggies sit waiting for me. I start with the onions since I know Chef Dan likes to get them on the flat-top first. Between each onion, I look around the room. Sylvie and her mom are making batter for cookies in the colossal floor mixer. Roman brings the salad bar crocks from the cooler to the prep table, where a cutting board and knife await. He is three feet away from me, rolling his eyes as Lu gives him specific and detailed instructions on what to do with the produce in the crocks. He ignores me. So far, so good.

"This is our version of cleaning out the fridge and doing something creative with the leftovers." Lu is saying. "I need you to empty each crock into a prep bowl." She waits for him to do something. Anything. "The prep bowls are under the table."

"I know."

"Get the prep bowls." She waits for him to reach down under the table and pick up a stack of stainless steel bowls. "Now, examine the contents in the crocks to make sure everything is still good." Again, she waits, but Roman does nothing. Lu sighs. "Pour the crock of carrot sticks into the prep bowl, Roman." He dumps the crock then returns it to the table with a loud thump. "Inspect the carrots. Are they discolored or soft? If so, throw them away." Roman extends a tentative finger, gives the carrot sticks in the bowl a half-hearted stir, and then shrugs. "They're fine," Lu prompts him. "Now they need to be diced on the cutting board and returned to the bowl so Chef Dan can easily add the carrots to his recipe. Once all of the crocks are empty, take them to the dishwashers."

"Where's the pudding?"

I stop cutting and look up when I hear Roman's question. Lu takes a breath, and I imagine she's counting to ten. "What are you talking about?"

"The bowl with the pudding in it."

We're a camp that caters to children and teens, so of course, we have chocolate pudding on the salad bar when we have campers. The staff rarely touches the stuff, so when it's just us, we don't bother to put it out.

"We emptied it after yesterday's dinner, remember? I told you to scrape the crock out with a spatula and take it to the washroom."

"Yeah, but it was still good, so I put some plastic wrap on it and put it back in the fridge. No use wasting it. We can just add more to it."

Lu's look is horrified. "No, we can't. We've talked about this. We replace the pudding crock every day. After dinner service, you get a new crock, put freshly made pudding in it, and put that new crock into the salad bar."

From his shrug, I can tell that he hasn't done that. I lower my eyes and go back to working my way through the last half-dozen onions.

"We do the things we do for a reason. You took the food-handling class. You know the steps that we take are to keep bacteria from building up and people from getting sick."

Roman mutters something about just asking where the pudding was.

"Stop with the pudding! It has nothing to do with what you're working on right now." Roman doesn't answer, and I'm not watching, but I imagine his usual shrug. "Get these crocks emptied and inspected." Lu continues. "I'll be coming along after you to double-check your work. I shouldn't have to do that. You should be able to follow simple instructions." I see Lu disappearing into the walk-in, and I know she is hunting down that pudding crock to deliver to the dishwashers. Roman mutters something under his breath, but I can't make out what he says.

I set the bowl of onion slices on Chef-Dan's prep counter next to the flat top. "Onions are done." Then I go back to the station to start on the mushrooms. They don't smell right. Mushrooms are earthy, but not this earthy. It is evident that someone, most likely Roman, poured the mushrooms from their flat directly into a prep bowl. Manure still clings to them.

I'm wrist-deep at the prep-sink, washing poopy mushrooms and tossing them into a colander as fast as I can when I hear Lu's frosty voice, "Why is Rose washing the mushrooms?" she asks Roman.

There's no answer, so I'm assuming a classic Roman shrug.

"You were supposed to wash them."

Again, silence

"Did you wash them?"

"They looked fine to me."

I imagine Lu grinding her teeth together. "Did you wash them?" When there is still no reply, she continues, "You have to clean mushrooms before we can use them. They grow in manure, and it clings to them."

"That's why I don't eat them."

Just a beat of silence on Lu's part then, "But other people do. This job is about others. Not about you. We prep and cook food for staff and campers, and we need to do our best for them."

"I'm staff."

I want to throw mushrooms at his head. He's the most frustrating person on the planet. Lu doesn't say anything, so Roman repeats, "I'm staff." I know where his brand of logic is taking him. He is trying to get Lu to agree with him that because he is staff, they should cook for his tastes. I turn just enough to catch Lu's eye and gave her a slight shake of the head. She isn't going to win this argument, not because Roman is too clever for her, he's deeply stupid, but because he won't admit when he's wrong. The worst thing she could do is lose her temper. He would see that as a win.

Lu catches my look and smiles. "Keep it up, and you won't be staff for long," she promises him as she sashays past me and out the kitchen door.

Roman's eyes follow her, and I see that her threat doesn't mean a thing to him. He's grinning. It's like I can see the gears working in his little-boy brain. He has no worries. He's a guy. He doesn't have to take orders from a girl supervisor.

I imagine my dad giving him a pat on the back.

$$\infty \infty \infty$$

If I could describe my brother in one word, it would be obnoxious. It was bad enough living with him, but working with him was a daily soul-suck.

At first, I blame my father. It is evident that in some ways, at least, Roman is trying to emulate him. After a few days, however, I can differentiate between his imitations and his personal brand of insufferableness.

That's a Jane Austen word, and it fits him to a "t." It might even replace "obnoxious."

I've started categorizing his insufferable obnoxiousness. Strangely enough, the least objectionable is when he acts like Dad — probably because he isn't armed with a giant spoon. Instead, his weapon is sharp sarcasm meant to raise psychological welts. He's learned to zone in on people's insecurities and make seemingly off-the-cuff statements or ask "innocent" questions to rattle their self-confidence. It's not sophisticated but still effective.

"Hey, Shaun, I was just wondering, what do you do on Father's Day? Do you take your mom out instead since she had to take over for him after he left? What? I was just asking!"

"I'd always heard that steam was good for the skin, but I guess you proved that isn't true. It seems like running the dishwasher all the time makes you break out more, not less."

"Sylvie, you make great cookies, but you might want to

limit yourself. You don't want to get fat like your mom."

"Chef Dan, do you think you'd work out so much if you were married?"

I nearly bit my tongue bloody during that first week.

When he first started staring at me, I thought he recognized me, but instead, he asked me, "Do you wear your hair like that because you'd rather be a boy?"

With my dark-fringed lashes, lip gloss, and feminine top, I knew I didn't look anything like a boy. It was just his way of trying to get under my skin. "I wear it like this because it's easy to take care of."

"So you can spend more time piling on the makeup? What are you hiding under there, anyway?"

I wanted to come up with something witty to say, but nothing was coming to me. Finally, from the bakery, Ms. Denise said, "I think she looks great."

"Thanks!"

Roman muttered under his breath, "Maybe she could give you some tips." I'm not sure if he was directing that at Ms. Denise or me.

His next level of obnoxiousness is when he acts like himself. He hums in staff meetings, just low enough to clarify that he's not taking anything said seriously. He also imitates people's walks and voices and makes up embarrassing scenarios for them, performing strange little skits whenever the object of his scorn is out of the room.

"Where's Chef Dan?" he asks, coming out of the walk-in. No one answers him because we know what is next. "Did he leave to go to the bathroom?" Again no answer, but that didn't stop him. "Oh, after all those protein shakes and salads, I'm going to be here for a while!" His crude imitation sounded more like Arnold Schwarzenegger than Chef Dan. "And how will I wipe when my big, overgrown muscles keep getting in the way?"

I'm embarrassed for my brother as he stands in the middle of the kitchen, miming a bodybuilder attempting to wipe his bottom. Not only did no one find it funny, but most of the workers also kept their eyes averted. Ms. Denise is angry and about to say something when Chef Dan comes up behind Roman.

"What are you doing?" Chef Dan looked like he already had a pretty good idea of what was going on.

"Nothing. Had an itch. How'd it go with you?"

"Get back to work."

"Yes, sir!" A mock salute, and off he goes to haul another flat of produce out of the walk-in.

That brings me to his highest level of ick — when he hangs out with Jack.

My Jack.

The boy I spent the last nine months dreaming I'd marry. One day watching him and Roman interacting, and I know it's over. I want nothing to do with either of them.

Jack finds Roman hilarious and gives him all the attention he craves. He doesn't participate himself, but he's the most receptive audience a comedian could desire. When Roman ratchets up the crazy, Jack laughs, egging him on until my brother is so out-of-control offensive, one of the managers or supervisors, or even Brother Topher himself, has to put a stop to it. When supervisors confront Roman, he opens his eyes wide and says, "What?" like he can't believe that anyone would think for a moment that he was doing anything wrong. Then, when the lecture is over, his grin is back, and he's basking in Jack's approving nod.

As I said, at first, I blamed my father for Roman's behavior, but I realized that I was doing the same thing as everyone else — assuming that good parenting made a good kid and bad parenting made a bad one.

Now I look at Roman and think, it's all you, Buddy-boy. You've decided to behave this way. You have the choice not to act like Dad, not to make fun of people, not to be virtually unemployable. It's all you — and I'm me.

Standing across from him at the prep table, resisting the

urge to throw watermelon rinds and stumps of romaine at him, I can't help but think I didn't turn out a decent human being because of my parents. But, I turned out okay despite them.

# Chapter Thirty-Two: Another Level of Freedom

"What are you going to do?" Lu asks after I tell her I'm over Jack.

"What do you mean?"

"You can't exactly break up face to face — at least not yet."

"Oh, that. No. All I have to do is this." I pull his contact up on my messaging app and type.

*Jack,*

*I want to thank you for being there for me during our senior year. Now that we've graduated, I think it's time for us to go our ways. I don't think marriage and a boyfriend are what I need right now. I wish you nothing but great things for your future, but I think we should break up.*

*-Julia*

I read the text to Lu, then hit send. "And that's it."

For once, Jack's response to one of my texts is immediate.

I show the lone, lowercase "k" to Lu, and we laugh, clanging our cans of diet strawberry soda together in celebration.

As I settle into bed that night, I wonder at my relief. I was the worst fiancée ever.

$\infty\infty\infty$

Two weeks later, the kitchen crew is starting to come together like a well-oiled machine. We churn out massive meals for two to three hundred campers a day. Then, on the weekends, we rush to get the work done in record time and enjoy most of the afternoons off.

There is only one problem — that squeakiest of wheels, Roman.

Lu has spent the past two weeks begging for insight from me. She's determined to "fix" Roman, but I told her he came from the factory defective. Lu doesn't believe me, and he becomes the focus of her job. Every time he messes up, usually on purpose, she takes it hard. I've never seen her so down.

This is my opportunity to be a better friend. I offer to go on walks with her. We go swimming. I listen while she rants. I buy the next case of soda for the mini-fridge — grape this time. I share my books.

Still, I know she cries at night when she thinks I'm asleep.

∞∞∞

Breakfast on Sundays is early, which means we are in the kitchen even earlier. Chef Dan keeps it simple. Muffins, fruit, yogurt, and coffee. Any complaints? Keep them to yourself, and be ready to get on one of the vans by 8:00.

The camp van sways and bumps as it carries us down the gravel road and onto the highway leading to town. Since the camp is the ministry of Crystal Falls Baptist Church, we all attend it during the summer months. The youth leaders and college and career teachers love having their numbers boosted by our sudden arrival in June. Now that I had maybe graduated, and I'm nineteen, I am in College and Career with most supervisors from the camp. It is nice getting to know them in a non-work setting. I sit with Lu, of course, and Sione goes out of his way to include me in their conversations.

I can't help feeling relieved, though confused, that Jack is in the youth group class. I can't help feeling that if he just looked at me — really looked at me — he'd know who I was. The most I ever got from him was a glance that made me feel equally relieved that he didn't recognize me and a little miffed that I was beneath his notice. He had told me once that he hated short hair on women, which might have something to do with it.

The College and Career director, Mr. Orange, is also a history professor at the community college. He loves the idea that the Bible comments on itself. He provides us with historical background and outside commentaries but always brings everything back to the Bible. I'm so busy with notes and cross-references and eye-opening revelations that I don't have the time, or even the desire, to write a sermon for myself. It's refreshing.

By the second hymn in the main service, I decided to join this kind of church. It reminds me of Nana's church. People are genuinely happy to be here, and it shows. They sing, they chat, and they listen to an engaging sermon that isn't full of hunting and sports metaphors but instead focuses on the teachings of Christ. I love it.

The only time I get distracted is when the sibilant whispering between Roman and Jack gets so loud that Brother Topher has to turn and give them both a look that quickly shuts them up.

"Hey, Rose!"

My eyes roll automatically toward the azure sky above the pines as Roman's voice follows me out of the back door of the mess hall. I'm looking forward to my two-hour break after being up at five for breakfast, attending church, and then getting right back to camp, working the lunch shift, and cleaning up. I don't have to return until dinner prep at four, and my bed is calling my name in a much more appealing way than Roman is.

I recognize his "playful" tone. I'm sure he's already done a warm-up of his newest act in the kitchen. I brace myself for another crack about my "boy hair" even as I step forward, intent on ignoring him.

"Rose!" he sings out, and I turn on the outside chance he has a message for me from Chef Dan or Lu. "Oh! It is you! I thought the kitchen had hired another guy!" He cackles and saunters back through the door. *What is wrong with him?*

Chef Dan is a quiet man, almost six-foot, blonde like a Viking, and covered in snaky muscles. He has happy deep-blue eyes and a close-cropped beard and mustache that are redder than the hair on his head. Dan doesn't say all that much but exudes calm, even in a busy and chaotic kitchen. He loves cooking, the ministry, and working out. Camp Galilee is a perfect place for him. He starts every morning lifting weights with some of the other staff guys at their gym next to the stables. Then, when he isn't making three meals a day, doing the ordering, and setting up cooking activities for campers, he's hiking on one of the trails, paddling a canoe, swimming, or riding a bike. The guy is always on the go and one of the most pleasant people you could meet. You wouldn't know that if you saw his face now.

Lu brushes by me as I return to work for the dinner service. I reach for her arm, but she shakes me off on her way out the door. I feel like I'm pushing against a wall of stress as I quietly slip my apron on and clock in for my shift. I try to be as unobtrusive as possible.

There are some behaviors you never forget.

I'm surprised to hear Chef's voice risen above his usual

quiet, conversational tone. He's not yelling, but he's louder than usual. I check the whiteboard for stuff I need to prep, keeping my back to Chef and Roman while keeping my ears open.

"I've been listening to you run your mouth since you got here. It's time for you to shut it and listen. That young lady," Chef Dan gestures toward the door through which Lu had exited, "Is one of the best workers I've ever had. It's why I hand-picked her to be the kitchen and dining room supervisor. She's doing a great job, and that's not easy since she has to put up with you. You don't know as much as you think you do. You are far, far out of your skill-set working in here."

"Then maybe I shouldn't work in the kitchen. Instead, I could work in the stables."

"The stables don't want you."

"Maintenance?" My brother sounds confused.

"They don't want you either."

For once, Roman is at a loss for words. Chef Dan doesn't say anything either. I sneak past them to get lettuce from the walk-in. Chef is standing with his knuckles resting on the prep table, staring at Roman, waiting for him to "get it."

He doesn't. "The pool?"

At that, Chef Dan lets out a bark of a laugh. "Not the pool. I suggest you avoid the pool area altogether."

"Why?"

"Because you've been nothing but rude to the supervisor's girlfriend."

"Who's his girlfriend?"

I see a glimmer of a smile on Roman's face and realize he's playing with Chef Dan. Unfortunately for Roman, Chef Dan realizes it too. The tall man straightens and turns away long enough to turn off his grill.

"Tell you what. You don't have to finish refilling the crocks ..."

"Good!"

"And you can go pack up your stuff."

"Why?"

"You know why. Go."

"I don't know why."

"You're fired."

Roman's smile is enormous. "So I can ask at the stables if I can work there?"

"No." Chef Dan's words are slow and deliberate as if he could make Roman understand if he just made himself clear. "You are fired from Camp Galilee. I'm sending you home."

That's the key. Roman's face blanches white. "Fine." His voice is brittle, touched with anger. "I'll do the job." He starts jamming uncleaned, uncut carrots into a crock.

"You don't have a job here anymore. Go pack up your stuff. We'll get someone to drive you to the bus station."

"No. I'm sorry, okay? I'll do whatever Lu-ser says."

In his frustration, he doesn't notice that his nickname for Lu slipped out.

"'Lu-ser'?" Chef Dan repeats back to him. "Are you talking about your supervisor who begged me to keep you on just a little longer to see if she could train you? Is that the 'loser' to whom you're referring? I was ready to fire you on day three, but Lu thought she could train you, and I wanted her to have the opportunity to try. I've got to say, I'm impressed. With her. You threw up brick wall after brick wall, and she kept at you, trying to help you see what you needed to do to become a successful worker. In my book, she didn't fail. You did. We can't keep babysitting you. We have work to do." Chef Dan turns his back, a final dismissal.

Roman tries to get back to filling salad bar crocks one more time, but he doesn't have the skills even after three weeks. He never pays attention to Lu when she gives him instructions, so every move he makes is haphazard. But at least he's moving. I glance over to look at his face.

That expression of anger is touched with terror and gives me hope that maybe he isn't as hard-hearted (headed?) as he seems. But I'm also a little sad for him. I wonder what life will be like for Roman now that I'm not home.

He silently appeals to Sylvie, and I wonder if there's something between them. She doesn't look angry or disgusted by Roman. Instead, she seems embarrassed for him. She doesn't say anything, though.

He shoots a single glance at me, and I wonder if this is the day he finally recognizes me. I guess not. He can't see past my "boy hair" and "heavy" makeup. He looks back at the crocks and seems to remember something. Roman rummages through a drawer for a peeler, lays it on the prep table, then heads for the storage room for something.

"You sure he's your brother?" Chef Dan mutters just loud enough for me to hear where I'm washing heads of romaine.

"Yes."

"Did your parents drop him on his head?"

I try to stifle a laugh and end up snotting a little. I turn off the water and head for the tissues. "Not that I can remember."

"How'd they do such a great job with you and not with him?"

I hate this avenue of logic: great kid = great parenting.

"It wasn't my parents." I throw my tissue away and wash my hands.

"Oh — sorry. Your, uh, guardians, then?"

Chef doesn't notice my head shaking because we hear Roman at the back door talking to Jack.

"Oh, good grief," I hear Chef mutter. "I'm stepping out for a minute. I can't deal with these two idiots right now."

My stupid heart stutters a bit when Jack strides in, followed by a puppy-like Roman. He looks good. A slight tan already. It brings out the crystal blue of his eyes under his almost black hair. "Yeah, I can talk to Frank about you working with me," he's saying to Roman, then, "Hey, Sylvie."

Sylvie blushes a deep red and looks up long enough to give him a shy smile and a quiet "Hi" before continuing to drop cookie dough onto baking sheets.

"Thanks." Roman's fear about going home is replaced with frustration that Sylvie responds to Jack but not to him. "What kind of cookies are those?" he asks, obviously trying to piggyback on Jack's conversation.

"Chocolate-chip." Sylvie gestures to the noticeable chocolate studded dough.

"My favorite."

Jack goes straight for the kill. "I thought snickerdoodles were your favorite. That's what you told her the last time she was making cookies." I know the two play-fight with each other all the time, but there is a quiet viciousness from Jack that I've never noticed before.

Sylvie smiles but keeps her head lowered. I can tell she's just trying to get her work done. She doesn't want to be a part of their drama. Roman glares at her and turns back toward our prep table. He doesn't see Jack slip a crookedly folded piece of paper under the laminated recipe on Sylvie's workstation.

I see it.

Roman isn't happy with how his life is shaping up and shows it by setting a few partially peeled carrots on a cutting board and cutting them into haphazard chunks with overly aggressive overhand chops. I check to make sure his hands are off the cutting board, and when I see they're clear, I don't interfere. Jack joins him, leaning his elbows on the prep table so he can face Sylvie.

"Why do you have to do that?" Roman complains as he loudly bangs the knife through an innocent carrot and into the board.

"Do what?" Even with my head down, I can hear the teasing smile in Jack's voice.

Now, Roman's voice lowers, "Embarrass me like that in front of Sylvie." Bang! Bang!

"You're embarrassing yourself."

A carrot rolls off the board and into the nearby trash. For some reason, Roman fishes it out, moaning at all of the garbage clinging to the outside of it.

Jack turns long enough to say, "That's nasty."

Roman throws it back into the trash and wipes his hand on his apron. "Why are you in here, anyway?"

"You asked me to come in and talk to Chef Dan about you transferring to the stables, remember?"

"He's not here."

"Then I guess I'm here to keep you company, Bro."

Chef Dan comes back, shaking his head, when he notices Jack hanging out at the prep station. He ignores him and moves to where I'm arranging the crescents of cantaloupe on the fruit tray and picks one up to taste. "That's good," Chef Dan says. I'm still uncomfortable with Jack's presence, so I don't say anything. Instead, I nod and haul a watermelon to the cutting board in front of me.

"Aren't you engaged to my sister?" Roman's suddenly loud voice crashes against every wall of our kitchen.

Everything stops. My knife hovers above the watermelon, and I stare in horror at the tableau before me. Chef Dan is staring at me, nearly choking on his mouthful of cantaloupe. Roman is looking past Jack at Sylvie. I know he's watching for her reaction to his bombshell. Sylvie is giving Jack a look that speaks of utter betrayal, and Jack's face has gone from being furious at being called out to sly to pseudo-sad in the fraction of a second, "I was — before she broke up with me." He drops his head and turns on his heel, muttering to Roman, "Have a good trip home." He turns back once to give Sylvie a sad puppy-dog look as he disappears out the door.

Sylvie stares after him, and I realize that she is completely taken in by him. Had I looked that idiotic? I knew I had.

I also knew I'd never look that way again.

I'm free, and it feels incredible.

# Chapter Thirty-Three: Taking Charge

By the time Lu and I are cleaning up after dinner, all the details are finalized. Chef Dan calls Lu and me into his office to give us the news. "Roman is going home, but not until next Saturday. We called his — your — parents, but they're out of town for this week, and they don't want Roman home alone. So they're going to pick him up on their way back to Sampson."

The thought of my parents showing up at the camp makes my skin shimmy. Lu must read my mind because she immediately begins to make plans. "That's no problem. Sione and I were planning to go into Crystal Falls on Saturday afternoon — you know, do our banking and have dinner together. We can go first thing in the morning instead and take Rose with us. Would you be willing to call us when Mr. and Mrs. Williams leave? Give us the 'all clear'?"

Chef Dan nods. "No problem. That's a good plan. I'll make sure you guys get your paychecks first thing in the morning." Usually, we get paid right after breakfast anyway, but it sounds like both Lu and Chef Dan are trying to hustle me out of camp at dawn.

As I listen to the two of them make plans, I realize I'm drifting again. I'm letting someone else make the big decisions while I sit silently. I clear my throat, and Lu breaks off mid-sentence to look at me. I don't know what I'm going to say, but I need to say something. It is my life, after all. It's time I start exerting myself.

"That's a good idea, Lu," I say lamely. I wrack my brain for a better plan, but I have nothing. Here, Lu is willing to give up her one day off to help me and I … And then it comes to me.

"Chef Dan, do you think it would be okay if Lu and I went into Crystal Falls on Friday night instead? We could stay at a hotel, and that way, Lu can sleep in on Saturday." I turn to her. "It's on me."

"That's doable. I'll run it by Brother Topher," Chef Dan says.

After the meeting, I can tell that Lu is relieved that there is an end in sight but frustrated that it isn't immediate. I know she's still beating herself up over not being able to train Roman. I think that bothers her more than anything. She's convinced that she's failed somehow.

We talk about it in our dorm. "Roman is not normal," I try to convince Lu. "He's always been willing to do whatever it takes to come out on top. The only thing he's ever been afraid of is my Father, and he learned long ago how to convince the man that he's close to perfect." Usually, by turning his attention to me as an alternate victim.

My words aren't enough to convince her. "Why couldn't Roman just do his job?"

"Because he doesn't want to. He can't see how it will benefit him."

"I can't wait until that butt-head is out of here!"

"Strong words, Lu. Strong words." I can't help laughing, and she finally smiles for the first time that day.

On Friday, the kitchen and dining hall are clean and deserted by seven, and I'm exhausted, but I practically run up the stairs to our dorm to change and pack my overnight bag. I've zipped it closed when I get a text from Nana. She's sent me her membership number for the hotel chain she frequents. I don't have a credit card, so I transferred some of my savings to Nana's account, and she made the reservations for the hotel. As a result, Lu and I get a discounted room, and Nana gets points. It's a win-win.

*Thanks so much, Nana!*

*No problem! Have a fabulous girls' weekend!*

At eight, Chef Dan pulls the camp van up at the foot of

our staircase. Sione jumps out of the passenger seat to carry our bags for us. He's sweet — one of the nicest guys I've ever met — but I think I've said that before.

No one says anything until we've made it onto the main road. I breathe a sigh of relief, and Lu laughs. "I feel like I'm in a spy movie," I tell her. "Sneaking away before the enemy captures me." I feel my smile fade, and things go blurry for a few seconds.

"Anyone up for ice cream?" Chef Dan offers.

Like we're going to say no.

We drive right by the hotel and into the downtown district of Crystal Falls. I wonder if every little mountain town has a historic district dedicated to gift shops and quaint restaurants.

The ice cream parlor is decorated in red and white striped wallpaper and shiny chrome tables. Sione and Chef Dan get banana splits the size of loaves of bread. I don't think I've eaten that much ice cream in my life. Lu gets a scoop of fresh strawberry, but I splurge for a hot-fudge brownie sundae.

Is there anything better than gooey hot fudge and brownie? No? Didn't think so.

The guys drop us off at our hotel. Because it's a chain, it looks almost the same as the one Nana and I stayed at in Dawes. It's really nice. However, Chef Dan insists on waiting until we've checked in before he and Sione wave goodbye.

Lu loves the place. I knew she would. We each claim a queen-sized bed, and I unpack my bag.

"What are you doing?"

I shrug at her. "Putting my stuff away."

"But we're only here for one night. Why bother?" Lu pops her overnight onto the luggage rack. "I'm just going to live out of my bag." Then she sighs. "I overpacked, per usual. I didn't know what I'd be in the mood to wear tomorrow." Lu unpacks two dresses and hang them in the closet, shaking out the wrinkles. I hang my new blue sundress next to hers as she flops on the bed and picks up the remote. "Want to watch a movie?"

"Sure. But I'm getting into jammies first."

"Good call."

We settle on the newer version of *Pride and Prejudice*. We decide it's good but not as good as the six-hour mini-series. By the time it's over, my eyes are heavy, and I'm ready to call it a night.

"What time is checkout?" Lu asks as she gets ready to set the alarm on her phone.

I've been waiting for her to ask this question. I grin at her like an idiot before saying, "Not until Sunday morning! Surprise!"

I can tell she's both pleased and excited. "Seriously? Two nights? That was okay with Brother Topher?"

"He said you deserved it. That you've been a trooper."

Lu goes quiet while the overwhelming thought floats through her mind. "So, tomorrow, we can really sleep in, I mean for as long as we want?" Sleep is the currency most desired at Camp Galilee, and Lu looks like she just inherited a Darcy-sized income.

"Well, until 1:00 at least."

"I doubt I'll sleep until 1:00 — wait — what's happening at 1:00?"

"Your regular Saturday date with Sione, except you'll have me tagging along. Unless you'd prefer I stay here. That wouldn't be a problem. I brought some books."

"Nah. Come with us. It will be fun."

We don't sleep until 1:00. We barely make it past 8:00 — the habit of waking early is hard to break. We decide to put on our swimsuits so we can hit the pool after the breakfast buffet. I love my swim shorts. They not only hide the scars on the backs of my legs, but they're also perfect to wear to and from the pool. I don't need to wrap a towel around my waist or wear a coverup. I throw a blouse over my shorts and swim top, and I'm dressed for breakfast. The buffet isn't as good as Chef Dan's, but then few things are. Still, we enjoy waffles — lots of waffles — and plenty of fresh fruit. We each grab a to-go cup of coffee and head out to digest on lounges by the pool.

I'm reading my new/old copy of *Catching Fire,* and Lu is eye-deep in *Tenant of Wildfell Hall.* After an hour in companionable silence, she drops her book to her stomach and turns her head to me.

"Can I ask you something?"

I set my bookmark and close the pages. "Sure."

"How can you afford this?" she makes a gesture at the hotel. "Two days?" she clarifies.

"I made some money when I helped at that wedding I told you about. And Nana has a membership that gets her good discounts."

"Still ..."

"By paying for two nights, I helped Nana get a free night the next time she makes a reservation, so I didn't mind doing it. Plus, I wanted to do something to let you know how much I appreciate all you've done for me. Not just at the camp but with helping me get out of Sampson, and being such a good friend. I wouldn't have made it through high school without you. Of course, work wouldn't be nearly as much fun either."

"That's just what friends do."

"I know. And so is this." I take a deep breath before I continue. "I'm trying to be better at this friend stuff. Not just taking all the time, but giving too."

"You don't have to be extravagant to prove your friendship."

"I know." I stand up and toss my book on the lounge. "But, one of the things I've learned from Nana is the importance of adding fun to my life." I don't expect the stings of tears in my eyes and nose and laugh it off. "I have a new life now, and I want to enjoy it. Let's swim."

∞ ∞ ∞

Lu's phone buzzes at 1:00 on the dot, and we head outside to find the camp van waiting for us. Sione didn't come alone. Chef Dan is driving, and Sione opens the front passenger door for me. "If you don't mind, I'd like to sit with Lu."

"I don't mind. Thank you." I haul myself up, careful to pull the skirt of my sundress around so it doesn't grab the seat and strangle me — girls who wear skirts and dresses understand the issue.

I end up plopping in the seat and wishing I was daintier, pulling the seat belt over my shoulder before I greet Chef Dan with a good afternoon.

"Having a good time so far?"

"Oh, yeah. We swam all morning.

"You have a little color."

"Do I?" I check the mirror on the visor. I smile at my reflection. There I am! The real me! The me I always wanted to be. My pixie cut frames my face with wispy bangs and brings out my eyes, boldly lined and mascaraed. And yes, I have color beneath my lightly applied foundation, powder, and blush. I close the mirror with a grin and turn to Chef Dan, who smiles back.

"Whatcha readin'?" He nods at the corner of the book peeking out from my purse.

"*Catching Fire.*"

"Oh. From the *Hunger Games* trilogy? Great books. Not so great movies. But I guess every book nerd thinks that. Hollywood hasn't seemed to catch on that we want a shot by shot remake of the the original texts."

"They do a pretty good job with Jane Austen's books."

"Yeah, they do. I wish the same respect for Austen were shown to other authors, though. They butchered *Twilight*. It made me embarrassed that I'd read the books, even though I like them. I thought Meyer's allusions to *Pride and Prejudice*, *Romeo and Juliet*, and *Wuthering Heights* were genius. Not sure about what she was trying to allude to in the last book, though. Left me stumped."

"I've only read the first book so far."

"And you're already reading another series?"

"I like to read several books at a time."

"Me too. It helps keep me focused. If one book gets slow, I put it aside, read something else, and then go back to it instead of trying to plow through it. I find that usually, the 'slow' issue is my mind drifting."

I nod. I'd never met anyone else who read my way. Even Lu insisted she could only concentrate on one book at a time. Mom discouraged me from it. She said my reading patterns were a sign of a confused and chaotic mind. But then, she said the same thing whenever I wanted to rearrange the furniture in my room. So I just hid my stacks the best I could and kept reading at least two at a time.

"Where do you guys want to eat?" Dan addresses the van in general.

None of us has a clear plan, so we start looking out the windows for a restaurant sign that inspires us.

And then there's a low "Ohhhh" from Chef Dan, and the van pulls smoothly into a parking spot. "You guys mind trying this place?" The sign over the outside dining area reads "Verdant." We all agree and hop out of the van.

I'm stepping down when Chef Dan is in front of me, his forehead crinkled. "Oh. I was going to get the door for you."

I reach back in for my purse. "Why?" I step back while he closes the door.

"Um — because It's the polite thing to do."

"Oh."

Lu snickers and I wonder If I offended Dan. "Sorry."

"You don't need to apologize," he says, half laughing. "Come on! Let's see what they have."

They have charcuterie boards with various smoked

meats and pickled vegetables paired with fresh salads topped with herbal dressings. Chef Dan and Sione barely come up for air, but Lu and I aren't much better. The breakfast waffles were a long time ago, and everything here is fantastic. When we finally push back, Chef Dan points out that the planters are all fresh herbs. When the waiter stops by to leave the check, Dan asks about them.

"We grow all our herbs and some vegetables — the tomatoes, carrots, cucumbers, radishes, spinach, and lettuce for the salads — they're all on the premises."

"That's really cool. So everything's in boxes?"

"Yes. And a greenhouse the owner put in a few years ago."

"Smart."

"Can I get anything else for you? Some dessert?"

"Sure, what do you have?"

I guess Chef Dan doesn't hear the rest of us groan. I'm stuffed.

But when the berry cheesecake arrives, we squeeze it in.

"Oh, yeah. We also have a wild berry patch," the waiter says to Dan with a chuckle. "But it was here before the restaurant. The advantage of a town set in the middle of a forest."

We sit for longer than is comfortable because we're too full to move. I won't need to eat again until tomorrow. Sione shifts in his seat and pulls a paperback copy out of his jeans pocket. "I can't sit on that anymore."

"Louis L'Amore?" I ask. I've not heard of him.

"He wrote westerns," Sione says. "Good writer. Not deep, but enjoyable. And most of his books are small enough to be portable."

"Unlike this," I pull my hardback copy of *Catching Fire* out of my purse.

"Exactly. I can't fit that in my pocket."

Chef Dan taps his phone. "You guys need to embrace the digital age."

"Kindle app?" I ask.

"Yep."

"I have that too, but I still like bringing a book with me."

"Like a security blanket?" he teases.

I smile at his tone, then pull myself up short. I let the other three talk while I unravel that statement. Is it a security thing? I don't think it is. When I needed security the most, I wasn't allowed to carry a book with me. Not openly. If I had a book, it stayed deep in my school bag or purse. I usually didn't bother to take it out, even when I was alone and waiting for someone, knowing I'd be scolded for not paying attention and the fear of having it taken away.

But I always had one with me, even if I didn't read it. It felt good having one within easy reach. It made me feel in control — about one thing, at least.

Huh. It turns out it's a security thing after all.

# Chapter Thirty-Four: A Good Day

Chef Dan drops us at the entrance of the historic district then heads back to camp to prepare and serve dinner. "Let me get the door," he says as I reach for the latch. I drop my hand and watch him cross the front of the van to open the passenger door for me, holding it while I attempt to get out gracefully. Sione and Lu don't wait. They're already in the first store. "Hey, I wanted to apologize."

I turn to Chef Dan, surprised. "For what?"

"That crack I made about the book being your security blanket. I didn't mean to offend you. I was just messing around. I didn't mean anything by it."

"I wasn't offended."

"Oh. You got kinda quiet."

"I was thinking."

"About?"

"About what you said. I concluded that you were right. It is a security thing. Always has been. I just never thought about it before."

"But — you're not mad?"

That makes me laugh. Why in the world would I be mad about that? "Of course not!"

"Whew!" Then, "I have to get going, but I'll see you this evening, okay?"

"Okay." I take a few steps away from the van as he closes the door and gives me a wave before getting back in and driving away.

Sione and Lu come out of the sweet shop, and we pass a salon on our way to the toy shop to browse. I stop to read a poster in the salon window. "You can go on ahead," I say to Lu, and I walk back to the door and step inside before I can talk myself out of doing something I've always wanted to do.

Fifteen minutes later, I have sparkly aquamarine studs in my newly pierced earlobes.

Si and Lu are sitting on a bench outside. Lu is grinning, so happy for me. "Let's see 'em!" she demands, and I turn my head. "Oh, those are cute!"

I nod but can't say anything. All my words are stuck.

"Oh, hey, it's okay! You did it! You got your earrings." She dabs with soft fingertips at the tears that have escaped my eyes. "You're your own woman. You can have earrings if you want."

My inhale squeaks horribly, and it makes me chuckle. "I know." I try another breath in, and it shudders rather than squeaks. I'm making progress! "I know," I say with more confidence. "I like them."

"Good. Good for you."

"I'm happy, Lu." I mean the words, but somehow my brain has crossed its wires because the few tears turn into sobs while Lu pulls me close to cry on her shoulder. She repeats, "I know, I know," while she holds me.

When the storm passes, Sione stands so that I can sit on the bench next to Lu. I shake my head, embarrassed and apologetic. "I'm so sorry. I must look a mess." I dig my compact out of my purse and wipe away the tracks tears have cut through my foundation. Mascara is still good, though.

We carry on visiting nearly every store in the district, not talking about my mini-breakdown. By 5:00, my feet are killing me. I think Lu's are too because she readily agrees when I suggest we sit on the grass in the park. We attempt a conversation, but nothing sticks, and we silently agree that this is a perfect opportunity to read. I sit criss-cross applesauce with *Catching Fire* balanced on my ankles and enjoy the sunshiney breeze.

I don't look up until a man plops down next to me. I look

up in alarm, then relax when I see Chef Dan's kind smile. "Don't let me interrupt."

"Hey!" Sione says. "How'd dinner go?"

"Easy-Peasy."

"Really?" Lu looks skeptical.

"Nah. But it was slightly easier than pulling teeth. I missed having you ladies on my team tonight."

"Sorry," I say.

"Don't be. It's not your fault the team hasn't completely gelled."

"I feel like it is," Lu admits, and I see the worry on her face.

"I get it," Chef Dan assures her. "But you're doing an amazing job. You can't control another person's actions or determination to do wrong when the right way is obvious."

"Did he make much of a fuss when our parents picked him up?" Honestly, I don't think Roman will be the one who makes a scene. It will be my father.

"They haven't come yet."

I check the display on my phone. It's 7:30.

Chef Dan continues, "Brother Topher can't get through to them on their cells. He's wondering if they can't get a signal because they're coming through the mountains on their way to the camp. At this rate, though, they'll probably have to stay the night at the camp in a guest cabin. It's a good thing you planned for two nights in the hotel."

I nod and scramble to my feet when both Lu and Sione stand, jamming my book and phone back into my bag at the same time. Sione stretches, stifles a yawn, then says, "I'm starving."

I'm hungry but not starving. Wherever we go, I'll eat light. We end up at a pizza place with a salad bar. At first, I'm determined only to eat salad, but the pizza looks so amazing, I can't resist.

Is there anything better than really cheesy pizza? That tangy sauce paired with salty cheese and chewy crust? My one piece turns into three, and I make no apologies, not to my friends — and yes, these three wonderful people are my friends — and not to myself. I'm enjoying my dinner.

But now I'm stuffed. Pleasantly so.

I pay my share of the bill, then Lu and I head to the bathroom before leaving. I'm passing the waiters' station across from the kitchen when I see it.

An oversized wooden spoon and fork set is hanging on the wall over the cubicle where menus, plastic cups, and bundles of napkin-wrapped flatware are stored.

My stomach lurches, and I run the few steps to the women's room door. I make it to the toilet in time to vomit. Lu is standing behind me, holding my forehead as I wretch. She doesn't say anything, but it's a relief just having her near. I flush and heave and flush again until there's nothing left.

Lu whispers, "Do you think it was something you ate?"

I clamber to my feet, getting tripped up in the hem of my sundress. "No. Wooden spoon."

"What?"

"There's a wooden spoon over the wait station. Like the one Dad used."

"Oh!" From her tone, I knew I don't have to explain further.

While Lu goes into another stall, I rinse my mouth and wash my face at the sink. No touch-ups will repair the damage crying, vomiting, and sweating have done to my look. Avoiding my eye makeup, I use a paper towel to wipe away the streaky remains of foundation, blush, and powder. I look pale, but there's nothing I can do about it now.

I make way for Lu so she can use the sink. "How are you feeling now?" She asks. The concern on her face is genuine.

"Angry." It's the first thing that pops into my mind.

"Angry?"

"I had a good day. I was happy. I was with friends — if you can count a boss as a friend — and then everything was ruined by a stupid wooden spoon."

Lu turns to talk to me instead of my reflection. "Every-thing wasn't ruined. You still had a good day. You were still happy." She pulls me forward and points to me in the mirror. "You got your ears pierced — something you've wanted to do for ages. And, yes, a boss can be your friend — and maybe more than a friend."

All thoughts of the wooden spoon whoosh out of my mind. "What in the world are you talking about? Chef Dan is like thirty years old!"

Lu laughs at that. "No, he's not! Dan's twenty-four! He just looks older because of his beard — and maybe because of his muscles, but he's nowhere near thirty! And I think he likes you. Here, have a mint."

That non sequitur brings me back to my vomit situ-ation, and I gladly take the peppermint she offers.

"Has he said anything to you?" I whisper as we make our way back to our table, my eyes firmly on the tile floor, so I don't see the spoon again.

"No. And I won't say anything to Dan about you. I'm not trying to push you into a relationship, but I wanted you to know that a nice guy is attracted to you. That information should be a part of your 'good day.'"

I don't know what to do with that news, so I don't say anything. When Chef Dan opens the van door for me, I mutter, "Thanks," but wonder if that was a signal that he liked me or if it was him being polite. I'd heard of guys opening doors for women, Sione opened doors for Lu and me, but this was the first time a guy did it specifically for me. He opened it again when we got to the hotel and wished me a good night.

"We'll pick you up tomorrow at 9:00," Sione reminds us. They're going to stop by on the way to church to collect us. I nod, and Lu smiles up at him.

"Thanks! See you tomorrow!"

In the hotel room, Lu and I both toy with ideas for the evening's entertainment, but it's soon clear that neither of us has the energy to do anything but sleep. Our big "girls' weekend," and we're asleep by 10:00.

# Chapter Thirty-Five: Back at Camp

The alarms go off at 6:00, and we shower, dress, put on makeup, pack, and hit the breakfast bar before checking out. We're outside and waiting when the van arrives.

The van is full except for the passenger seat and space next to Sione. I feel my face warm when Chef Dan opens the door, and I realize he'd saved this spot specifically for me. I think I catch the sound of hooting from the very back of the vehicle, but I ignore it.

At the church, Lu grabs my elbow and hisses, "Come with me!" She walks me over to a giant pine tree near the end of the parking lot. I'm surprised to see the anger on her face. "He's still here!" she snarls. I turn to follow her line of sight, and my heart sinks when I see Roman exit the second van.

"Why?" I groan.

"Your — no HIS — parents never showed up. They sent an email saying they couldn't make it and to please make arrangements for Roman to stay until the end of the month."

"But, he was fired!"

"Yes, he was, but Brother Topher can't send a sixteen-year-old back to an empty house against the wishes of the minor's parents. Sione said that Brother Topher even contacted Dr. Jeffers to see if he'd take responsibility for Roman."

"I take it he said no."

"He said no and that if Brother Topher didn't drop it, the church would drop the camp."

"What does that mean?"

"No more campers or workers or financial support from Sampson. Jeffers even hinted at getting other churches to boycott."

"So he's staying."

"He's staying."

"What are we going to do?"

"I'm too angry to think right now." Then a scoff from Lu. "I'm too angry to even pray about it."

"Then let me." While the church lot fills, I pray for Lu, myself, the camp, and, finally, for Roman.

∞∞∞

Lu and I run into our dorm just long enough to pull our still-damp swimsuits out of our luggage so they can finish drying and then change into work clothes.

Chef Dan, Lu, and I are in the kitchen for staff lunch prep and cleanup afterward, so everything works smoothly.

We are out by 2:00, and Lu asks if I'll go swimming with her. Our suits, which had hung in the hotel bathroom for almost a full day and were still damp when we packed, had suddenly dried in the two hours we'd been at work. I pull on the swim shorts and tankini top, sliding into my flip-flops before following Lu down the stairs. I know that part of her hurry was to see Sione, but I am happy for her and don't mind tagging along.

I swim some laps while Lu hangs off the edge of the pool and talks to Sione. I've missed swimming. Now that I'm in the water every day, I'm working on perfecting the different strokes I learned when I had taken the Red Cross classes growing up. Dad had insisted we learn to swim correctly, but as soon as I hit puberty, I was suddenly not allowed to participate in "mixed bathing."

I first heard that phrase from a visiting preacher who condemned any family who allowed their children to participate in pool parties where "mixed bathing" was akin to letting them go to an orgy — his word, not mine. He also clarified that if girls were going to swim, they should dress modestly, wearing dark-colored t-shirts over their suits.

Dad wasn't taking any chances. Swimming became forbidden — for me. Roman could swim at his friends' homes and, I know for a fact, he went to several swim parties where — *gasp!* — girls were also invited.

Now, I'm flying! Okay, I'm swimming, but for me, swimming is like flying in the water. I'm weightless. I'm free. I delight in the push and pull of my muscles as they work against the water's tension. It's meditative, and I love every minute of it. This is what I'd wanted to feel when I played "anywhere but here." I've arrived.

I do a hundred laps, feeling great about my accomplishment, then sit on the pool's steps, watching Lu as she crosses the water using the front crawl. Now that I'm not moving, I shiver. I see a chaise lounge standing in a patch of sunlight. That looks like the perfect place to warm up. I get out, wrap a towel around me, grab my book, and stretch out.

I'm a few chapters in, but the book isn't grabbing me. I close it and look around, wondering what to do next.

Sione comes over to sit in the chair next to my lounge. Lu is the only person in the pool, and he can watch her — as a lifeguard — from here as easily as from his platform/chair.

"Ah, you must have finished *Catching Fire*," he notes, seeing *Mockingjay* book in my hand. "Liking it so far?"

"Not really. I liked the first two books better."

"Me too."

Lu switches to butterfly, a stroke I have yet to master, and Sione asks me what other books I brought with me. I tell him about shopping with Nana. "I'm jealous. Remind me of the bookstore's name at dinner some night so that I can write it down. I go to the university in Dawes, so I'll check it out when I go back in the fall. When you finish the books you brought, I've got some you can borrow, and the library in Crystal Falls is pretty great. I go every two weeks."

"Library?" Lu has finished her laps and is resting her

arms on the edge of the pool. "We're going next Saturday after we get paid. Do you want to go? Just for a couple of hours, though," she clarifies with a grin.

"And no historic district," Sione says. "We've done that to death. Instead, we can deposit our paychecks, go to the library, and have lunch at the Mexican restaurant afterward. Sound good?"

"Oh — well, it sounds great, but I don't want to butt in if it's a date."

Sione shrugs. "We have to have a chaperone anyway, and you're not annoying, so that's a plus." He smiles at me and wriggles his eyebrows at Lu, making her laugh. It's pretty evident that the two of them genuinely like each other.

"I'd love to join you. I promise not to be annoying."

"Don't make promises you can't keep," Lu teases and pushed off the wall to backstroke to the shallow end of the pool.

"You can invite Chef Dan if you want," Sione suggests, and I stare at him. "Or not. Whatever."

"Has he said anything to you?"

"Nope. Just making a suggestion."

"What does he ..." but before I can finish the question, Sione cuts me off.

"Nope. If you want to know something about Chef Dan, ask him. Lu and I won't be your go-betweens."

"No, you'll just invite us on your dates." I don't attempt to hide my sarcasm and am gratified when Sione laughs.

"Lu's glad to have you here." Sione's voice lowers as he changes the topic. "She told me the two of you have been close for a long time."

"I couldn't ask for a better friend."

Before I leave the pool, I hand Sione the bookmark with Twice Turned Books' information on it, keeping place temporarily with my finger. Then, on our way back to the dorm, I ask Lu how much Sione knows about me. I'm curious.

"That we've been best friends since we were eleven and

that we were in two different grades because you started school a year after I did. That we both love to read. That we planned to go to college together when you graduated. That you had a thing for Jack — which he does not get, by the way — and that your different look and different name are the results of hearing that Jack was hitting on somebody else, and you wanted to see him in action for yourself."

"What? That's not true!"

The look she gave me was genuinely perplexed. "Isn't it? I mean, at least partly? Why else would you be in disguise?"

"Duh! To help you out, remember? To keep tabs on what's been going on in the kitchen."

"But that's just the excuse we made up. I thought the real reason was so you could spy on Jack.

"No, actually, it was because of Roman. I didn't want him to call Dad and Mom to come to get me as soon as I showed up."

"Huh. Ms. Denise assumed it was because of Jack."

"Yeah, well, Ms. Denise thinks my parents 'did a great job' with me, so I wouldn't put too much stock in her instincts." It comes out harsher than I intend, and I can see the reproach in Lu's eyes. I try to backtrack immediately. "She's sweet, but she has no idea why I left home. I'm pretty sure she just assumed my parents were trying to keep me from Jack and sent me to live with Nana."

"How is your Nana?"

"Awesome as usual. She told me I could live with her as long as I want."

"How long will that be?"

"Not sure. Why?"

"Just wondering if you'd given any more thought to joining me at Palmdale. You know, now that Jack is in your rear-view mirror.

"What was he up to? Before I got here, I mean." I'm finally ready to hear it all.

"Other than encouraging Roman to act like a world-class butt-head? Mostly trying to get Sylvie to give him the time of day. I think she likes him, but her mom stays pretty close to her in the kitchen."

"I caught a look between them earlier."

"The sad puppy thing?"

"Yeah."

"He should get it trademarked."

"I think she's falling for it."

"It's pretty convincing — 'poor me, everyone's against me, only you can see the real me.'"

"I never felt sorry for him," I assure her.

"You didn't need to. Back in Sampson, he's the golden boy. Outside, he's the problem child."

"How did I never know that?"

"His good looks and charm blinded you," she says dryly. I don't answer, but my face warms with embarrassment. It is true. When he paid me the least little bit of attention, I didn't stop to think about his character. I was wowed by his height, the depth of his eyes, his firm jaw, and the way he moved so fluidly as a natural athlete. I couldn't believe that Jack was interested in a plain Jane like me when he had so much going for him. "He was a big fish in a small pond," Lu continues. "That's why I said you should wait until you get to college and get a better idea of how many types of guys there are in the real world."

"But you ended up with a guy you already knew," I protest.

"True. But it wasn't until I met some of the duds at college that I realized what I wanted in a guy."

"So — go to college so you can identify duds?"

"No." She pauses for a long time, and I don't prompt her to continue. I can tell she's thinking about what she wants to say. "Not every guy on campus is a dud. I don't mean that at all. But the losers make themselves — prominent. They practically yell when they talk about — well — anything. They are the first to chat up the girls at a party, but they always act like a first meeting is an interview process. I did make some friends my first year. We spent our time studying and talking quietly about important things. We sat in chapels together, took notes, and discussed what we'd learned afterward over coffee. The others — well, as soon as special speakers took the stage, they'd applaud and whistle and stamp their feet. They yelled, "Amen!" at every pause in the sermon, even if it wasn't about something spiritual or biblical. Afterward, they'd crowd the platform, trying to get a word with the visiting honorary doctors. Chapels were about networking to a lot of them."

"Yeah, I can't picture Sione doing that."

She gives me a slight smile. "Which is why I like him so much. He's real, but he's also spiritually-minded. I respect him."

"How does he feel about the group of friends you made?"

"What do you mean?"

"He's not jealous that you're talking with other guys at college?"

"Oh, good grief! No way! He's no control freak. Besides, he knows a couple of guys in the group — and their girlfriends. I'm the only 'single' in the bunch, and that's fine with me. I keep him posted on our conversations, usually while we have them, and they like hearing what he has to say and have me relay their messages to him. It's like Sione is part of the group too. So if you decide to attend Palmdale next year, they'll accept you as well."

"I don't see that happening. My Dad cleaned out my account, remember? So I'm not going to have enough for even the first semester, much less for four years."

"So — I take it we shouldn't have done our girls' weekend?"

"Why?

"You spent a lot of money on that hotel."

"It was less than you probably think, and it was worth every penny. Did you enjoy yourself?"

"Absolutely!"

"Feel rested and ready to conquer the world?"

"Um — not quite, but I'm ready to dominate your brother."

"Close enough."

"You could work your way through," Lu says, bringing us back to our college talk.

"If I can find a job that's still open on campus. It's kind of late in the year to start the application process."

"Late, but not too late."

"I'll think about it."

"Pray about it."

I don't say anything else, but when I step into the quietness of the shower, I thank God for hot water and then ask for His leading about college.

# Chapter Thirty-Six:
# His Next Target

"Hurry and get your shoes on! We've got to get downstairs to help transport the stew to the bonfire pit." Lu says, even though she can see me fumbling with my shoelaces. "There are s'mores for dessert," she teases in a sing-song voice.

I groan. "Of course, there are. I can't escape the curse of the s'mores."

"Not if you're working at a campground every summer."

Chef Dan's stew is better than any campground s'more, so I ignore the promised dessert and focus on his roast beef in a bowl, soaking up the gravy with a flaky buttermilk biscuit. It isn't a fancy meal, but it's scrumptious.

I don't stay long around the bonfire. Even after my relaxing weekend, I feel worn out. Tomorrow we are scheduled to get a busload of campers at 10:00. That means a busy morning setting up registration tables on the porch of the mess hall, complete with snack bags and bottles of water for our new arrivals. Kids come off buses like they haven't had food in a week. Lu and I will be down in the kitchen before 7:00, making trail mix and washing apples. I nudge Lu with my elbow. "I'm going to head back up to the room."

"Okay. See you in a bit."

The sun had set, and I kept my eye on the bouncing yellow ray from my flashlight. I give a little jump when a salamander saunters across my path and a big jump when a voice to my right says, "Hey."

My beam lights up Jack's face, and I quickly return it to the ground at my feet. "Hey." *So he's finally figured it out.*

"Going back to your dorm?"

"Yes."

"I'll walk with you."

"You don't need …" My voice fades into nothingness, and I wonder if this is when he'll finally confront me, asking me what I thought I was doing at Camp Galilee with my short hair and makeup and new clothes. Who did I think I was pretending to be? I'm genuinely surprised that my light beam holds steady. It should be shaking as much as my insides.

"I don't mind." He gestures for me to continue moving and falls in step. "I'm Jack, by the way."

I look at him sharply, but he's staring at the ground, obviously concentrating on where he puts his feet.

"I'm Rose."

"I know. It's a pretty name. Where are you from?"

"Um — Posting. Posting, California." It's not a lie. I live with my Nana now. He doesn't say anything, and I find myself curious to know what he tells people about himself. "How about you?"

"I'm from a little town about two hours away from here called Sampson."

"Like the guy in the Bible?"

"No. Like the guy who led troops during the Spanish-American War. A lot of these little mountain towns are named for military guys, haven't you noticed?"

"I have to admit I haven't."

"Yeah, Sampson, Prescott, Dawes, Decatur. Of course, Crystal Falls isn't named for a military guy — but Hamilton is. Although I guess that's a given."

I had no idea Jack knew so much about our state's towns. "You like history?"

"Yeah. I'm a history major at Dawes University."

"Really?" I keep my tone casual, but I'm thinking, "Liar, liar, pants on fire."

"Uh-huh. Where do you go?"

"I'm not in college. I just graduated high school."

"But — you're going to go to college, right?"

"I'm not sure. I've been toying around with the idea of working for a few years first."

"That's cool."

"It's necessary. Can't go to college without the cash to pay for it."

"True."

"So, how come you don't go to the college and career class at church?"

"Oh — uh — I'm just, you know, helping out the youth leaders."

"Ah."

Now that I've caught him in a lie (or two), I'm curious to see what else he'd make up. "Do you have a girlfriend at college?"

He gives me his dazzling grin, the one that used to make my knees shake, and I realize too late that he assumes I'm asking because he thinks I'm interested in him as a potential boyfriend.

"No. No girlfriend at college."

"Just focusing on your studies, huh?"

"No. It's not that. I do have a girlfriend — just not at college."

Okay, now I'm confused. I'd broken up with Jack. He doesn't have a girlfriend at all anymore. He continues, saying, "Actually, she's the reason I'm here." Finally, he stops and gives me an intense look augmented by the moon, filtering through the trees and the flashlight's glow. "I think she's pretty special, but I've been getting the impression that she's ready to move on."

I try to stop trembling as I wonder if he sees right through me. *Does he know it's me?* I break our eye contact. I don't want him to read the truth in my eyes, but I can't help asking, "What is she like?"

"Boy-crazy."

*What?*

He starts walking again and continues, "I think she wants to play the field a bit before she settles down. I've tried to talk to her about it, but she keeps pushing me away. Of course, it doesn't help that her parents don't like me all that much. They think she's so innocent and assume that I'm going to lead her astray. If they only knew what she was really like."

I keep my voice steady. "What is she really like?"

"She flirts with everyone. You've seen her in the kitchen making eyes at Roman. The guy's a total dweeb. He's from my hometown, so I know him pretty well. I introduced him to her, to be nice, you know? Next thing I knew — flirt city. I think it's the real reason Brother Topher fired Roman. He's not going to fire his own daughter, but Brother Topher can't exactly let that kind of flirting go unchecked, so he's getting rid of Roman. But if Roman goes, Nick and Andrew need to go next."

*He's talking about Sylvie!* I try to play it cool. I'm relieved it isn't me, but I'm ticked that he's dragging Sylvie's name through the mud like this. Sylvie is a lovely fourteen-year-old girl — much too young for Jack and too shy to be at all flirtatious.

"The dishwashers?"

"I'm telling you — she flirts with everyone."

"Then why are you trying to work things out with her? Why not just break up?" I ask the question even as I remind myself that this whole story is a giant load of manure.

"That's just it. I'm trying to, but Sylvie won't talk to me without other people around. I want to be a decent guy and break up privately, but ..." He lets his voice fade and stops, waiting for me to slow and face him. "Maybe you could say something."

That pulls me to a complete stop. "You want me to break up for you?"

"No. Nothing like that. Just tell her to meet me, I don't know, at the stables, maybe? After a dinner service. That way, it wouldn't interfere with either of our work schedules, and we could finally talk things out."

I start walking again. Jack's feet scramble under him, and he's back at my side before I've gone ten feet even though I'm stalking away as quickly as I can.

"Hey. Hey! What's the matter?"

"I'm not comfortable with this."

"With what? Asking my girlfriend to meet me at my job so I can break up with her privately?"

I'm not a violent person, but at this moment, I want to punch Jack's face until it's swollen like a balloon. I feel the heat in my face as I mentally interpret his seemingly innocent request. He wants me (his real former girlfriend/fiancée) to tell his fake girlfriend to meet him at the stables (near the edge of the woods) after work (when it's dark), so he can break up with her privately (when all of the other workers have gone to their cabins) and the two of them will be alone together.

Just like we are alone together right now.

The hair on my head raises with a tickle, and I run my hand through the shagginess of my outgrown pixie cut.

"By the way, I like your hair."

I speed up, thankful when the porch lights on the mess hall begin to twinkle through the trees.

"All the girls in Sampson wear their hair long. I mean, really long. Like they're still living in prairie days."

"Does Roman's sister have long hair?"

"Roman's sister?" He repeats the words guardedly.

"He said you were engaged to his sister. Does she have long hair?"

"Uh, yeah, but we're not engaged."

"Seems like a weird thing for him to say."

"Yeah. Well, Roman's family is messed up."

*That's true.* "How?"

"His sister is weird. No. That's not politically correct. She's mentally ill. It's sad. I don't think Roman knows how bad it is. *Huh. I'm mentally ill.*

"My senior year, she told everyone that we were engaged. When her parents told her to stop harassing me, she called the cops on them and told them they beat her. Fortunately, the same cops go to our church, so they knew better than to believe her."

"That's sad." The ridiculous lie is sad, not me. *I'm praising God every second that I'm not stuck with you, you compulsive liar.*

"Very sad," he agrees. "She got so bad this summer that they had to hospitalize her."

*Oh, good grief!*

"Roman doesn't know, though, so don't say anything. He thinks she ran away."

"Is that why you told him she left you?"

"Exactly." He seemed pleased that I'd paid attention to what had gone on in the kitchen when I'd first arrived. "Roman came to the camp to take her place. They couldn't trust her around the knives in the kitchen."

"Interesting. I'm going in now. Early day tomorrow." With that, I walk to the stairs at the back of the mess hall.

"So — will you do it?"

I sigh as I realize he's still following. "Do what?"

"Tell Sylvie to meet me."

"I don't think so. You'll have to break up with her in public." I'm three steps up when he pulls me back to the bottom by my elbow. "Hey! Let go of me!" I try to pull my elbow away, but his fingers have curled themselves into the flesh around my bone, pressing into the muscle and nerves. I gasp and try to yell, but the pain is so intense I can't catch my breath.

"You don't have to be so rude," he growls at me. Then, with a sudden flinging motion, my elbow flies up as if of its own accord and slams down on the railing, hitting squarely on the humorous. I pull my numb and aching arm to my chest. Jack fixes me with a wicked grin and melts into the shadows.

# Chapter Thirty-Seven: Ms. Denise

I push the door shut and lock it with a trembling hand. My string-tight nerves squash any plans for getting to sleep early, and I lie awake on my mattress. I give a little yelp when something crashes into the door, but Lu's voice pulls me to my feet immediately. I open the door for her.

"Why'd you lock it?" she complains, rubbing her shoulder. She'd gotten so used to turning the knob and entering at the same time that she'd run right into the door.

"Sorry," I mutter and get back in my bed. Now that Lu is here, I fall asleep.

∞∞∞

The alarm goes off at 5:00. Devotions, showers, hair, makeup, and dressing are all done in record time, and we're both downstairs by 6:30. I start my day hauling cases of bottled water from the storeroom and setting them on the walk-in floor, where they'll cool quickly. I wash my hands when I'm done and join Lu in the bakers' corner to help make the camp's trail mix. We combine roasted salted almonds, mini-chocolate chips, raisins, and pretzels in a giant mixing bowl, then scoop the mixture into individual snack bags. Working with the other women from the kitchen helps me move past last night's scary encounter with Jack. I especially love chatting with Ms. Denise and Sylvie.

Sylvie is a sweet girl, and I can't imagine her with Jack. I wonder if she even likes him or if that was just another one of his lies.

Ms. Denise asks us about our girls' weekend, and I mention that the only thing I wish we'd included was a trip to a salon for more than my ear piercing. "I didn't realize my hair would grow out so fast." I love the short do, but it's already starting to get out of control.

"I can cut it for you," Ms. Denise offers.

"Mom works at Tress Beautiful in Crystal Falls," Sylvie says with a smile.

Lu and I exchange a puzzled look. "You work at a salon?" I ask.

Ms. Denise nods. "Part-time. I have some time-slots open on Saturday, so I can book an appointment for you if you want."

"That would be great." I can't wait to get my pixie cut back.

"I didn't know you had a second job," Lu says.

"Oh, yeah. I've had two jobs for years. I love baking, but I was a cosmetologist before we came to work at the camp. I went to beauty school right out of high school and had been working my way up at a salon for years while Topher was away at college. After we got married and relocated to the city where he was hired as a youth pastor, we realized that there was no way we could live on his salary alone. So, I applied at the swankiest salon in town and got hired. I started at the bottom of the heap but worked my way up over time. I also offered deeply discounted or free haircuts in our home for Topher's fellow ministry workers."

"How did you end up baking at a summer camp?" Lu asked.

"The pastor of our church wanted the youth group to come here. He believed it was the best camp around, but it was pretty far away from where we lived and much more expensive than closer camps. Still, he insisted. So Topher and the youth group worked their heinies off, raising money so every kid in the youth group could go. I contributed as much as I could, including my vacation time, so I could help Topher take the kids to the campground. The beauty of this place struck us. It felt homey right from the beginning. We got our kids safely delivered to their cabins and had a little prayer time with them before we were off to enjoy different activities."

Ms. Denise gets quiet as she pinches the seal on another snack bag closed. No one says anything. We all know there is more story coming.

"That night at the campfire, we saw our old youth pastor." Ms. Denise takes a deep breath and exhales slowly. I know that move. She's calming herself. Without thinking, I reach out and cover her hand with my own. She turns her hand over and grasps my hand with a sad smile, then lets go to seal another bag.

"I'm going to share something with you girls. It's not a secret — just something I keep private until I know I can trust people with the information. I can trust you girls."

We all nod, assuring her that we're all trustworthy. Sylvie's eyes are enormous with anticipation and worry for her mother. I wonder if she already knows what her mother is about to say.

"My youth leader was a very charming man. My friends and I were heavily involved in his youth group, and we loved him and his family. When I was in my sophomore year of high school, my parents went through some financial difficulties. It caused a lot of stress in our home. Tempers were very short. While my parents scrambled to pay our bills and keep our house from going into foreclosure, I babysat to pay for youth group activities. That way, I could escape the dark cloud perpetually over our family. The problems lasted through my junior year, and I couldn't wait to get a 'real job.' The summer before my senior year was the worst. We sold my mom's car and had a huge yard sale where we got rid of just about everything we owned just to pay that month's mortgage. My parents told me that I wouldn't be graduating with the friends I'd gone to school with my whole life because they could no longer afford my Christian school's tuition. I understood, but it hurt just the same.

"Hanging out with my friends and attending youth group activities were my lifeline. When my youth pastor announced we would have free youth activities every Friday that summer, I was excited. When he offered me a weekly babysitting opportunity, I jumped at it. I'd be out of the house every Saturday night, and I'd get paid.

"These were the days before everyone had cellphones, so he'd call the house to remind me of our 'standing appointment' and chat for a few minutes. Then, he'd pick me up early, get me a drink or even a meal from a fast-food place before taking me to his house. Afterward, he'd drive me home and hand me an envelope with cash and a note thanking me for babysitting.

"Then he started slipping me notes even when I hadn't worked — at youth activities or church. Of course, there was always a little money included. And he started calling more, always during the day when he knew my parents were at work. Sometimes, he'd pick me up and take me for ice cream or a slushy. It felt good knowing that there was someone who cared about what I was going through."

I scoop some trail mix into a bag, trying to suppress the shiver going through me. This story is starting to sound familiar. It was one thing when I was getting notes from a cute guy at school (even if he turned out to be a jerk), but Ms. Denise is talking about an adult — her youth leader — her married youth leader — and it's creeping me out.

"It happened very quickly. He told me that his marriage was a mistake, that he had married outside of the will of God, and if he had just waited, he knew that God would have led him to me. He courted me, and because I was desperate for love and — to be honest — financial security — I fell for him. He convinced me that I was in love with him.

"He continued writing me notes. They were longer, more detailed. He talked about our future together. He said that he and his wife were married in name only. That they even had separate bedrooms, and he was lonely whenever the two of us were apart. He expected her to leave and return home to her parent's house any day, and then he and I could be together.

"He asked me to write notes back to him. 'Tell me that you miss me. About how much you love being with me. Tell me how I make you feel.' What I felt was awkward, writing down my innermost thoughts. Admitting that I liked it when he kissed me, touched me. I didn't add that it also made me feel incredibly guilty. We were doing the very things he preached against at every youth group meeting.

"At first, I felt a sense of pride that this leader of men was paying attention to me. Then guilt when I thought about his hands on my body and my body's automatic responses. The guilt was compounded by some of the stuff he said. He tended to be crude, and he laughed when he saw it made me uncomfortable. Then he'd hold me close and croon in my ear that he loved me until I relaxed again.

"Now I know that what he was doing was called 'grooming' or 'testing.' He was an adult in a position of power who was preparing a young and innocent girl for his sexual pleasure. It was manipulation pure and simple. I'm sharing this with you three so that you can understand what this grooming looks like." I see Ms. Denise flick a look at her daughter, and I realize that she's sharing her story primarily for Sylvie's benefit. Still, I pay close attention. The information is essential for all of us.

"Because he was a person I admired, a person I looked up to as a spiritual leader, I could not believe that what he was doing was harmful. Whenever I considered reporting him to the pastor or telling my parents or friends what was going on, I thought about what it would do to him and his reputation and career. I wasn't thinking about what this abusive relationship was doing to me.

"But I did worry about what people would think of me if they found out I was fooling around with the most dynamic youth pastor our church had ever employed.

"But then, when we were alone, he began saying that I was no longer 'pure,' but that it didn't matter since we were destined to be together. He wouldn't tell anyone that I was 'damaged goods.'"

Damaged goods. One of Mom's phrases. "I can see your bra strap. Put another t-shirt on. I'm not letting you out of this house looking like a piece of damaged goods!" I hated that. I look down at my soft gauzy blouse, cut to give my up-and-down shape the appearance of gentle curves, and once again, I'm thankful for my freedom.

"I shudder to think of how much control I would have given him over my life and body had everything not been exposed before mid-summer. He demanded more and more explicit notes. Finally, I slipped him one at the end of a Wednesday night service, which he immediately placed inside the cover of his Bible. I guess it fell out because his wife found it and confronted my mother with the evidence that I was 'stalking' her husband. What followed were some of the worst days of my life."

Oh! I can relate! Stupid notes! They did me in too! "I'm so sorry," I sympathize as I reach again for her still-busy hand and grasp it. "I know exactly what you went through," I assure her, then I bite my lip in concern. "How bad was it?"

Ms. Denise gives me a look that lets me know she appreciates my empathy and squeezes my hand in return. "It was bad. So much yelling and crying and blame. I felt like the biggest whore in the world. My father completely shut down, so upset as if I'd betrayed him personally, ruined the family name. Mom was more vocal. And more intent on learning everything that occurred. She demanded I tell her all that happened, no matter how embarrassing. When I mentioned his notes, she tore my room apart until she found his letters to me. She called our pastor and told him the other side of the story. She was still angry, but gradually, she became my advocate, demanding Pastor fire Mr. Rayne. Implying he should even be arrested.

"The 'arrested' stopped everyone in their tracks. Did my

youth pastor do something illegal? Was it really against the law for him to kiss and touch one of his sixteen-year-old students? What would an arrest or investigation do to his reputation as a pastor? To his family?

"While everyone debated what to do, the Raynes packed up their stuff and moved. They were gone by that Sunday. I was too broken up about the notes to go to church. I found out they were gone when my best friend called to see why I hadn't shown up for services."

I give a significant look at Lu. See, I'm not the only one who had to stay home because of a nasty beating.

"I was still so wrapped up in him that I cried when I heard he'd left town. It especially hurt when I heard that the excuse he gave in his resignation letter was that his wife was pregnant, and they were moving closer to her parents since she'd had trouble with her previous pregnancy. He'd told me they were sleeping apart and living as roommates. He'd lied to get me to do things he knew I wouldn't do otherwise.

"My home church was ready to call an end to the investigation. Mr. Rayne was gone, so everything could go back to normal. Except, I couldn't. My life was turned upside down. That's when Topher showed me who he really was. We'd known each other since preschool; we even had crushes on each other throughout our childhoods, but never at the same time. Now, he started coming around, always when my parents were home, to sit with me on the porch and play Uno, making me feel normal again — reassuring me that no adult had the right to touch me — putting the blame solely on Mr. Rayne. 'He used us both,' he'd say. He finally told me that he'd been going to counseling with Mr. Rayne, who made Topher feel like he didn't deserve to be around me — that he needed to let me go. It turned out Mr. Rayne was keeping Topher and me apart because he wanted me for himself.

"During our senior years, Topher continued at the Christian school we'd attended our whole lives, and me and my best friend, Cindy, went to Rhodes High, the public school. I blossomed that year. I'd already finished most of my required courses and took some that my little Christian school couldn't offer, like home economics and art. Then, in my second semester, I only had to attend in the mornings, so I checked out the local cosmetology school and started taking classes there in the afternoons. By the time I graduated, I was almost done with my certificate and already working part-time as a hair washer in a salon in downtown Rhodes.

"Topher and I spent the summer together before he went off to college, and I started working full-time at the salon. I made enough money to get an apartment near where I worked and put some away in savings. Topher and I dated whenever he was home from college, and when he graduated and got a job, he asked me to marry him. So, of course, I said yes. Not only did I love him, but he'd also proven that he would always be there for me. I wanted to do the same for him.

"I didn't mind being the breadwinner of our new little family. I wanted him to concentrate on his career, thankful that this was one youth group with a genuinely spiritual leader, not just a wolf in sheep's clothes. But I had a hard time with our head pastor. Something about him didn't sit right. He was, too — well — everything. Too loud, too boisterous, too braggy, too demanding. Topher was working insane hours and was on call 24/7. And then it was 'I want these kids going to Camp Galilee,' and Topher had to make it happen. But he did, and the kids were so excited.

"Then, on that first night, while sitting at the bonfire, Topher and I saw a couple sneaking off into the woods. Topher gave me this look like, 'Ugh, why me?' before getting up to follow them. I knew he was hoping that all he'd have to do is tell them to get back to the group. It wasn't that easy, though. The next thing I knew, Topher was back at my side with a shaking teen girl. 'Take our kids back to their cabins. This is Sasha. Take her with you. I'll be back as soon as I can. Pray for me.' We hadn't had the promised campfire treat yet, so everyone was confused and disappointed when I quietly told them we needed to head back to the cabins, and I'd explain everything shortly. No one argued, though. I kept my arm around Sasha's shoulders as we walked, listening to her weep and my mind racing about what must have happened to this poor girl."

"Back at the cabins, I put a blanket over her shoulders and gave her a bottle of water before addressing the youth group. 'I'm not exactly sure what is happening, but right now, Pastor Topher needs our prayers. That's all I got out before the kids formed little clumps and began praying together. It was a beautiful thing to see. They were a special group.

"It was a good hour before Topher returned. By that time, the sky was lit up with flashing blue and red lights, and he looked stressed. Behind him was a policewoman, looking grim. She knelt in front of Sasha and began whispering to her while Topher pulled me aside. The boy walking into the woods with Sasha wasn't a boy at all. It was her youth leader, Mr. Rayne. Topher called the police immediately and kept close to Mr. Rayne's side until they arrived. The camp director was furious with Topher and called our pastor, who yelled at Topher over the phone. Both said he'd gone 'out of order' for how to deal with a 'church issue.'

"Mrs. Rayne showed up at our cabins and began yelling at Topher for ruining her husband's life. Then she saw me and called me every name in the book. She told our youth group that I'd seduced her husband when I was a teen and that I was probably still a whore. She demanded that Sasha come with her, but the policewoman told her that Sasha would be coming with her, and Mrs. Rayne needed to leave our cabin immediately.

"I spent the rest of that evening telling our youth group what I've just told you and realized that this kind of behavior needed to be exposed or it would keep happening. I had just seen it repeated right in front of me. Unfortunately, Mr. Rayne didn't have to face any consequences after what he did to me, other than losing his job, and he just continued his behavior. I didn't sleep that night, wondering how many other girls he had abused. I believed with my whole heart that if no one stopped him, he'd do it again.

"The following day, our pastor showed up before breakfast. Mr. Rayne's pastor showed up next, followed by the pastor of Crystal Falls Baptist. You know him. Pastor Taylor. Pastor Taylor had just started. He was our age and the only one who sided with Topher. He was upset with the camp director for assuming that an attempted sexual assault was something he was qualified to address on his own instead of calling the police.

"The camp director was an older man who'd been here for years before Pastor Taylor took over Crystal Falls Baptist. He was belligerent, claiming that Pastor Taylor didn't understand how 'some of these girls act like little harlots.' Topher told me later that those words set Pastor Taylor off.

"He fired the camp director. The man was given a very generous severance for his years of service and a week to move off the property. Our pastor fired Topher and took over the youth group while at camp. The kids were heartbroken, and that made our pastor furious. He wanted them to forget that Topher and I even existed. The Taylors invited us to stay with them in their tiny apartment until everything settled down.

"We grew very close that week, and now I consider Kelly Taylor one of my closest friends. After getting to know us better, Pastor Taylor asked Topher if he wanted the camp director job. I was all for it. I could see Topher being a tremendous asset to this camp. We said yes. Topher stayed in Camp Galilee, learning the ropes, while I rented a car and returned home to give my two-week notice and pack up our apartment. We've been here ever since."

Lu's forehead is wrinkled as she asks, "Didn't it bother you to give up your career that way? Just pick up and move?"

Ms. Denise gives her a one-shoulder shrug. "I didn't give up my career. I left a job. I worked in the salon in Crystal Falls for two years before Sylvie was born. With a cosmetology license and my years of experience, I can work pretty much anywhere. The baking, though? That was a new thing for me. After Sylvie was born, I cut my hours at the salon and spent more time at the camp."

"Our baker was a sweet woman who was very encouraging to me as a new mom, so I gravitated to the baking corner to hang out with her and then started helping out, with Sylvie in a sling on my chest. Before long, I realized I enjoyed baking even more than my work at the salon — and I loved my work at the salon. Mrs. Luntz, our baker, told me not to think of the two career paths as 'either/or' but as me expanding my skill-set. That helped me clarify what I wanted."

"What did you want?" Lu wants to know.

"I wanted to have a successful marriage. I wanted to be an awesome mommy. I wanted to be a spiritual leader. I wanted to be a cosmetologist. I wanted to be a baker. With Mrs. Luntz's advice, I started viewing my life as a series of skill-sets and decided that I could be all of those things. I had Mrs. Luntz train me in the basics needed for our camp bakery, and then I did some online courses to learn more. I kept my cosmetology certificate up to date and continued working part-time at the salon in town. I spent quality time with my husband and daughter and worked with Kelly Taylor in her women's ministry at Crystal Falls Baptist. Sometimes all the pieces fall into place, sometimes they stick and have to be worked on, but overall, it's a balanced and full life. I'm a happy camper." She smiles at her own joke. We smile too, but Lu's forehead is still crinkled, and I'm still heavy inside, thinking about the beating Ms. Denise must have had to endure. Sylvie impulsively hugs her mom and tells her she's an awesome mom.

Skill-set mastered.

I continue my prep work, no longer worried about Sylvie. With a mom like Ms. Denise on her side, she's too intelligent and protected to be fooled by guys like Jack and Roman.

# Chapter Thirty-Eight: Rushing

Once we finish the trail mix, we help Chef Dan with breakfast. Sylvie and her mom whip up another batch of biscuits. Last night, I ate four of them with my stew, but my mouth is watering, thinking about having them again at breakfast. "I've got to get that recipe from you," I say to Ms. Denise as I haul a case of melons past her on my way to the prep table.

"I keep copies for normal batches in the office. I get a lot of requests from counselors at the end of their camp weeks."

"Maybe you should write a cookbook."

"There's an idea."

"Make that your winter project this year," Sylvie chimes in. "Another addition to your skill-set."

Chef Dan comes in with his yellow legal pad to-do list and says, "You guys making plans for winter projects already?"

"Mom's going to write a camp cookbook."

"I said I'd think about it," Ms. Denise clarifies, but she's grinning. "And I'll only do it if Sylvie promises to help out. I'm not doing it alone!" Then she gives her daughter a searching look. "It's about time you started building your own skill-sets, young lady."

That gets Sylvie buzzing with excitement and throwing out ideas of recipes to include. I slice honeydew and cantaloupe while Lu cracks eggs into a bowl and Chef Dan greases up the griddle. "What are you doing for your winter project, Dan?" Lu asks.

"I'm trying to talk Brother Topher into building a greenhouse, like the kind they have at Verdant. Even if we can't grow enough for the campers, we should raise plenty for the staff. He's given me the go-ahead to scout out locations and research crops, but there's no guarantee it will happen."

"I don't know," Ms. Denise said from the baking corner. "He seemed pretty excited about the idea the other day."

"He did?" Dan looks thrilled at the news.

"Oh, yeah. Topher even called his mom to get some suggestions about what to grow here. She ran a very successful garden center before she retired."

"I made an appointment to talk to the owner of Verdant. Think Topher would want to go?"

Ms. Denise smiles and nods, saying, "Why don't you ask and find out?"

I'm laying out peeled orange and green crescents of melon on a tray when I ask Chef Dan, "How are you going to get all of that done before you go home for the winter?"

Chef Dan pours a few ladlesful of scrambled eggs onto the flattop and fluffs them up with the constant movement of his spatula. "What do you mean? This is my home."

"Oh. You live here year-round?" I knew that the Stades lived permanently at the camp but wasn't sure who else did. Now I know one of the full-time resident workers is Chef Dan. "What do you do when there are no campers?"

"We have camps all year long — not as big or as busy as the summer program. When we have open weeks, we all pitch in to do maintenance."

Lu is slicing tomatoes for lunch and points at the gooey seeds littering her cutting board. "Of course, this winter, you'll be trying your hand at gardening. Want me to save these for you?"

Chef turns, rolls his eyes at her, then narrows them. "Hmmm. Maybe."

"Seriously?" Lu laughs.

"Maybe not those particular seeds, but it's something to think about." He stops moving the eggs long enough to jot something down on his legal pad.

I gesture with my elbow at the eggshells in the garbage. "Might want to save those too."

Dan turns to see what I'm talking about, and his forehead crinkles. "What?"

"The eggshells. They're great for starting seeds."

"Oh. I didn't know that." He again stirs the scrambled mounds of eggs on the flat top before making another note.

While placing trays of hot breakfast sandwiches on the buffet, I can see Brother Topher and Roman setting up the tables on the dining hall porch. I'd wondered why my brother hadn't shown up in the kitchen this morning, but I didn't miss him.

By 10:00, staff breakfast is over, and the clean-up is complete. We've set the tables up and loaded them with snacks and water. As each camper gets off their bus, they get sustenance, a cabin assignment, and a schedule that begins at 11:00 with a chapel service.

The week in the kitchen is busy but smooth. After Friday breakfast, the campers frantically try to pack and organize themselves enough to get on the busses before noon. Then, while Brother Topher, Roman, and Jack break down all of the tables, Lu and I scrub the dining hall floor. We put some music over the speakers and sing along while we work. When we finish, the dishwashers will wax and buff the entire hall.

"What are you doing this afternoon?" Lu asks.

"Not sure. My back is killing me. I might take a few Tylenol and crash." I'm glad our library trip isn't until tomorrow.

"Come swimming with me instead."

"Okay."

"Really?"

I laugh at her. "Yes. Swimming sounds great. It's almost as relaxing as a nap. I'm still taking Tylenol first, though."

The pool is a rectangular blue crystal reflecting the clear summer sky. The water envelops me in a cool embrace, streaming off my head and shoulders as I rise from my shallow dive.

"Oops! Mascara is running!" Lu is rubbing her eyes. I wear waterproof, but it tends to flake after an hour in the water. Lu reaches into her swim bag and pulls out a package of makeup removal cloths, handing me one and gently dabbing at her own eyes. I use mine without thinking, then haul myself out of the pool long enough to throw away our black-streaked wipes before using the steps to ease back into the shallow end.

In a boiling group, the guys from the stable come pouring through the pool gate, joined soon after by the guys from the kitchen. Lu and I swim into deeper water, continuing our conversation while we tread. Sione mounts the lifeguard chair, smiling in our direction and crooking a finger toward Lu, calling her to him silently.

"Be right back," she says while I stare after her.

Sione pulls off his sunglasses and tosses them into the water near Lu, nodding his head in my direction. Lu looks at me, her eyes widening as she pulls swift strokes to get back to my side.

"Put these on," she directs. I see a glimpse of myself in the mirrored lenses before I turn the glasses around and slip them over my eyes. Without my makeup and my hair slicked back wet, I look like the old me. I would be easily recognizable to my brother and my former "fiancé," who are among the guys in the group. I mouth "thanks" to Sione, who lifts his chin slightly in a cool-guy nod.

We swim the afternoon away. Sione lets us know when it is 4:00. Lu sticks to me like glue, standing between the crowd in the pool after I slip the glasses off my face and hand them to Lu to return to Sione and head back to my room, praying I won't see anyone on my way.

∞ ∞ ∞

We're doing cleanup after staff dinner when Chef Dan enlightens me about Roman's new job. "Brother Topher didn't feel like it would be fair for anyone else to have to deal with Roman, so he's made Roman his assistant. Roman's going to learn pretty quickly that Brother Topher works harder than anyone else here."

"I doubt very much that Roman will learn anything quickly." I say it like I'm joking. I'm not.

"Brother Topher is assuming that Roman will remain for the rest of the summer. That there will always be excuses made about why he should stay."

I nod. That sounds about right. I feel bad for Brother Topher, though.

"He won't be invited to come back again to work, though," Chef Dan says firmly. "This is it for Roman."

"Sorry."

"For what?"

"If I hadn't gotten in trouble, Roman wouldn't have been here this year."

"You don't need to apologize." He stops scraping the flat top and gives me a puzzled look. "You do that a lot, you know?"

"What?"

"Say you're sorry."

"Oh. Sorry."

"Now you're just messing with me."

I force a laugh, but the second sorry was a reflex, not a joke.

On Saturday, we serve breakfast to the staff and get the dining hall swept and mopped before lunch. Chef Dan makes sloppy joes while I set up the salad bar, and Lu begins cleaning the walk-ins. I break for lunch just long enough to inhale my sandwich, then head back to the kitchen to slice onions and mushrooms for tonight's stir-fried rice. As soon as everyone has finished using the salad bar, I set the crocks on the prep table and chop the leftover vegetables, putting them in a stainless steel bowl, ready for Chef Dan to toss onto the mounds of leftover rice we always seem to have.

As soon as the now-empty crocks are in the dishwashing room and I've wiped the prep table down for the thousandth time, Lu and I clock out and jog to our dorm to change. Finally, we get the afternoon off.

I'm exhausted, though. I've been rushing to get everything done so I can spend three hours in town. My back is killing me, and my feet are swollen. I take a few Tylenol and drink a bottle of water while I change. I slip off my tennies and sweat-soaked socks and put on a clean pair of jeans that don't smell like mop-water and kitchen cleaner before strapping on my sandals. For my blouse, though, I choose my fanciest new top from my and Nana's Walmart trip. It's a light green color with silver studs on the yoke. It floats right at my waistline and makes me look ultra-feminine. I double-check my sparkling blue studs and smile when I see that they don't clash with the color of my blouse.

I lay on my bed for a few minutes, taking all the pressure off my sore feet. I sink into the mattress and relax until a horn beeps outside, and Lu says, "The guys are here. Let's go!"

They drop us off at the salon, where Ms. Denise welcomes us with a smile and offers us a menu of the different services provided. While I sit waiting for my color to develop, I watch as Lu gets her feet massaged and her toes painted bright pink. I recheck the menu for information on pedicures. I've never had one, but my feet have been screaming at me nonstop for almost a month now. They could use a hot bath and a massage. I decide to splurge.

Sitting in a massage chair with my new strawberry blonde pixie cut, having the pain in my feet massaged gently away, I decide this isn't a splurge. It's a medical necessity. The muscles in my back are stretched and kneaded by the chair until I'm a puddle of relaxation. "Drink some water," Ms. Denise says as she materializes by my side with a cold bottle. "A good massage releases toxins, and you need to flush them out of your body." I down the bottle, relishing its sweet taste. I'm feeling good.

Lu texts the guys that we're ready while I pay my bill, tip Ms. Denise and the woman who gave me my pedicure, and go to the bathroom before we head out again.

The relaxation I'd achieved at the salon disappears like smoke in the wind. We race to the library, where I get a library card using the camp's address. It's my first library card. My mom didn't trust libraries. "You don't know what kind of books they may have on the shelves!" "You don't need to go into a place where half the books may be inappropriate." "It's a waste of time. You have books at home." And, of course, the ridiculous excuse of, "I don't know those librarians." Well, guess what, Mom? I actually do know one of the librarians! It turns out that Kelly Taylor, the pastor's wife, is the assistant librarian in Crystal Falls. She's not there today, though. It's her day off. I check out a pile of books that Lu and Sione recommend. I'm giddy.

Then we rush to the bank to deposit our paychecks. We slow down a hair to enjoy some stellar chips and salsa at the local Mexican restaurant, but I feel like I'm constantly rushing despite spending the afternoon with my friends.

Even back at camp, I don't slow down until after the dinner service. As soon as my duties are complete, I wish everyone in the kitchen goodnight and clock out.

Chef Dan looks surprised. "You're not going to the movie tonight?" Brother Topher has invited the staff to a movie night at the camp amphitheater to watch *The Wizard of Oz*. I'd planned to go — I've never seen *The Wizard of Oz* since Mom thought a movie about a wizard "Doesn't sound very nice." Unfortunately, I'd forgotten all about the film in the excitement of the day. I'm ready to drop, but I attempt to rally some enthusiasm.

"Um, sure. See you there."

I throw myself onto my bunk and set the alarm on my phone for 8:00 when it's finally dark enough to show a movie outside.

∞∞∞

I wake disoriented, wondering if it's morning or night when I remember that Chef Dan expects me to show up at the movie. I go to the bathroom, brush through my hair, and brush my teeth before slipping a hoodie on and heading out. The woods are lovely, "dark and deep," and eerily quiet despite all the summer staff currently on the grounds. I walk faster, remembering how Jack had come out of the dark just a couple of weeks ago. Fortunately, I make it to the amphitheater just as the opening credits start. I look for the familiar face of Lu in the reflected flicker coming from the screen and instead see Chef Dan turned to me with a smile, waving me over. He's been watching for me while Lu and Sione are already absorbed in the names on the screen.

"Popcorn?" Chef Dan offers.

"Thanks. Sorry, I'm late."

He responds with a humorless chuckle. "You don't need to apologize."

"Right. Sorry."

He doesn't say anything else but shakes his head and offers the popcorn bucket again.

The final frame flits into darkness, and camping lamps and flashlights blaze to life three long hours later. I'm ready to trudge back to my bunk when Brother Topher cheerily announces that hot chocolate and a sundae bar are available in the dining hall. I don't object out loud, but inside, I'm crying with exhaustion. Still, I let myself get swept along in the slow-moving exodus toward the promised sugar rush.

"You feeling okay?" Chef Dan quietly asks as he sits next

to me with a ceramic mug piled high with mini marshmallows.

"I'm fine. Just tired." I sip at my chocolate, topped with whipped cream.

"Maybe you should have skipped the movie," Chef Dan suggests.

"Honestly, I'd planned to make an early night of it."

"Why didn't you?"

"Well, because you asked if I was going to be there."

"And?"

"And I said I would."

"But — you could have easily said you weren't."

I shrug. It hadn't occurred to me to refuse. On the contrary, it was ingrained in me to:

Be there every time the church doors are open.

Be there for every youth activity.

Be there for every church event.

Be there for ...

Me?

No. What kind of person would I be if I abandoned those I cared about just because I was tired? I slug another swallow of hot chocolate and force a smile.

# Chapter Thirty-Nine: When is a Day Off Not a Day Off?

I have today off.

But it's Sunday.

A busy day even if I don't have to work.

I dismiss my alarm and groan as I push to get out of bed and into the shower. "Thank you, God, for hot water" has been my daily prayer for as long as I can remember.

Lu is already downstairs, putting the pre-packaged foods on the buffet for staff to grab and go on their way to the camp vans.

My feet are hurting again, but the baby pink nail polish looks cute on my swollen toes as I squeeze them into my sandals. I pull the black and purple dress I'd bought in Dawes over my head. I take a moment to revel in wearing so few clothes. A simple dress over a bra and panty set, and I can walk out the door. No heavy denim. No half-dozen layers of cotton t-shirts. Just blissful freedom.

I run a comb through my fresh pixie cut and smile at my reflection. There I am! I'm getting used to seeing the real me in the mirror.

Downstairs, I make myself a small cup of coffee — just enough to get me started — and stick a bottle of water and granola bar in my purse for later. Then, while I wait for everyone else to gather, I munch on a pink-lady apple.

Chef Dan bustles out of the kitchen, unplugs the coffee pot, and rolls down his sleeves, buttoning the cuffs as he scans the room. When he sees me, he answers my smile with one of his own and comes over. "Good morning! Get some rest last night?"

"Yes. You?"

"I'm feeling good. Are you ready to go?"

"Yup. Just waiting."

"Then, come on." He gestures for me to follow and leads me straight to the van, opening the passenger door for me and the sliding door for the staff piling into the back.

While everyone chats, I'm in the front next to Chef Dan, a guy I've known only as my boss for three years. Now, however, he's more — interesting.

Before I can think of something to say, Dan starts. "You live with your Nana?"

"Yes. In Posting, California."

"What do you do in Posting?"

"Not much yet. I helped a woman from her church get the place ready for her wedding and did some odds and ends for her. I was serving at the reception when I saw Brother Topher and Ms. Denise, and they invited me to return."

"I'm glad they did. I don't know what I would have done without you here this summer."

"Thanks." That was a nice thing to hear, but can I take a compliment with a simple "thanks"? No. I have to get all warm and shy.

"What are your plans for the off-season?" Dan wants to know. "Off-season" is camp talk for winter.

"I'm not sure. I'd planned to go to college, but I'm not sure if I can afford that now. So I might have to get an actual job and raise some cash first."

"I'll write you a recommendation — a glowing one — you shouldn't have a problem working wherever you want."

"Thanks." I will the newest flash of heat away from my face and add, "I appreciate you offering."

"Not a problem."

"What about you? Any news about the possible greenhouse?"

"I have an appointment with Brother Topher this afternoon, but I've been jotting down notes whenever something occurs to me. I think we can make quite a few cost-effective changes that will be beneficial to the camp." His tone is more excited than his words, and it makes me smile.

"How long have you been working at Camp Galilee?"

"This is my tenth year." He laughs at my surprised expression, probably not realizing that, in my mind, any possibility of the two of us developing any kind of relationship has just ended. There is no way he's twenty-four.

"My mom and I moved to Camp Galilee after my dad passed."

"Oh. I'm sorry."

He doesn't acknowledge my sympathy and continues, "He was the mechanic overseeing a fleet of busses and vehicles for a big church in Texas. My mom was one of the church secretaries. I was the typical staff kid who rode my bike all over the church grounds and got tagged for every grunge job there was. I hauled trash, moved furniture, shampooed carpets, basically, anything I was asked/told — to do. I was free labor."

"When Dad died, Mom discovered that he'd discontinued his life insurance policy. She wasn't sure if it was a faith thing — you know, 'God will take care of my family' — or if he just couldn't afford to make the payments."

"You know how you don't realize how poor you are when you're a kid? I had no idea until after it was me and Mom alone. That's when it hit me. The church offered to pay for my uniforms and curriculum fee for one more year at their school — my tuition was already free since Mom worked there full-time — but any chance of extras was out — no sports, no field trips, no camp. Her salary covered rent, but that was pretty much it. Most of our groceries came from the church pantry. Then, to 'show my appreciation,' I was expected to work for hours after school doing janitorial chores. It was way more than the occasional odd jobs; it was back-breaking full-time work. That was a rough year, but I had no idea what my mom was facing."

"Losing your dad must have been rough for her." Based on the context of Dan's story, I assumed that the father was someone they liked.

"She started making plans for us to leave, and I was so angry with her. I wasn't happy doing grunge work, but that church and school were the only life I'd ever known, and now she was all, 'We've got to get out of here, but don't tell anyone.'"

My scalp begins to prickle as the hair rises. I would recognize this change of tone in the story even if teenaged Dan didn't. "Somebody was — bothering — her," I stammer.

Dan takes his eyes off the road for a fraction of a second to flick a look at me. "Yes. There was a teaching — I'd never heard it from the pulpit, not ever — but my mom heard it plenty that year, and I had no idea."

"What teaching?"

"It was — weird. Have you ever heard anyone say that if a woman was divorced or widowed, she was considered the church's ward? So the church would take care of her?"

"I've heard of churches helping out widows. And the Bible teaches caring for widows."

"Okay, but this went a step further."

"In what way?"

He grimaces before he finally spits it out. "That the pastor takes over the responsibilities of the husband."

Silence settles between us. On my part, I'm filtering the information through my mind, wondering if I'd ever heard such a thing. I shake my head.

"I hadn't heard it either. A few years later, Mom told me that her boss, our pastor, had 'counseled' her on how she raised me, how she spent her money, even what she wore, and how she did her hair. The more time went on, the more personal he got, and that's when she started talking about 'getting out.'"

"How did she hear about Camp Galilee?"

"Pure luck? God's direction? She was Googling jobs for

church secretaries — it's all she'd ever done, and she wasn't quite ready to break the mold. Then, she saw an online ad for the camp. She sent her resume and a letter explaining our situation — being widowed and having a kid, not the pastor as husband thing — and the next weekend, we did a video interview with Brother Topher and Ms. Denise. As soon as school was out, Mom quit, and we drove to Arizona."

"It must have been hard leaving your friends that way."

"It was at first. I cried when we left, but none of my old friends were even talking to me within a month. I guess people assumed we left the church out of 'rebellion.'"

"One of the old stand-by excuses," I note.

"So stupid."

"Very."

"I don't get that vibe from this church," I say as we pull into the parking lot.

"Nope. This is a good one, praise God!"

Our conversation abruptly ends as he opens his door and hops out. The sliding door opens behind me, and the rest of the staff pour out, but Dan is waiting to open my door for me. It's sweet. Very sweet. And inappropriate for this older man to be paying so much attention to me. Then it all clicks into place. As soon as he opens the door, I blurt, "How old were you when you and your mom moved to camp?"

"I was fourteen."

I smile, feeling the relief pour through my veins. "And you started working right away?"

"Absolutely. Brother Topher encouraged me to try a little bit of everything my first year and paid me to do it! Eventually, I gravitated toward the kitchen. When I turned nineteen, the cook left, and we got a new one, but she ended up leaving too — mid-season — so I stepped in and proved I could do the job. I love it."

We are walking into the building when I remember something. "Wait! What happened to your mom? She's not at the camp, is she?" Even if I don't have much contact with some of the other departments, I know everyone, at least by sight.

"Nah, she left a couple of years ago. She got remarried to a nice guy. He owns a tire shop." Then he grins. "She's his receptionist now. Want to meet her?"

"I'd love to meet her someday."

"I meant now. She's right over there."

A pretty short redhead with deep blue eyes is waving at us and trying to extricate herself from a conversation so she can head our way. She gives Dan the biggest hug, which is kind of funny since he's over a foot taller than her and has to bend way down.

"Mom, this is Rose."

Dan's mom extends a hand, "It's so nice to meet you, Rose. I'm Donna."

Dan and Donna talk for a few minutes, including me, in their chat, and I realize that these are two people who genuinely love each other. Donna is nearly buzzing with happiness, and I find myself grinning at her. I know how she feels. Leaving a soul-crushing situation and experiencing freedom makes one giddy. I'm pleased to see her so excited years after her escape.

The lightness I felt when getting dressed this morning floods back. I resist the powerful urge to twirl in the foyer of this lovely church. Of course, I'd never do such a thing, but shouldn't we be happy in church? Excited? Airy, light, and free?

I say yes to all of the above. Dan and his mom hug and promise to talk again after the morning service, then Dan escorts me to our Sunday school room.

Sitting next to him, I let myself feel content, and I open my Bible, ready to learn.

I skip lunch after church. The euphoria of the morning hasn't worn off, but exhaustion is making my happy brain buzz with static. I just want to sleep. My feet scream when I peel off my sandals. I get as far as pulling my dress over my head and letting it settle in a puddle on the floor before crawling into my bunk. Then I sigh and haul myself to the bathroom to empty my bladder before I crash.

Under the blankets, I'm warm and comfortable, perfectly at peace when the screaming starts. There are no words, just angry elongated syllables emitting with flecks of foam from my father's distorted lips. He's coming for me, and he's going to kill me.

I wake in the dark, dripping sweat. I push the suffocating covers off and turn on my bedside lamp. I'm safe. In this empty dorm, I don't have to worry about being beaten.

Lurching to the bathroom, I step into the shower for a lukewarm sudsing, letting the smell of stress-sweat wash down the drain. I pray the whole time.

I'm thankful I'm out. That is not my life anymore. I'm living the life I want. I'm happy.

And then, out of nowhere, memories come slamming back to knock me off my feet. I can't always control my emotions, and I can never gauge what will set them off. My tiny blue studs sparkle in the bathroom mirror as I rub the towel over my wet hair. I see the red flush make its way up my chest to my throat, and I hitch a dry sob. I'm still embarrassed that I cried when I got my ears pierced. Only Lu would understand what that meant to me.

When Lu got her's pierced for her thirteenth birthday, she was excited and couldn't wait to show me her little gold heart-shaped studs. They were adorable, and I wanted some for myself, so I did some extra cleaning and made an elaborate dessert for dinner before asking Mom if I couldn't get my ears pierced too.

"No."

She didn't offer any explanation, and I knew better than to question her decision. But, that didn't stop me from wondering why. Mom's ears were pierced. So were the ears of most women at the church. And the girls at school, including every girl in my learning center. Mine were the only ones that weren't

A month later, an ear-piercing kiosk opened at Walmart, offering free piercing with the purchase of a pair of earrings. There was a pair of silver studs available for seven dollars. I had that in my babysitting funds at home.

"Mom," I gestured at the sign. Mom barely glanced at the counter before passing by. "I can pay for it myself...," I began when she stopped mid-aisle to glare at me.

"What did you say?"

"I — I can pay for it myself. I have the money at home." I stopped talking when I read the fury in her face. She stared me down, then handed me the key to the car.

"Go." She turned her back on me and continued shopping.

I knew I was in trouble and tried not to cry until I was safe in the back seat of the family car. I didn't know what I'd done wrong, but I knew it was bad. Really bad.

An hour later, Mom was pushing the cart toward me, and I jumped out of the car to open the trunk. Mom parked the cart near the vehicle, pulled the key out of the trunk lock, and swept past me to get into the driver's side. I loaded the groceries and returned the cart to the corral before hustling back to the car, too afraid to drag my feet.

Mom let me unload and put away the groceries at home while she had a "talk with your father." They appeared like magic as soon as I placed the last can on the pantry shelf.

Dad's hulking form blocked me from leaving the pantry, and I felt my belly clench, trying hard not to pee.

"You confronted your Mother in public?" It sounded like a question, but I knew better than to answer. Dad grabbed me by the shoulder and hauled me out. "You told her you could do what you want — despite the fact she told you no?"

"I — I didn't ..."

"And now, you call your mother a liar?"

I missed church the next day. On Monday, Lu asked how I felt. "Are you completely over the flu already? Was it just a twenty-four-hour bug?" I realized that my parents had lied about why I wasn't at church the day before. While walking laps on the field during P.E. that day, I told Lu the truth — even about my "spanking." I still didn't know the big deal about getting my ears pierced, but Lu decided that it was because my parents didn't want me to grow up.

"Dad said I was too independent," I say, finally connecting those two ideas. "Independence" was always paired with "rebellion" in my house.

"My dad says that about me too, but Mom says it's important for a woman to be independent," Lu assures me.

"I don't think my mom believes that."

"Probably not." We walk a few minutes in silence before Lu clarifies, "So you didn't have the flu?"

"No. I — had to stay home after — you know — getting in trouble." I wish for her to understand what I don't want to say.

"So you were grounded?"

I didn't correct her assumption. I was in bed, unable to move until the swelling on my thighs and butt went down. I sat on my sweater at school that day, trying to cushion my bottom without calling attention to my discomfort. The walking made it feel better, but I stiffened up again on the ride home. I never asked to get my ears pierced again. I even avoided looking at the jewelry cases as we passed by them in the store.

It didn't stop Dad from buying Mom pearl earrings for Christmas that year.

Now, looking at my reflection in the steamy mirror, I have little sparkles in my earlobes that proclaim my independence.

I run a comb through my shiny red hair and exit the bathroom. I stay in my towel until I put on my makeup — my skin has cleared up, so I skip the foundation and focus on moisturizing, powder, blush, a sweet pink eyeshadow, and, of course, my glorious mascara.

After dressing in jeans, a long-sleeved pink peasant blouse, a purple hoodie, and tennis shoes, I reach for the door to head on my way to the Sunday night bonfire when I stop short. I hear voices.

From the window near the door, I see Jack and Roman sitting on the bottom step. I can't understand what they're saying at first, but they're in an intense conversation. My hand drops from the doorknob. There is no way I'm opening the door right now. Very quietly, I turn the lock and back away, looking through the tiniest crack between the curtain and the window frame. As I still my breathing and racing heart, I can make out what they're saying. I'm shocked at the liberal peppering of curses and crude dialog passing between them.

Jack swears at Roman, accusing him of "blocking." Whatever that is. Roman's smarmy grin is wide. "Hey, it's not my fault Mom came home early! You had your chance!" Roman laughs like a hyena.

"Two can play the blocking game. Let's see how well you do with the next one." There is a challenge in Jack's voice.

"Shouldn't be a problem — except getting her alone. Her parents put the hell in helicopter."

"Clever. How long have you been waiting to work that into a conversation? Besides, a girl will find time to be alone with you when you do it right. So let her do all the work getting away from her parents."

"If you're talking about my sister, you hardly had to do anything. Mom always said she was a sex fiend."

"Anything but. Julia was as frigid as they come. I wasted a whole year with her."

"I never thought you'd pull the proposal trick."

"Didn't have a choice. She was all, 'Oh, I love you!' 'I want to spend my life with you!' Good grief. Just give it up already." Jack punches Roman on the arm a little too hard to be playful. "And then you go and ruin all that hard work by calling your mom."

"I swear I didn't! She came home early."

"I was this close to getting her upstairs."

"But you didn't, and I'm still ahead three to two."

"Ugh. I can't believe you got Polly."

"What can I say? She thinks I'm cute."

"The chick's a mental defective, but she's hot."

"Yes, I know." Roman's suggestive tone turns my stomach.

When the Stade family walk by on their way to the bonfire, Brother Topher invites the guys to walk with them. Roman answers with his fake look of wholesome innocence, but Jack turns a bit when he stands so I can see him rolling his eyes before turning back to Brother Topher. I wait for several minutes after they leave before I finally open the door.

I'm not sure what I just heard, but those two make me nervous. I decide to take the longer path to the bonfire, my eyes following the flashlight beam at my feet as I pick my way along the trail. I exit the woods next to the stables and move to the light and voices on the other side of a tiny, dense copse.

I dish out a bowl of stew and grab a couple of biscuits. My stomach growls, reminding me that I'd slept through lunch. Dan catches my eye and waves me over.

"Get some sleep?"

"Yes. Just woke up. I'm feeling much better."

"Good. I'm off tomorrow, but I don't think I'll be sleeping." Even in the dim light reflecting off his face from the campfire, I can see the excitement in his face.

"That right, you had your meeting with Brother Topher this afternoon," I remember. "I assume it went well?"

"Better than I ever expected. Brother Topher jumped at the idea of us growing some of our stuff. It will require a large initial investment, but we can do most of the manual labor ourselves. Eventually, it will be cost-effective. He likes the idea of our making the camp more self-sufficient." He chuckles like he can't contain his happiness. "He and I are going to Verdant tomorrow for lunch. I want to show him the place and talk to the owner to get some tips."

"That's great. Have you guys decided where you're going to put the greenhouse?"

"Not yet. I suggested near the kitchen, but Brother Topher would prefer a less-trafficked area. There are several little meadows throughout these woods that we could utilize. You know, make a bunch of smaller greenhouses that would fit in with the environment without having to clear big sections."

"Think about composting too. We could easily separate the trash in the dining hall into compostable materials."

Dan gives me a searching look. "You've done some gardening?"

"Every year." Part of my extensive chore list every spring break.

"Okay, so what do you need for composting?" He looks so eager that I don't mention that this might not be the best topic for dinner. Instead, I scrape the last bite of stew from the bottom of my bowl and shove it in before I begin.

"You'll need a place, a bin, in the shade and close by a water source, oh, and far away from where you might be able to smell it. Put all your kitchen scraps in it — well, the green stuff anyway. Add some brown stuff — paper, cardboard, woodchips — and stir it up and water it occasionally, and you'll have new soil in about a year." I can't help smiling at his excitement. His fingers are drumming on the sides of his bowl, and I get the impression he wishes he could write all this down. "We have plenty of kitchen scraps," I point out unnecessarily. We fill the kitchen dumpster a couple of times a week. I've wished we had a compost heap for years, but there was no need for one without a garden nearby. "All those trimmings from when we prep fruits and vegetables don't need to go anywhere near the trash. We could compost instead."

"Yes. That — that's good. Come on." Dan starts from his seat like he'd been sitting on a coiled spring. I follow him to Brother Topher, where I share my wealth of composting knowledge.

∞∞∞

I miss Dan the following day, but I love my time with Lu in charge of the kitchen. She's an excellent manager and lets us do what we do best. I'm slicing melon, regretting every rind I toss in the garbage. Dan's assistants are dishing up scrambled eggs and pulling trays of bacon out of the oven. Sylvie and Ms. Denise are making both their famous buttery biscuits and muffins with fresh blueberries.

The staff eats quickly, knowing that we have only a few hours before the next campers arrive. We've already made the snack bags and set up the registration tables. Water is chilling in the walk-ins.

"Okay," Lu calls us to attention after we've cleaned up after staff breakfast. "We need twenty-five rounds set up in the dining room. Lunch is macaroni and cheese and tostadas, with the usual salad bar and brownies for dessert. Campers are due at 11:00, so they'll start with lunch right after getting their cabin assignments, be prepared to have them trickle in as early as 11:15." She turns to me. "You might want to keep the salad bar in here until we're ready to serve." I nod, knowing that she's referring to the strange phenomenon of kids, and their counselors, grabbing carrot or celery sticks while waiting for lunch to officially start — as if sticking their hands into the crocks is perfectly acceptable.

While we start our assignments, Lu writes everything on the kitchen whiteboard. I head for the storage closet off the dining room and start rolling out the heavy tables. Andrew and Nick leave the dishwashing room to help me unfold the legs from the bottom of each table and set them up. Once twenty-five tables are in place, we pulled out the rack of folding chairs and set eight around each.

My back is aching, but the job continues. Andrew and Nick take their twenty-minute break while I stay behind to spray each table with cleaner, wiping them with terry cloth kitchen towels. I'd already swept the floor after breakfast, so the dining room is ready for the campers' arrival.

"It looks good," Lu says. "Take your twenty before you start on the salad bar."

"Thanks. I'm going to the dorm. Need anything?"

"My Chapstick, please. I left it on my nightstand."

"You got it."

I jog to my room. The faster I get there, the longer I can stay. I jam Lu's Chapstick into my pocket so I won't forget, set the timer on my phone, and swallow two Tylenol before I lay down on my bed to stretch out and let my back rest. Fifteen minutes later, I wake from a doze and dismiss the timer, jumping up to head back down to the kitchen, handing Lu her lip balm as I walk in the door.

We have two hundred campers and counselors and our fifty full and part-time staff, so I bring produce out by the flat. I start with making the lettuce mix for salad. I wash multiple heads of romaine and iceberg, two of purple cabbage, and a pound of carrots. I cut everything, dump the mix in a bucket and cover it with ice water, letting it sit. Meanwhile, I prepare more carrots and celery, cucumbers, broccoli, cauliflower, snap peas, mushrooms, bell peppers, and red onions. I regret every stump, root, and limp leaf I have to throw away. I hope the compost idea is adopted.

Once everything fresh is in its appropriate crock, I pour the salad mix into a large colander to let it drain. I get a giant stainless steel bowl, set it on a rolling cart, and dump an industrial-sized box of instant chocolate pudding into it, whisking in whole milk until it's smooth and soupy. I push the cart into the walk-in so it can thicken.

Now comes the easy stuff: pickles, olives, beets, and raisins, as well as a larger than usual bin of cheddar cheese shreds since we're having tostadas. I scoop the now-thickened pudding into its crock and set it in line with the others on the prep table before pouring the now-drained lettuce mix into its presentation bowl.

I notice that the tempo of the kitchen has picked up, and I step into the dining hall. There are already some guests milling about. I unplug the chilling table and roll it into the kitchen, where I assemble the salad bar.

Lu comes in as I finish. "The steam table is ready," she says to the cooks, and they pass by me with basins of mac-n-cheese and refried beans. Lu picks up the bin of tostada shells and follows them out, saying to me as she passes by, "The salad bar looks good. Need help getting it out?"

"If you could just get the door," I suggest, then move to the far end of the bar and push to roll it forward. Once it's in place, I plug it in again, then stand guard against a possible rush. I remain close by until Brother Topher has a chance to welcome the campers, give them instruction, and lead them in the blessing. When the people at the first table rise, I head back to the kitchen and down a water bottle.

Lu sticks her head in the door. "Rose! There's no liner in the garbage cans."

"Oh! Sorry!" I throw my empty bottle in the recycle can and grab a couple of trash bags. I've got them lined just in time for the first campers, who must have inhaled their food, to scrape their salad and tostada remains into the bins and shove their trays into the window for the dishwashers, who are waiting to begin their steamy job. I stand by, reminding campers to scrape their plates first and pointing out the tubs for silverware to soak. As soon as the garbage cans are three-quarters full, I haul the bag out, set it on the ground, and replace the liner. Only then do I tie up the old bag. Unfortunately, guests don't seem to notice when there is no liner in the bin and will chuck stuff in without looking — which means an extremely gross job for me later.

I'm walking two bags out to the dumpster when Brother Topher and Dan drive by on their way out of camp. They're off to their lunch at Verdant. I pray that God will give them insight into the greenhouses, gardens, and compost. As I stand back to get a good swing to lob the bag of garbage into the dumpster, I wonder how much of what I'm throwing away could be salvaged. Of course, it would be more work for me. I'd have to be constantly on point to ensure that the proper items went into the suitable cans, but it might be worth it.

An hour later, lunch is over, and cleanup begins. I start with covering and refrigerating the leftovers in the crocks. Then clean the salad bar and the steam table before wiping down each table and chair. By the time I've swept the dining hall, I'm ready to drop. I get a bottle of water and clock out. I've got a few hours off.

∞∞∞

Dinner is lasagna, so it's an easy prep for me. I top off crocks for the salad bar, then help the cooks by cutting thick slices of crusty loaves of Italian bread that came out of the bakery oven an hour ago and spreading them with garlic butter. I fill tray after tray to hit the ovens long enough for the butter to melt and brown.

After the last guest leaves for their program's evening chapel service, the staff gathers for their evening meal. I center a square of lasagna on my plate and nestle a piece of bread at its side. I skip the salad for now. Dan gives me a wave and gestures to the chair next to him with a questioning look. I head his way. Of course, I want to sit with him. Intelligent conversation with a genuinely lovely person? Sign me up!

Dan fills me in on his lunch with Brother Topher and their plans for bringing an agricultural element to Camp Galilee. I listen and nod while shoveling saucy lasagna into my mouth.

"Feel up to taking a walk with me tomorrow afternoon?" Dan asks.

"Sure. Where?"

"I'm going on the hunt for clearings we can use for

greenhouses. I'll ask Sione and Lu to join us; otherwise, it can look a little sketchy." Yes, a couple of workers taking off into the woods together can look suspicious.

I sit back, happily full but a little disappointed that now I have to get up and clean. It's like Dan can read my mind because he says, "You have a few minutes yet. Relax. Tell me what you did today."

"Same old, same old. Set up tables, did prep work, supervised lunch, cleaned, started a new book, did more prep, supervised dinner, procrastinated getting up after eating because I don't want to start cleaning ..."

"What book?"

"*Frankenstein.*"

"Like it?"

"I don't know. It's not what I expected. So far, it's letters from an explorer to his sister. He just met Victor Frankenstein in the Arctic, so I thought things were going to pick up, but then Victor starts his story with his parents' romance."

"He does backtrack. Or I should say, 'she' since the author was a woman. Anyway, stick with it."

"I will. The language is charming."

"Mary Shelley was only nineteen when she wrote that book."

"Same age I am now. Hard to believe."

"Talent knows no age."

"Who said that?"

"Um — me, I guess. I mean, I wasn't quoting anyone."

"I wish I had a talent like that." Did I? I hadn't thought of it before.

"What is your talent?"

"Not sure. Right now, I'm enjoying ..." I let my voice fade.

"Enjoying what?" Dan's forehead is crinkled, but he's smiling encouragingly.

"My freedom," I say simply.

I'm shocked to see his smile fade, and his eyes begin to

glisten.

"I'm glad," he whispers, then clears his throat. "I'm glad you're happy."

"I am. Well, I'd better get started." I push away from the table before things start getting awkward.

I put my dirty plate in the dishwashers' window, grab a clean one and assemble a salad without dressing. I cover it in cling film and set it on an upper shelf in the walk-in before I begin the last cleaning of the day. Two hours later, I've added ranch to my salad, and I'm eating from my chilled plate on the steps leading up to my dorm, enjoying the cool evening breeze.

As soon as I've finished the after-lunch clean-up the following day, I join Lu, Sione, and Dan on a trek through the woods. Dan seems to have an idea of where to go because we end up in a clearing just fifty yards from the camp's main road. It's a good size. Dan pulls a printed page from his front pocket and a tape measure from a clip on his belt. While he and Sione measure and take notes, Lu and I sit on a felled log and talk. Before we leave to hunt for the next location, Dan asks me where I'd put a compost bin. I choose a shady spot and remind him of the need for water. "Not a problem," he assures me. "We'll have to run an irrigation pipe anyway." And we're off and walking.

We find three other locations, none far from the main camp but hidden enough that most people wouldn't see them from the road or pathways.

We stumble on a patch of wild blackberries, and Dan hoots. We pick a few and pop them into our mouths, warm from the vine. Dan loves them, but I don't care for the watery tartness I always associate with berries. I prefer sweeter fruits like apples, oranges, and melons. Dan seems a little disappointed at my lackluster reaction to the blackberries, but as far as I'm concerned, he's excited enough for both of us. He's planning a blackberry shortcake for Saturday's staff lunch.

Dan is out of the kitchen for the rest of the week as soon as lunch is over. He and Brother Topher oversee the clearing of each glen and the building of compost bins at the future greenhouse sites.

Roman comes to every meal covered in dust and looking exhausted. He usually sits with Brother Topher and his family, but sometimes Jack joins them as well. They still hang out together, but now they're both working. They can be found at the stables in their off time, often with Sylvie joining them for go-carts and dirt-bike racing. Roman and Sylvie are googly-eyed over each other and have even gone on a double date with her parents, after which Roman and Jack didn't talk for a couple of days. The whole thing makes me uncomfortable, but as long as they're under the supervision of Frank, the head of the stables, and Brother Topher, I know Sylvie is safe.

Every two weeks, I deposit paychecks in my account like clockwork, taking out only enough to pay my tithe, going out for an occasional lunch with Dan, Lu, and Sione, and maintaining my short do. My daily hairstyling is five minutes at the most, but I get it trimmed every two weeks to keep it looking good. Of course, I also use that time to park myself in a massage chair to relieve the pain in my back while I treat my feet to a more hands-on experience.

Everything is going so well we don't see the bad stuff coming.

# Chapter Forty: The Bad Stuff

The staff has finally gelled — over a month later than it usually does — and now we're running the camp like it's a well-oiled machine. We're diligent cogs turning with perfect timing.

We get the campers on the buses in record time on Saturday, so Lu and I do a deep-clean on the walk-ins and store-room. Lu tasks Nick and Andrew with waxing the dining hall floor. The kitchen crew isn't the only one doing extra clean-ing. The stables do some track repair and a mass wash of all the vehicles. There is a general pick-up of the campgrounds themselves, and everyone uses the excuse of looking for litter to drift over to the various clearings to gawk at the brand-spanking-new greenhouses. They are still empty, but Brother Topher and his crew have already installed the plumbing and electrical. The greenhouses stand vacant, ready for their raised garden beds, tables, and benches to be added. Dan is itching to break them in but told me he knows he'll have to wait until the summer programs at the camp end. In the meantime, he's watching gardening shows on his phone at every opportunity. He's given me the go-ahead to start composting all our vege-table waste.

After serving the staff lunch on Sunday, Lu and I join Dan in the kitchen to prep the usual Sunday night bonfire meal. He works on his twelve-hour roast beef stew while Syl-vie and Ms. Denise make their melt-in-your-mouth buttermilk biscuits. Lu and I prep a green salad and a bowl of fruit that we cover and put in the walk-in. We are all out of the kitchen by 1:30 — our personal best.

A couple of hours at the pool followed by a hot shower and a nap, and I'm ready for the bonfire at sundown. Everyone tears into the food, like we haven't eaten in days, and as a result, we have no leftovers. Great news for me because that means cleanup is a breeze. I load the last pan into Dan's golf cart and turn the key. The lights come on, illuminating Roman standing in the middle of the path, squinting in the beams. He jogs over to me and demands, "Did you see where Sylvie went?" He looks nervous and angry.

Roman hasn't said much to me since I arrived at Camp Galilee, and most of what he has said has been pretty rude, but it's obvious right now that he doesn't care who he's talking to. He just wants information. Now. He reminds me of dad.

I turn away with a shiver, trying to disguise my discomfort by scanning the faces glowing in the firelight on the floor of the amphitheater. "Um, I saw her earlier. I told her the biscuits were good, so I know she was here. Oh. Didn't her mom leave because of a headache? Maybe Sylvie went with her."

"No. I told the Stades I'd walk Sylvie home afterward."

I turn back and narrow my eyes at him, but he doesn't notice. He's still peering into the darkness of the forest. I can't believe that the Stades would okay Roman walking Sylvie home through the dark woods. He's come a long way, but he's still Roman.

"I haven't seen her. Just stick around the fire. She probably just went to the bathroom or something."

"Yeah. I checked the bathroom. She's not there." He looks worried, but there is no need to be. Sylvie grew up at Camp Galilee. She knows this place better than any of us.

I blow past the weirdness that he checked the bathroom and say, "Have you asked Brother Topher?"

Roman's head snaps around, and his eyes bore into mine. "No! I — I don't want her to get into trouble."

"Why would she be in trouble? She probably just went to the bathroom, and you missed her. Or she went home with her mom. She probably just forgot to tell you. Ask her dad," I suggest with more force.

"I don't need to bother him. She's around here some-where." I watch a scowl creep over his features, and he growls something about Jack under his breath.

"Why would she be with Jack?" I ask cautiously. He doesn't answer, so I say, "You know where he would be better than anyone. Go check his usual haunts." He starts skulking away, but I call after him, "But touch base with Brother Topher first!" That stops him, and he shifts his weight as if to walk back to me but pulls himself up short, and I see him form the weird fake mask of pseudo concern that he'd put on to convince adults that he was a good guy.

"I'm just a little worried. Jack has been coming on a little strong lately."

I'm looking for the deceit, but I can't quite connect what I know I'm seeing with what I'm hearing. "I'm sure Sylvie's fine," I say lamely. "Most of the camp is down here."

"Yeah. I guess if Jack was going to do something, he'd go somewhere else."

That sends a shiver through me. "What are you talking about?"

He doesn't give me the expected oily grin, but there's something in his eyes I don't trust.

"Just make sure she gets home," I tell him. I see Dan walking up the stairs to the golf cart. I get in the passenger seat and remind Roman again to check in with Brother Topher before taking off for the dining hall.

At the kitchen, I help Dan unload the dishes off the golf cart and into the dishwasher. Then, while he adds soap and programs the giant washer, I quickly go through the kitchen to ensure everything is in its place.

You know that moment when you see something wrong, but it doesn't register at first? You try to tell yourself that what you're seeing is a mistake? It was the corner of a piece of notebook paper sticking out of Sylvie's cookbook. It could have easily been a scrap she'd torn off for a bookmark, but I knew it wasn't. I pull a neatly folded sheet of notebook paper from between the laminated pages of her binder. I don't hesitate to spread it open on the table in front of me.

    *Deer Sylvie,*

    *Meat me after diner at the stables. I need to talk to u.*

    *-Jack*

Except it isn't Jack's handwriting. Or the way he folds his notes. The misspellings take me back to my childhood home kitchen, and I know I'm looking at Roman's work. Mom never pushed for Roman to excel in spelling (or anything else, for that matter). To do so would be to admit she had room for improvement.

    I shove the paper into my jeans pocket and tear out the door. Dan and his golf cart are already gone. I wonder if he'd said anything to me before he left. I would have been too preoccupied to notice. I don't bother with the curving dirt path that eventually leads back to the fire pit and the stables. Instead, I jog in a straight shot through the woods, fighting against every tree root that seems intent on grabbing at my feet as I pick my way through. In minutes I'm at the top of the amphitheater. I look down at the people still basking in the ring of light. Jack and Sylvie are indeed gone — as are Roman and several other junior workers. It is primarily supervisors and managers in crash mode around the blaze. Lu sees me and sits up straight. Sione follows her gaze in my direction. I don't give them any sign that I notice them and back away to double-check the bathroom. The cinderblock building is dark, but I wave my hand over the motion sensor to wake the fluorescent lights and check each stall. The place is indeed empty. I don't hesitate to run into the men's room to check it as well.

    I'm back at the entry to the amphitheater and see that Lu is now on her feet staring at me as I check the faces of the people below one more time — willing Sylvie to appear. My nose burns, and I sniff back the tears. There isn't time for that right now.

    I quickly scan the woods standing thick around me and

hear the low growling of motocross bikes in the distance. I run into the woods closest to the stables, mentally yelling for Lu to follow me since I can't seem to talk around my panic.

The stables are lit up, busy, and loud. Nearly every staff member under eighteen is either racing or watching and cheering. Unfortunately, Roman, Sylvie, and Jack aren't there. I remember how Jack wanted me to direct Sylvie to the edge of the woods near the stables, and I turn back to the bordering forest I'd just run through. Did I miss them?

I see a glimmer of bouncing beam — a flashlight. I take off in its direction, slowing when I hear voices in front of me.

"If I'd know you liked her that much, I would have given her to you!" Jack is saying with a mocking laugh.

"You know I like her." That's Roman. I creep forward until I'm at the edge of a small meadow. The circle of trees filters the moonlight, but a lantern makes the small circle glow. Jack is holding his jaw. He takes time to spit to the side before grinning at his supposed best friend. The boys face each other, Jack loose-limbed and smiling, Roman furious and shaking, looking so much like Dad in one of his fits that my knees start to shake.

It's when I hear a little mewling sound that I notice Sylvie. She sits on a stump a few feet away from me, hidden in the shadow of the surrounding trees. I edge my way over to her, trying to think of how I can get her attention without scaring her.

I stifle my own panic when Lu slips a hand over my mouth and whispers, "It's me. Don't scream." I nod and gesture toward Sylvie. We carefully work our way to the crying girl, and we must be unbelievably stealthy because when Sylvie finally notices us, she yelps in surprise. Fortunately, the guys are too busy punching and pushing and cussing each other out to catch us.

"Come on," I whisper to Sylvie, and I see she's shaking so badly, she's having trouble even moving. I grab her elbow, and she yelps again. I recognize that sound. Quickly, I release her elbow and pull at her wrist and hand instead. "Sorry. Let's go."

Lu takes her other hand, and we pick our way through the trees toward the nearest light source. Finally, we show up outside the stables, but I feel Sylvie pull back. She's not ready to see a crowd of people just now. I look over at Lu and nod in the general direction of our dorm. She nods, and we find the path that leads us home.

When the dining hall comes into view, Lu finally speaks to Sylvie. "Want us to walk you home? Or do you want to hang out with us for a while?" Sylvie doesn't answer but leans toward the wooden stairs leading up to our dorm. We follow her silent movement and welcome her into our safe space.

# Chapter Forty-One: Triage

Sylvie doesn't say anything for the longest time. Lu and I sit quietly on either side of her on Lu's bed. Our room is comfy, but we don't have room for anything extraneous like chairs or a couch. The beds are the only places to sit.

Lu and I exchange serious looks, but neither of us knows what to say. Finally, I get up. "Be right back."

When I return from the downstairs kitchen with three bottles of water and three pre-packaged cups of ice cream, they still haven't moved, but Sylvie reaches her hand out for the dessert as soon as I enter. She eats it robotically, going through the motion of dipping the little wooden spoon into the ice cream and bringing it to her mouth. There's no indication that she enjoys the flavor or texture, just a slight pause, a swallow, and then back for more. When the ice cream is gone, Sylvie sits with the cup cradled in her hands and whispers, "He threatened to rape me."

The already quiet room stills even more. It is Lu who recovers first.

"Who?" She asks the single word while slipping a comforting arm around Sylvie's shoulders.

"Roman." She breathes out a shuddering sigh before she continues. "He told me I was an idiot for falling for Jack. That Jack was engaged to his sister and that he was using me. I — I told him I wasn't falling for anyone and left to go to the bathroom. He was waiting for me when I came out and pulled me behind the building. He tried to kiss me." She shudders. "And — and he grabbed me." She drops her empty ice cream cup and crosses her arms over her chest. "I told him 'NO!' just like we learned in defense class." She throws her arms forward as she demonstrates the stance she was told to take after shouting the magic word meant to repel most attackers.

"But he didn't stop. He grabbed me again. It hurt." Her arms return to her chest, the memory of the pain Roman inflicted prompting her to revert to protecting her breasts from another violent attack. "Then he put his arms around me and shoved me against the wall. He held me so tight; I couldn't move. I tried to knee him, but he was too close, and I knew I should do the — you know," she pumped her partially closed fist in a swift upright jerk meant to break an attacker's nose, "but he was holding my arms against my chest. I couldn't do anything!" Sylvie drops her head to her knees and wails.

Finally, the sobs subside, but Sylvie still doesn't raise her head. We have to lean in to hear her. "Then he said that he could make me his. That Jack wouldn't want me anymore after he was done. He let go of my arm so he could — could unbutton my jeans, and that's when I hit him. I didn't do it like I was supposed to, I didn't get his nose, but he let go anyway, and I said 'NO!' again and tried to run away, but he grabbed me again and — he — he was too strong!" Her sobs are quieter this time and punctuated with long sniffs that prompt me to get a long line of toilet paper from the bathroom. She raises her head to blow her nose and takes a deep breath. "Then Jack came and pulled me away from Roman, and we ran. I tried to get back to the bonfire, but he had my hand, and we ran right past the amphitheater. I thought we were going to the stables, but he said we should stop in the woods to ensure our safety. I said no. I wanted to go back to the campfire and find my dad. He kept trying to hug me. Telling me everything would be okay, but I kept pushing him away, saying I wanted my dad."

"He said he'd call my dad and have him meet us. I tried to see his phone, but he held it away from me so that I couldn't watch him dial. He said he sent a text because there wasn't a signal. Then — it was so weird — he lit a lamp. It was already there. There were water bottles and snack bags all over, and I realized that this was a place he hung out."

"Then Roman found us, and Jack pushed me behind him. I thought he was protecting me, but he — " Her voice dropped to a whisper. "He — he — started laughing. It was a joke to him. Roman tried to hit him, but Jack ducked and hit him first." She gestured to her belly to show where the blow had landed. "I tried to run away again, but this time Jack grabbed my arm, hard. Here," she lifted her short sleeve, and I saw the red fingerprints, so much like the ones he'd left on my arm when I refused to have Sylvie meet him, but deeper, redder. "He grabbed me and pointed to a stump and said, 'Sit there,' and I did. I couldn't think of what else to do." A shudder goes through her as her eyes meet mine. "Then Jack said, 'If I knew you wanted her that bad, I would have given her to you' like I was some — some — thing!" She says it with fury.

Lu nods at her. "It's okay to be angry. They were wrong. What they did was evil. You did nothing wrong. Don't let them make you feel like you did."

Sylvie nods her head, but I can see the doubt in her eyes. I feel like I know what is going through her mind.

"I found the note on your workstation."

"What note?"

"This one." I pull the paper out of my jeans pocket and open it.

"Oh. I — I've never seen this one. I asked Jack to stop leaving me notes. At first, I thought they were sweet, but he's old and acts like a jerk sometimes. He kept writing that we should date, but I said I was too young. I'm not allowed to date yet." She reached for the note in my hand. "He wrote another one anyway?"

"Jack didn't write it. My brother wrote this."

"Your brother?"

I realize I'd just unmasked myself, but it doesn't seem at all important at this point. "Roman is my brother. It's me, Sylvie. Julia."

"Julia?" Her eyes widen as she mentally strips away my

new make-up, imagining me with long hair and scrubby hand-me-down jeans made into skirts topped with layers of t-shirts. Finally, I see the recognition slowly come over her. "Julia! You look so different! Why? — I don't get it. Why did you tell everyone your name was Rose?"

My mouth goes dry. What do I say? How much of my past should I share?

A knock on the door splinters the silence. Sylvie and I both go pale and automatically freeze. Only Lu has the presence of mind to spring up and look out of the window next to the door. We watch her wave to someone and then turn the knob.

Brother Topher stands in the doorway, looking embarrassed. He usually doesn't go anywhere near girls' dorms. Then his expression changes, and he charges right in. "Sylvie! Oh, thank God! We were looking for you everywhere!" In a fraction of a second, he takes in her tear-streaked face and moves to Lu's vacated place on the bed, pulling his daughter close to him. "Oh, baby, what's wrong?" he croons.

I don't anticipate the flash of jealousy that comes over me. My father had been a man to fear. He never touched me in a way that anyone would think of as "loving."

I expect Sylvie to quietly evade her father's questions, shyly dropping hints as to what had happened, avoiding the embarrassing subject of her near-rape. Instead, the words flow from her like water from an unkinked hose. She names names and freely shares her thought processes. She hands him the note, insisting that she hadn't seen it before, but "those guys were planning something" and explains everything the way she had presented it to us. This time, though, I notice that she's angry and growing angrier by the minute. Her father never stops her rant, and his face keeps its expression of sympathy. I back up across the room until I felt my mattress at my knees. I sit heavily on my bed, knowing for the first time that this is how a father is supposed to act.

The door opens again, and Ms. Denise runs in with Lu

right behind her. I hadn't even realized that Lu had left. Now she sits next to me as Sylvie and her parents hold each other close.

While Sylvie tells her mom about her ordeal, Brother Topher pulls out his cell phone and dials three numbers. I don't say anything, but I shoot a look at Lu and see the same surprise on her face. Brother Topher isn't calling a specific police officer from his church to come "handle things." Instead, he calls the 911 dispatch — a number I was told to only call if there was a fire. His voice is clipped but urgent. He seems satisfied by what he hears, and with a "thank you," he hangs up and dials another number.

"Dan, we found Sylvie. I need you and Frank and Sione to get Jack and Roman into the office ASAP. Don't say anything to them except that I want to talk to them. So if they talk, let them, but don't engage. I'll explain everything in a few minutes. Thanks."

Brother Topher slips his phone into his shirt pocket and sits next to Sylvie again. "The police will be here in twenty minutes. They're going to want to ask you some questions about what happened tonight."

"Do you want me to go to your office too?"

"No. I'm going to have Mom take you home. The officers can talk to you there. Don't change your clothes or wash your hands. Stay as you are until after they interview you. You tell them everything you told you've mom and me. You going to be okay?"

I notice that Sylvie is starting to shake, but she nods determinedly. "I'm fine."

Brother Topher walks his family out of our door, stopping long enough to nod his thanks to us. Lu and I follow them out onto the porch and lean on the rail, watching them walk to their nearby cabin. Sylvie and Ms. Denise go in, but Brother Topher closes the door after them and makes a bee-line for the office. Lu and I walk to the edge of the porch, unable to let him leave our view just yet. A second after he goes inside, light floods out of every window. Dan, Frank, and Sione, three hulking men who start each day in a makeshift gym working out together, silently herd Jack and Roman to the office door. They silently ignore Jack's attempts to explain himself. Roman slouches along next to him. As soon as the door closes after the mismatched group, Lu and I go back inside.

"What do you think is going to happen?" My question comes out in a whisper.

"I don't know." She turns to me with an expression of awe. "He called the police."

"I know."

"I'm glad." She looks more scared than glad, but I know what she means. Somebody is doing something. Brother Topher's instinct isn't to cover up but to expose. We weren't used to that.

"Think Roman will be arrested?" I ask. She shrugs, and I say, "They'll have to call Mom and Dad."

"Yep."

"Are you going to call your Nana to come to get you before your parents come up to the camp?"

I don't answer at first, and Lu doesn't push. Finally, I say, "No. I can't keep hiding from them." I swallow the lump in my throat. "I can handle them," I say experimentally. I'm not sure if I believe it, but I want to.

Lu and I sit on our beds in silence until we hear the distinct crunch of gravel and a single *blurp* from a police siren. We return to our perch on the porch.

The police car sits in eerie silence with red and blue lights flashing, coloring every staff member's face as they silently stand in a half-circle around the office. There are two officers. We watch one of them talk to Brother Topher, but we can't hear what is said. Then Dan opens the office door and waves them in.

Usually, the camp bubbles with sound, but tonight, it is only the sighing of a slight breeze through the treetops. My mind feels like spinning gears, all skipping and missing their connections in a whirl of chaos, preventing the forming of words or even thought. That makes it difficult when one of the policemen comes to "take our statements" as witnesses.

A silent eternity passes before the same policeman walks with Brother Topher to his family's cabin. Lu and I move to the steps where we can sit down as we wait. When the door finally opens again, everything happens in a rush. Sylvie and her family get in their car and start down the road. The police put my brother and my former fiancé into the back of the squad car.

Silently, I go back inside my dorm and crawl into bed. The day was too much for me to handle. Eventually, I fall into a fitful sleep.

∞∞∞

I wake to my usual alarm. I strip off yesterday's makeup in the shower and return to my bunk scrubbed clean, ready to put on a fresh face for a new day.

It's Monday, and we're expecting campers in six hours, but neither Sylvie nor her mom shows up to work. So instead, Chef Dan and one of his line cooks help us fill the snack baggies and help us put up the tables we'll need for the week. While I appreciate Dan's help, I am also uncomfortable. He is across a table from me, and still, it feels too close. He's so tall and his hands so large, I cringe whenever he gets too close. If he ever hit me the way my father did, I'd be on the ground at the first blow.

Sylvie couldn't protect herself against Jack and Roman. I know that if Jack had ever forced me, I probably wouldn't be able to defend myself against him either. I definitely couldn't protect myself from Dan. I find myself wishing he would find something else to do. He tries to start a conversation a few times, and Lu has no problem engaging, but I can't think of a thing I want to share. I just want him to stay away.

I keep my head down and do the work, but I'm barely hanging on.

Brother Frank, from the stables, stands in for Brother Topher to greet the campers and give them instructions on how to find their cabins and what the schedules are going to be.

Could Brother Frank ever turn on one of us girls?

We get the lunch prepped and served without missing a beat — except, instead of the fresh-baked cookies on the menu, Chef Dan switches them out with ice-cream cups. Hopefully, the three I took the night before won't matter. After the campers leave, we clean up a bit and then get ready to eat our staff lunch when Chef Dan approaches Lu and me. I don't want to look at him. Mentally, I push him back a few steps. He's too close. I always thought he was a nice guy, but what if I was wrong all this time? What if there are no nice guys? Chef Dan stops in front of me, but I keep my eyes on the ground at his feet and take a step back.

"I just got a text from Ms. Denise," he says, gesturing with his phone. "She'd like to invite the two of you to lunch in their cabin. Don't worry about lunch clean-up. I'll make sure it gets done. I'll see you at 4:00 for dinner prep." Lu thanks him and leads the way out the dining hall door. I don't lift my eyes until we climb the entrance to the Stade's porch.

The camp director's "cabin" isn't as rustic as the name implies. Although it has horizontal wooden paneling and flagstone floors, it also has giant windows to let in the dappled light of the forest, a remarkable collection of cobalt blue glass, and soft jewel-toned rugs in every seating area. And then there are all the books. The great room walls are a giant library embracing a living room, dining room, and kitchen combo. I want to grab the nearest volume, sink into one of the comfy-looking chairs near the fireplace, and lose myself in a great story.

Ms. Denise welcomes us with hugs and an offer of tea. She brings it to us on an actual tea tray and pours it into delicate china cups. I'm relaxed once I realize that it's only her and Sylvie in the house. Then she says, "Topher will be here in a few minutes. He had some stuff to take care of in the office first. I hope the two of you like tomato soup and grilled cheese."

Lu nods enthusiastically. "My favorite comfort food."

I nod too, but not as eagerly as Lu. I'm already stressing about seeing Brother Topher again. Yes, he was kind to Sylvie last night, but what if that was an act. My father could act friendly sometimes too.

I try to focus on what Ms. Denise said about grilled cheese and tomato soup. It was one of the meals Mom made when I was sick and couldn't cook. The combo tasted okay, but it wasn't my favorite. The tomato soup was always lumpy and never hot enough, and mom always made her grilled cheese with the heels of the bread that I had to dunk into the soup to get down my throat. Still, I could fake it for a day. The Stades were such a sweet family I could enjoy their company even if I didn't like the food.

And I'm almost positive that Brother Topher will be kind when he comes in.

Lu and I both offer to help Ms. Denise, but she waves at us to remain seated and bustles off to her open kitchen to do her thing. Sylvie takes a dainty sip and says, "Mom and Dad wanted me to invite you over to say thanks for all you did for me yesterday." She looks like she's about to say more but stops abruptly and takes another sip. Lu assures her that, of course, we'd be there for her. My mind jumps to the "what if we hadn't been" scenario. I don't trust my brother, but I'd never thought of him as a potential rapist. I thought I'd loved Jack, but he turned out to be a womanizing scumbag. I am coming to realize I might not be the best judge of character. I can't help but think about all the "good guys" I know. Are they capable of this too? My father's face crosses my mind. He'd be capable. But would Brother Topher? Or Sione? I shoot a guilty look at Lu as if she can tell I'm evaluating her boyfriend.

Or Chef Dan?

He seems nice, but what if he's not. What if I've never

seen the "real" him?

I'd always wanted a boyfriend. A fiancé. A husband with whom I could start a happy home. But what if that was a lie? What if the guy I chose was only nice to me when we were dating and turned into a monster after getting married? Or after we started having kids? Then I'd be trapped with a person I couldn't stand, raising his kids with no way out. Was that how my mother felt? Would I start acting like her?

I thought that Sylvie was protected because her parents loved her. They were always in her corner, encouraging her. Involved. And it didn't matter. She was still targeted. It could happen to anyone. By anyone.

Ms. Denise breaks into my anxious thoughts. "Topher just texted saying something came up and to start without him."

I follow the other girls to the table and take my place in front of a satiny bowl of tomato soup. After Ms. Denise prays, I lift the spoon to my lips for a sip. It is hot, creamy, and lump-free. Next, she passes the platter of grilled cheese sandwiches. These are not my mother's grilled cheese. Instead, these are masterpieces of crusty sourdough, melted butter, and sharp cheddar cheese. My sandwich is a flavor bomb that explodes with each bite.

Listening to the others talk while I savor every bite of the best lunch ever, I wonder if my earlier thoughts were the hysterical musings of a disturbed mind. Ms. Denise seems genuinely happy. It's obvious she loves Sylvie and Brother Topher. Her home is warm and inviting. She doesn't act like someone who is trapped.

Mom did. Her every movement was stilted, frustrated. During my last days at home, I realized for the first time how often she was gone. She could escape all day with me to cook and clean, only returning because she felt she had to. I almost feel sorry for her. I got out when she couldn't.

"Rose?"

I look across the table to see Sylvie staring at me. "Are

you okay?"

"Yes. Sorry. I was daydreaming, I guess." I try to chuckle, but it comes out as more of a throat-clearing. "I didn't catch what you said."

"Last night, you started to tell me about why you changed your name."

"I didn't really change it. Rose is my middle name."

"But, why go by Rose instead of Julia?"

I set down my spoon and wipe my mouth with my napkin. Sylvie had been so brave last night, standing firm, telling the truth about what happened to her. I wanted to be that brave.

"Because what Roman said about Jack and me was true. We were engaged. We had planned to elope right after graduation and move to Dawes where we would get jobs and go to college."

The confusion on her face is reflected in her voice. "But Jack came here, and you didn't. Not at first, anyway. What happened?"

I shudder. Lu and Nana were the only ones who know what happened, but after Sylvie had so bravely spoken about the attack, how can I stay silent? I look over at Lu, who nods her encouragement, and then at Ms. Denise, whose look of surprise is mingled with compassion. I'm among friends here. I can trust these women.

"When my parents found out that Jack and I were engaged, my father beat me." The words come out in a monotone as if a robot has taken over my nervous system. It's as though once I decide to share, I am shunted off to the side, and my story takes on a life of its own. "Dr. Jeffers and the deacons knew he did it, but didn't see anything wrong with him hitting me over and over again with a giant wooden spoon, the kind people hang on the wall as a decoration, while they sat in our living room and listened. That night, after they left, he beat me again. I was kicked out of school before graduation, but Jack was allowed, encouraged even, to stay since he was valedictorian. We still planned to run away. We would get on the bus for camp and get off in Dawes instead, but when Mom discovered my packed bag and a check from my grandmother, Dad beat me again. It was even worse than the first two times. That night, when my parents were at church, I called my Nana to come to get me, and I moved in with her. When Nana gave me a cell phone, I contacted Jack at the camp, but it was obvious that he had changed his mind about me. He had no plans to marry me, and by then, I didn't have any desire to marry him."

"Why?" Sylvie's eyes are openly curious. "What changed your mind?" I have to think about her question. What had made me finally decide that Jack wasn't who I wanted?

"I met some people who were actually in love. They cared about each other so deeply, and, at first, I lied to myself that my relationship with Jack was like theirs. The truth is, Jack and I never had a deep relationship. It was note-passing and a few fireside chats surrounded by the rest of the youth group on church outings. We'd never really had the chance to develop a friendship. I learned that people need to be friends if they're going to live together as a happily married couple."

*And they have to trust each other. I don't know if that will ever happen to me.*

"But I was still willing to develop a relationship. Willing to build something deep, something strong. I made it a point to pray for Jack. To write to him. To text him. One day I sent him messages letting him know I was thinking of him, praying for him. I shared a word of Scripture I had read that morning for devotions."

"The four texts," Lu comments knowingly.

"Yes. I sent a total of four texts throughout the day. In the last one, I asked him to text back when he got a chance. He texted back a few minutes after that and told me to stop bothering him. That was it. That was when I knew that I didn't want to spend another day with Jack as my boyfriend, and I didn't want to spend a lifetime with him. Or anyone else at that point." Do I still feel that way? Right now, yes.

Lu breaks in and says to Sylvie and Ms. Denise, "Remember the day on the first week we came back that Jack stood in the doorway the whole time, messing with me because I kicked him out of the kitchen? That's the day of the four texts." Sylvie's eyes widen, and she nods.

Ms. Denise gives me a compassionate look, letting me know she understands and approves of my decision to let Jack go. "What are your plans now?" she asks.

"I'll go back to living with Nana and get a job. After that, I'd like to save up some money and go to college. I told Lu I'd be her roommate." I smile at my best friend. "I'll get there as soon as I can," I promise.

"I know you will. I'm just glad you'll be in a safe place. On the other hand, I shudder to think of you ever going back to your parent's house."

"That will never happen. I'm out for good." I take a sip of my now-cold tea from its china cup and revel in the bliss of friends and freedom. My terror is fading. I can think a little clearer now that I've spoken openly about what happened to me.

I assure myself that I do know good men. Brother Topher is one of them. Sione is incredible and treats Lu with utmost respect and care. Chef Dan is kind and has never done anything to prove it otherwise. So I can feel safe around them.

I address Ms. Denise. "Knowing that you went through that kind of stuff at home too and were able to get out and live a happy life helps. It's encouraging to know that eventually the memories of beatings pass."

"I'm sure," Ms. Denise says cautiously. "But, Julia, I wasn't beaten."

I'm shocked by that revelation. When she'd told us her story and how her parents had been so angry about the notes, I'd assumed that when she said things were "bad" she meant physical punishment that got out of hand. Now I turn to Lu. I know she'd been spanked, but that's the word I'd always used too. "Lu?" She shakes her head. Sylvie follows suit. I force a humorless chuckle. "Just me then?"

Of course it was just me. The unwanted, invisible one that no one could stand.

The front door swings open, we turn as one, expecting Brother Topher's arrival, but it is my father that barrels through. Never slowing, he grabs my arm and yanks me away from the table with so much force that the chair I am sitting on bounces twice as it falls over onto the hardwood floor.

"What did you do to your brother?" my father roars, spittle flying and spraying my face. Any thoughts I'd had about "handling" my parents are long gone. I'm stumbling, trying to get my feet under me while he keeps me off balance with bruising jerks. "You run away from home and reappear only to wreck your brother's life? You think playing with a person's reputation is a game?" I don't see the blow coming, but I do feel the explosion of knuckles against my skull. My knees buckle from the pain. I hear screaming, but I am pretty sure it isn't me. It's hard to tell. Everything is grey somehow.

# Chapter Forty-Two: Going Forward

You know those old television shows where someone wakes up, surrounded by beeping monitors, doctors, and nurses, and the first words out of their mouth are "Where am I"? Yeah. I always thought that line was stupid. How could a person not know they are in a hospital?

It's dark in here, but the display on the monitor glows green and red as it measures my blood pressure and pulse. I'm obviously not at a grocery store or library. I fumble for the button I know has to be on my bed somewhere. Every hospital bed on TV has a control that calls a nurse. I'm still feeling for it when a soft hand covers mine, and I yelp with surprise and heart-stopping panic.

"Hey, Sweetie." Nana's voice is low and calming. I grab her hand with both of mine, and before I can even register the emotion, I start sobbing. Thirty seconds in, and I wonder if I'm crying because I'm relieved that it's my Nana in my room and not my parents, or if I'm crying because of the pain. My head thrums like a big bass drum played with sticks of exploding dynamite.

Nana helps me sit up and holds me close to her, rocking me back and forth like she did when we got the calls that my visits to her were being cut short. "Everything is going to be okay," she whispers. I nod my head against her chest, but that sets off a new explosion deep inside my skull. I groan, and she lays me back down before locating that elusive nurse's button.

"Yes?"

"My granddaughter is awake."

"I'll be right there."

Nana's cold fingers stroke my forehead, and it feels incredible. I try to focus on her, but she's still fuzzy in the dark room. It hurts too much, so I close my eyes. There is so much I want to say, but when the words make it from my bruised brain to my mouth, they come out in barely coherent short bursts.

"Nana?"

"Yes, dear?"

"Can I still live with you?"

"Of course. For as long as you'd like."

"I want to go to college."

"We can make that happen. There's a great community college in the next town over."

"Palmdale. With Lu."

"We'll see about getting some applications."

"Police here?"

"Not right now. I'm supposed to call when you wake up."

"I'm awake."

"Let's check with the doctor before you talk to the police."

"Reporting this time." I feel her squeeze my hand.

"Good."

"Should've last time." Another squeeze.

"I'm sorry we didn't. You're right. We should have." There is a slight catch in her throat, and it makes me sad.

"Don't cry."

A sniffle and a deep breath before a shaky "Okay."

Then I say, "We start here. No going back. We go forward."

"We go forward." Nana agrees.

I fall asleep before the nurse comes in.

Two days later, I'm released from the hospital with instructions to rest often and avoid bright lights, loud noises, and reading. I can handle the first two since exposure to either feels like being stabbed in the brain.

But not reading? That's just sadistic. Nana reminds me that I can still listen to books, and she sets up an Audible account just for me. The doctors at the hospital want me to come back for periodic checkups over the next week. Brother Topher has given us the guest cabin closest to theirs, so we have a place to stay.

I'm so tired that I spend most of my time sleeping. When I'm awake, Nana starts my Audible app. I can't look at my phone's screen.

I'm allowed to have people visit for fifteen-minute increments, and a few people come now and again, but Lu stops by every day to talk. I feel horrible about leaving her shorthanded in the kitchen. I tell her I hope to be back to work soon, but she shakes her head at me.

"You're done for the season — doctor's orders. Right now, you need to rest and let your brain heal. You got knocked around pretty badly. If Chef Dan hadn't gotten to you when he did, you'd …" her voice trails off, but I can see from her expression that she'd planned to finish the sentence with "be dead."

"Chef Dan was there?" I didn't remember seeing him. I don't know anything after Dad punched the side of my head.

"He pulled your dad off you and held him in a reverse bear-hug, pinning his arms to his sides while your dad kicked him and yelled and slammed the back of his head into Chef Dan's face. Dan wouldn't let go, though. Kept him pinned until the police showed up." I feel Lu squeeze my fingers in the dim light. "You should invite him over for a visit. He's been worried about you. He told me the worst thing was seeing you laying on the floor, not moving, and not being able to get to you because he had to keep your dad away."

"I had no idea."

"No. You wouldn't. You were unconscious." Lu stops and squeezes my fingers again. She doesn't say anything for a minute, and I hear a squeaky moan. She's started crying. "I was so scared, Julia," she says with a shaking voice. "You looked so bad. I thought — I thought you were dying — maybe even dead already. I didn't move you. I just checked to see if you were breathing. Ms. Denise told Sylvie to call 911 just as your mom came in and started screaming at Chef Dan to let your dad go and trying to push past Ms. Denise to get to you. It was so scary."

"I'm okay now," I try to sound reassuring, but I'm trembling at the scene playing through my bruised brain.

"Yeah. You'll be fine, but you have to take it easy for a while. Don't try to push yourself to get back to work. If you have to wait until the spring semester to join me at the college, I promise not to make you feel guilty. I just want you to get better."

"I'll be good," I promise. Before Lu leaves, I have her download *Frankenstein* on my Audible app and find where I left off in the physical book. I thank her as I put my earbuds in, then as she gets ready to walk out the door, I ask for one more thing.

∞∞∞∞

Once the sun goes down, I can sit on the porch with the light off and enjoy the fresh air. The guest cabins all have rockers out front, but the back and forth motion makes me nauseous right now. So Nana wrestles an overstuffed comfy chair outside for me instead. I see the shape of someone coming toward me, and though I can't see his face, I can tell from the silhouette who it is.

"Hello, Dan." My voice is a papery whisper as I greet him.

His "Hello" is just as quiet, and I'm thankful. Every loud noise is a spike of pain.

"Lu told me what you did."

He doesn't say anything, so I continue.

"Thank you. You saved my life."

"I'm just glad I was there."

"Me too."

"So. Are you angry with me? About your dad?"

"No. Why would I be?"

"Because he got arrested."

"He deserved it."

"Yes, he did."

"I'm pressing charges this time."

"This time? He'd done this before?"

"Yes."

"I'm sorry."

"Don't apologize. You didn't do anything wrong." It's weird repeating the words that Dan said to me throughout the summer.

"I'm relieved to hear you say so," he says. "I'm glad you're going to be okay."

"I'm just sorry I'm leaving you short-handed."

"Being short-handed is the least of my worries."

"Why? What's going on?"

"I was worried about you." He says it simply, but there is a sense of caution in his voice.

I spent the afternoon after Lu left thinking about what she told me happened after Dad knocked me out, about Dan stepping in, about how he was so concerned.

I have to rethink my treatment of him the day of the attack. I had shielded myself against him. I had lumped him in with all men, based on the tiny and poor sampling I'd been exposed to in my life.

I knew better. This was my fourth year working with Dan, but this was the first year I'd gotten to know him as a friend. I can trust him.

"I don't think you need to worry about me," I assure him. "The doctor said that I'm recovering well. It just takes time. I have to stay quiet. Can't read or watch T.V. or stare at my phone screen."

"You must be bored."

"I thought I would be, but I spend most of my time sleeping. And I'm listening to *Frankenstein* on Audible."

"What part of the story are you at?"

"Victor is in Scotland putting together the creature's bride."

"Oh. It's getting good."

"I loved the part where the creature talks about living in the pigsty near the cabin of the French family."

"Makes you feel sorry for the poor guy."

"It really does."

"I'm glad you're getting better, but I was sorry to hear that you're not going to be sticking around."

"We're leaving on Saturday if we get the final all-clear from the doctor."

"I'll miss having you in the kitchen." He goes quiet for a few seconds, then follows it up with, "I'll miss hanging out with you after hours too. I enjoyed spending time with you in Crystal Falls on our days off."

"Me too. I've never had so much fun with a group of friends." Come to think of it, I've never had a group of friends.

"Think you'll come back next year?"

"I hope so." We both go silent again, but I break back in. "I'd like for us to keep in touch, though."

"Oh. Okay." I feel like I can hear the smile in his voice.

Now is my time to share with him what I've been thinking. "This year has been different for me. I came to camp feeling freer than I had in my previous years. I looked the way I wanted and acted in a way that finally felt normal to me — not just how I thought I was supposed to act. I've always been close to Lu, but this year I branched out and got to know my coworkers better. I had several conversations with Sione, and I'm happy for him and Lu because I know he's a great guy and perfect for her. I got to know you better too. I think we talked more this year than in the previous three years combined."

"You used to come into the kitchen with your head down, powered through your work, and left without saying a word," Dan recalls. "It was almost like you were invisible, like you didn't want anyone to notice you. This year, when you came in, I was shocked, not just at your new look — which I love, by the way — but by your whole attitude. You had your head up. You talked to your co-workers. You laughed. And walking around Crystal Falls with you, I realized that you were this really interesting person, and I wanted to get to know you better."

"I had a great time with you too." I'm quiet for a moment, then pretend that I'm brave and push on. "I'd like to keep talking to you. Lu keeps in touch with Sione through texts while they go to two different colleges. I'm hoping to join Lu at Palmdale this year. Can I text you while I'm there? If I get in, that is?"

"Of course! And if you need recommendation letters, let me know." Dan goes quiet and I wonder if maybe I didn't make myself clear. I'm interested in starting a relationship with him and he's talking about the application process. But then, he breaks into my thoughts. "But are you sure about going to an AFB college?"

"AFB? What's that?"

"You know, American Fundamental Baptists."

"Oh. Yeah, I guess so." I'm not sure why he's concerned, or why he's calling the loose circle of independent churches the AFB. I'd never heard that before and I've been in church my whole life. I know Dr. Jeffers has always bragged about being an American Fundamental Baptist, but it's not like it's a denomination or anything. It's more like an idea. Our church would only fellowship with other congregations of "like faith" but each group was independent and run by a pastor who was in total control. It really depended on the pastor whether or not the church was a good one. Crystal Falls was one of the best I'd ever attended and when I'd visited Palmdale for College Days or youth rallies, I thought it was pretty good too. I feel Dan looking at me, waiting for me to elaborate, but I don't know what to say except, "I've always wanted to go to Palmdale with Lu."

"Then you should. I'll help however I can. And yes, I'd love to stay in contact with you."

∞∞∞

Nana drives the whole way home and I sit quietly on the passenger seat, wearing almost black sunglasses and trying not to throw up. The concussion has messed with my equilibrium, so I'm easily nauseated.

"I talked to Brother Topher yesterday," Nana is saying, and I focus on her voice so I won't upchuck. "He's called a friend of his at the admissions office at Palmdale. There's still plenty of room if you apply right away. Topher is getting letters of recommendation for you from all of the supervisors at the camp. I'll call your high school for your transcripts."

I start to shake my head but stop just in time. "I don't know if they'll say I've graduated. I don't have my diploma anymore."

"We'll work it out. You concentrate on getting better, and I'll concentrate on getting you into Palmdale. Deal?"

"Deal."

∞∞∞

For my application essay, I compare biblical Christianity with traditional Christianity. I use my Nana as my example of the biblical. She lives in Christ. Every part of her being exudes the love of God.

I use my parents as my example of the "vain traditions of men." They were so concerned with looking the part from the outside and yet were dead inside — the perfect representation of those "whitewashed sepulchers" mentioned by Jesus. I say that I hold no bitterness toward them, and I don't, but that doesn't mean I trust them. I have restraining orders against my parents, my brother, and my ex-boyfriend/fiancé. I'm starting my life over with Nana and Lu in my corner — oh, and Dan too.

"Your mom called late last night. She's upset that Roman's lawyer is pushing for him to go to Alpha-Omega Ranch. It's a strict military-like Christian boarding school. It's for guys only and, from what I understand, the students don't interact with each other. They use the same workbooks you used in your old school, and he'll have jobs he's required to do on campus. She's upset that most of the boys who attend the school have criminal backgrounds. Your mom was angry because when she pointed that out to the judge, he held up Roman's file and said, 'That is true, ma'am, and since your son also has a criminal background, he'll feel right at home.'"

I don't laugh at that. It's sad and laughing still hurts. "Is Dad out yet?"

"She had him out as soon as he was arraigned. So he's at home until he can work out his plea deal."

"Have you heard anything about Jack?"

"Not yet. Ms. Denise told me she'd keep us in the loop."

After two weeks at Nana's, I'm almost back to normal. I am allowed limited screen time but still wear dark sunglasses every time I walk outside. I read texts from Lu, Dan, and Ms. Denise in fifteen-minute bursts each day.

Nana is standing as my champion between my parents and me. Some days, I want them both punished to the full extent of the law, no matter how long it takes. Usually, though, I just want them to let me go. Completely. Nana understands this and is helping me to break the power they still had over me. The first thing was my transcripts. They were sent to Palmdale immediately, complete with the notification that I had graduated. I expected Nana to demand I get the money I'd saved for college, but she went a few steps further. My father had to cough up all four years' worth of tuition. It's in my savings account now. Nana encouraged me to keep as much in there as possible over the next four years so it can grow with interest. Lu and Dan hooked me up with a job on campus, cafeteria, of course, so I'll be using that money for living expenses. I'll dip into my savings only when tuition is due.

The last thing Nana insisted on was the restraining order. My parents are to have no contact with me at all except through a lawyer. All of this in return for a plea deal for my dad. He's on probation instead of in jail for years of abuse.

Now that my brain is nearly healed, I'm feeling behind. I've got college clothes to buy, books to pack, and school supplies to check off my list. Lu and I are sharing a dorm, and we've agreed it will be the most beautiful dorm on campus. She came down for a visit, and we got our matching bedding, lamps, and bookcases at Ross. We're going with a white and grey theme with a pop of color provided by a throw rug that will cushion the floor between our two beds.

The best part of her visit though, was when Nana and her best friend, Marie, took us to Martha Green's The Eating Room for their "Rustic Tea." Between the tower of finger sandwiches and the elaborate mini-desserts, Lu and I ate like there was no tomorrow. I felt no embarrassment, no guilt for enjoying every bite. For enjoying my life.

It's strange. For a month, I couldn't do anything other than sit in a darkened room listening to audiobooks on low volume. Except for visiting lawyers' offices, I didn't get out much. Still, it was good for me. It was more than my brain that healed. It was my mind. I made an effort to decide who I wanted to be, where I wanted to go, how I wanted to live my life. For the first time, I became comfortable in my skin.

I have Nana, the most awesome grandmother in the world. I have Lu, a best friend who pushes me to succeed. I even have a potential boyfriend. After four years of working with Dan, I realize that he's a good man. Since I left the camp, we haven't seen each other, but we write to each other every week and talk to or text each other every day.

I'm looking forward to next summer to see how our relationship develops.

Most importantly, I have Christ, a Savior who watched over me even through my darkest times and showed me the truth about what being a Christian means. There is great comfort in knowing He lives in me. There is a relief, comfort, and deep-seated happiness in knowing that I live in Him. Having Him on my side means I can strike out with confidence. I can understand what I want and push to be successful. I can trust Him not to leave me stranded. And I know that because I belong to Him, no one has the right to hurt me. I will fight for my freedom, my health, and my well-being. God gave me those gifts, and no one will ever steal them from me again.

God sees me for who I am and for who I want to be. In turn, I see myself through His eyes.

I am no longer invisible.

# Acknowledgements

I want to take this opportunity to say a special thank you to my team, whose selfless sacrifice allows me to write and publish the books that God has laid on my heart.

Theo Skwarczynski--husband, partner, and sounding board: thank you so much for your support as I embark on this new career. I love you and appreciate all that you do.

Esther Vander Vegte--financial wizard extraordinaire, friend, and sister by birth and choice: thank you so much for your encouragement and help. I couldn't do any of this without you.

Kaylene Ranee Skwarczynski from Ranee Designs: I have the prettiest book covers in all the land thanks to you. I am blessed to have a woman of such talent in my family. Your work is fantastic!

Marc Skwarczynski--my IT genius: without you this book would have been a goner! Or at least been delayed. It is a comfort to know I have you in my corner when the tech side of writing wants to send me 'round the bend. And, yes, I have tried turning it on and off again.

Carrie Smith--editor, friend, and colleague: thank you for being so kind about getting my frantic emails asking you to "put a pin" in one project to work on another and being willing to reread my books almost as often as I do. Your insights and suggestions are invaluable.

My Readers: thank you for taking time out of your busy schedule to read my books, write reviews, and suggest my novels to friends. Your encouraging messages and posts on Facebook, Twitter, and Instagram mean the world to me.

Finally, I cannot sign off on an acknowledgements page without taking the time to thank God for allowing me to practice this gift He's given me. I'm happier than I've ever been, doing what I am made to do. Thank you for this opportunity. My heart is your habitation.

# About The Author

## Marbeth Skwarczynski

Though born on the east coast, I spent most of my life in the American Southwest, eventually settling in California, where my husband and I raised two sons. Later we welcomed two fantastic daughters-in-law and four grandchildren into our family. After teaching history and literature for eighteen years, I resigned to  write contemporary Christian fiction full-time. I keep my characters grounded in the real world and the real problems that Bible believers face today. While they grow, learn, and find possible solutions to their issues, my characters must also deal with the residue of the past. I write what I know, either firsthand or through close observation, injecting the joy, happiness, and humor that comes with spiritual freedom and love.

# Books In This Series

*The Rose Collection*

## Plague Of Lies

The cover-up didn't have the desired effect. The lies could not be contained and rippled throughout the community.

The sense of betrayal hit seventeen-year-old Scott the hardest. He had planned out his entire life based on the teachings of his spiritual mentor. Discovering that his mentor was living a lie sent Scott into a swirling abyss of anger and frustration. He lost his faith and unconsciously followed in the steps of the man he'd learned to hate—until she came into his life.

Lauren knew two things about her father: he had demanded she be born, and he left when she was an infant. He was the first adult in her life to let her know she was unwanted, but not the last. Her very existence was the reason her grandparents were perpetually angry and that her mother was doomed to a dead-end job. Then, on her eighteenth birthday, a letter from her father arrives, inviting her to meet him. Is it possible that her family had lied about him all this time?

## Twists, Turns, And Curves

Caroline Taft did her best to live a life of service and sacrifice, "above reproach," but when her teaching career at Benchmark Baptist Christian School is cut short, she discovers that she hasn't lived much of a life at all. Despite going on visitation every Saturday, teaching Sunday school, singing in the choir, directing children's music, leading Wednesday's Bible club, and, of course, teaching fourth grade (her actual job), it isn't enough to keep her on. She wonders if it isn't what she has or hasn't done or if it's her weight. Caroline is one of the few plus-sized women in her church and the only one on staff. Despite her discipline and hard work, her weight has made her a target. She has no savings, no apartment of her own, and her only close friend is the fellow teacher assigned to be her roommate. Her love life is non-existent. But maybe, just maybe, this abrupt change is just what she needs to break out of the mold she's was shoved into for so long. It's time for a new job, new clothes, a new home, and a new chance at love.Maybe it's even time to approach Ty Lang, the uncle of one of her students and a man she's secretly admired for two years. He's kind, successful, and sweet—and entirely out of her league. Her life may hold some twists and turns, but now it's time for Caroline to throw some curves of her own.

Made in the USA
Monee, IL
04 February 2025